ABOUT THE AUTHOR

Geoff Aird was born in Berwick Upon Tweed in 1960. He served five years in the Royal Navy then lived in London before joining the Fire Service in 1986. He lives in Edinburgh and when he's not cycling, he writes short stories and is currently working on his second novel.

WITHIN THE WALLS

GEOFF AIRD

Matador
9 Priory Business Park,
Wistow Road, Kibworth Beauchamp,
Leicestershire. LE8 0RX
Tel: 0116 279 2299
Email: books@troubador.co.uk
Web: www.troubador.co.uk/matador
Twitter: @matadorbooks

ISBN 978 180046 130 7

British Library Cataloguing in Publication Data.
A catalogue record for this book is available from the British Library.

Printed and bound in the UK by TJ Books Limited, Padstow, Cornwall
Typeset in 11pt Adobe Garamond Pro by Troubador Publishing Ltd, Leicester, UK

Matador is an imprint of Troubador Publishing Ltd

To Lorraine

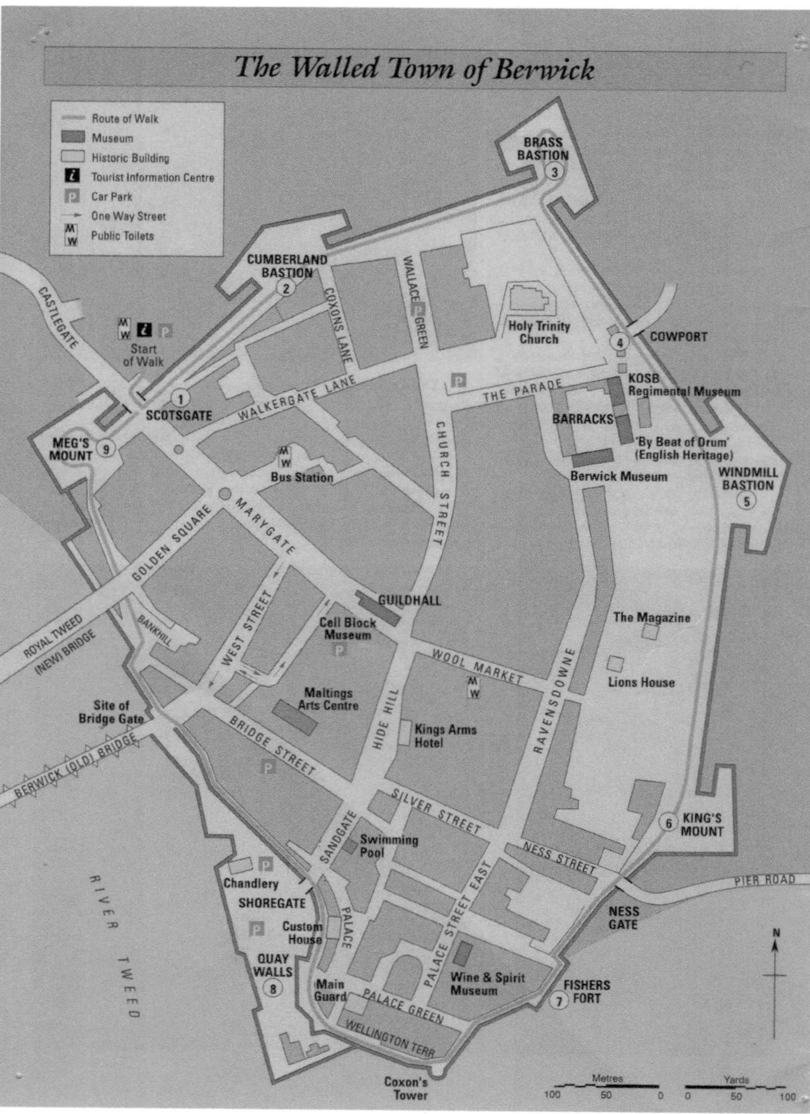
The Walled Town of Berwick
Route of Walk
Museum
Historic Building
Tourist Information Centre
Car Park
One Way Street
Public Toilets
BRASS BASTION
3
CUMBERLAND BASTION
2
CASTLEGATE
Start of Walk
COXONS LANE
WALLACE GREEN
Holy Trinity Church
4
COWPORT
KOSB Regimental Museum
1
SCOTSGATE
WALKERGATE LANE
THE PARADE
BARRACKS
MEG'S MOUNT
9
CHURCH STREET
'By Beat of Drum' (English Heritage)
Bus Station
Berwick Museum
WINDMILL BASTION
5
MARYGATE
GOLDEN SQUARE
GUILDHALL
ROYAL TWEED (NEW) BRIDGE
BANKHILL
WEST STREET
Cell Block Museum
The Magazine
WOOL MARKET
RAVENSDOWNE
Lions House
Maltings Arts Centre
Site of Bridge Gate
HIDE HILL
Kings Arms Hotel
BRIDGE STREET
BERWICK (OLD) BRIDGE
SILVER STREET
6
KING'S MOUNT
SANDGATE
Swimming Pool
NESS STREET
PIER ROAD
RIVER TWEED
Chandlery
SHOREGATE
PALACE
PALACE STREET EAST
NESS GATE
Custom House
QUAY WALLS
8
Main Guard
Wine & Spirit Museum
FISHERS FORT
7
N
PALACE GREEN
WELLINGTON TERR
Coxon's Tower
Metres
100
50
0
Yards
0
50
100

CONTENTS

CHAPTER 1

FROM THE SOUTH

SATURDAY

Elijah Bootle's day started early, started bad and started a long way away. And it seems a long way from where he is now: sitting in the back of a taxi while the driver blethers away in what Elijah thinks is a quaint and likeable accent. That's if he can make out what he's saying, the guy's talking that bloody fast! The weather, parking restrictions at Berwick Railway Station, frequency of trains and the cost of taxi licences are some of the subjects delivered with machine-gun speed.

'Have you travelled far today then, pal?' asks the cabbie.

'Yeah… London, actually. A long way and a long day,' responds Elijah, and hopes his voice and bedraggled demeanour look sufficiently exhausted to stifle any further conversation. However, the driver prattles on, now it's London landmarks he's visited on city breaks with "the wife". He doesn't realise that most Londoners have never been to places like the Tower of London, the National Portrait Gallery or Madame Tussauds. The sheer pace and noise of the city causes most locals to scurry home after work, shut the front door, open a bottle of wine and breathe a sigh of relief.

Christ, I hope they don't all talk this fast, he thinks to himself. Elijah is weary but his sense of courtesy causes him to give the odd monosyllabic response and occasional nod as he can see the driver eyeing him in his rear-view mirror. The taxi suddenly screeches to a halt, causing Elijah to jolt forward. It's a set of traffic lights and he wonders if they've been recently installed and the driver's forgotten about them. He must have been reading Elijah's thoughts, as he turns to him and says, 'Aye, until aboot fifteen years ago there were no traffic lights in this toon. But this is 2014, mate. We've had to come oot o' the Dark Ages,' said with a wry smile and a degree of sadness. He winds down his window to let some cool air in on this warm afternoon. The sudden waft of fish and chips drifts up Elijah's nostrils and he immediately feels ravenous.

The taxi moves on down Castlegate, under the Scotsgate and into the old, walled town of Berwick Upon Tweed. Elijah sits up and looks out. He's getting the impression that the only two things that move fast around here are this taxi and its driver's staccato dialogue – which suits him fine. London has burnt him out. London's pace, London's noise, London's violence. Especially the violence.

The driver slows as he negotiates the high street. It's a Saturday and market day. A row of stalls line the street and run parallel to the usual assortment of retailers found on any high street these days. Elijah sits forward and cranes his neck to look up at the imposing town hall as they drive past its right flank, then a sharp left and up Church Street.

'...but that's the north/south divide for you, eh? Here we are, pal, mission accomplished! That'll be... eh... three pounds, twenty, please.'

Elijah hands over four pounds and tells him to keep the change. *Christ, he's still talking.*

'...You've got everything you want on your doorstep here. Tommy's Newsagent just doon there, which is open all hours. Then there's the Cannon chippie on your left, best fish suppers in town. It's just past the police station, and there's a pub just down there. It's called the Queens Head, also known as the Burglar's Arms, and I'd gi' it a miss if I was you. Especially as you're not local and... well, you divn't look local, if you see what I'm saying, mate. Nae offence, like. Talkin' of the police, they've got their hands full just now. This town only gets about one murder a decade and it was a couple of weeks ago!'

Elijah leans forward and says, 'There's been a murder *here?* In this town?'

The cabbie spins round to look Elijah straight on. 'Aye, there's been a murder here, mate. A guy was killed on one of the beaches. About three weeks ago. And I don't think the police have a clue who did it so... aye, the killer's still out there.'

Elijah responds, 'Good God. Well, I hope they find him soon. Or her.' And he thinks, *I don't bloody believe this. I got out of London to get away from murder and they've had one here. Am I the Angel of Death, or what?* He turns to get out the back of the taxi; it's a struggle to get his legs out behind the passenger seat that's been pushed back, until the driver sees his plight and moves it forward.

'Nae need tae sit in the back of these taxis, pal. You're no' in a black cab now!'

On the pavement, Elijah reaches back in to collect his holdall, then gently shuts the door. Leaning in towards the driver at his open window, he says, 'I'm gonna be in Berwick for a while and I'd like to use you for getting about if that's okay. Do you have a card?' The driver is already digging around in the glove compartment, retrieves one and hands it over. It says Morrison's Cabs.

'That's me, Savage Morrison. Eh… aye… everyone in this town has a nickname.'

'Thanks… err… Savage. My name's Elijah.' They exchange handshakes through the open window.

'Elijah, eh? I've never met an Elijah.'

'Well, err… I've never met a Savage.'

Savage roars and laughs, then engages first gear and explodes up the street, brakes at speed then turns left and disappears. Elijah Bootle pockets the business card and stands watching the taxi disappear from view. The sound of its roaring engine seems obscene in this quiet street. He turns to face a tall, whitewashed guest house displaying a "No Vacancies" sign in the window and, behind the sign, a cage containing what looks like an African Grey parrot. It's sitting motionless, giving him the evil eye, and Elijah smiles back. The formidable front door is painted a brilliant black sheen, and a brass knocker protrudes boldly out of its centre panel.

He's about to approach the door when he sees a young girl skipping along the pavement towards him; she's about eight years old. She's running then skipping and the exertion has flushed her cheeks which bookend a huge grin. She passes

Elijah without really noticing him and dances on down the street. Elijah's gaze follows her. It's the blue and white checked dress and white socks that suddenly rock him with a jolt. Clammy sweat gathers on his hands and forehead, and nausea sweeps over him as he's transported back to that filthy flat off Bermondsey Street in south east London. That girl had been wearing a blue checked dress when she was found… and a sock which had once been white. Violated, blinded, repeatedly raped over a period of days, then murdered. It wasn't his last case, but it was the one that nearly destroyed him.

He thought he was okay. Then it started. Vivid flashbacks where he relived the incident. Intrusive thoughts of the child's abused little body. Sweaty, sleepless nights. At his annual check-up at the Metropolitan Police Occupational Health Unit, the nurses had been concerned about his physical condition. He'd lost weight and looked tired, and his health questionnaire showed increased drinking and trouble concentrating. He'd been referred to a doctor, who'd diagnosed post-traumatic stress disorder. Take a holiday, the doc had said. Elijah had booked a fortnight off.

And this town seems just the place to kick back, relax and get my mindset healthy again. Just two weeks away should do it, he figured.

He knocks on the door while wiping sweat off his brow with the back of his arm. The door opens almost immediately, and a middle-aged woman is standing looking at him with a furrowed brow. 'Sorry, we've no vacancies. Sorry.'

She begins to close the door without waiting for an answer when Elijah responds, 'I've booked a room for a fortnight. My name's Elijah Bootle.' He thinks, *Yeah, I'm black. Fuckin' problem?*

'Oh, I'm sorry... eh... yes, Mr Bootle. Yes, of course. Come in, come in.' She turns and waddles back into the house. Elijah picks up his holdall and follows her in, gently closing the door behind him. She leads him down a dimly lit corridor to a small, snug reception all boarded out in oak with a staircase leading off it. They deal with the administration and Elijah pays up front. His laid-back manner and easy temperament cause most people to warm to him and this landlady is no exception. Beaming now, she says, 'Okay, Mr Bootle. That's all the paperwork done. My name's Mrs Barraclough but you can call me Lily. Here's your keys. This one fits the front door and that one's for your room. You'll find it up on the second floor.'

'Oh, thanks, err... Lily. Much appreciated. I saw the 'No Vacancies' sign in the window. You must be busy?'

'It's the middle of the tourist season, Mr Bootle. The town's jumpin', man!' she laughs.

Elijah shoulders his holdall and treads up the stairs. He unlocks the door and enters his room. It's bright and clean and decorated in a tasteful mushroom and cream. He tips his holdall out onto the bed and looks at the contents. It's the usual jumble of shirts, jeans, underwear and toiletries. A couple of books lie underneath a crumpled white linen shirt. He picks one up. It's by a pioneering criminal profiler. There's a comfortable-looking bed settee along the back wall but he chooses the armchair next to the window and sits down on it without taking his eyes from the book's bound cover. He'd bought it earlier on today at a bookshop in King's Cross. It looks different from other forms of profiling as the focus is on the nature and behaviour of the criminal. It adheres to the examination of the facts, which appeals to Elijah's personal approach. He becomes aware of the chair's deep comfortable upholstery and smiles. He twists the chair round so it faces the window and envisages many peaceful hours here, reading and occasionally looking out over the street.

He casually flicks through the book then gets up and retrieves a map of Britain from a side pocket of his holdall. He hadn't realised it was in there but came across it when rummaging for a pen on the train. Laying the map on the chair seat he sees the coffee-making facilities on a tray in a shelf beneath the television, so puts the kettle on and makes himself a cup of strong coffee. He throws the decaffeinated sachets into the waste bin under the sink. A cup of that rubbish always makes him feel cheated and ripped off.

Coffee made, he settles down again and opens up the map, balancing his cup on an arm of the chair. It's an AA map of Britain – old, well-thumbed, with strips of Sellotape holding together sections where the creases have caused the paper to split. He looks down at London then slowly traces his way up the map until he gets to the town of Berwick Upon Tweed. He nods slowly in confirmation that this town is so far away from London and its dregs. Although he's focusing on the map he's thinking about the murdered child. He sees her abused little body… lying there like a discarded doll. It's now preoccupying him, invading his thoughts like sharp spikes to the temple, which causes him to furrow his brow and lose concentration. On the day she was found, Elijah was called into Southwark Police Station for a briefing and to look at the photographs taken by detectives. They had questions for him.

Elijah sits back in the armchair with the cup in both hands and poised on his bottom lip. Motionless now, he sees the photographs again in his mind's eye. The dress, the filthy white sock, the sightless orbits, the dark-red caked blood. Hunger has now deserted him. He rises slowly, and from a small pouch on the bed he retrieves his stash of weed: Amnesia Haze. His drug of choice. He's always liked a smoke and recently it's been good for curbing his anxiety. He folds up the map onto his lap and, with methodical routine, places a long cigarette paper on it then rolls a conical-shaped joint. He holds it between thumb and forefinger and nods in appreciation. He lights it before realising he's no ashtray to hand, so drains the coffee in one big gulp then flicks the first traces of ash into the empty cup. It comes slowly – not a rush but a mellow loosening of tensions and emotions. He sinks further into the seat and finds himself drawn to a woman across the street, looking into an antique shop window. She's dressed eccentrically, with brogues, green knee-length socks, a short summer coat and what looks to Elijah like a leopard-skin shawl or stole around her neck. This item fascinates him. Every time she moves the fur seems to ripple around her neck like a living beast. The sunlight has blurred the colours of brown, beige and black rings into a subtle, gentle shade and Elijah wonders how soft the material must be to touch.

He finishes his joint and thinks he should open the window but can't be bothered to move. From a pocket in his loose-fitting cords he retrieves an MP3 player, complete with earphones. He eases lower into the seat and lets the weed sedate and comfort him. There's an escapism with marijuana that you don't get with alcohol. A Picnic bar lies on the bed and he could devour it right now, but he chooses to stay where he is, lost in the tranquillity of narcotics and the slow, hypnotic reggae beat.

Yellow beams of warm afternoon sunshine stream in through the window as he drifts off, dreaming that he's lying on a fur coat with soft, delicate hairs. But the dreamworld freedom is only temporary because no cage can restrain the human mind. In his dream he's lying on the coat, and next to his head is a filthy, blood-encrusted child's sock.

CHAPTER 2

FROM THE NORTH

SATURDAY

Jez Guinness throws his holdall into the back of the cab then follows it in.

'Waverley, please.' The taxi scoots along Restalrig Road, clearly breaking the speed limit.

'Nae cameras on this street!' the driver announces with a sneaky chuckle. He shoots his fare a look in the rear-view mirror. He looks like Robert De Niro. A De Niro look-a-like taxi driver! In Edinburgh.

Jez looks out the rain-spattered window. *Aye, nae fuckin' tourists either.* Black water gathers in the gutters. Locals shuffle along the pavement under coats and brollies, avoiding clumps of dog shite and blown-away litter. Overfull wheelie bins stand like sentries in front of shops. The roller metal shutters are pulled half down, displaying brightly coloured graffiti.

'Goin' anywhere nice?' asks the cabbie.

'Just down to Berwick for a few days,' replies Jez. 'It's my hometown. I'm gonna catch up with a few old friends.'

The driver's still eyeing him in the rear-view mirror, then says with a wee smile, 'Aye, so you're English, then?'

'Eh… well, no' really.' Jez can't be bothered to get into a conversation regarding his nationality so wipes condensation off the window and watches the rain-washed streets pass by. *Aye, I bet you're one of the thousands who belt out Flower of Scotland at Hampden and Murrayfield. O'er land that is lost now! The only land that Scotland's lost is my home town, and if you don't want it back stop singing songs about us.* Then Jez says, 'Has anyone ever said you look like Robert De Niro?' The cabbie twists his head round and gives him a full-on impression of De Niro's character in *Goodfellas*, complete with a faint smile. He obviously enjoys the comparison. Jez laughs and says, 'It's Jimmy Conway in *Goodfellas*!' The cabbie smiles as he turns back, and Jez wonders how often he practises that look in the mirror.

He doesn't want to share this with De Niro, but the reason he's going to Berwick is to attend the funeral of an old friend, Kevin Devine, who was murdered in the town three weeks ago. Shock fizzes through him every time he thinks about his death. And the manner of his killing. He'd known Kev for most of his life and they'd both knocked about together as teenagers. Most of Jez's mates had stayed in Berwick but he'd joined the Royal Navy when he was eighteen, although he'd kept in touch – weekends home, the odd reunion, Hibs games and New Year's Day drinking sessions around the pubs of Berwick, that sort of thing. Kev was only forty-eight. It's still hard to believe he's dead.

Down the ramp and into the bowels of Waverley railway station. He pays the driver and adds the obligatory tip, then walks over to Platform 10 to wait for the one o'clock train. Not too busy for a Saturday, and he vaguely recognises a couple of elderly women from his home town, maybe friends of his mum's. The train pulls in and they all pile on. He finds a spare seat and stuffs his holdall in the overhead luggage area. He'd originally planned to spend the weekend in Berwick, go to the funeral on the Monday then return to Edinburgh the following day, but as it's school holiday time he thought he'd stay a bit longer, so packed accordingly. He's got some marking to do and then preparation for the new term but he can crack on with that when he gets back. A teacher's life, eh? Everyone thinks you get six weeks off in the summer to piss about but it's not like that.

Just as they pull out, the two elderly women bustle themselves into the carriage and sit down opposite him. He thinks, *Do I know them?* They're blethering away in that soft, half Geordie, half Scottish accent with a bit of gypsy slang thrown in. Definitely Berwickers. He's by the window and sits up then tucks his legs under the seat to make more room for them. It's no fun having long, gangly legs on public transport. *Oh Christ, they can talk!* He's now hoping he *doesn't* know them. They take about five minutes to get their shopping bags onto the table then delve about in them to retrieve sandwiches, bottled water, chocolate and newspapers while a queue of people stand behind them in the aisle getting agitated and twitchy. The train lurches as it gathers speed and everyone standing is forced to grab hold of seat headrests and tables to stay upright.

Thank fuck I'm off here in about forty minutes, Jez thinks, and looks out the window at nothing in particular just so he doesn't have to enter into any kind of conversation. A dull pain begins to form in his head, just behind the left eye like it always does, so he fishes out a couple of ibuprofen and swallows them neat. He closes his eyes and feigns sleep. His mind drifts back to the long, hot summers of his adolescence. Life had been one long adventure back then. Playing football in the street, sometimes twenty a side. Down on the beach chatting up girls on holiday staying at the nearby holiday camp. Trekking up the river to hunt for fish and explore deserted fishing shiels. The salmon industry's all but finished now; even the poachers are struggling.

And of course, the obligatory hanging about with the gang on street corners, on the town hall steps, in public parks, doing nothing much at all. He now realises that hanging about doing nothing is doing something when you're a teenager. There's all that posturing and posing as they subconsciously find their positions in the gang's hierarchy. And Kev is always there in these warm, treasured memories. *And the clothes we wore, smart like!* He can now see Kev sharply in his mind's eye: Harrington jacket, Ben Sherman shirt, two-tone Sta Press and his regulation oxblood Doc Martens – a clone to the movement, battle dress for the "BUNDIG Boys".

But he was alright was Kev. Not as mental as, say, Wacka Short, a psycho of the highest order. He was a friend too, but you couldn't trust the fucker. Like, you could take the piss but not too far. He was a hard guy with a propensity for violence so you had to be careful. Even his close mates were wary of him due to his unpredictable temper and tendency to lash out at anyone who crossed him. Aye, Wacka Short, he's on a fuse as long as his name.

Jez first heard about Kev's murder the day after he was killed. He received a phone call from another old friend, Johnny Bang Bang, and he replays the conversation in his head from three weeks ago. Jez wasn't a big fan of Bang Bang, with his greasy hair, yellow teeth and dodgy dress sense. He also didn't care for him because he always thought him weak, the butt of everyone's jokes but unable to do much about it. But, to cover up his physical weakness, Bang Bang always carried a weapon, any weapon, and was not afraid to use it. He got called Bang Bang because he was born without ring fingers and pinkies, and from a distance he looked like he was carrying a gun in each hand.

The train begins to pick up speed and suddenly lurches right and left as it passes through the Meadowbank area. Jez gazes out onto the rows of tenements flashing by. He catches a glimpse of a window with a filthy, ill-fitting net curtain and wonders who lives behind it. He hears a newspaper being opened by one of the elderly women opposite him, so lazily opens one eye. It's a broadsheet and he immediately recognises the publication: The *Berwick Advertiser*, or the "Berwick Liar" as it's affectionately known. He can only see the back page, which headlines 'Last gasp equaliser saves 'Gers!"', which is referring to Berwick Rangers' latest exploits in the Scottish footballing wilderness. The 'Gers do have two claims to fame though. Putting the "Big 'Gers" out the Cup back in nineteen hundred and frozen to death and the fact that they are an English team playing in the Scottish league.

He hears a voice from behind the newspaper. 'Aye, so that's how he died. Drowned. It's frightening, it really is,' says one of the old women, referring to something she's reading on the front page.

Responding to the cue, the other woman puts her glasses on and is now leaning over to get a better look at the page. She blurts out, 'Look, it says there he was found on Murphy's Beach. I'd heard he was in one of the caves next to the harbour wall.'

The other woman replies, 'Well, I'd heard he was found further along, you know, near to the outdoor pool.' Jez finds himself smiling and slowly shaking his head as he hears the phrase: "I'd heard". He bets every gossip in town is prefixing their sentences with that comment just now! Because it gives you power, you see. You can say anything, anything at all, regardless of how fantastic it is, without fear of recrimination. It's not the speaker's view, you see, it's something they've *heard.*

Even though his murder was weeks ago, the inquest was only last week, hence the headline story in the *Advertiser*. And, as the press are allowed into the public gallery, the full details of his grisly murder are now known. He'd been beaten unconscious on a beach then tethered to a wooden stake and left to drown by the incoming tide. He was found the next morning by a couple of kids who'd gone to the beach to pick winkles. And Kev's death was always going to be headline news. Berwick's a small, seaside town with little crime so a murder was a huge story. Jez knows his town; the rumour mill will be going into overdrive as people speculate on motive, cause and culpability. He's keen to see the article and finds himself concentrating on the back page as if it will somehow open a channel to the front page like the wardrobe to Narnia. But all he can see is a photograph of a footballer and a ball in the air near an empty net.

Time passes and the gentle sideways rocking of the train causes him to drift off. He wakes to see the distant fringes of Berwick: first the lighthouse out at the end of the pier then the new industrial estates on the town's outskirts. It used to be about three miles from the border but over the last decade or so the town has crept northwards, courtesy of these new units, waste disposal sites and other ugly buildings. What a contrast to the old town, enclosed within its proud, stout walls boasting historic buildings, Georgian townhouses, upmarket coffee shops and quaint cobbled streets with shops selling antiques, bric-a-brac and Celtic jewellery, as well as the usual assortment of tacky outlets catering for the summer tourist trade.

The sudden squeal of the train's brakes jolts him out of grogginess. The two women are already up out of their seats and collecting shopping bags and what's left over from their little picnic. *What are they panicking for? There's plenty of time.* As the train draws into the station he looks down and sees the grassy embankment on the opposite side to the platform. As teenagers they'd hitchhike up to Edinburgh to see Hibs then jump the train home and hide in the toilets if a guard was around. As they pulled into Berwick they'd open the doors then leap out and land on the embankment before running off, usually giggling with fear and excitement.

He stands and stretches, resists the urge to yawn out loud, then reaches up and collects his holdall before making his way to the end of the carriage. He waits by the door as the train slowly comes to a stop; there's a pause before the hydraulic doors hiss at him then open, inviting him to step out onto the platform. He walks to the steps which lead up and over the tracks and reminds himself to buy a copy of the *Advertiser* in the shop near the exit.

Another train has pulled in on the opposite track. It's the London train heading north to Aberdeen. Half a dozen passengers have alighted and are now embracing friends who have been waiting patiently. Jez sees a tall black man with short dreads and a goatee beard making his way to the steps. He buys the newspaper then walks outside to the taxi rank. Above, the rain clouds have passed and the sky gleams with the brilliance of blue enamel. It's such a nice day he decides to walk instead, so slings the holdall over his shoulder and heads for the New Road, which is a path along the river into town. The bag is heavy but there's no way he's going to buy one of those trolley bags, complete with wheels and a telescopic handle! He's a man! A gadgee! He doesn't own a softie trolley bag. Imagine if someone like Wacka saw him prancing down the high street pulling one of those! Alone now on the path into town, he laughs out loud at the abuse he'd receive. But his laugh peters out as his thoughts return to his dead friend and the reason why he's back in his home town.

The riverside path takes him under two of the three bridges that span the River Tweed and then onto Bridge Street where he's booked his accommodation: a wee guest house sandwiched between an Indian restaurant and a small, single-room art gallery. He arrives at the front door and knocks so hard his knuckles ache. He hopes his room's okay as it's booked for a week. So, he's got the weekend, then it's the funeral on Monday then… *Well, what are you going to do? See your mates, visit your mum, go to your sister's grave. And your dad's.* The thought of cemeteries brings him back full circle.

One of your oldest friends has been murdered. Are the local police up for this type of crime? The last time someone was murdered in Berwick, Methuselah was a boy. He's still pondering this thought when the door opens.

CHAPTER 3

AFTERNOON

SATURDAY

'Hi, I'm Jeremy Guinness. I've booked a room for the week.'

The landlady smiles and says, 'Yes, I know who you are. It's Jez, isn't it? I was talking to your mum in the hairdressers last week and she told me her son would be staying here. Yeah, she taught me English at the High School. God, it must be years since I last saw you.'

Jez shakes his head and smiles. This is life in a small town. You sneeze in the high street and by the time your home you've got the bubonic plague! She extends her hand and says, 'I'm Lesley Abercorn. You won't remember me though. I must be ten years younger than you! Come in, Jez.' He likes this woman immediately; you know when you meet someone and instantly feel comfortable with them. Introductions over, he slings the holdall over his shoulder, all macho-like, and follows Lesley into the property. He thinks, *Good-looking woman, classy.* And inevitably his comfort is already beginning to erode as it always does when he's in the company of an attractive woman. He suddenly feels tongue-tied and is sure his face has reddened slightly. *Christ, Jez, get a grip, for fuck's sake.*

'So, you're up in Edinburgh now, then?' asks Lesley.

'Yeah, I've been there for a few years now. I'm teaching Maths at a High School. My mum's in sheltered housing now down West Street so I can't stay there.'

'I know that too!' she responds, then leads him along the corridor and points into a room. 'Breakfast room's on your left and we serve a full range from 7.30am until 10am.' He peeks in. There's a huge mahogany table and he realises that breakfast will be a communal thing, where the guests sit round the big oak table and make small talk. He can just see the kitchen door leading off it. 'And on your right is the sitting room which you can use at any time.' He looks in and it's dark and comfy looking. The shelves are stacked with books and there's an assortment of leather chairs and settees. The upholstery has that ancient leathery smell which oozes out into the corridor. They're about to go up a flight of stairs when Lesley turns and smiles, saying, 'Yes, this isn't a boutique bed and breakfast. It's a proper, old-fashioned B&B built for comfort!'

'I like it, Lesley. Aye, I like it a lot. Loads of character. How many guests have you got staying?'

'Well, there's only three guest rooms, and I've got a Dutch couple (she starts counting on her fingers, like people do), a Norwegian family, and you,' she says, smiling, before leading him up the stairs which has a bannister and dog-leg. 'Your room is at the front overlooking the street. It's not double-glazed but Bridge Street's quiet at night so you'll be fine.' He follows her up the stairs; her black jeans are tight with no belt and each time she climbs a step a tiny gap appears between her jeans and her back and he gets a glimpse of the top of a pair of black, minute-looking knickers. Every time, and he feels himself flushing again. Now along the first-floor corridor he can see the door to his room is open. She walks in first then holds the door open and extends her other arm, inviting him in.

Jez dumps his holdall on the bed and looks around. 'Oh, very nice. Yes, very nice.'

'Okay, I'll let you settle in, then. There are three keys on that fob (pointing to them on the bedside table). One's for your room and the other two are for the main door. A Yale and a mortice so you can come and go as you please. We don't lock up shop at eleven o'clock so just treat the place as your own,' she says, smiling.

'Oh, that's good. Thanks,' he responds, sounding like a daft wee laddie.

Lesley walks away and he shuts the door and faces the room. It's airy and spacious. Smells of clean linen. The en-suite bathroom is on the left and next to it is a walk-in wardrobe. He walks to the window and draws the vertical blinds to one side. *Christ, it's one of those old double sash windows!* Hidden behind the curtains are two sashes so he grabs one and raises the bottom window. The hidden counterweight clanks in protest as he secures the sash, then he pokes his head out to see what's happening in Bridge Street on this fine summer's afternoon. The sun flits behind a cloud then begins to reappear, and he watches as the cloud shadow is swept away, chased along the street by the sun's rays until it reaches him and he's zapped, and it feels warm and luxurious. He looks along the street to the bottom of the junction with Hide Hill, then the other way where the street veers off left to cross the River Tweed. It's business as usual. This street is nothing like the busy high street, which is like "Clone Town" with its poxy WHSmith, Boots and Burger King interspaced with depressing looking charity shops. *Aye, I hate the way these big companies have their signs sticking out at right angles to the shop. I don't want to see a crappy "New Look" sign from half a mile away. No, no, no, no.*

By contrast the best word to describe Bridge Street would be "nostalgic". Businesses here have been passed down from one generation to the next. There's a couple of family run bakers, independent butchers, hairdressers and oldy worldy antique shops. They've been there forever. And to give it a real bohemian feel, a couple of art galleries have sprung up on the street, alongside quirky little coffee shops and eco-friendly grocery stores. The fascias above these shops aren't bright and gaudy so don't detract from the character of the buildings. Not many holidaymakers from the camp get down here; there's not a "bucket and spade" shop in sight. This street is like a secret for Berwickers and they want to keep it that way. He gets a faint whiff of Indian food from the restaurant next door and starts to salivate. *Christ, I'm starving.*

He returns to the bed and opens up the holdall, wondering if he's brought enough clothes to see him through the week. The wardrobe has an assortment of coat hangers so he hangs up his black shirt and suit brought for the funeral, a couple more shirts and jeans and then the obligatory T-shirts and light jumpers. A shower's required to wake him up but hunger's taken hold. He's suddenly got a hankering for fish and chips so makes do with brushing his teeth, splashes some water on his face and he's ready to go.

Picking up the keys he sees the *Berwick Advertiser* in his holdall so takes that too. If he lived in Berwick he probably wouldn't read this paper, but as he visits infrequently he can happily spend an hour or so devouring every page. Except the farming section. He stares at the headline: "Beach Murder Victim Was Drowned". The inquest was last Tuesday, and the report takes up most of the front page and gives a breakdown of Kev's movements on the night of his death. The headline confirms that although he had suffered serious blunt trauma injuries, the cause of death was drowning. Even though he's aware of these details, to see the words in print causes him to shudder at the barbarity of his death. The injuries sound gruesome, and extreme violence was used against his friend. His fingertips dampen as he holds the paper and digests every gory detail.

He's still preoccupied with these thoughts as he locks his room and makes his way downstairs, and he hopes he doesn't meet anyone. He's tired and in one of those moods where you struggle to formulate sentences; you know, like when you're hungover and the brain's become sluggish and disjointed. Out into the street he pulls the heavy front door shut and listens for the click of the Yale lock. As it's such a lovely day he decides to walk along Bridge Street then up Hide Hill, past the town hall and up to the Cannon chippie on Church Street. He loves Hide Hill; it's wide, like an avenue, with steps up to the pavements on each side. And the cars don't park parallel to the kerb or even at right angles. No, they're all parked at about a thirty-degree angle to the pavement so from the bottom of the street it looks like a multi-coloured car chevron. There's a couple of bars, a wine lodge, estate agents, an Italian restaurant and, at the top, ice-cream parlours and cafés.

Jez likes the pace of the street too; like Bridge Street there's a gentle calmness, and people are stopping and blethering to each other like they've got all day, and probably have! He's looking in a jewellery shop window. Not to admire the merchandise, you understand, but there's a big chrome-bordered mirror behind a display and he checks himself out and thinks he's ten years too late for that "Just For Men". A quick look up and down the street and no one's looking so he ruffles his hair to try and make it, and him, look more youthful. The hair is speckled with grey and he's lost a bit of weight around his face. *Okay for forty-eight*, he concludes with a trace of a nod.

'Aye, you're still an ugly bastard!' He freezes. *Fuck!* He drops his cigarette and stamps it out without turning. He's still looking in the mirror but sees the funny side now. He spins round and sees a taxi driver sitting in his taxi, looking chilled with an arm hanging out the open window and smoking what looks like a roll-up cigarette, although he won't know for sure until he gets closer.

'I was just checking the jewellery, Savage.'

'Fuck off, I saw you posing there. What were you doing like, checkin' your George Michael stubble?!'

Jez smiles and walks over. 'None o' *your* fuckin' business, SLAPHEID!' He's now at the car and has his hands on the roof, and his head's bent down and partly in the open window. If they were strangers this would be too close, but they've known each other since they were snotty little gits together. 'Ahh, Savage. Long time no see, pal. How's it goin'?' The driver puts the cigarette in his mouth and they shake hands. You know the way, when only the thumbs cross, as if they're about to go head to head in an arm wrestling contest.

'Ticking over, Jez, you know. No prizes for guessing why you're home.'

They release their grip and Jez pulls out the newspaper he'd jammed under his armpit and shows him the headline. 'Funeral on Monday, pal.'

'Aye, I'm taking the day off work. The wake's in The Brown Bear like, so it might turn into a right session. I was talking to Kev just a couple of days before, you know. Unbelievable, Jez.'

'What's the craic, then, Savage?'

'What? Who killed him? Fuck knows. Rumours are rife, like. They must have used something like a fuckin' baseball bat, you know. His mam wasn't allowed to see his face it was that bad. Not that she'd recognise him, like. Apparently his heid was swollen to twice the size. I feel sorry for the two young chavas who found him.'

'Fuck's sake. How's his mum?'

'Oh, she's in a bad way. I feel heartily sorry for her. I tell you, Kev's death's been the talk of this taxi for nearly a month.' Savage's mobile phone starts ringing. The ring tone's "You've Got My Number" by The Undertones at about 140 decibels. 'Hang on, pal.' He takes the call then turns to Jez and says, 'Gotta shoot, pal. Listen, I might catch up with you over the weekend for a pint. Where you staying?'

'IN A B&B ALONG BRIDGE STREET,' shouts Jez as Savage reverses wildly, spins the car round then accelerates down the street.

Jez raises his hand and watches him disappear down the

road then shoots a left. He carries on up Hide Hill, now preoccupied with thoughts of Kevin Devine. But that Kevin Devine, that guy is no longer. What's left is a battered, broken, pulverised mass of dead skin and bones. He turns left at the top, then crosses behind the town hall and on to Church Street. The chip shop is halfway up the street but he can smell it from here. *I think I'll head up to The Brewers Arms tonight. See some old faces. See what's goin' down.*

There are quite a few holidaymakers about. You can tell the guys a mile off with their baldy heids and tattoos, accompanied by overweight, loud women sporting bleached, straw-like hair and screeching at a couple of kids who have names like Chantelle, Madison or Kylie. And wearing a football strip is de rigueur attire, with no gender preference. He sidesteps a Geordie family wearing identical Newcastle United replica shirts, then passes a gaggle of pasty-faced Hearts fans staring in a traditional butcher's window like they'd never seen meat before. He arrives at the Cannon chippie and pushes the door open, thinking *When was the last time I had a sit-down fish and chip supper in here?*

It's chock-a-block, with no free tables. But you don't know this as each table is situated in a small booth, so he has to walk down the aisle looking in each one from side to side. For some reason he begins to get embarrassed. Fuck knows why. He reaches the last two booths. In one is a loved-up couple snogging over their pie, chips and mushy peas. In the other is a large black man with the remains of a meal in front of him. Jez thinks, *Christ, he's the guy I just saw up at the station before.* He's nursing a huge mug of coffee and reading a newspaper.

Jez asks, 'Do you mind if I sit here?'

CHAPTER 4

THE CANNON CHIP SHOP

SATURDAY

The diner looks up hesitantly from his newspaper then gestures with an open hand for Jez to sit down. They exchange polite smiles. Jez chooses the aisle seat so they're diagonally opposite. There's a menu on the table so he picks it up and starts to scan down the list. From here he can see right down to the front of the shop, with the entrance door at one side, the serving counter on the other and a huge frying range behind it. The floor-to-ceiling plate-glass window which serves as the shop's frontage is heavy with condensation. Two kids are looking in from outside, close up to the glass. Grubby hands enclose their faces to block out the sunlight glare, like they've both donned snorkels.

His memory transports him back to his own youth, when he would press his face up to windows at chip shops, sweet shops, bakers' shops. *Remember that joke shop down West Street?!*

Kev, Wacka, Johnny Bang Bang, Cement Shoes, Bob, CD and Fish Heid were all there. When they were kids they would bring empty lemonade bottles back to this chippy and get money for them. Sixpence each – about two pence in today's money! In his mind's eye he can see the transaction taking place at the counter, circa 1978. They'd watch the staff tipping freshly cut chips into the huge fat fryers. They'd ask for bags of "scraps", which were tiny bits of batter that had been gathered up and placed on the top shelf of the brightly lit range, just along from the battered fish, haggis and jumbo sausages.

'I recommend the fish and chips,' says the diner, smiling at him.

'Oh, err… yeah, okay,' Jez responds and then feels he needs to add something. 'I was miles away there. Err, is it table service or do you order at the counter?'

'It's table service, with a notepad and pen. All very traditional.' The diner is slowly nodding with a lopsided, likeable smile. As he's saying this, Jez sees a waitress approaching wearing a white staff coat and trousers under a blue and white bib apron and matching baseball cap. They make eye contact and he smiles as she gets to the table, pad and pen at the ready. *She's about my age. Don't know her though. Bonny woman. Redhead too. Very nice.* He looks her straight in the eye.

'Haddock and chips, please, with beans and two buttered rolls. Oh, and a tomato ketchup sachet as well. No, make it two.' He holds up two fingers and wonders why as he's just told her.

'Oh, so you like tomato ketchup, then?' She raises her eyebrows, scarcely disguising the flirtation in her voice and expression. Immediately she's got the upper hand and they both know it. He's flustered now as he knows the guy sharing his table is privy to the scene. She nods at the table saying, 'That not enough for you?' He follows her stare and sees a huge, round plastic tomato ketchup holder, complete with green plastic stalk, next to the salt, vinegar and tartar sauce. He catches the other man's eye, who immediately looks back at his newspaper, smiling away to himself!

She's writing on the pad now. 'There's nae haddock left. We've got cod though.'

'Nah, they're bottom feeders. You got plaice?' enquires Jez, now trying to recover the situation.

'Naw, sorry. I can put haddock on, but it'll take ten minutes, like.'

'Okay. I'll have that. Better get your skates on, then.'

She walks away then stops and turns back to him, laughing now. She has a wide, full grin showing beautiful, sparkling teeth. Jez replaces the menu into its wooden base and notices the man smiling at the joke, which gives him the cue to open a conversation. 'Aye, you have to be a "coasty" to get that joke.'

'Well, not necessarily,' responds the diner, shaking his head. 'I'm a Londoner and that's inland… but my dad worked as a waiter in a fish restaurant. Hey, I know my fish! We used to have it for breakfast!' He laughs again, almost in a quiet way, as if he's reminiscing to himself.

Jez smiles then says, 'Actually, I think I've already seen you today. Weren't you up at the railway station before?'

'I *was* at the railway station earlier, yes. What *are* you? A cop? Are you following me or something?' He's still smiling, although there's a slight apprehension in his voice.

Jez is laughing now. 'Naw, mate, no. I've just got off a train myself and I thought I recognised you.'

'I must stand out,' replies Elijah. He looks round and catches the loved-up couple opposite staring over at him, and they quickly divert their gazes elsewhere. He looks back at Jez and says, 'You better not be a cop.'

Jez laughs out loud, almost too loud. 'No, no. I'm a teacher. Maths. Not here though, up in Edinburgh. But this is my home town. By the way, my name's Jez.'

He extends his hand and, as they shake, the diner replies, 'I'm Elijah. Pleased to meet you. Ah, Edinburgh. I love that city. Who doesn't?! And there's a feel to the place, like you *feel* safe. Not like… other cities I know.' He feels on edge and vulnerable but feels the need to add something. 'I've… I've spent a few weekends up there. And hey, what city has an extinct volcano just off its main street?' he says in little more than a whisper now.

'Well, two, if you include Arthur's Seat,' Jez replies. 'But it's got its problems like any other city, you know: drugs, deprived areas—'

'Ah… but the kids must be easy to teach, though. Surrounded by all that history and culture.'

'Listen, I'm at Liberton High, not George Heriot's! They're schools in Edinburgh, by the way. Anyway, I try not to think about work when I'm on holiday. No' that I'm home for a jolly. I've got a funeral to attend on Monday.' He retrieves the *Berwick Advertiser* from the seat next to him and shows the brutal headline. A wave of concern crosses Elijah's face but it passes so soon Jez barely sees it. 'This guy who was murdered,' he says, pointing to the black and white image next to the story, 'I grew up with him. Kinda known him all my life, you know. We used to come in here as…' The conversation is suddenly drowned out by the noise of an automatic potato peeler starting up in a back room off the passage behind him. Jez doesn't want to raise his voice over the racket of potatoes clunking around so moves his head closer to the man, who responds in kind. From a distance you'd think they were being conspiratorial. The loved-up couple in the booth across the way nervously glance over. Jez clocks them and thinks, *Do you think we're a couple of fuckin' gangsters, like, arranging a heist?* Thing is, they did look like two hard men talking business.

'Aye, we used to come in here as kids. Through the back behind me there's a room with a pool table and juke box. Spent a load of time there. Wasted a load of time there, really. Anyway, he was murdered a few weeks ago and the funeral's on Monday.' Elijah nods with a sympathetic frown but looks uncomfortable, so Jez changes the subject. 'Well, you're a long way from home. What brings you up here, then? Weekend break?'

'Well, it's a break and it's a bit longer than a weekend. I'm staying for a fortnight. Staying just up the road in a B&B. And what brings me up here?' Elijah puffs his cheeks and blows out slowly. He looks anxious now and less self-assured. He remembers the doctor telling him that it's "good to talk"so he steadies himself and says, 'Put it this way. Your line of work is teaching, yeah?' Jez nods, serious now as the mood has changed. 'Well, umm, mine's… it's… death. Murder, actually. I work for the Met, plain clothes. And, err… well, death and dead bodies can mess with your head, man. Sometimes you just need to get away, y'know? Sometimes. I think they call it gardening leave.'

'Oh right. You said you were plain clothes? Are you a detective, like?' Jez replies, sounding impressed and interested.

'Well no, not exactly. Not in the traditional sense of the word. I'm a criminal profiler.'

'You're a criminal profiler?' responds Jez, drawing out the words like he's surprised. 'Well... I wasn't expecting you to say that. Ah mean... you don't really look like—'

'I don't really look like a criminal profiler,' cuts in Elijah. 'I've been hearing that shit for years, man.'

Jez understands the message behind Elijah's comment and smiles. Then he says, 'I've gotta say, it sounds like an interesting profession. I mean, apart from those aspects you've just mentioned.' The potato machine suddenly stops but he remains close to Elijah's face, lowering his voice. 'I was gonna say, good job you showed up then, but obviously not after what you just told me.'

Elijah's already shaking his head. 'Hey, pal, it's not my manor! And I'm on holiday. Vacation, you know. Convalescence! And, umm... I kinda want to keep it that way. No offence, mate. Anyway, they won't need me. On a case like that (he nods towards the paper lying between them) they'll have an investigation team put together from this region. And part of that team will be the local CID. And some local officers. And I'm sure they'll do a good job.'

'The local police?!' replies Jez. 'Christ, they're still on bloody pushbikes! Aye, they do a good job chasing kids playing football on the school field or arresting drunks fighting on a Saturday night, but this,' he says, pointing to the paper, 'this is right out of their league, man.' Elijah takes the paper and starts to read the article, although, after what he just said, Jez assumes it's out of courtesy. As he's talking, he sees the waitress approaching with his meal. Her hips are swinging rhythmically. Now at the table she lays a huge plate of haddock, chips and beans in front of him then lays down a smaller plate with the buttered rolls. She bends forward and he can see her breasts straining at the bib apron. She's smiling right at him and holding the position a moment too long.

'There you go, Jez! That'll keep your energy levels up!'

'How do you know my name? Do I know you?'

'I don't think you'll remember me, but Fiona knows you well.'

He looks down the shop and see the manageress behind the counter. An old friend, she's married to a mate of his. 'What's your name, then?'

'It's Josie,' she replies, looking right at him again. 'Enjoy your meal.' Full lips and a great jawline. He's not the only diner checking her out as she slinks back down to the counter.

'Looks like someone's checking you out, my friend,' says Elijah. Jez pulls a face like he's thinking about it. He's keen to return to the subject of Kev's murder investigation but can see Elijah getting ready to leave.

'Well, it's been nice talking to you, Jez. Enjoy your meal. I might see you around. And… err… I'm sorry to hear about your friend's death. Hopefully his family will get some closure after the funeral.' Elijah rises now, pushing his chair back, its backrest banging against the booth wall behind him.

'Well, I hope this wee holiday does you some good… and err…' Jez trails off, not knowing how to convey the "get well soon" message. 'You said you were here for a fortnight. Might see you around, then.' He's looking up at him and realising how tall this guy is, like he's looking at him properly for the first time.

'Yeah, two weeks. Might stay longer. I'm kinda liking the smell of the sea air.'

'Okay, see you, pal,' replies Jez, filling a roll with chips. The big man nods, then walks down to the counter, pays for his meal and exits. Jez watches him. He's deep in thought. *Well, would you believe that? A guy's been murdered – battered unconscious, tied up, then left to drown on a beach – and I bump into a criminal profiler! From the Met! In the Cannon Chip Shop!*

He tucks into his meal with relish, cutting into the batter with a crisp crunch. He thinks about Elijah and the horrors he must have witnessed.

He thinks about the funeral on Monday.

He thinks about his sister's funeral. The years melt back like a spring snowdrift. Not that her funeral was springlike. It was the middle of January, in late afternoon darkness. Snow buried the base of tree trunks, and snowflakes stuck to the hard soil. The tarmac paths were rutted with ice. Mourners huddled together under black coats and brollies angled down to protect them from a freezing wind which bit their faces. He can see those faces now. Close family, relatives, schoolmates and friends. All the BUNDIG were there, Kev amongst them. Mostly in ill-fitting suits and scuffed shoes. But they were all there. Even Fifty Fifty, who was recovering from cancer at the time.

He looks over at the loved-up couple in the booth across from him. Apart from the odd nervous glance over they've spent their entire time giggling, smooching and slobbering over each other. Everything the guy says seems to be a cue for his girlfriend to either touch his face or burst out laughing. She's got her hands cupped around his face now, and she's leaning over, pulling his face towards hers, and it becomes a full-on open-mouth job. Jez looks over while his tongue tries to dislodge a renegade bean that's taken refuge between his teeth and cheek, like a ball in a pinball machine that the flipper can't quite reach. To no avail. A quick look round, no one looking, he puts his pinky right up into the recess and retrieves the annoying little bastard.

Meal over, he hides behind his paper, burping silently. He wanted to read the paper from cover to cover but he's not in the mood now. He can't concentrate. He sees Josie at the counter by herself so makes his move. Walking purposefully down the aisle he notices that the booths are still busy, left and right. Nearing the counter, he hears the sharp, high note of frying chipped potatoes.

'Aye, you can run, son, but you cannae hide. How you deein', Jez?' He spins round and sees Fiona behind him with a tray of dirty plates. She's half Scottish, half Italian and not someone to tangle with.

'I'm fine, Fiona. Fine. Hey, I thought *you* were the boss round here!' he says, pointing to the tray, which is piled up high.

'I am, Jez!' She laughs, now near to Josie at the counter so she can hear. 'I think one of ma staff's bein' distracted!' She sidles up to him and whispers, 'She's fancied you since school. Honest!'

Jez feigns naivety and approaches the counter. 'How much?' he asks, holding out a tenner. She smiles, takes it and turns to the till behind her. He absorbs the view. She spins her head round, sees he's looking at her and smiles at him.

She's biting her bottom lip. He smiles back and feels

a stirring. She returns to the counter and dabs a hanky at her forehead. 'You won't remember me, Jez, I'm a few years younger than you, but you know ma brother, Monty. He lives out in Spain now.'

'You're Monty's sister! Right, right. I vaguely remember you now. Aye, you've got the same colouring right enough.' They talk about her brother and how he's doing.

She places the change into his outstretched hand and says, 'Okay, I'll tell him you were asking for him. There's enough change there for a pint on your way home.'

'Is that it?' He feigns incredulity. 'It's obviously been a long time since you bought a pint!'

'It's a long time since I've been on a night out. And err… you can read that later.'

Among the change is a yellow note, folded in half. She's blushing furiously now and grabs a cloth before making her way down the shop. Jez smiles, pockets the note and cash, gives a stupid, cheesy grin and turns to leave. Just then the shop door bursts open and a police officer marches straight up to the counter.

'Eh, it's Fiona, yes? Fiona Rossillini?'

'Yes, what's wrong?' replies the manageress, a hand involuntarily going up to cover her mouth in anticipated shock.

'It's your son, Mrs Rossillini. He's in the nick next door.'

'Oh Christ! What's happened? What's he done, like?'

'He's assaulted a guy. Outside the Pilot Inn, this afternoon. No' sure if he's getting charged.'

'Ah, well, that'll be another pub he's barred from, then. Well, look… thanks for taking the trouble to come in and tell me.'

'I'm not. He wants a fish supper.'

'He what?! He wants a fish supper?! I'll gie him a fish supper when I see *him*, the little shit! Are you serious? He's asked you to come in here and get him a fish supper? And he's in the nick next door for fighting? Nah, forget it!' She's furious. The cop's still at the counter, now rummaging about in his pocket, as Jez makes his exit, slowly closing the door. *I wonder if they do that at the Met? Y'know, go out and get a prisoner a fish supper!* He stands on the pavement and looks up Church Street as the afternoon shadows lengthen. He's deep in thought.

Elijah's staying up there. I wonder which B&B he's in.

Could he solve this murder?

Does he want to? I doubt it. Not after what he told me.

CHAPTER 5

NIGHTFALL

SATURDAY

Jez retraces his steps back down the street then onto Hide Hill. The town hall clock chimes six times. He loves this time of day in Berwick, especially on a Saturday. The transition from day to night isn't just physical, with the shops shutting, streets emptying and shadows lengthening. No, there's an atmosphere of anticipation. It's Saturday night and he senses a gut elation from the shopkeepers as they turn down their lights and lock up their premises. It's not like this in Edinburgh where, like any city, it's open for business round the clock. There doesn't seem to be that demarcation which separates day from night, with the usual city latenight shopping, twenty-four-hour gyms, permanently open fast-food shops and taxi drivers who must sleep in their cabs.

He thinks about the night ahead. He's due to meet up with some of the old BUNDIG gang. Not that he's planned it, he just knows they'll be in The Brewers Arms on the high street like every other Saturday night. And being a teacher means getting a load of stick from these lifelong friends. To some of them, teaching's a cushy occupation, remote from any sweat, grime and physical toil. A "soft" job. So they take the piss and he finds myself in the hot seat more than most, until he can deflect the attention to someone else.

Anyway, most of his mates became steel erecters, scaffolders, welders. You know, *men's work.* But they grew up together and grew up equal. Free school meals, free school uniforms, second-hand clothes. Badges of hardship. As kids they gravitated towards each other and became feral children. The BUNDIG bonded them. The gang had a core of about twenty back then, with another half a dozen hangers-on. They were all Hibs fans and started travelling up to home games as a mob. That was about 1982. So long ago now. BUNDIG – Berwick United Never Defeated In Green. Although most of them came from the south side they weren't territorial. There were half a dozen other gangs of boys based in the West End, Prior Park and Spittal, but their main rivals came from the tough Highfields Estate in the north of the town. Known as the Men Of Berwick, aka the MOB, they were a Hearts gang.

Jez walks down Hide Hill. There's been a wedding at the Kings Arms, and he sees a group of guys in hired kilts with "whisky glow" faces smoking outside the main entrance. They're puffing furiously. *Must be between courses,* he contends, now lighting up a cigarette himself and guessing he's got time to smoke it before he reaches his B&B. The roof of his mouth has a thin film of fish batter coated on it and he reminds himself to brush his teeth when he gets in. Seeing the Kings Arms reminds him of an incident donkey's years ago when Berwick played Newcastle in a pre-season friendly. A gang of Geordie skinheads spilled out the pub and chased Johnny Bang Bang up the street. When the first boy reached him, Johnny pulled out a nine-inch nail and stabbed the guy in the stomach before nashing up the high street to safety. This earned him a mental reputation which he thrived upon. Aye, he's a dangerous little bastard is Bang Bang.

He lets himself in as the Indian restaurant next door opens, and already there's a spicy aroma emanating into the street. But a stomach weighed down with fish and chips isn't receptive to these delicious smells. Walking along the corridor towards the staircase he hears Lesley singing quietly in the kitchen. The sitting room door is ajar, and the warm, humid day has intensified the musty odour of old books with their glued spines, and this warm, homely smell accompanies him up the stairs to his room. He brushes his teeth then empties his pockets onto the bedside table. And there's the note that Josie squeezed into his hand. He opens it up to reveal her name and a mobile number. A warm feeling rushes up from his stomach.

He's lying on the duvet and pulls half of it over him as sleep beckons. He sets the clock alarm on the bedside table for 7pm then drifts off. The dream commences almost immediately, like a hand-delivered note from his subconscious mind. He's at home in Edinburgh, brushing his teeth in the bathroom. He looks up and realises there's no reflection. He looks closer, then suddenly, behind him, people are passing the open bathroom door. They're talking and laughing, clearly oblivious to him. They're removing his furniture, books, guitars, clothes. Then

Kevin Devine fills the doorway. He's smiling widely, then bursts out laughing. Then his open mouth spews out wet sand and stones onto the bathroom floor. But he's still laughing. And now he's on his knees, retching in front of Jez, who shouts out "KEVIN" and he knows he has, even though he's still asleep. Consciousness comes slowly, his mind still picking through the dream events. He wakes in stages then lies there, head to one side. He'd left the window open from the afternoon and a cool chill has filled the room, along with the subtle aroma of spices from the restaurant next door.

His headache's returned. Stronger than when he was on the train earlier. He gets up slowly, shuffles to the bathroom and downs two more ibuprofen with a glass of water. He gets these blinding headaches occasionally. Sometimes he gets a migraine and has to go to bed and sleep it off. But he's got Sumatran for those bastards, and they do the trick, so he always keeps some handy. Migraines, fuckin' migraines. They don't come often but when they do they put him in a bad place. He's been getting them for nearly thirty years now, ever since he was attacked, which left him with over forty stitches in his head. His ear was hanging off. He was a twenty-year-old sailor on a night out in Plymouth. The man was a piece of filth. He'd smashed a dimple pint mug across his head in a pub. The judge described it as an unprovoked attack on a complete stranger. Sneaked up behind him to do it too, the cowardly little fucker.

He decides to ring Wacka. He's not really sure why. Maybe a protocol from years ago when he was the "de facto" leader and tended to call the shots. The last time he'd spoken to him was the night after Bang Bang phoned to tell him about Kev's murder. He taps in a number and waits. 'Wacka, it's Jez here.

How you deein', pal?' He instantly lapses back into the local dialogue.

'Fuckin' hell, it's Pythagoras himself, the great mathematician. Long time no hear. Where are you?' A typical Wacka telephone response: no warmth, no small talk and the usual sprinkling of sarcasm.

'I'm in Berwick, staying at a B&B in Bridge Street. You oot the night?'

'Aye, there's a few of us meeting up in The Brewers, why? Gonna grace us with your presence, like?'

'I'll be there, pal.' A pause. 'Wacka, what's the latest on Kev's death? Like, what are the cops saying?'

'The *Keystone Cops*? They haven't got a fuckin' clue, Jez. Mind you, they've no' got much to go on. He was underwater for a good few hours, like. No' really much left in the way of evidence, you know. Nae murder weapon, nae footprints, no' even a fuckin' fag end. He was left to drown. Tied to a stake and left to fuckin' drown! I felt sorry for the two kids who found him. They were called as witnesses at the inquest last week. Still sounded shocked when they were giving their evidence to the coroner. I was there, up in the public gallery. Surrounded by fuckin' ghouls, man. And that includes the poxy press, desperate for a story.'

Jez tries to calm him down and softens his voice. 'I know, pal. I know.' There's a pause in the conversation, then Wacka starts again, quieter now.

'Aye, there's an old, rotten fishing boat at the far end of the beach and it's jumpin' wi' fuckin' rats. When the tide went oot and left him there, the rats got to him and bit the flesh off his ears and his nose and lips. Bit his keekers oot too. Fuck's sake, eh? I didn't know this when I spoke to you after he died. But word got round. You know Berwick.'

'Christ almighty, Wacka. How long had Kev been doing this sea fishing, like?'

'Oh, maybe two, three years. Did it all year round. Fuckin' stupid pastime if you ask me. Standing on a poxy beach casting a line aboot a hundred metres into the North Sea. What's that all aboot, eh? What was he hoping to catch, like, a fuckin' conger eel?'

'What do you think, Wacka? Did Kev have any enemies?'

'We've all got enemies cos none of us are angels. Not even you, Mr Nice! But what sort of fuckin' psycho would do that to someone, eh? Eh? Cos this is off the scale, man. I'll tell you one thing though. If I find Kev's killer before the police, he's going down.'

'Aye, and that'll be you locked up. Welcome to Durham Prison. Again.'

'It beats Saughton. Anyway, they won't catch me. Whoever killed him is a dead man walking. He's the enemy. And a dead enemy is a thing of beauty.'

Jez finds himself smiling at that last sentence. *Maybe Wacka feels like he* should *act; it would appeal to his violent personality and fearsome reputation.*

'Oh… absolutely, Wacka. Absolutely. There might be a queue though.'

'I'll be at the front. Catch you later.' He rings off. Jez looks at his mobile phone then puts it down on the bedside table thinking, *He is so rude, eh? Triple nipple!* Wacka had a slight deformity: a third nipple located in the middle of his chest, higher up than the other two. Now, this was no-go territory with the piss-taking. Unless they were all stoned out their nuts, then they'd shout, 'Oi! Triple Nipple!'; and because he was wrecked he couldn't take you on and he'd be too embarrassed to mention it the next day!

He picks up the phone again and decides to text Josie.

Hi Josie. Jez here. Thanx for your number. Luv u in that bib apron and hairnet!

He takes the phone into the bathroom and places it on the shelf above the sink. The shower has a powerful jet which is invigorating as he lathers up. There's one of those spongy things jammed behind a plant pot in a corner unit but he chooses not to use it. *Aye, probably been roond someone's scrotum at some point so give it a miss, eh?*

Three distinct beeps signal a text has been received. He hates that noise! It's like the phone's summoning him! *Fuck off, phone.* He has his shower then picks up a folded towel from the shelf and dries himself off. He needs a shave but decides not to bother, partly to deflect the squeaky clean teacher look later on in the pub and partly because he kind of likes it. He picks up the phone and reads the text.

Cheeky bugger! Yeah still at work x

He sends another.

Aye well get those dishes done! Are u up for some food 2moro nite?

Five minutes later.

Love to! Need to finish course essay during day 2moro

She's doing a course, eh. I wonder what in?

Homework Josie! Teacher's impressed! Would u rather do homework or come hang out with me?!!

Two minutes later.

Think I'd rather hang out with you! X

Okay. Will ring 2moro xxx.

Looking forward to it… xxx

He likes the three dots after the word "it". It makes the comment open-ended, like she's arching her eyebrows.

* * *

Twenty minutes later, he's dressed and ready to go. Nothing trendy. Nothing "George Street Man About Town". Nothing to attract the attention of his piss-taking mates. A black Italian zipper jumper, black jeans and boots. He tidies the duvet, checks the windows are shut then leaves his room. His boots make a racket as he clambers down the stairs, sliding his hand down the bannister as he negotiates the dog-leg.

As he makes for the front door, Lesley emerges from the dining room. 'Oh, I say! Very smart, Jez! You must be going to that posh wine bar on Hide Hill, then.'

'Eh, The Brewers Arms in Marygate, actually, Lesley,' he replies, raising his voice as he says her name in an attempt to sound friendly yet authoritative. 'What are your plans for tonight?'

'Well, that's the dining table laid up for breakfast tomorrow, so all jobs are done now! No, it's a quiet one for me tonight. Watch some TV then off to my bed with a good book, I think. As you know, there's no curfew here, so have a good night and I'll see you at breakfast. And I do a full English *and* a full Scottish, so whatever you fancy.'

'Err… oh, the Scottish please, if that includes black pudding and a tattie scone.'

She's climbing the stairs now and laughing, then turns to him and says, 'It does, and if that's what you like, you can have two of each. That's if there's enough room on the plate. Goodnight.'

'Bye,' responds Jez. She's still wearing the tight, black jeans and again he finds himself sneaking a look as she makes her way up the stairs. There's a swaying, rhythmic elegance in her movement. It's like her hips are saying 'Come chase me!' *Christ, it's enough to make a bishop kick a hole in a stained-glass window,* he contends as he lets himself out, her image still full in his mind. The Royal Bengal is busy as he ambles past and a chicken jalfrezi aroma wafts up his nostrils. They didn't have Indian restaurants in Berwick until about twenty years ago, so his first experience was the Vesta Beef Curries his mum brought home when he was a teenager. *Aye, a Vesta curry with garlic bread. International cuisine or what?!*

He's turns up West Street and hears the town hall clock chime eight times. He's uneasy about meeting up with the old team. He hasn't been in their company for a while and tonight will be different as the talk will be on Kev's death and the funeral on Monday. And, as the night wears on, alcohol-infused theories about his killer. Tonight could be heavy, it could be emotional, it could be difficult. He stops and lights up a cigarette. He's in no hurry to get there.

I wonder what that Elijah's doing tonight? I bet he's been involved in some heavy duty cases. Interesting though. He reaches the top of the street then turns left onto the high street. *Well, interesting until it gets to you. And it's definitely got to him. I felt for him in the chip shop today. There's no way he'll wanna get involved in Kev's murder, that's for sure.*

A car suddenly beeps its horn. He jolts and looks up. Savage Morrison is driving down the opposite side of the street with a fare, but he still stops and shouts, 'You're no' in poxy Edinburgh now, y'knaw. You divn't have to dress up here, Jez.'

Jez stops and raises his hand, slightly embarrassed at being the centre of attention. 'This is me dressed down, Savage.' And he thinks, *That's twice today he's had me, the cheeky bastard.* Savage smirks, pulls on the hand brake and emerges from his taxi. Jez thinks he's coming over to speak to him, but no, he runs round the front of his car to a burger van and has a quick conversation with the vendor. Something's exchanged between the two of them then he hurries back to his car, smiling now and shouts over:

'Livin' on the edge, Jez. Livin' on the edge, pal.' He gets back in the car, exchanges a couple of words with his passenger, then accelerates down the street. Jez approaches The Brewers Arms, thinking, *This is some fuckin' town.*

CHAPTER 6

POSTERS AND POWERHOUSES

SATURDAY

Elijah Bootle emerges from the chip shop and glances at his watch. It's five thirty, and he's in no hurry to return to his lodgings, so decides to walk off his meal and do some exploring. He looks up the street and decides to walk that way, past his B&B, and see what's up there. He's surprised at how comfortable he was with that teacher, especially as the conversation included a murder. It's a good sign, as lately the idea of talking to people has filled him with dread.

Although he's only been here a few hours, Elijah's already feeling a slight loosening of tension. He's still getting the intrusive thoughts. Well, not thoughts. More like an intrusive photo album, with distressing, grotesque images. He doesn't want his mind to open the album now, but it does, and he feels the panic and horrible sense of impending doom. Sweat beads on his forehead and runs down his back. He slows his walk and focuses on deep breathing. Five counts in, hold it, then five counts out. After a minute or two the images subside as calmness takes over. He checks he's got his room keys for the umpteenth time. He's developed mild OCD, a side effect of his PTSD. He thinks, *Fuckin' OCD, man. Once it gets a grip of you.* But he knows he's not a slave to the rituals. Just keys and doors actually.

He looks up the street and thinks, *Maybe I could do a loop and walk back down the high street.* Then he spots the newsagents across the road, the one that Savage referred to before. He enters and buys a copy of the *Berwick Advertiser*, along with a couple of Picnic bars. Elijah likes the idea of a weekly, local newspaper and looks forward to reading it when he settles down in his room later on tonight.

A wind has picked up and, as he walks, a light sea mist blows towards him. The sun shines brilliant white light through its smoky swirls. The big man flares his nostrils and breathes in its sharp, minty fragrance. It reminds him of family holidays down on the south coast, places like Bognor Regis and Margate. Certain smells act like a memory portal on Elijah, and sea air, seaweed and candy floss transport him back to those childhood seaside holidays. They went to the Isle of Wight one year when he was very young and his dad convinced Elijah and his brothers that they were abroad! His dad's salary as a waiter wasn't great, so Mum did a couple of cleaning jobs to make ends meet. *But we were happy! Christ, we were happy. Well, we didn't know anything else, did we?* Although his parents were poor, they understood the power of education and where it could take you, so they encouraged their kids to stick in at school. Elijah completed a degree in Forensic Psychology at Uni which kickstarted his career as a criminal profiler. He ambles up Church Street at a slow, comfortable pace. This is a man in no hurry. And now it's other smells he's thinking about from his childhood, like Play-Doh, roast dinners and cut grass. He's still smiling. *Savage was right. That must be the best fish and chips I've had in a long time.*

He stops suddenly and wheels round to look at a window. A police appeal poster stares out at him. Looking up, he sees the blue and white 'Police' sign. It's big, bold and square, unlike London police station signs which resemble lanterns and a throwback to Victorian times of gas-lit street illumination. The poster has been roughly stuck onto the inside of a window, and Elijah gets up close to read the content. The bold headline announces "MURDER", then underneath is a colour photograph of Kevin Devine. He looks at the victim. The photograph shows him from the waist up standing in front of a silver car. He's wearing a black Harrington jacket half zipped up to expose a red tartan lining. Underneath he's sporting a plain white T-shirt. A clean-shaven nondescript looking guy, Elijah contends. To the left of the photograph is a short narrative.

CAN YOU HELP?

Kevin Devine was murdered during the evening of Friday, 27th June, 2014.

A forty-eight-year-old married father of two from Berwick Upon Tweed, Kevin was found on Murphy's Beach at approximately 9am on Saturday, 28th June.

We'd like to hear from anyone who was in the area between 6pm on Friday, 27th June and 9am on Saturday, 28th June.

Anyone with information, please call us on 101 or contact Crimestoppers anonymously.

Elijah looks back at the photograph. An important aspect of criminal profiling is getting to know the victim. Familiarity with the victim can uncover connections or relationships between victim and killer. The connection could be geographical. It could be work or hobby related. It could be sexual. Understanding the victim's lifestyle enlightens the profiler as they can discover where the victim could have been exposed to danger. And that brings the profiler closer to the killer.

Elijah bends forward and reads through the dialogue again but this time in a more detached manner. The intensity is reduced. It's like the reading voice in his head is distant and unfamiliar. It's because he doesn't want to get involved. This is not his case. This is not his problem. *Don't climb into my head, Kevin. My head's full of mince just now so don't do that. Or is it "ma heid's full o' mince"!* He stifles a chuckle at his lame attempt at the Berwick accent.

It looks to Elijah as if the poster was stuck on in a hurry. It's not straight and the scraps of Sellotape stuck on each corner are peeling off. It looks scruffy. Not a professional job. *Well, if it's not straight then it must be bent,* he thinks, smiling at his private joke. A career working with the police has given him a cynical edge regarding some of his uniformed colleagues' unlawful ethics. The abuse of power for money and sex, protection of criminals for financial gain, fabricating evidence and intimidating witnesses are just some examples of the systematic corruption Elijah has encountered. *Oh, and racism*, he thinks, with a slow nod.

Something moves in the room behind the poster. He sees a big guy in plain clothes sitting at a desk, reading through a sheaf of papers. Memories he wants to forget now flood his mind. He turns abruptly and strides away up the street, his long legs and big feet pounding out a quicker than usual pace. He thinks again about the eight-year-old girl. The grisly scene. Head down, his thoughts become a voice and he speaks them out loud to the pavement, like a muttering vagrant, 'And that's why profilers and detectives sometimes like to detach themselves from the victim. Y'see, it puts distance between you and the horror.' A furtive look around but no one is near to receive his spoken thoughts.

He stops and gazes into a shop window. It's one of those classic seaside town shops combining hardware and holiday paraphernalia. He sees electric plugs, tools and cleaning products. There's a tall glass cabinet full of keyrings and cheap ornaments. And on the pavement outside the shop are carousels displaying postcards and badges, including yellow "smiley" badges. They were the universal icon for the acid house youth culture back in the nineties. Unlike nowadays, where they mean something far more innocent – a happy, smiling emoji. He thinks, *I bet there have been a few rave parties in this happy holiday town.*

He continues walking up the street. Over the road is his B&B, with its solid front door and motionless parrot in the window. The street tilts upwards and bends slightly from right to left. He soon reaches the top and is pleasantly surprised to find that it opens onto a huge square. To his left stands an imposing, spired church with the town's walls partially showing behind it, giving the area a real sense of enclosure.

He looks back down the sinuous curve of shop frontages on Church Street and realises the police station is on a bent street! He stands there on the corner with a sombre-looking building behind him and surveys the scene. Opposite the church he sees Berwick Barracks, home of the now defunct King's Own Scottish Borderers regiment. Between the barracks and the church is a grassy park. There are a couple of picnics on the go, with shoppers and lovers occupying the park benches scattered randomly around. Nothing stirs, except the shifting canvas of seagulls poking about on the lush, green grass. Then something causes him to spin around and he eyes up the building behind him. Square-shaped, built of sandstone, with stained-glass windows, and above the huge, formidable front door is the Freemason symbol, cut into the cold brickwork.

Well, would you believe that?! We've got the church, the Freemasons' hall and the barracks, all in full sight of each other. Imagine that, eh? Around this peaceful park are the military, civic and religious power houses of the town, all facing each other like a bloody Mexican stand-off! I wonder who shoots first!

He turns along Walkergate Lane, guessing it will take him back towards the high street. He's still thinking about the three buildings and likening them to the scene in the *The Good, the Bad and the Ugly*, where Clint Eastwood, Lee Van Cleef and Eli Wallach confront each other in a triangular shoot-out. And now he's got Ennio Morricone's soundtrack on his mind and whistles a few bars. Arriving back on the high street he makes his way down the town's main thoroughfare. Market-day stallholders are packing up their unsold wares into side-opening transit vans. The streets are deserting. The imposing town hall looms up before him and he slips down its left flank where the sun can't reach, before turning back up the now familiar Church Street to his B&B.

He lets himself in and treads slowly up to his room on the second floor. The heat of the day has left a warm, woody odour which Elijah finds appealing. It's a peaceful, still smell that reflects his newly found melancholy mood. There's a small bookcase above the bed settee containing holiday brochures, pamphlets and a few books left by previous occupants. He sees a book entitled *Berwick Upon Tweed, A Visitors Guide*, so picks it up and begins to thumb through it. The back cover shows an aerial photograph of the town and Elijah sees for the first time how enclosed this place is, with its formidable Walls wrapped round the western and northern flank, the sea to the east and the river's estuary to the south. And within these physical boundaries are the densely packed streets, linked together by cobbled lanes and spindly alleyways. Even in this photograph the town's Walls look magnificent, and he decides to walk round them tomorrow morning, after breakfast. It might become a routine. The doctor did tell him that exercise was good for his PTSD, and he's looking forward to it already.

The armchair by the window beckons him so he slips off his shoes and settles in it. The wooden arms have retained heat from the afternoon's sun, and he sinks deeper into the warm fabric upholstery. He idly starts reading the book and becomes fascinated with the town's bloody history. Berwick's strategic position meant it was at the centre of the Anglo–Scottish Wars of the Middle Ages. Battles over nationality. Battles over territory. Carnage in the streets of the town. Elijah shakes his head as he reads the lines from a poem written after the final sacking of Berwick in 1482 by the English. 'The gutters of Berwick ran red with the blood of eight thousand men. Under Longshanks the townspeople were put to the sword for shielding and housing Scottish troops. There was even religious conflict in this region during the 1600s as the Scottish Presbyterian Covenanters stood up against King Charles I and Catholicism.' Elijah reads on but sleep beckons. His right elbow slides off the arm of the chair and he wakes with a fright. Drowsy now, he looks out over the street, then upwards to the terracotta pantiles of the facing buildings. His brows begin to furrow. Bolt upright now, he sits motionless. He digs out his mobile phone, then retrieves a business card from the bed and punches in a number.

'Savage, hello. Elijah Bootle here. You dropped me off at the B&B this—' He's interrupted by the taxi driver talking over him at a hundred miles an hour. Elijah smiles and waits for an opportunity to resume.

'... Yes, I... I know that, pal. I know. Savage, could you take me to Murphy's Beach?'

A minute later he hangs up and looks at the blank screen. That appeal poster at the police station has pricked his interest. It was the method of killing that's intrigued him. Drowning as a cause of murder is so rare. So he's interested now. And as this murder is so different from the one in London, he figures that taking an interest in this case might stop him dwelling on the London murder. He'll treat it as a little sideshow to keep him occupied. Nothing heavy. Just an interesting distraction.

* * *

Detective Constable Gordon Mackay looks at his watch. He's

on the back shift, two till ten, and it's just gone five thirty. *How slow is this day going, eh?* He shuffles a loose sheaf of papers in his shovel hands, checks the page numbers again and confirms to himself that they're all there. A colleague is using his office to interview a suspect so he's sitting in the main reception office.

He lays out the papers on a desk so he can see all the information. He likes it that way. Draining his coffee mug, he places it to one side. The mug was a gift from his girlfriend after he complained that the crockery at the station was chipped, stained and manky. Emblazoned across it is "Goagsie's Mug" with a cartoon character of a police officer lying flat out with huge feet. He got it last Christmas, and six months later it's, well, chipped, stained and manky. Goagsie used to hate this shift when he was a beat constable. It's stuck in the middle when nowt happens! Early shifts were good on a Saturday because he picked up anything that happened the previous night. Night shifts too, as most of the action in Berwick occurs during this shift – mainly fights, criminal damage and other alcohol-related crimes. During the rugby season he plays for the Berwick Second XV on Saturday afternoons so if he's on night shift on a Saturday he turns up at 10pm, buzzing with endorphins. Even though he's now a detective he still finds these slow Saturday back shifts a drag.

He picks up a sheet and is about to read when a movement causes him to look out the window. A tall, imposing-looking black guy is reading the Kevin Devine appeal poster. *Big guy. He'd take some arresting!* Their eyes meet momentarily then he returns to his paperwork. A quick glance at his watch. *Okay. Bawheid said he'd be here at six so get concentrating on this, Goagsie boy.*

He looks at the first page of the autopsy report, carried out following Kevin Devine's death. His photograph shows him clothed, with the same jacket he's wearing in the appeal poster. In addition, Goagsie has photographs from the crime scene. On the right side of his head there is evidence of severe violent trauma, with swelling around the impact area. The pathologist confirms a fracture to the skull with bone emerging from the open skin. The external examination also reveals ligature marks around both wrists where the victim had been restrained with a plastic cable tie. Evidence of sand is visible on his clothes, hair and hands. Removal of the victim's clothing shows blunt trauma wounds to the victim's back and shoulders. There is severe bruising and swelling beneath both knees. Further investigation reveals open fractures to both tibias. Goagsie winces and slowly shakes his head as he looks at these limb injuries then back up to the vivid head wound. *Christ, he's been given a right hiding. For fuck's sake.*

The pathologist discovered a quantity of sand and stones in the mouth and concludes that these were deliberately stuffed into the victim's mouth. *Maybe to stop the poor guy shouting for help?* wonders the young detective. Further examination of the respiratory system shows both lungs clogged with seawater. The victim's stomach contents reveal seawater present plus the remains of a partially digested meal. In the section titled Evidence Collected are the clothes that Kevin was wearing on the night he died, plus the car keys found in his pocket. In addition is the cable tie and the metre-long wooden shaft that he was tethered to. Now Goagsie's nodding slowly. *That stake is too short to leave him standing so he must have been tied to the stake in a sitting position. That's why his legs were broken.*

The report's final section outlines the pathologist's opinion regarding time and cause of death. Rigor and liver mortis, plus stomach contents, give the approximate time of death between 8pm and 10pm on 27th June. Cause of Death is given as drowning and, below it, the Manner of Death section has one word: Murder. Off the record, the pathologist has informed the Major Investigation Team that the likely instrument which caused the blunt trauma is a ball-pein hammer, probably weighing about two kilos. This information has been kept from the public and doesn't appear on the report. Goagsie's scanning back through the paperwork, looking for toxicology information, when the custody sergeant pops his head in the office. 'We're letting Rossillini out, Goagsie, so there's a free cell. I think he's sobered up now. That fish supper must have done the trick!'

'You're charging him, though?'

'Oh aye, we're charging him. ABH. He's admitting it, like, so it's a done deal. By the way, the guy he beat up… Turns out he's a nephew of Kevin Devine.'

'Did he say why he attacked him?' asks Goagsie.

'Naw, he's saying nowt. Anyway, we cannae keep him in so, as I say, there's a free cell.'

'Okay,' replies Goagsie, 'I'll pass that on to the Investigation Team. You never know, it might be a good lead. Fuck's sake, we could do with one.' The custody sergeant starts to make small talk but Goagsie cuts him short. 'Sarge, I'm assigned to a murder case here, man. I've no' got time to blether. And the DCI's on his way for a meeting at 6pm so let me get on, eh?' He turns back to scan the report and confirms that there's no alcohol or illicit drugs in the victim's system.

There's some noise in the corridor as Detective Chief Inspector Alan "Bawheid" Hazelwood has arrived and there's the usual sycophantic rush to make him welcome, make him tea, make him feel like he's fuckin' special. It could be worse. As the Senior Investigating Officer on this case, he reports directly to Chief Superintendent Jack Mills, and when *he's* around it's Bawheid who becomes the toady, servile flatterer. 'Honest, it's embarrassing,' Goagsie mutters to himself as he organises the sheets into order. *Aye, one of those meatheids that think having a degree in Social Science means you're somehow better at solving crimes.*

A Major Incident Room has been set up in the conference hall and he's here to talk to the investigating team about last night's operation. Last night was exactly a month to the day that the murder took place, and the whole beach area had been under surveillance, hoping that the date was a triggering stressor for the killer and he'd return to the scene of the crime. But to no avail. Apart from an elderly couple walking their dog and a group of rowdy teenagers from the nearby holiday camp, there was no sign of anyone or anything suspicious. The DCI also wants to use this briefing to elaborate further on the victim's injuries and scene of crime issues. As far as Goagsie's concerned this has all been covered, and he thinks this is Bawheid panicking before the victim is buried on Monday, in case they've missed something. *Aye, too late then, Bawheid, and that would be your promotion chances up the spout, which is what's driving you. Frightened of your own fuckin' shadow.* It's clear to the Detective Constable what's happened: the victim's been struck on the head with a blunt object, knocked unconscious, then received further blows to the body and legs. Then he's been tied up, tethered to a stake and left to drown. *Aye, Bawheid's great at telling us what we already know. 'Let's recap,' he's always saying with his dodgy Durham pit-yacker accent. Let's fuckin' recap. Let's just get on and find the scumbag that did this, eh? Or scumbags.*

With all the information in his file, Goagsie slips it under his armpit and heads off for the briefing, stopping only to pick up a tide timetable that had slipped out his folder and onto the tiled floor.

CHAPTER 7

WAITING

SATURDAY

And in among the shadowy, dark alleys and cobblestoned streets of this old town the killer waits… and waits.

And the killer thinks about fear. *What is fear?*

The killer smells fear. It has a cold, metallic odour… like blood in your mouth. And it has colour – purple, red and black.

The killer looks at the Stanley knife in admiration. The single screw has been unwound to part and reveal the knife's cold, grey interior. Two blades have been placed together, separated by a single match. The killer screws the knife back together then pushes forward the slide to reveal the double razor blade. The killer sees an image of slicing through skin, dripping droplets of crimson blood. And he thinks, *There's not a surgeon in the world gonna be able to stitch you up. Not when I'm finished with you.*

CHAPTER 8
REUNION
SATURDAY

Jez checks his watch, confirms it's accurate by the town hall clock, then approaches the door to The Brewers Arms thinking, *Christ, how many times have I walked in here with Kev, eh? Fuckin' hunners!* He peers through the door's clear glass and then the bay window, shrouding it to see how busy it is inside. In the old days the glass was frosted, which gave the place a cosy sort of sanctuary – a visible demarcation between the drinking clientele and the busy high street outside. About ten years ago the bar had a makeover. Away went the rough-and-ready look, along with the smells of yeast and ready rolled. Now it looks like a Wetherspoons, with mahogany panelling and private alcoves. He still feels surprised whenever he walks in – and disappointed. He's yearning for the old days when they came in here as young men. It was more basic then, with small Formica tables along the left-hand wall and a big long bar along the right-hand side. It had a symmetry to it. There'd be a row of older gadgees sitting along the back wall supping pints of Heavy, often with a whisky chaser. It was never a "beer and dominoes" pub, more a "beer and men's talk" sort of place. Hard-drinking, hard-working men. It used to be wild, but somewhere along the way someone swapped the dartboard for a food menu.

It's early for a Saturday night so the pub's quiet, with a few punters propping up the bar. They're in various stages of sobriety, depending on the length of time they've been in. High up in the corner is a large TV showing a match with the volume up loud. The steady drinking regulars are idly watching, while making small talk. Opposite the bar there's a large alcove where a group of men have gathered.

Jez walks up and gives the obligatory: 'How's it goin', lads?' He hasn't seen some of them for a couple of years and this would normally be the cue for some cheeky piss-taking but their response is uncharacteristically subdued. He's smiling, as you do when you meet old friends. He scans them all and thinks, *Christ, I've known these guys that long and called them by their nicknames for so long I can't remember some of their real names!* A few of the boys smile back and nod, say hello, but it looks laboured. They look tired… weary.

'What you having, Jez?' He turns and sees Fifty Fifty at the bar, with drinks in front of him, so he walks over and they hug. Fifty Fifty looks at him with glowing eyes, then pats his shoulders and breaks into a smile, as if he's really pleased to see him.

'Oh, a Stella, please, Fifty. Cheers. Here, shall I take some of these over?'

'Aye, hang on a minute. How you deein', son? Good to see you. When did you get doon here?'

'Got here this afternoon, Fifty. Staying at a B&B in Bridge Street. Apple House, it's called. Aye, I'm fine. I suppose.' Jez slowly shakes his head and Fifty understands.

'I know, Jez, I know. It's been a fuckin' nightmare since Kev was killed.' He looks at Jez and says, 'Still cannae believe it. Can you? I suppose you've seen this week's *Advertiser*? The inquest was last week so we know a bit more now. Wacka, Hammer and Bang Bang were there, in the public gallery. So... err... it's good to see you anyway, son. Here, take some of these over. It's Stella, Amstel and Guinness. Oh, and that's a gin and tonic for CD.'

He always calls everyone "son" even though he's a year younger than most of them. Just his way. When he was about nineteen, he had testicular cancer and it spread to his lymph glands. It's a rare condition for someone so young. Jez remembers his mum really suffered with the worry of it all. He's an only child and she thought she was going to lose him. But he responded well to the treatment, including the ugly side effects, and beat it off. When the cancer was at its most aggressive the consultants said he was "at best, fifty-fifty" and the name kind of stuck. And since then he's had this laid-back, fatalistic approach to life. Like, he just rolls with the punches. Not as horizontal as, say, Cement Shoes, but near. Says what he wants. Does what he wants, really. His wife, Angie, runs a florist shop at the top of Castlegate and is known and loved by them all. He's wearing a green T-shirt with a picture of Don Logan shouting, "Yes, yes, yes, yes, yes!" – from the scene in *Sexy Beast* when Ray Winstone's getting it tight from Ben Kingsley.

Jez picks up the drinks with ease and makes his way back over to the alcove. He lays down the pints and places the short in front of CD. The padded bench seat along the alcove's back wall is taken: Wacka, Fish Heid, Bang Bang and The Hammer, with CD sitting on a stool facing them, his back to the bar. Jez plonks himself down next to him. Pleasantries over and he's feeling comfortable among this crowd again, even though they all know it's going to be a tough day at the funeral on Monday. He decides to try and lift the mood a little so puts the boot in first. 'Fuck's sake, CD, you'll no' get chatted up with your back to the bar! Unless they're after that dodgy Italian shirt.' Everyone gets on the bandwagon, slagging him off with no holds barred. And they mean it, but they're laughing too because they all love the posing bastard. Jez goes to ruffle his hair but stops as he doesn't want his hand covered in product.

'Good taste's like common sense, Jeremy. You've either got it or you haven't. And you haven't.' CD has the confidence of a good-looking man who knows he's good-looking. Even sitting down he has a swagger about him. He's one of those guys who married young, then got divorced and now lives the life of a twenty-something again. Real name: Christopher Driver. A one-man shagging machine. When he was chatting up holidaymakers he would tell them his name was Christian Dangerfield. The initials added credence to his dodgy *nom de plume*. He would go missing in action for a week every July when the single mothers' Gingerbread Club came to town and stayed at the holiday camp. He loved that place. Jez remembers CD telling him that one night he met a woman from Sunderland and she took him back to her caravan. She was up for the weekend with her mate. Big girl, like. Nice and fleshy. Anyway, they were in bed and she had her arse in the air and her tits in his face and was just telling him that her man was the leader of a Hells Angels chapter down on Wearside when the unmistakable sound of a muckle fuckin' motorbike drew up outside. In his desperation he climbed out through a small window in the bedroom as the husband was coming through the front door. He fell head first onto one of those big, red Calor gas cylinders and nearly knocked himself out! Got away though; he always did. Women just loved him, and he was always getting the twice over.

The conversation moves on to what constitutes common sense, but Jez can see CD wants a blether. He's not seen him in ages. 'How's life in the Big Shitty, Jez?' he asks with a straight face.

'Same old, CD, same old. Still a peasant in the Big Shitty,' Jez responds, recognising The Stranglers connotation. 'I've no' seen you at Easter Road for a while, pal.'

'Honest, you're still going? I fell out of love with them, mate. Playing "hoofball" for that bastard Tory tractor driver. Just got too much, Jez. Last game I was at was the play-offs. Drove up wi' Fish Heid.' He nods in the direction of the Big Man, who acknowledges the comment with a slow shake of his muckle, medicine-ball heid. Fish Heid loves a moan and this was his cue.

'It's disgraceful what's happened, Jez. Honest, we were challenging for sixth place in aboot March and two months later we're doon. We're fubbed now, like. I couldn't bear to look at the fixture list when it came oot,' he concludes with another shake of his mighty heid. Jez keeps a straight face with Fish Heid and his verbal eccentricities. As an ex-fisherman he's retained certain superstitions which the fishing community hold dear – like not swearing when fishing or saying the word "pig" at sea. Plus his wife, Alice, converted to Jehovah about twenty years ago so swearing, or "cursing" as she calls it, is a sin. As a result he doesn't swear at all. Instead he makes words up like "fubber" instead of "fucker".

Bang Bang chips in. 'Awright, Fish Heid, for fuck's sake. Honest to God. You'd make a fuckin' onion cry.'

Jez smiles and adds, 'Think yourself lucky, Fish Heid. You live in Berwick. I'm up in The Burgh with the Jambo Glee Club. Honest, if they go straight back up, we'll never hear the end of it.'

'Aw, forget those douchebag fubbers,' Fish Heid replies, laughing now but only because he's smarting at Bang Bang's abuse regarding his miserable demeanour.

'Boys, if they go straight back up first time they'll be calling themselves the Gorgie Galactacos! Self-proclaimed of course,' contends Wacka. He suddenly looks past Jez towards the door. 'Talking aboot common sense, here come Bob and Cement Shoes!' They all laugh now and turn towards the newcomers. The Hammer and Bang Bang are in the corner of the alcove and have to sit forward and twist their heads to get a look.

Fifty gets up and shouts over to them as they approach, 'My round, lads. What you havin'?'

Bob answers with a question: 'Has Bang Bang got a round in yet? Because when he does we should all get a pint and a chaser and see how many times the little fucker has to go back and forward to the bar!' Bob's now got his fingers looking like Bang Bang's. He walks up close to him. He shoots two imaginary bullets, then blows imaginary smoke from his imaginary guns, places them in his imaginary holsters, laughs and shouts over to the bar:

'Gie's a pint of 80 Shilling, Fifty.'

'Me too, my man,' adds Cement Shoes, pulling up two more stools.

Bang Bang takes a slow sip of his pint, seems to savour it, then concentrates hard on replacing his glass in the exact centre of the round beermat and pretends he's not bothered. But he's fuckin' furious. And while Bang Bang is one of Jez's least favourite mates, he finds himself shaking his head at Bob's insensitivity. But he's smiling like he doesn't give a fuck either. He scans the table again and wonders what his teaching colleagues would think of this company!

Wacka leans forward and asks a question: 'We're just talking aboot common sense, Bobby boy. How would you define it?'

'Eh, like walking into a bar, sussing oot who the psychopath is and givin' him a wide berth. That's why I'm no' sitting next to you!' Bob claps Jez on the shoulder, partly as he's pleased with his response and partly as a kind of hello to him. He carries on talking. Because for Bob, *not* talking is the effortful activity. He gets a whiff of CD's cologne. It's a robust night-time fragrance.

'Fuck's sake, Chris, what aftershave are you wearing?' CD knows Bob will then proceed to answer his own question. He usually does. 'I didn't know they still did Hai Karate! Listen, pal, here's some advice from a style guru. Put it in your hoover, it'll make a good air freshener!' We're all howling now. CD smiles, then nods slowly like he's about to kick off, then sips his G&T. He's above all this. But Bob realises he's struck a raw nerve and is now defusing the situation. Colour runs into his cheeks like a tide on fast forward. He knows CD's a bit handy. 'Just a bit of fun, CD. No honestly, decent threads, like. Tidy shirt. You look dressed to kill. Dressed to kill.' The belly laughs around the table slowly become stifled. Jez doesn't know where to look and feels embarrassed for Bob now. Wacka, Bang Bang and Cement Shoes just look at him like he's an arse.

Fish Heid breaks the silence. 'Bob, have a flippin' word with yourself, eh?'

The Hammer gets up, says, 'I need a piss,' to no one in particular and marches off, violently kicking over Fifty's stool.

Fifty's still at the bar and sees the commotion. 'Hi, Hammer! What the fuck you playing at? Eh? You fuckin' radge.'

The Hammer stops, turns to face Fifty, raises his hands like he's about to start a football chant, then shouts out to the whole bar: 'Up the fuckin' BUNDIG!'

The manageress stops pouring and shouts over, 'Now, enough! That's enough! Or you're barred. Do you hear?' But The Hammer just ignores her and carries on walking to the toilets, arms still outstretched like a stag's antlers. The other regulars at the bar look around, then look down at their feet, look at the TV, look down again – look anywhere but at Fifty Fifty, The Hammer or any of the BUNDIG. There's an uneasy silence. Jez feels uncomfortable, but not as much as Bob, who's now sitting forward, elbows on table with his hands cupped around his face.

Fifty returns from the bar with the two drinks and places them in front of Bob and Cement Shoes. He retrieves his stool, and as he sits down he's shaking his head at The Hammer. He's unaware of Bob's faux pas but senses his mood and sarcastically jokes, 'What's wrong, Bobby boy? Just come up on the Lottery?' He's still smiling at his joke, then realises the atmosphere's changed and has become dark and heavy. He nods, looks around, then asks, 'Okay, it's the elephant in the room, is it? Well, let's get down to it, then. Let's get it out.' A pause. They look at him intently. 'Kevin. Kevin Devine. Our mate. Our mate who was attacked and left to die on a beach aboot four weeks ago. What's the latest? Who's hearing anything? And I don't mean the crap I'm hearing about town, boys. Jesus Christ, according to my missus *I* was in the fuckin' frame as his killer at one point. She overheard two women in the hairdressers last Saturday. They weren't local so didn't know who she was. Didn't take her long to put everyone right, like.' He laughs but is still shaking his head in disbelief.

'We all know Angie, Fifty. Have those two women stopped running yet?' asks Cement Shoes with some sincerity. The atmosphere eases slightly. They're smiling at the scene in their heads. Fifty's wife takes no prisoners – ever. Even when her husband's out of order she'll back him to the hilt. They all love her for that.

Bob, eager now to make a meaningful contribution, pipes up, 'I mean, it's not like he was punched in the face on a Saturday night and fell and banged his heid. Fuck's sake. He was battered unconscious then tethered up and left to drown. Who the fuck would do that, eh?' He looks around the table with a hopeful expression but knows that's the big question. It's been asked a thousand times in their town – friends, family, colleagues, acquaintances, the police, everyone – and the answer eludes them all.

It's still early and there's not too many punters in so Jez quickly guzzles down his pint, confirms the order and goes to the bar. His round. He likes to get it in early as it's no fun standing three deep waiting to get served with half a dozen pints of Stella inside you. And it gives him a little respite from the heavy discussion on death and murder. He feels a big, heavy hand on his shoulder and it's The Hammer.

Jez looks up at him. 'Where you been, pal? I thought you were just away for a piss? Pint of Stella, aye?'

'Oh, make it a snakebite, I've got a thirst on. Here, I'll take these over.' He walks off to the table carrying four pints. Jez calls the barmaid and changes the order. He'd clocked The Hammer's eyes and he's obviously been snorting something. Coke, he hopes. Not that he's a fan of it. He's shaking his head and thinking, *I mean, a bit of weed's one thing but that stuff's for losers. All that ecstasy shite, and ketamine and M-KAT. Laced with fuckin' talcum powder or rat poison to bulk it up. The school was awash with it a couple of years ago.* He takes the drinks over and settles back down on his stool.

The conversation is quieter now. It's about the case, yes, but it's also about him. The man. Kevin Devine. On the overhead TV the match ends and loud music suddenly fills the bar. They involuntarily move closer to each other, their heads close together like they're about to scrum down. And without anyone saying, they like it. They like the physical proximity of each other. They can feel it. It's like they're back in their teens again. And they talk about Kevin. About his death and who would want to kill him. And why in such a brutal way. Jez is listening and contributing and enjoying the feeling of friendship, despite the sadness and anger that weaves through their conversation. And, as he often does when a person is taken too soon, he finds himself thinking about his sister, Mandy, and her death all those years ago.

The drink flows and the volume rises. Now they're talking about his life, and they're all trying to talk at once, swapping stories, butting in on other stories, shouting people down and reliving the past with embellished accounts of their youth. The Hammer's hyper and can't stop talking. He's giggling and cuddling whoever's near him. At six foot four no one complains, not even Wacka, whose never been comfortable with male physical contact. Well, except the contact of fist on jaw, knee in ribs or boot in bollocks. The Hammer's at the bar again, even though he's just bought a round. CD's just suggested they all go on shorts so it's G&Ts, single malts, and vodka and Irn Brus all round. Bob's back on form and holding court. He's got the "four-pint glow" and is recounting an incident circa 1978. 'Aye, Kev had a thing aboot sheep, like! He was a fuckin' pervert, that boy! Mind when he rustled one from a farm oot by Chirnside. Aye, he drove home with it on the back seat of his Zephyr 6. Kept it in his coal cellar for a week, then CD let it go cos he felt sorry for it. Remember?' They all burst out laughing. Cement Shoes puts a comforting arm around CD's shoulders.

'Aye, I remember the car, like, cos it was maroon. Fuckin' traitor,' replies Bang Bang.

'I mean what's a Hibby doing drivin' aroond in a fubbin' maroon car, eh? It's just not normal behaviour that, like,' adds Fish Heid, pulling a face like he's just downed a rancid pint.

'Eh, boys' says CD, raising his hand as if about to swear an oath, 'you're forgetting the main thrust of this story. The sheep.'

'Fuckin' thrust?!' replies Bob. 'You cannae string two sentences together, you, you dirty fucker, without some reference to shagging!' They're all roaring and laughing but CD maintains a mock straight face.

'The sheep… It was last seen on Tweedmouth Main Street. Near the docks.'

'Fuck's sake, it would have been safer in Kev's cellar!' shouts Cement Shoes.

'Aye, it's a funny thing,' contends CD; 'after I let it go it was missing for a couple of days. And, coincidentally, so were you, Cement Shoes. Were the two of you cohabitating or what?'

Cement Shoes replies with mock outrage, 'Mr Driver. What do you take me for? A barbarian?'

More laughter and Jez shouts over the noise, 'There's no way that sheep was a virgin! You know those Chirnside boys. They love a good frolic in the hay with a Borders Longhorn.'

They roll about howling. They're all pissed. Jez spills beer onto his jeans and Fish Heid shouts over, 'Hi, Jez, shame you've no' got your hairdryer with you to dry that off. I was talking to Savage before and he saw you posing in a shop window this afternoon.'

'Fuck's sake, Fish Heid! What a town, eh? I'm only home for a few hours and I've got Savage doing a character assassination on me!' Fish Heid's now got his arm around Jez and talking quietly. And when Fish Heid talks to you, he focuses on you and looks straight at you, oblivious to anyone or anything else around him. He's talking about Kevin again. He's getting emotional. In Jez's drunken haze he suddenly realises he's got to look serious with him. He sees tears standing in his friend's eyes. Not tears of grief. No, these are tears of loss, tears of nostalgia, tears reminiscing the passage of time. He's slurring and his breath stinks of garlic and whisky. Jez waits for an opportune moment then excuses himself and goes to the toilet.

Standing at the urinal he fishes out his mobile and checks for messages. Well, checks for messages from Josie. But there's nothing. He feels a light stab of disappointment in his stomach. He thinks, *Should I text her? No, Jez, nothing stupid now. Leave it till tomorrow.* The Hammer and Bang Bang barge in, laughing and pushing each other, then both disappear into a cubicle. They're both talking at a hundred miles an hour. Then Bang Bang shouts out, 'I'd ask Jez if he wanted some, but he's a fanny!' Pure rage rises up Jez's face. The anger throbs in his temples. He finishes at the urinal, walks to the adjoining cubicle, stands on the toilet and looks over the partition. There's four lines of cocaine on the cistern. Bang Bang's bent over it with a rolled-up fiver at his nose.

Jez says, 'Ya sounding like a hard man, Bang Bang. Makes a change for you, eh?' Bang Bang's still bent over like he's frozen. He looks up. Jez says, 'See that knife in your pocket? Eh? Any more of your cheek and it'll be hangin' oot your fuckin' keeker.' The Hammer just looks on with a daft grin on his face. Because he knows. He knows that back in the day it was him, Jez, Wacka and Cement Shoes who did most of the business. Jez gets down then takes a while to wash and dry his hands – partly because of personal hygiene, partly to wait on Bang Bang to emerge, but he doesn't.

He walks out, banging the door shut so violently the frame judders. Walking back through the bar he checks his phone again to get the time. Eleven thirty. He sees the alcove but only Wacka, Cement Shoes and Fish Heid are sitting there. The group's dwindling. The night's deteriorating. Fifty and Bob have already left. He passes CD who's deep in conversation with two thirty-something women, one of whom has her hand on his hip. *No' see him again tonight.* Suddenly Jez wants to go home to his B&B. He's talked out. He's tired. He's pissed. He squirms his way past a throng of noisy people and gets to the alcove, leans his hands on the table and says, 'Boys, I'm... I'm gonna go. I'm... you know. I've had enough.'

He expects some abuse but it's fine. Even a thumbs-up from Wacka, who responds, 'See you Monday, kid.'

'Aye. See you Monday. See you Monday, lads.' He makes for the exit. Young men stand in his way, looking arrogant and aggressive. Not that this bothers him. He glares aggressively at them as he barges his way to the door. He needs to escape the pulsing neon spotlights and heavy bass beat.

Outside it's bucketing down with rain. One of those summer showers that lashes the streets with random clatter before rushing down the drains in a torrential hurry. It smells fresh and earthy. He shivers, like a wee boy on a scruffy step, so zips up his jumper and, with head down, quickens the pace and sets off. He yearns for the big bed in his room at Lesley Abercorn's. The rain drums a violent, chaotic beat on the roof of a parked van.

CHAPTER 9

WALKING THE WALLS

SUNDAY

Jez slowly comes to and feels heat from the morning sun as it pierces through a gap in the thick curtains. He lies with his hands behind his head and pieces together events from the night before. It starts to come back. *Oh, I feel like shit, man.* Blurred vision, thick head and a furry mouth. He needs a couple of headache pills but can't be bothered to move. From the kitchen below, the aroma of cooked sausages and bacon has gone walkabout, into the hallway, up the stairs and into his room. These mouth-watering smells remind him of sunny Sunday mornings at home when his sister and he were young. At Mum's request, Mandy would burst into his room and prise open the curtains, then shout, 'What's your breakfast order?!' before rushing out again, usually squealing with laughter. Sometimes she'd relieve him of his pillow and batter him with it! Even when they were kids she was always an early riser and seemed charged with energy. He lies there and thinks about Mandy, wallowing in nostalgia.

'Yeah, forty years ago. I'd have been eight and she'd have been six,' he says out loud to himself. His mind drifts off and he thinks about Mandy. He doesn't want to. Not now. Not when he's nursing a hangover and feeling lonely inside. But he does. He thinks about the last time he saw her alive. He thinks about their last conversation. At home, a Sunday afternoon. He was travelling back to Portsmouth later that day to his ship. Jez, his mum and Mandy had sat and blethered and drank coffee, if he remembers correctly. Innocent, trivial stuff. She died a week later. Death came to Mandy early. The pain of her death has scabbed over without ever healing. He still misses her. He closes his eyes and really concentrates but can't remember her voice now and her face only returns in the form of old photographs.

He pulls the duvet over him, seeking sanctuary in the dark. Hollow, squeaky footsteps sound on the stairs, like walking on a polished floor. And quiet, hushed voices. Then in the distance a church bell tolls. Guessing it must be nine o'clock he decides to haul himself out of bed. He draws the curtains then hoists the window and pokes his head out and it's all quiet. Bridge Street has that Sunday morning feeling. The overnight rain is long gone, leaving a sharp smell in the air like wet sand. Turning back into his room he recognises the stale whiff of alcohol. He quickly showers and gets dressed, then makes his way down to the dining room.

A middle-aged couple are seated at the mahogany table, the remains of breakfast dishes in front of them. Jez manufactures a smiling face to greet them. They're the Dutch couple Lesley mentioned yesterday, and they start talking across a range of subjects: British food, Berwick's bridges, and Den Helder, their home town. Lesley enters from the kitchen. Over a lilac polo neck and jeans she's wearing a black apron with the *TopGear* logo on it, except hers says TopGirl. Her full breasts are pushing the logo into beautiful contours. Jez imagines her naked on top of him – in charge of him – calling the shots. And that's another thing about a hangover – he craves dirty sex.

'Morning, Jez. And how are you?' she asks, with a warm smile flickering over her full lips.

'I'm good thanks, Lesley… err… despite last night's excesses,' he replies.

'Well, as long as you had a good night, that's the main thing. Now, what can I tempt you with this morning?' Filthy thoughts fill his mind. But it's all just in his mind. Lesley Abercorn is completely oblivious to her guest's lewd thoughts. A hardworking businesswoman, she's just getting on with the day in her usual friendly yet professional manner.

Jez feels her eyes on him and gets flustered in his fragile, hungover state. 'Oh… err… I'll have the full English please,' as he's forgotten if the "full Scottish" includes salmon which he couldn't stomach right now. She disappears into the kitchen, leaving the door open, and he watches her while making small talk with his fellow diners. The kitchen looks bright and clean, with yellow walls and a white lino floor. The tantalising smells are now bolstered with "comfort food" noises: bacon sizzling in a skillet, eggs being cracked open then dropped noisily into the fat. The Dutch couple are telling him that they often have pancakes with blueberries for breakfast, but he couldn't care less about their poxy, healthy European diets just now. He wants that fry-up!

The breakfast room looks out onto the street and bright sunlight floods in, bouncing off glasses, cutlery and crystal on the decanter, causing shards of light to ricochet around the room. Five minutes later Lesley enters with a huge plate of heart-attack heaven. 'You'll need to do some walking to lose all these calories,' she says, placing the plate in front of him.

He picks up his cutlery to tuck in, looks up at her and replies, 'You know, it's such a beautiful morning, I think I'll go for a walk around the Walls.'

* * *

Half an hour later he's out in the warm, fresh air and walking along Bridge Street, then it's up Bank Hill to start his walk at Meg's Mount, a formidable bastion on the western corner of the Walls. He's got a spring in his step – probably that glorious breakfast – and he's smiling broadly now. *She can cook, that woman.*

He slants forward and pushes his way up Bank Hill, panting quietly with beads of sweat forming on his forehead. Pausing halfway up to catch his breath he gazes over at his family's church: the austere Presbyterian church he attended as a child every Sunday. Leaning back against a railing he looks at the church in all its dark solemnity. His mind reverses forty odd years. He can see the rows of pews and can feel how uncomfortable and hard they were to sit on. No cushions there; they had to suffer and feel the pain. As Christ did. His mother and aunties would always look like they were listening intently to the minister as he preached, whereas Jez, his sister and cousins were just confused by it all. The smell of the place was alien, like musky clothes. After the service they went to Sunday School in the annexe next door which was okay. And it's where he met some of his lifelong friends; Wacka, Bob and CD used to go too, and he's smiling now at the memory of those innocent boys.

Rest over, he strides up the remainder of Bank Hill, then it's a dozen steps up to Meg's Mount, and he stands there, breathing in the panoramic view of the river, the three bridges and across to Tweedmouth, the area where he grew up. From here he can see the densely packed rooftops of the old town, held captive within the Walls. He finds it odd that the Walls were built to keep the Scots out yet within the Walls the town has a distinctive Scottish flavour in its architecture, customs and history. He's reading a large information board when something prompts him to look up. A man has emerged onto the Walls. It's Elijah, the guy he met in the chip shop yesterday. Hurrying now, he clambers down from Meg's Mount and picks up his pace to catch him, as he's walking away from him, his broad shoulders swaying rhythmically, like a sailor's march.

'ELIJAH!' he shouts, and the big man pauses, then looks around, and even from about forty metres Jez sees his face turn into a smile. A broad smile. He nods in acknowledgement and waits until Jez catches him.

'Morning, Jez. Walking off those fish and chips from yesterday, I suppose?' he inquires.

'Partly that, Elijah. And partly to walk off a raging hangover that a full English breakfast couldn't shift,' he responds. 'How's your B&B?'

'I like it. Yeah, decent room, and a lovely landlady who cooks a damn fine breakfast. I had scrambled eggs and salmon this morning. Beautiful, it was. And now I'm going to spend an hour or so walking around these magnificent Walls,' he responds with a sweeping arm gesture.

'Well, that's kind of my idea too, Elijah. Mind if I join you?'

'Do I mind?' He laughs. 'No, I'd like that. You can give me a guided tour on the way round. Anyway, how's your B&B?'

'Can't complain, pal,' responds Jez. 'Decent little place. It's called Apple House, along Bridge Street, which is a lovely part of town. Aye, good breakfasts too, I have to say.' They set off along the Walls and Jez points to the car park down to their left and explains that walled towns usually have parking problems and Berwick's no exception. 'And up ahead is Cumberland Bastion, named after Butcher Cumberland, who passed through Berwick in pursuit of Bonnie Prince Charlie's Jacobite army.'

'Yes. I saw a map of the Walls in a book I was reading in my room last night,' replies Elijah. 'I love the shape of these bastions. They're like the arrows at the start of *Dad's Army*. How many are there altogether?'

Jez laughs at the *Dad's Army* memory of those black arrows pushing the Nazis back towards mainland Europe. 'There's five of them. The Walls are like a stone ring, set with five gemstones. That map you mentioned would show the town encircled by these Walls, and most of the structure's still intact.'

Elijah's nods, patiently waiting for his companion to finish before adding, 'Yes, it gives a foretaste of modern Europe, I think. You know, territory and protection. And fighting over boundaries and borders.'

'And power Elijah, and I think these ramparts take you

back to a time when Berwick was a thorn in the side of English kings and queens.'

'Yes, very interesting. Very interesting. Well, if someone had said a week ago that I'd be walking around these Walls today on this lovely Sunday morning, well, I wouldn't have believed them. And with someone who knows their local history, too.'

'And where were you a week ago today, then?'

Elijah slows a bit and looks down, then says, 'I was in London a week ago today. And I was in a bad place, my friend. I really was.' He casts his mind back to the previous Sunday morning in his flat in Islington. He'd woken scratchy eyed and agitated. He'd felt angry but didn't know why. A close-up photograph of the child's body had become a recurrent, distressing memory. An exhibit of atrocity.

He shudders involuntarily then looks around him as if seeing the place in a new light. He nods, almost in confirmation, then continues, 'And can I tell you something? This town feels like a million miles from there.' He cranes his neck upwards and focuses on some squalling gulls in search of food.

Jez says, 'Aye, you see a lot of gulls on a Sunday morning. They come in looking for fast-food rubbish from last night, before the council gets around to cleaning it all up. The only other time is when there's a storm at sea and then there's hunners of them.' Elijah's looking at him. Jez elaborates, 'Aye, if there's a storm at sea it drives the fish down from the surface so the gulls come inland looking for food. Nae chance of that today, like. It's goin' to be a roaster. Well, I mean a "roaster" for Berwick. Might hit twenty-two degrees, about seventy in old money.' Elijah smiles but says nothing, which Jez likes. He's getting the impression this is a man who contemplates. He muses. He deliberates.

They amble along the footpath towards Brass Bastion, before scrambling up the grass then stand at the top to take in the views up and down the coast and out to sea. The big man breathes in a huge lungful of air, then slowly exhales, saying, 'Ah, the joy of being out in air so fresh you could wash your face in it! And it's got a smell, you know, like mint up your nose. Yeah, it's a different "smellscape" to being inland. Or in the city.'

Jez nods in acknowledgement while looking out to sea and it's glimmering like a sheet of glass. On the horizon it's hazy, like there's a sea fog lurking out there, waiting to advance and smother all before it. He looks north up the coast and knows that just around the headland is Murphy's Beach, where Kev was murdered. 'I was telling you in the chip shop yesterday about the funeral I'm going to tomorrow. Well, just around those cliffs (he nods in a northerly direction) is where my friend was murdered.'

Elijah turns slowly and looks at him, as if he's absorbing what he's saying. He breathes in another lungful of air then blows out noisily, puffing his cheeks. 'I know,' he replies. 'I went there, last night. Took a taxi. Savage Morrison's.'

Jez spins around and says, 'You went to Murphy's Beach last night? What for?'

'I know, I know. I told you yesterday afternoon that I wasn't interested. I know. Well, after I left… Oh, by the way, that lovely girl who served us seemed quite interested in you. I hope you got her number.'

'Eh… yeah… I did, actually. I know her brother. We've… err… texted,' Jez responds, sounding like a daft teenager. 'How do you know Savage?' He's keen to get back to the conversation.

Elijah's grinning. 'She's a lovely looking woman. That dark auburn look isn't too common around my parts. Now then, I know Savage because he picked me up from the railway station yesterday afternoon. And we had a good conversation on the way down to my B&B. Well… he talked and I listened. Do you know him?'

Jez laughs and imagines the scenario. Savage talking twenty to the dozen to a complete stranger. 'Yeah, I know him. He's fuckin' mental, him, like.'

'Well, he gave me his card. The first I heard of your friend's death was on that taxi ride from the station. Said it's been the talk of the town for weeks now. Anyway, after our meal yesterday I was walking back up the street and I passed the police station. There's an appeal poster stuck on a window. There's a photograph of your friend and… well… I found myself looking at it. And… I found myself looking at the man. And without really realising it, I was, kinda, trying to get to know him. You know, the who, what, why, when and where type of questions.' Elijah looks at Jez, purses his lips then shrugs his shoulders.

Jez is looking at him with interest as he doesn't really know where the conversation is heading. Then he says, 'Listen, pal… I know I only met you yesterday and this is none of my business but… well, do you really think you should be involving yourself with a murder? Ah mean… after what you told me yesterday in the chip shop.' He lightly pats the back of Elijah's shoulder. 'If I were you, I'd focus on you and your health.'

Elijah looks at Jez. 'It's not involvement, man. Not involvement. Just a bit of light interest… you know, to take my mind off things. But hey, I appreciate you saying that.'

They walk on in silence, immersed in their own thoughts. Then Elijah continues, 'Anyway, to answer your other question, I took a trip to the murder scene for a look about. I didn't go down on to the beach. I could see it all from the clifftop. In fact, I preferred it that way.'

Jez can see the beach in his mind's eye and adds, 'The tide will have been in and out a hundred times since the murder so I doubt there will be much in the way of evidence.'

Elijah says, 'It's not just that. A crime scene isn't just a few metres around the body. It's not micro. It's macro. It's "big picture" stuff. And standing there on that headland gave me the perfect view of the murder scene. There are steps leading down to the beach, but then again, if it was low tide the killer could have gained access to it by simply walking round the headland, from either north or south. That would be the discreet approach, so I'm gonna assume that's the way the killer arrived on the beach.'

Jez looks at Elijah and says, 'You're really getting into this, aren't you?' There's a pause as Jez mulls over everything Elijah's just said, then adds, 'Kev was there to do some sea fishing so it wouldn't have been low tide. It's unlikely he'd traipse out a quarter of a mile with all his fishing tackle. So, I guess he was found further up the beach.'

Elijah turns and smiles. 'Hey, I like it. I like it. Also, I guess the tide would be on the way in when he was killed to minimise the time between him being attacked and drowning. Can you get me a tide timetable?'

Jez replies, 'Shouldn't be a problem. The Tourist Information Office should have copies, or that week's edition of the *Berwick Advertiser* will have tide information.'

Elijah has an expression of intrigue around his eyes. He says, 'So… did the killer bring his own stake for the job… so he could choose exactly where to position the victim? The report in the paper you showed me was sketchy about that and what weapon was used to inflict the trauma injuries. I did see some rusty old anchor points, but they were above the high tide mark. Oh, by the way, I'm using the word "he" as I assume it's a man who carried out this crime, by the power used to inflict the injuries.'

Jez shakes his head then replies, 'No idea where he was found except it had to be below the high tide mark.' He focuses on a red and white cargo ship steaming slowly northwards. *I wonder if it's going to Leith? Then maybe on to somewhere like Venezuela or Puerto Rico. Sounds better than teaching maths to gobby teenagers.* He suddenly wants to go home to Edinburgh. But these thoughts are just his mental C drive flicking through a folder in the back of his mind. By comparison, his A drive is full-on, listening intently to his Sunday morning companion.

But Elijah isn't looking at him. He's looking over his shoulder at the huge Trinity Church which shelters in the angle of the Walls – a drab, spireless monolith surrounded by hundreds of centuries' old headstones. He nods at the church then says, 'Strange church, that one. No spire.'

'Yeah, you're right. It is strange looking. No spire, no bells, no tower. It was built during Cromwell's time. And when it was built it didn't even have stained-glass windows. I think the style's known as "Severe Puritan". Actually, that church is where the funeral's being held tomorrow morning. Eleven o'clock. And the burial afterwards.'

Elijah falls silent. Now he's nodding and says, 'Yeah, you

definitely know your history.' Jez looks out to sea, but the cargo ship has disappeared from view. Elijah asks, 'Do you know about the Covenanters?'

'The Covenanters?' Jez shakes his head. 'Some bunch of religious fanatics back in the day. At least that's what I remember from my history classes at school. Long time ago, mind.'

Elijah says, 'Yeah, I read a guide book on Berwick last night and it mentions them. You're doing them a disservice. They were an actual army. The Army of the Covenant. They were Scottish Presbyterians who disagreed with King Charles I. Acted like a "de facto" government in Scotland for about a decade in the 17th century. The King hated the Covenanters and had his army hunt them down and executed.'

'Hi, I'm impressed. You know your history too,' replies Jez.

'Actually, the reason I'm telling you this is because in the guide it says that one method of execution was to tie them to posts fixed in the sand within the flood mark of the sea and when the tide came in they were drowned.' He's looking at the church, then he turns to Jez and says, 'Just like your friend. And bearing in mind he'd been viciously beaten, at least that's what it said in the paper you showed me, why go to the trouble of tying him to a stake and leaving him to drown? It's either the killer's signature or a very odd MO. Very odd. Don't think I've ever come across it.'

'MO?' asks Jez, not sure what the acronym means.

'Modus operandi. A loose translation would be a particular method of doing something. Many killers have their own modus operandi. Let's walk on, shall we?' They set off, past Windmill Bastion, which has a cannon set inside, and on to King's Mount, last of the five jewels in this medieval stone ring.

Jez says, ‘So… you think that the drowning was significant. You must have dealt with drownings before.’

Elijah responds, ‘Well, the usual type of drowning murder. You know, unfaithful wife in the bath, shaving her legs. Husband enters and drowns her. Although usually the cause of death in that type of scenario is strangulation. But I’ve dealt with other drownings. I was once involved in a case where the mother strapped her baby into a car seat and drove to a lake. Then she got out, released the handbrake and let the car roll down and into the water. Took two days to find the car and recover the body.’

‘Why would she kill her own child?’

‘The court had granted custody to the father. Tug of love gone wrong. The woman’s in a nuthouse now. But in that case the drowning was merely a means to an end. But this one here is different. The killer didn’t have to drown Kevin Devine. He could have just battered him to death. Easier, quicker. That’s what’s intrigued me. Water may be the connection. Water might be the key to solving this murder.’

Jez digests this information. The pace of their walk slows to a contemplative crawl. He wants to tell Elijah again that maybe he shouldn’t be getting too involved in this but it’s awkward as he doesn’t really know the guy and doesn’t want to sound pushy and forward.

Elijah talks on: ‘But to beat a victim unconscious then go to the trouble of restraining him and leaving him to drown, Jez. That’s unusual. Very unusual. The killer took a chance in order to convey a message. So, this aspect of the case has intrigued me. And reading about the Covenanters being killed in a similar way got me wondering.’

'Do you think there's a connection?' asks Jez.

'Fuck knows,' he responds with a rueful smile. 'But the killer certainly wanted your man to die by drowning, that's for sure.'

They walk on and up to Coxon's Tower, which overlooks the river's estuary and is a great vantage point for views across to the south side. The Tweed's dark waters are flowing out fast, finally able to get lost within the ocean's depths. And down on the newly exposed, stinking mudflats they see the hideously bloated shape of a dead dog, void of hair, jaw hanging open in a silent scream. The stench of the animal's rotting flesh attracts rats that are swarming and squirming all over it: lunging, nipping, biting, ripping. More rats dart about amongst the limp, reposing bladderwrack and foul-smelling debris. Jez casts his mind back to the telephone conversation he had with Wacka, when he told him that rats had got to Kev and had bitten into his lips, nose and eyes. He's staring down at this grotesque scene then says out loud, almost to himself, 'It wasn't reported in the paper, but Kevin's body was attacked by rats. Aye, even in death he was violated.'

The big man's looking out over the tranquil, waveless sea, then turns to Jez, puts a hand on his shoulder and says, 'I'm sorry about your friend.' There's real sincerity in his expression and body language. Then he says, 'Do you fancy a pint?'

CHAPTER 10

THE BARRELS

SUNDAY

'It's a bit different in here,' says Jez, pushing open the door to Barrels public house. Opening time was about fifteen minutes ago but already there are a few people in. They're all at the bar, either sitting on stools made out of barrels, or standing and leaning over the bar counter, as if in deep conversation with the barman. It's cool and quiet and Elijah's looking around him and adjusting to the dim, atmospheric light. From somewhere Etta James sings an old blues number, "I'd Rather Go Blind". The clientele has a pleased look about themselves. Not for them the Sunday morning routine of washing the car, trimming the hedges then off to a retail park with the missus. No. These dudes have beaten off suburbia. Bit like going to the pub on Boxing Day night, leaving behind the chaos of Christmas. They've escaped.

'What you havin', pal?' asks Jez.

'Oh, now. Usually it's London Pride but… oh, are those real ales there on draft?' Jez and the barman nod in unison. 'Never heard of that one before! Okay, give me a… oh, a pint of your best… Orkney Dark Island, my friend.' Elijah purses his lips like he's just made a monumental decision.

'So, that's an Orkney Dark Island and an Amstel for me, please,' says Jez. The barman reaches up for a couple of glasses and begins pouring.

Elijah's looking around the place then asks, 'Is that what I think it is?' pointing to an old dentist's chair which resides at the end of the bar.

Jez replies, 'As I said, it's a bit different in here.' The big man's still absorbing the scene. Sections of the bar are made out of barrels, as is the high shelving which runs round the walls of the pub like a tidemark round a bath. Displayed on the shelving are signs in different languages, an ancient radio set and a small collection of antique binoculars. Jez pays for the drinks then they walk to a table in the small snug area by the window. Jez takes the seat with the wall behind him as he prefers to look out onto the bar. Above them, a puppet rides across the ceiling on a marlin.

They make a drama of their first sip. Elijah's impressed. 'Mmm, now that's what I call a pint of beer. What's its strength?'

'It'll be strong, pal. Those Orkney boys are all fishermen descended from Picts and Vikings so it'll be super-charged stuff.'

Elijah asks, 'How's that chemically enhanced dishwater you're drinking?'

Jez laughs in mock indignation then responds, 'Listen, this is Dutch beer, proper hard drinking beer, this is. Straight out the River Amstel. Straight out of Amsterdam, one of my favourite cities. You must have been there.'

'Oh yes,' Elijah responds. He sounds like the dog on the Churchill Insurance advert.

They exchange smiles, then Jez says, 'Aye, I've been in a few coffee shops in Amsterdam.'

'You're talking to the converted here,' responds Elijah. 'Ever been in one called Rookies?'

'Oh, I know Rookies!' replies Jez. 'Aye, just off the Leidseplein. Know it well, and what a laid-back atmosphere. Aye, they do a lovely milkshake too.'

'In addition to a brilliant weed menu,' says Elijah, 'and I like the way they categorise their produce by stars, you know, denoting the strength of the crop.'

'Super-chilled-out place,' replies Jez. 'Truth is, I've never taken anything stronger than weed. To be honest, all that cocaine and pill-popping stuff frightens me. You don't know what it's cut with, don't know how you're going to react. At least with weed you know what you're getting.'

'Hey, if it grows out the ground, it's fine by me,' responds Elijah. They both laugh out loud and some of the regulars turn and look over, and Jez can see their outburst of humour has put smiles on their faces too. He vaguely knows a couple of them and waves over.

He turns back to Elijah and says, 'I wonder if any of them get involved on Oliver Reed Day.' Elijah looks at him bemused.

'Aye. Oliver Reed died on 2nd May about fifteen years ago. I remember the date as it's always on a Bank Holiday weekend. Anyway, each year a gang of boys gather here to celebrate his life. Aye, it's a full-on all-day session. Obviously, it gets right out of hand. Not violent, they just get absolutely roaring drunk. One year the police were called because some of them had shinnied up the drainpipes outside and were all on the roof! And by the way, there's a three-storey tenement above this pub.' Elijah's laughing and shaking his head. Jez continues, 'If I lived back in Berwick this would probably be my local. Do you have one down in London?'

'Not really. I'm not much of a drinker, although I like a real ale. Especially on holiday.'

They sip their pints and Elijah now has a white, frothy upper lip but Jez doesn't know him well enough to point it out. They're quiet. Jez is thinking about the alcohol-fuelled night he had last night and nearly says something about "hair of the dog" but that only prompts a memory of the dead, hairless dog that they saw lying on the riverbank so quickly flips his brain elsewhere. He casts his mind back to when he met this man yesterday and asks, 'You mentioned in the chip shop yesterday that you were here for a couple of weeks. So, why choose here?'

'A couple of weeks, yes,' he responds, but Jez can see he's miles away, like in a trance. He's talking but looking at his pint. 'Well, I chose this town because it looked on the map like Berwick was about as far away from London as I needed to go. I thought about Edinburgh and, as I said yesterday, I love that city. But I wasn't looking for that. I was looking for somewhere smaller. Not a city. Some place where I could get some peace and quiet. Where I could walk the streets at an easy pace, with my own thoughts. I don't mean rest and recuperation. More like rest and repair. So, I booked a B&B, got on a train and didn't look back.'

'Yeah, you called it gardening leave yesterday. I see,' responds Jez. A pause, then he says, 'Why? Was it just a cumulation of things or…' The sentence dies in the air and trails off to nothing. He suddenly feels awkward, as if the question was too personal for a guy he only met yesterday.

Elijah looks troubled. Then he says, 'I told you about my job.' It's a statement, not a question. So he begins. 'Well, about six months ago I was assigned to a murder case. So what? We get about a hundred murders a year in London and at any one time I've got at least a couple on the go. Anyway, I became involved with an investigation into the murder of a young girl. A child. Eight years old.' He looks at Jez and opens his mouth as if to speak but doesn't. He takes another sip then inspects his glass. The white froth on his upper lip is still there, more substantial now. And, despite the cool, dark shade of the snug, Jez sees sweat forming on Elijah's forehead. A single shake of his head, then he continues. 'She'd been abducted more than a week earlier. The Met turned the city upside down looking for her. Some cops worked on their days off, even though it was Christmas. Anyway, I was contacted the day her body was found.' He stops and pulls a large, white handkerchief from his pocket and begins to dab at his face.

'There's froth on your lip, pal,' Jez quietly points out to him.

Elijah takes his time with the handkerchief then emerges froth free. 'Freezin' cold day it was. The roads were slick with ice. I remember driving to the scene. I went with a blood spatter analyst. When we got there, to the house where she'd been kept captive, well, she'd been dead for a couple of days, you know.' He's looking at Jez, who nods even though he's never seen a dead body that's lain for two days. 'We know that because of the level of rigor mortis. It's a very reliable way of estimating the time of death and it occurs in the first forty odd hours after death. And because it was the middle of winter and so bloody freezin' in the property there was no larvae infestation. You know, maggots.' Elijah continues but his voice begins to waiver. Then he shakes his head violently and says, 'And, erm, oh look. I shouldn't be bothering you with these things. You've got your own problems with your friend's funeral tomorrow.' He raises his glass and takes a huge draft of beer.

'Elijah, it's fine. And if you want to talk about it then I'll listen. It's no problem. I'm fine.' Elijah looks unconvinced, so Jez adds, 'Sometimes it's easier talking to someone you don't really know. You know, like a stranger on a train. So, if you need to get it out, then get it out.'

'Are you sure?' responds Elijah. 'I mean, this isn't normal Sunday morning chat, y'know?' He takes another drink then wets his lips and continues. 'Okay. Yeah, when she was found she was… she was… oh, pure white. I don't just mean she was a white girl. I mean it was like every drop of blood had drained away from her. It was like… like porcelain. So we started doing our work, me and the blood spatter analyst. The cause of death was strangulation, but we didn't know that then. She'd been strangled with her own knickers. And… erm… they'd blinded her.' Now he's looking at Jez hard. 'Hear what I'm sayin', man?' He's talking like a hard black man, toughened to life in an inner city combat zone.

Jez nods, but knows it's not a question. He can see Elijah getting agitated and wonders where this is going. *Jesus Christ, I only came oot for a fuckin' walk.* His companion suddenly looks like he's struggling to keep his composure. Jez thinks, *This man is fucked up. This poor man.*

They're still holding eye contact. Seconds pass, then he continues. 'And… and… this child… this child who should have been bursting with joy and life and noise… she just lay there… like a doll picked up by a child and flung across the room. Her legs were… Oh Christ, no.' He looks away then stares at the floor. Two minutes ago Jez didn't know him well enough to tell him he had froth on his lip, but not now. He reaches over and places a hand on Elijah's forearm. He doesn't speak, just looks at him. Elijah breathes out hard then says, 'The silence was awful, man. It was heavy, you know. Did I tell you… did I tell you they blinded her?'

'Yes, you did,' Jez responds. He's looking at Elijah as if to say, *"Go on".* He does.

'They'd poured neat ammonia into her eyes. Then she'd been raped… multiple times over a period of days. That dog we saw on the shore. Rats were all over it. Reminded me. Reminded me why I came here. Those men… those depraved, vile creeps were all over that child, like rats in a fuckin' frenzy.'

Jez asks, 'Christ, how did they find her?'

'Suspicious neighbour reported it. There'd been a steady stream of men to the property and she thought it was drug-related, like maybe a crack house, so didn't want to appear too curious. Then nothing for a couple of days, so she thought it safe to contact the police.'

'Were they caught?' asks Jez, anger rising inside him. Elijah grips his pint glass and looks at him.

'No. No, they haven't been caught. They were careful not to leave any evidence. Meticulous. After she was dead, they doused her with a solution of sodium hydroxide and ammonia. Those chemicals really goofed up the DNA samples. And the fibre evidence. So no, they're still out there. The investigation's ongoing.' He sits and stares at his pint like a defeated man.

Jez says, 'Well, I hope they're brought to justice soon. Cos filthy scum like that need to be kept away from the public.'

There's a pause as Elijah seems to absorb what Jez said. Still looking at his glass he replies in a slow, meaningful way, 'Prison's too good for these sub-humans. I'd have them castrated.' They look at each other and nod in agreement.

Another silence, then Jez asks, 'What was her name?'

'Hayley. It was Hayley. And you know what? It bothered me cos—' Just then two men barge in through the door talking loudly. Elijah spins round in startled shock, like the sudden noise scared him. He takes a few seconds to recover then starts again, almost in a whisper. 'It bothered me cos I knew she was dead but at that time her parents still hadn't been informed. They were still clinging to the hope she would be found alive. But I knew. I knew those parents were gonna be told later that day and it was gonna fuckin' destroy them, man. Change them forever. That bothered me. That I knew, and they didn't. I felt guilty, somehow.' He takes a drink then abruptly rises from his chair, mouths the word "toilet", so Jez points to the corner of the pub, and he heads off.

Jez watches him until he disappears through the toilet door then breathes out slowly. *This is heavy duty stuff, my man. Fuckin' hell. I feel sorry for him, I do. It's hard seeing a strong man broken down by grief or horror. Why the fuck he's showing an interest in Kev's murder is beyond me.* He fishes out his mobile phone and checks for messages. There're two. The first one's from Cement Shoes.

Good to catch up with u again pal. C u 2moro at the church. Wee drink after

Jez decides not to reply until later on, as every Sunday Cement Shoes takes his mum to Mass then has dinner at her house. Aye, he looks after his mum and Jez respects him for that. He's a decent guy. Well, now he is. Thirty years ago, the same man stuck a broken bottle in a man's throat then visited him in hospital and warned him if he grassed to the police he would kill him. Does time change people? Or do people change with time? Or do we just mature and change with age? Jez puts Cement Shoes in that last category. He thinks, *Christ, when he was in his forties he got a distance learning degree in Theology at St Andrew's University. What the fuck?!* The intense conversation with Elijah is causing his mind to sink to a deep place. Not unsettling, though. No, he feels strangely calm. He thinks about Elijah and how this horrific crime has affected him. *That murder has changed him. Aye, circumstances can change people too.*

The next text is from Wacka.

Get a haircut. Wake's in The Brown Bear

Jez thinks, *Cheeky bastard, eh? Well, you've no' changed, Triple Nipple. Still as rude and off-hand as always. Aye, he's definitely no' changed. Always has and always will be a violent, obnoxious bastard. Surprised he's no' killed somebody.* He pauses at this thought and allows it to sink in. Not deep, cerebral stuff, just sitting there in his subconscious… nagging away.

He scrolls down but there's no text from Josie. He smiles, thinking, *That little bugger's playing hard to get, eh? It wasn't that yesterday with her wee message, was it?* Then he realises that the last message from last night was him saying he'd text her today. He punches in a message.

Hiya it's Jez. How's homework comin along xx

A minute passes. *Where the fuck's Elijah got to?* Another minute then he emerges from the toilet and goes straight to the bar. He looks around at Jez with an expression of "it's my round". Jez raises his glass to him, as an affirmative. The phone gives that poxy "beep" sound.

I know. Got u in ma contacts! Homework done. Just references to add xxx

What u studying xx

Diploma in Nutrition xxx

What is it aboot qualifications, eh? Everyone's getting them these days. There's Cement Shoes with his theology degree and here's this lass aboot forty years old studying nutrition!

Talkin of nutrition. Food 2nite, with me? Xx

Yeah!!! Anywhere but Cannon chip shop!! Xx

But I luv a chippie!! Ok will ring u later. Bout 4 xx

Elijah's back from the bar and places another pint of Amstel in front of Jez, who looks up and says, 'What's that you're drinking?'

'It's called Pentland IPA. And it's a decent real ale, this one. I've had it before.' He looks over at the array of ales on display at the bar. 'I might try them all while I'm here… err, I don't mean try them all *today*. I mean, during my holiday, y'know.'

Jez laughs then his mobile beeps. It's a single x from Josie. He says, 'That was a text from the girl in the chip shop you saw yesterday. I'm meeting her tonight.'

'That gorgeous little redhead, you mean?' asks Elijah, with

a smile. And he feels okay. Talking about the incident and opening up on his demons has lifted his mood. The burden suddenly feels a little lighter.

'Yeah, that gorgeous little redhead. That's the one,' Jez responds, and he's glad because the conversation can move on now. He's drained with the thought of a frozen dead child. 'So, I'm seeing her tonight. Then, well, it's the funeral tomorrow morning and then the wake. I'm here till Saturday though. Thought I'd spend some time in the old town then head back to Edinburgh next weekend. I'm visiting my mum on Tuesday. She's on holiday just now.'

'Is that why you're at a B&B?' Elijah asks.

'Partly that and partly because she lives in sheltered housing. It's only a one-bedroom cottage so not really much room. It's just up there actually,' he says and points out the window towards the steep, cobbled street over the road. 'How long did you say you were staying here for?'

Elijah replies, 'A couple of weeks. And you know what? I've nothing in my diary so just taking each day as it comes. Loved that walk this morning so I'm gonna make it a regular routine. What time is the funeral tomorrow, by the way?'

'Eleven o'clock. And, as I said, it's at the Trinity Church we walked past before. The one with no spire. It was Kevin's church. Aye, he was just a normal Protestant. Not like me and a few of my mates that are Presbyterians. Proper hardcore Prods, us.'

'Not as hard core as those Covenanters, though,' Elijah replies, and Jez's mind drifts back to the conversation they'd had earlier this morning. Then, out of the blue, Elijah says, 'Who do you think killed your friend?'

Jez feels uncomfortable at the directness of the question. 'Who do *I* think? Oh Christ, Elijah, I honestly don't have a clue. I can't really think of anyone who'd want to kill him. I mean, I used to know Kevin really well but, you know, you grow up and take different paths in life. So, he might have enemies. I don't know. I rarely saw him these days. I'm up in Edinburgh, so it was the odd night out, occasional football match, that sort of thing. But that was about it.' He pauses then says, 'Who do you think it could be? I mean, like, from a profiling point of view.'

'Oh, now. Big question, that,' replies Elijah. 'Well now,' he says, sipping his pint then slowly placing the glass back on the table. And the way he does it, he looks hard as fuck. 'I think he knew his killer. Most victims do. So it's family, friend or work related. And he knows the area so he's local. What job did Kevin do?'

'He was a plumber. Aye, he left school, did his apprenticeship and ended up with his own business. One-man band, like. Never seemed to be out of work. He was a popular guy, you know. Well liked.'

'Okay, good. Well, I think our killer is blue collar too. The physicality of the crime points to that. Bludgeoning his victim then restraining him with cable ties to a stake suggests a person who works with their hands. But, as I say, what's interested me is why use drowning to kill him? Anyway, we don't know the killer, but we know the victim, so let's study him. That often throws something up. If, as you say, he was a popular man then we don't yet have a motive. No matter. Let's overlook the motive and focus on the evidence. And the most significant piece of evidence is Kevin himself. Before and after his death.

It would help if I could get a copy of the autopsy report. Oh, and a tide timetable; I think I mentioned that.'

'The tide timetable should be easy to get hold of,' replies Jez. He feels odd talking about his friend's murder like it's a classroom case study. 'There's probably one in the reception at your digs. I'll ask at mine too. But the autopsy, I mean… only the family, you know, next of kin would get that. I suppose his mother would have a copy, but it would be odd if I approached her for something like that. Having said that,' he says, smiling now, 'I've got a friend who knows Kev's mum well. Very well, actually. His name's CD.'

Elijah's looking at Jez and says, 'Well now, that's an option. Do you think he'll be seeing her anytime soon?'

Jez smiles then replies, 'Anything's possible. And I mean anything.' His mind drifts off thinking about various encounters CD has had with Kev's mother, including one night in the back of a car Jez was driving. She had her right leg resting on his bloody shoulder!

Elijah continues: 'Obviously, the cops working on this case will have access to that information. Would you know any of them personally?'

'I'm not sure, is the straight answer to that one. I only landed here yesterday so don't really know which of the local cops are involved. Ah mean, how many people get involved in a case like this?'

'Oh, dozens, Jez. Obviously the local CID would have been called to the scene after Kevin was discovered, but due to the nature of the crime it would have been given a Category A status and passed to a regional investigation team. So, maybe forty altogether.'

'Forty?! Jesus Christ. I didn't think there'd be that many. What do they all do?'

'Well, they're not all out playing Starsky and Hutch wannabies, that's for sure. Oh, there are so many different roles – forensics, fingerprints, crime scene investigators, search teams and all those types of hands-on responsibilities. Then there's the specific roles, like disclosure officer, interview advisor, crime scene manager. They'll be led by a senior officer, probably a Detective Chief Inspector.'

'Bloody hell, Elijah. It sounds very well organised.'

'It is. In theory. What jurisdiction does Berwick come under?'

'Northumberland,' Jez replies. 'Aye, it's still an English town.'

'Well, no doubt they'll have a Major Incident Room at Berwick Police Station and the investigation team will have relocated there.'

'Christ, the toon's swarming with cops and detectives and here we are, a month on, and I'm not really sure how much progress has been made.'

Elijah says, 'Believe me, they'll be keeping their cards close to their chests with this. And I wouldn't be surprised if they've kept some evidence from the public. I don't know, a murder weapon, a piece of forensic evidence, something like that. But the pressure's on for one single reason.' Jez looks at him intently. 'In case the killer strikes again. I doubt he will, as this looks personal so it's a one-off. But you never know. It may have been staged to look like it's personal. Clever fuckers, these murderers.'

'Not as clever as the combined total of forty law enforcement officers though, I bet,' replies Jez. He drains off his pint then says, 'Listen, I need to get a move on. Date tonight, you know. But what I'll do is, I'll ask my mate to ask Kev's mum about the autopsy report. If he tells her it might help find her son's killer, I'm sure she'll give him it.'

'You can only ask,' replies Elijah. 'Can I ask you something? Could you write a small profile on Kevin for me? Nothing in depth, you know. Hobbies, relationships, criminal past, that sort of thing.'

'I suppose so, although it's been a long time since I was close to Kev, so it won't be much. But aye, I'll put some words together. You've already said you think the killer's blue collar, lives locally and this murder's a one-off.'

'Yeah, I have.' Elijah moves his head close to his companion. 'Listen, Jez, I'm only gonna have a look at this case, that's all, pal. Okay? That's about as much commitment as I'm giving. Because, you know… I'm ill and I need to take this illness seriously. But this will give me an interest. A pastime to pass the time. As I've said before, it's not my manor and I'm on holiday.'

'Aye, well, just remember that,' replies Jez. 'You're on holiday, so take it easy.'

Elijah smiles and downs his pint. Then he gets up, saying, 'I fancy another one of these. Sure you're okay?' Jez shakes his head. 'Okay, do you fancy meeting up again later in the week?' He fishes out a business card and hands it to Jez. 'Oh, and thanks for walking round the Walls with me this morning. Really appreciated the company.'

'No problem,' replies Jez as he pockets the card. They shake hands and he walks out. A black and white framed print of an obviously drunk and dishevelled Oliver Reed stares down from above the door. Underneath his image it says, "Sobriety is Pointless". The afternoon sun belts down as he ambles back to his digs. He decides to compile the list of information on Kevin when he gets in, while the conversation with Elijah is still fresh in his mind. He feels like Janus, the Greek god of transitions, with two faces. One looking forward to the future, and one looking back – to the past.

CHAPTER 11

THE DATE

SUNDAY

Jez lets himself in and closes the heavy front door. He's expecting the familiar smells of leather and old books in the corridor, but instead gets lavender and cleaning products. Like an old folks' home, without the pissy smell. Lesley's obviously the "Bleach Queen" of Bridge Street. It's now early afternoon, and all's quiet in the house as he climbs the stairs. The room's been cleaned. He kicks off his shoes and flops onto the bed. The combination of alcohol today on top of the skinful he had last night is making him tired. He's told Josie he'll ring her about four, so sets his alarm, undresses, then slides in between the starched, cool sheets. He's soothed by the distant drone of a lawnmower and drifts off to this slow-paced summer soundtrack.

The dream is vivid. He's on Murphy's Beach. It's a beautiful day and the sea is glittering across its flat surface. He's on the shoreline, then suddenly he sees Kevin standing right out there, waist deep. He's shouting something, or is it the ocean's distant roar? The ground's not firm and he's sinking into the wet sand. Jez screams at him and beckons him into the shore – to safety. But he just stands there, shaking his head. He's sunk up to his shoulders in sand as the foaming waves lunge towards him. Rats emerge from the slimy seaweed and circle him. They get bolder, knowing their prey is trapped and helpless. They move in, flashing white dagger teeth. Kevin chokes and vomits up bile and sand. The waves surround him with dirty white scum. Jez watches as he slips under the churning mass of growling water. There's nothing he can do. He shouts out and wakes suddenly in jerking movements, gagging on a scream in his throat. Cold sweat runs out of his hair. He lies there, feeling shocked and vulnerable. The silence snaps as a car accelerates along Bridge Street. He drifts off again. Deep this time.

Just before 4pm he wakes and feels refreshed. Leaping out of bed he dives into the shower then shaves at the basin in the corner. He retrieves Josie's note from the bedside table, sits on the edge of the bed and punches her number into his phone. His fingers are sweaty. He thinks, *Christ, I'm nervous. Hope I don't get tongue-tied. She might be a man-eating cougar!* He's trying to work out roughly how old she is when he hears a click, then her voice. It's quick and breathy, like she's dashed to answer it.

'Hello?'

'Hi, Josie. It's Jez here. How y'doin'?'

'Ooh, hiya, Jez. Sorry, I had to run to get my phone. How are you?' I sense she's smiling and breathless as she asks the question.

'I'm good. Aye, I'm good. Met up with a few friends last night so, err… yeah, good night. Sore head this morning, like, but a've been oot for a walk roond the Walls. So no' bad now.' And he's always surprised at how quickly he reverts to a broad Berwick accent when talking to a fellow "townie".

'Good job you had those fish and chips yesterday then, before venturing out, eh?' she replies. 'I thought I'd impress you with the biggest piece of haddock I could find! And it *was* lovely and sunny this morning. Not that I've seen much of it to be honest.'

Jez lets her talk. He's thinking about yesterday in the chip shop when he first saw her approaching his table. That tomato ketchup incident where she played him like a wee laddie. 'Yeah, I loved that meal, Josie. And the fish *was* impressive!' He laughs and tries to sound casual and relaxed but can sense his flushed face so changes the subject. 'Whereabouts in town do you live?'

'I've got a flat on the Walls. Just along from the Scotsgate.'

'Oh. Well, I walked along there this morning and if you'd been looking out your window you would've seen me. Aye, I was with a big West Indian guy. You might remember him. We shared a table in the chip shop yesterday and got talking. He's a Londoner. Interesting guy, actually.'

'Yeah, I do remember him. Polite. Lovely smile. Yeah, good-looking guy. So, you didn't know him before, then?' she asks.

'Nah. Just met him yesterday and then bumped into him this morning. Anyway, I gave him a tour of the Walls and we ended up having a pint in The Barrels. I've got him on the local hard stuff.'

'Hair o' the dog, Jez. Hair o' the dog! Barrels, aye. Been in there. Long time ago, mind.'

Jamming the phone in his ear he lies back on the bed and props his head on a pillow. He likes Josie's easy manner. He sees her face and a rush comes up from his belly. He responds, 'Yeah, you said yesterday that you hadn't been out for a while... err... just before you gave me your number.' Not wanting to make her feel uncomfortable he quickly adds, 'Which I'm glad you did by the way.' He senses she's smiling *and* blushing now.

She responds shyly, 'I thought I was being a bit forward, then I thought, *Go for it, Josie!*' And now they're both laughing out loud. Any lingering nerves have disappeared.

'Erm... I'm actually here in Berwick for a funeral tomorrow, Josie. Kevin Devine's. You'll have heard.'

'Oh, yes I'm so sorry to hear that, Jez. Christ, what a shock that was. I mean, people don't get murdered in Berwick, you know.'

'I know, I know. I got a phone call up in Edinburgh from a mate of mine. It knocked me back.'

'He was just a young man, Jez. Then when we heard *how* he'd died, well, that's sick, isn't it? It's frightening actually. To think someone's out there capable of doing something like that. I've got my locks on at night, I can tell you. Bit nervous, y'know?'

'Aye, I can understand that,' says Jez. 'I mean, although Kev and I go back a long way, I've not been close to him for a good few years now, so I don't know if he crossed someone or if it was a random attack, y'know? I'm not even sure the police have worked that out yet.'

Josie replies, 'God, the whole town's been knocked back with his death. He was so well known, you know. And liked. Aye, I remember him from years ago. Bit older than me though.

Fiona mentioned in the shop yesterday that you were probably here for the funeral. Aye, the last time I saw Kevin was a while back. He was with Fish Heid in Marmaris.'

'What? Turkey?'

'No! The kebab shop on West Street!'

They both burst out laughing at the same time. And it feels good for Jez. Like a release of tension. Then he says, 'Aye. Anyway, the service is at eleven o'clock. At the Trinity Church just along from you. But I'm here till Saturday then heading back up the road.'

'Aye, Fiona said you're a teacher up there. Maths.'

'That's right, yeah. Been teaching for years now. So… err… what else did Fiona say about me, then? Nice things I hope.'

'Mmm… very nice things, actually. She says you're a good guy. Well, you are *now*!'

They both laugh again and he's really liking this woman. 'Aye, well that's a back-handed compliment if I've ever heard one. I've known Fiona for a long time. She's married to a mate of mine. Aye, it's a funny thing, Josie. All my mates were tearaways when they were young, but they've all settled down now. It's their wives who are mental!' He takes a deep breath and cuts to the chase. 'So, did you finish your essay?'

'Yeah, all done,' she happily announces.

'Well, do you fancy getting your glad rags on tonight and having some food with me?'

'Oooh, I'd like that. Actually, I don't really do glad rags. What about skinny jeans and heels?'

'To be honest, I fancied you in your blue apron and hairnet!' They both laugh then he says, 'Would you like to go to Limoncello, the Italian on Hide Hill?'

'Oh I'd love that! Mmm… yeah,' she responds.

'Tell you what, I'll meet you outside the Advertiser at six thirty.'

'The Advertiser. Oh, that's so 1980s, Jez! Okay, then. That's ideal for me.' The Advertiser is the printing works for the *Berwick Advertiser* and is located at the top of the high street. Couples have met there for decades.

'See you there, then,' says Jez.

'Okay. Bye.' The word "bye" is said softly. Enticingly. And in his mind's eye he sees her full red lips forming the word.

He hangs up, then remembers the texts from Cement Shoes and Wacka so taps in a response. Well, he responds to Cement Shoes. Triple Nipple can do one! His hands are still sweaty from the conversation with Josie. He phones the restaurant and books a table. And he feels good, even though he's preoccupied with tomorrow's funeral. There's a notepad on the bedside table with the B&B's name as a header: Apple House. *Okay. Let's write this bloody list on Kevin. His family, friends, associates, job, hobbies…*

Kevin Devine

Age – 46

Physical characteristics – about 5 foot 10 inches tall. Approx. 14 stones. Fairly fit.

Family – Married to Colette. Two young daughters. Homeowners. All Church of Scotland.

Parents – Dad is a retired long-distance lorry driver; Mam works as a minicab receptionist.

Occupation – Self-employed plumber. A one-man band. Good reputation, reliable, always in work. No obvious money problems.

Hobbies – Sea fishing. Hibs. Played Sunday league football.

Miscellaneous – Lived in Berwick all his life. Well liked, no known enemies. Made a couple of court appearances in his teens and twenties. Fighting, breach of the peace. Used to like a drug. Unaware of any problems, e.g. financial, relationship, health.

Is that it? No' much of a profile, eh? Well, if Elijah wants to know more, he can ask someone who knows him better than me. Maybe Savage. He must hear some juicy gossip in his taxi.

The sun's rays penetrate his room and seem to say *Do something!* He dresses then decides to go out for a wander before meeting Josie. At the foot of the stairs a movement causes him to turn, and through a window behind him he sees Lesley on a sunbed in a small garden. He shuffles quietly up to the window. Laying his hands on the cold shoulders of a cast-iron radiator he looks at her. She's in full recline, a book in her hand and head leaning over to one side. Amber sunlight bathes the garden in warmth. At the edge of the lawn is an apple tree and a wooden wheelbarrow filled with flowers, all hemmed in by a tall creosote fence. He looks at Lesley and thinks, *Where's your man? Where're your kids? Where's your family?*

He suddenly feels sorry for her. She looks lonely, in a way. And maybe her easy chat and ready smile obscure the reality of a solitary life. On the outside windowsill there's a jam jar half filled with water, and chunks of jam smear the inside. It's a wasp trap. He looks closer. The lid has holes punched in it – just wide enough for a wasp to crawl in but not be able to get out again. The surface is blanketed with drowned, disfigured wasps, and then he sees one, treading water among the carnage.

There's no way out. Others have sunk to the bottom and become hideously bloated. He looks at the crawling, desperate, barely living creature and wonders how long it has to live. In a minute it may go under. Or an hour. Or two hours. He wonders if it knows. Like Kevin did.

He makes his way to the front door, still thinking about Lesley. Then the crankshaft in his brain clicks over to Josie. She's single too but there's no burden of loneliness with her, just happy, positive energy. And *her* fire could engulf him. He lets himself out then heads along the street to Sally Port, a narrow, cobbled lane leading down under the Walls to the small harbour near the river's estuary. The tide's running out fast. He stands on the jetty and scans the river's surface for seals that journey up here from the Farne Islands to prey on salmon.

And now he's forty years back to when they were wee boys. Saturday matinee at the Playhouse then down here on their way home. Kids were often here fishing for eels around the sewer outlet. They used hand-held wooden frames with orange catgut wrapped around them. He remembers being fascinated if an eel was brought up, writhing and dancing on the end of the line. He was scared of them! And as a backdrop to all this would be a running commentary of the film they'd just been to see. And he still hates those Persian bastards for what they did to the three hundred Spartans. Aye, him, Wacka and Bang Bang were going to start a war with them, if he remembers rightly. They even practised ambushes along at the One Tunnel.

He walks up the cobbled slope. The late afternoon heat is still fierce, and sunlight glints off broken glass. Then it's a right, past The Barrels and up West Street with its steep incline. Near the top he's breathing heavy with the effort so stops and peers into Tropica pet shop. Not that he's into the dwarf iguanas in the window, it's just that he needs to halt the sweat running down his back. *I cannae meet Josie stinking like a heifer. Mind you, the smell of sweat on a man can be quite erotic.* After a minute the nape of his neck develops a cold dampness so it's okay to proceed. He makes it to the high street and immediately looks over and there she is at the Advertiser, looking in the window at a selection of photographs. And although the elegant, Victorian building is four storeys high, the insignificant person standing on the pavement next to it is more important to him.

Nearing her now and still unnoticed he shamelessly checks her out. Tight denim jeans, high heels and a fitted white shirt. She's bending forward to look at something in the window. Her figure curves with sex appeal. Then she looks up, sees him and smiles. He blushes and smiles back, nodding his head in approval. She walks towards him like a graceful, confident animal, and Jez says, 'Hi, you look gorgeous.'

She responds with a quiet, 'Thanks,' then adds: 'Well, you certainly scrub up well,' pretending to give him the once-over. And he realises she's as nervous as him. Her smile betrays an innocence and he senses the note yesterday was in the heat of the moment, safe in the haven of her work.

Her stiletto heels have brought her up to about his height, so he kisses her on the cheek while his hands rest on her hips. And, as he always does when he kisses a woman who's his height, he blushes slightly in the knowledge that they'd be this height if they were horizontal in bed. She returns his kiss and he feels her hands on his shoulders. The mood is shattered by the blaring sound of a car horn. It's Savage, careering round the corner and up Marygate. He pokes his thumb out the open car window in a gesture of approval. Even from here Jez can hear "Princess of the Streets" by The Stranglers blasting out.

'Do you know him?' asks Jez.

'Everyone knows Savage Morrison,' she replies in mock indignation.

'Aye, but I bet you didn't know he went to see *Abba The Movie* three nights running at the Playhouse when it came out. Denies it now, like.'

Josie throws her head back and laughs out loud. She looks comfortable now and so does he. They start to head down towards the restaurant. They're making small talk and it feels easy and natural. And as a backdrop to their conversation he has the lyrics of that Stranglers song in his mind.

She's real good looking, she makes me sigh. Blue jeans and leather, her heels are high.

Turning into Hide Hill they're met with the thick aroma of garlic, its bold pungency hanging in the still evening air. They're about to cross the street when he turns to her and says firmly, 'Okay. Teacher says give me your hand. We're crossing the street. C'mon.'

'Okay, sir!' she replies, with mock submissiveness. They join hands, cross the street and enter the restaurant.

* * *

Hours later and he's lying in bed, hands behind his head and searching for sleep. The alarm clock says 2.30 in harsh red light. The evening's memories return, giving him a warm glow inside. What she wore. What she said. The smell of perfume on her neck. Snippets of conversation. Her nutrition course. *Christ, what I didn't know about broccoli!* He loved her humour, clever and insightful. Oh, and they've both visited the same coffee shops in Amsterdam! Yeah, she's a wee stoner! Just recreational of course, which suits him fine. Her hair is dark red, like cherry, and not as loud as under the fluorescent glare of the chip shop yesterday. Even the walk back to hers was enjoyable, as was the kiss on her doorstep and the plan to meet again, later in the week. He thinks, *Christ, the thrill of the chase, man!*

The clock says 2.45 and he thinks about the funeral tomorrow. He tries to capture the atmosphere in his head: the musky smells, the hushed conversations, the quiet psalms. And he thinks about the congregation. Faces filled with grief, disbelief and anger. The BUNDIG have lost one of their own and he sees them filling up the pews with their wives and partners. Wacka, Bang Bang, Bob, Fish Heid, CD, Cement Shoes, Fifty Fifty, The Hammer. Savage will be there and the cops working on the case will show face. *Aye, the cops who seem no nearer to catching the killer than on the night Kev was murdered.*

Jez lies there and thinks about his friend, Kevin Devine. Not the man, the child. A kind, gentle child. He can see him now in his mind's eye. They're about five years old and it's a rainy day on the beach at Spittal. He can see his mum and Kev's mum. They've taken cover in a shelter on the promenade. The bench seat is high, and their feet swing with a carefree rhythm. Childhood. A place where no one dies.

* * *

Elijah Bootle sits in his room. After Jez left The Barrels, he had another pint of Dark Orkney. Then he went up to the

Kings Arms on Hide Hill and had a bar lunch. He got back to his B&B in the late afternoon and slept fully clothed on his bed until about nine o'clock. Now he's showered and changed and settled into his comfy armchair by the window. He rolls up a "mighty joint". Sleep now eludes him but he's not bothered. He puts on the TV and starts channel hopping. A remote in one hand and a joint in the other. 'Now, this is being relaxed,' he says out loud to himself and stretches out his long legs. Intrusive thoughts begin to enter his mind. Images of Hayley, the child. The remote feels sweaty and slippery. But before these scenes sharpen their focus, he propels them away from him. His thoughts turn to the scum responsible for her murder. They're still out there, somewhere. His marijuana-induced state allows his mind to move effortlessly from one theme to another, like moving through rooms in a house. He thinks about Kevin Devine. Slow-burning thoughts flit around the periphery of his conscious mind. *Why deliberately drown a man? Was the murder staged to confuse and mislead the investigation? Or to send a message to the police. What message?* He'd like to see that autopsy report. His brow is furrowed. He thinks about the Covenanters. About Freemasons. About the victim's family and friends.

CHAPTER 12

THE FUNERAL

MONDAY

Jez stands outside the black, wrought-iron gates of the churchyard and looks in. He'd been a choirboy here for a couple of years, when he was about nine or ten. In his mind's eye he sees the boy now. Crimson cassock and white ruff. An innocent kid living in innocent times. But that boy is long gone. Pockets of black-clad people stand about making small talk. The steady grey drizzle has prompted most of the congregation to take their seats already. He checks his watch. He needs a cigarette so digs out a packet and lights one up.

'Got a light, boy?' said in a mock West Country accent. It's Fish Heid. He worked as a fisherman down in Brixham for a couple of years and has the Devon accent off to a tee.

'Hi, Heid. You just want under ma' brolly, don't you?' Jez replies. 'No' that it's mine, like. Ah borrowed it from the B&B.'

Fish Heid joins him under the brolly's black canopy. Jez offers up his lighter and he inhales furiously, trying to light the soggy ciggy. 'Aaw, light, you fubber!'

'Here, chuck that away and have one o' these, for Christ's sake.' Heid takes one and Jez jams the brolly between his shoulder and head and cups his hand around the lighter, although there's not a breath of wind. Fish Heid breathes in, tilts his head back and exhales a long stream of smoke towards the heavy, leaden sky. Then he says:

'Well, this is it, Jez. The Big Day. And I cannae say I've been looking forward to it.'

'Me neither, Heid, me neither. I was just thinking before there, Kev's the first of the BUNDIG to go.'

'Aye, I know. Jesus Christ. Dead at forty-eight. Sometimes I still can't take it all in.' He looks lost and confused. 'And until we know who did it, who took him down, I don't think there'll be any closure. Ah mean, his killer could be here today for all we know. Alice is worried.'

Jez looks at him and thinks, *Who took him down? Odd way to describe it.* Then he says, 'Alice is worried? What aboot?'

'Death, Jez. She's worried aboot fubbin' death. She's worried aboot me. She's worried aboot all of us. It's the not knowing, you see. Aye, she's doon at the Kingdom Hall now. Praying for Kevin. And all of us.'

They smoke on in silence. Fish Heid's looking over at the churchyard while Jez looks down at the wet tarmac ground between them. If they weren't old friends, the silence could have become awkward. 'You'd think they'd clean up all this poxy chewing gum, eh? Look at it,' says Jez, gazing down and around them. But Fish Heid doesn't answer. He's just standing there, staring at the church like he's about to sit an exam he hasn't revised for.

'Okay, time to go in,' Jez says and blows out noisily. They stamp out their cigarettes then join the small band of stragglers on the narrow path towards the church entrance. As they walk through the churchyard Jez remembers some of the cracked and leaning headstones from his youth – like moss-covered sentries forming a nostalgic guard of honour. The rain suddenly strengthens and is followed by a clap of thunder which rolls across the sky. They quicken their step and take cover inside the church foyer. From here they can see the congregation. The smell of wooden pews and candle wax mixes with the odour of damp clothes. The front pews are empty for the family, and behind them it looks full, so they take seats near the back. There's a soft, quiet murmur. Someone coughs. The hard, wooden pews creak as people try to make themselves comfortable.

Jez looks towards the front of the congregation and sees the BUNDIG Boys huddled together with their wives and partners. A head turns and it's Cement Shoes, talking to someone behind him. He sees them and waves over, then motions that there's no room for them to join them. Fish Heid acknowledges him and gestures that they'll see him later. Jez makes himself comfortable then looks about. He sees Kev's friends and acquaintances, neighbours from his estate, football and fishing buddies. Mates from school. All here to pay their last respects. He vaguely recognises some faces from the past. He sees a guy who was in their year at school. *Fuck's sake, I thought he was deid.*

As the minutes tick down the small talk quietens to a

whisper. People are acknowledging others with head nods and hand waves. Jez thinks, *Aye, funerals are as much about the living as the dead.* A rustle of activity causes him to look around. He sees the coffin. Kev's cousins are the pallbearers, in position, taking the strain. In front of them is the minister, and behind the coffin Kev's family have gathered. The cortege begins to slowly move down the aisle, and as they pass Jez he briefly looks over. Kev's mum is tastefully dressed in a dark suit and simple jewellery. Half a step behind is her husband who looks a broken man. His suit looks worn and shiny although his shoes are well polished. He watches as the family take their seats in the front pews. The minister is talking to the organist. Centre stage is the coffin. Jez can't look at it. But he can't ignore it. The ultimate elephant in the room. And he knows that in that box is the barely recognisable body of Kevin Devine – the shell that's left of him.

Something makes him look around and he sees two uniformed police officers who've arrived late. They've entered from a side aisle and taken the back pew. Jez isn't sure about police rank markings but they've both got silver diamonds on their epaulettes. One of them looks like an ambitious young man, with his fresh face and rosy cheeks. Fish Heid leans close to Jez and whispers, 'Colette's had him dressed in a Hibs top, jeans and a pair of brogues.' Jez nods in approval. He likes that. You know, just in case there's somewhere we all go to. Suddenly the organ bursts into life with the first few bars of the opening hymn. Everyone stands abruptly and there's a feeling of relief that the service is finally underway. The hymn sheet tremors in Jez's hands as he looks at the words and begins to sing. And he thinks, *My God, this is it. All these weeks of waiting since he was murdered, and here we are.* The congregation sings out loud, almost too loud, as if in defiance at his death. Jez is singing but can only make out Fish Heid's monotonous tones next to him. By the third verse he stops and just looks at the words on the page.

The hymn ends and the minister pauses, allowing the last notes from the organist's fingers to resonate around the church. Then he asks the congregation to be seated. He walks to the pulpit. The eulogy begins: 'We are here today to show our love and respect for Kevin Devine, and to pay tribute to him as a husband, father, son and friend. And in doing so we can bring some comfort to those closest to him who have been deeply shocked and hurt by his death.' He continues bleakly and describes Kevin's premature passing away as "having the pages ripped out of a young man's life".

He talks about Kevin being born in this proud town. A Berwick man born into a proud Berwick family. The minister's deep voice echoes around them, then up high in the rafters. Jez looks at Colette. She looks defiant and resolute. Her elder daughter is sitting upright next to her, looking straight at the minister. Her focus on him is unwavering, as if he's personally talking to her, telling her that death is part of life and that her dad is now with God. The younger one sits on her mum's knee looking around. She's twisting a ringlet of blonde hair around a finger, looking fragile and unsure. Jez hopes that when she's older this won't be her earliest memory.

The minister's eulogy moves on to Kev's first day at school and the friends he made there – childhood friends who became lifelong friends and stood the test of time. To reinforce his comments the minister looks out over the congregation until he sees the BUNDIG Boys and scans them all. 'Yes, Kevin had many friends; and although he didn't see as much of them as he used to, he still kept in touch with them, safe in the knowledge that they were there for each other… if needed.'

The minister's now talking about how Kevin lived for his family. Colette had told the minister that he hated working away from home because he missed his family too much. Fish Heid turns to Jez and whispers, 'Missing getting his leg over with that accountant who does his books for him, more like.'

'Yeah?' Jez furtively inquires out of the corner of his mouth. Fish Heid purses his lips and nods his muckle heid once in silent acknowledgement. Jez thinks, *What a bastard, eh? There's the minister slavering on about how much of a family man he was. Talking like he personally knew him. What a fuckin' sham. He's never met Kev in his puff.* The minister's now talking about Kevin's hobbies: fishing, playing football and following Hibernian Football Club. Jez cups his hand over Fish Heid's ear and whispers, 'Aye, another Hibby that didn't get to see them lift the Cup.' Fish Heid shakes his muckle heid, as much to confirm his team's pathetic Cup record as anything else.

The eulogy continues as the minister gives testimony to the life of Kevin Devine. He speaks fondly of a man he didn't know. Then he finishes. Jez looks around thinking, *Is that it?* Then the minister says, 'I'd like us all to spend a few moments in silence so you can remember Kevin with your own thoughts in your own special way.' And these words serve as a memory portal as Jez thinks back to his primary school days, to where he first met Kevin. And he sees him. Not in the classroom, but out on the school field wearing the red and white of their primary school football colours. Kev was small for a Number 9 and the kit always looked like it was hanging off him! He didn't sprout up until he was about ten or eleven. Then he remembers his terrible dream from yesterday where Kevin was sinking in the sand surrounded by rats, then going under, and there was nothing Jez could do.

In a quiet voice, as if awakening a child, the minister informs the congregation that the site of internment is in the eastern part of the church grounds. He then leads them all in The Lord's Prayer as the pallbearers take up position then hoist the coffin onto their shoulders. A church official leads the procession out into the churchyard. The family then rise and leave through a side door, and someone is there, handing out black umbrellas as protection against the soft, slimy mist. A respectful pause follows before the rest of the congregation gets to their feet and files back out the main entrance.

Jez and Fish Heid wait outside until the BUNDIG Boys emerge and begin to gravitate towards each other. Wacka walks up to them and looks at Jez and Fish Heid as if to say, *'You were nearly late.'* His bottom jaw is moving around, indicating teeth being ground. The Hammer is whispering something to CD who looks up at him and smiles. Even Bob, who always has something to say, seems all talked out. A wind kicks up then, almost apologetically, falls short and dies away again. Johnny Bang Bang joins them, blows out his cheeks and shakes his head. Then Fifty Fifty ambles over. No, he shuffles over, like an old man. His stride seems shortened, as if restricted by imaginary shackles. All they do is exchange nods. Nothing else to say.

Savage is outside the vestry door behind them, having a smoke. Jez is about to go over to him when Savage is approached by another guy and they begin to talk. It's Fergal Owens, also known as Fatlad. What you'd call a "well kent face" around Berwick. A church official requests that everyone follows him to the graveside. They fall in line and walk along a meandering path to Kevin's final resting place. The coffin has been set down next to an open grave, with flowers placed around it. The minister says the prayers common to the rite of burial. Then Kevin is lowered into the ground. His cousins take their place next to the family on one side of the death trench. Kev's mum has inky tears staining her face. Colette stands tall and strong as her daughters clutch her hands.

The mourners stand in silence. Jez feels a hand resting on his shoulder. It's Fifty Fifty. Jez puts his arm behind him and pats the small of his back. Then something makes him look up and behind the church. And there, standing high up on the Walls, is Elijah. Just where they stood yesterday when he was telling him about the history of this church. When Elijah told him about the Covenanters and the cruel way they were put to death: tied to a stake and left to drown under the incoming tide. He's standing under a huge black golf brolly. His position provides him with a panoramic view of the churchyard. Jez turns to Fifty and is about to whisper something about Elijah and what he does for a living. But Fifty's brows are furrowed. He looks tense and preoccupied. Jez follows his line of vision. He's looking at the flowers. And amongst the green and white floral tributes and beautiful wreaths, Jez sees it too. A single black rose.

The service ends and the family are making their way to a fleet of black funeral vehicles parked outside the main entrance. The mourners stand about and wait. Jez looks again at Fifty, then at the black rose. Then over at the Walls, but Elijah's gone.

The BUNDIG Boys form up before following the rest of the mourners out of the church grounds. And over the hushed, dignified conversations Jez can hear Fatlad talking to Bang Bang. He's too loud. He sounds like he's just been to a wedding, not a bloody funeral. Now he's laughing at something.

'Remember that cocky fubber?' asks Fish Heid, nodding towards him.

'Aye, a' mind him well, Heid. A sycophant. A' mind he did a lot of drugs in the past. Distributed big time, too. Aye, he liked his pills, did Fatlad.'

'I think those days are long gone now though, Jez,' replies Fish Heid, with some conviction.

'But that's the thing aboot memory, Heid. It's like writing with a pencil. Over the years you can rub it out and create new versions.' Jez loops his arm round Fish Heid and says, 'Aye, Heid. You always see the best in people.' Fish Heid's arm winds round Jez's back and they slowly walk on, like two lovers. Except this is about loss, not love. Loss of an old friend.

'Hang on, guys.' It's CD. He must have been the last one to leave the graveside. Jez and Fish Heid unlink and wait for him to catch up. He's jamming a white hanky into a trouser pocket. Outside the main gates people are talking quietly, dabbing their eyes with hankies and gently hugging each other. Partly in grief. Partly in farewell, until they meet again. Maybe a wedding. Or a birthday bash. Or another funeral. Jez sees the two police officers talking to Colette. Passing on their condolences, no doubt. The officers begin to walk away when Wacka and The Hammer go over to them. A conversation starts and it becomes heated. Jez can't make out what's being said but Wacka looks raging.

They begin to walk down to The Brown Bear. CD says, 'Colette put a couple of hundred quid behind the bar when she went to book the wake. No' a bad bung, like.'

'Probably last half an hour,' replies Fish Heid. Jez motions to them that he's checking his mobile and lets them walk ahead. The phone powers up and he searches for the meaning of a black rose. He stops and waits for the response. *Eh? What the fuck's this?* This flower is the symbol of death and farewell. And vengeance.

CHAPTER 13

THE WAKE

MONDAY

Jez jams the phone back inside his trouser pocket, cursing its size. A heavy thunderclap growls overhead. Seagulls swoop low, before heading off, carving the skies to ribbons. The rain starts up again, so he opens up his brolly and heavy raindrops begin to smack off its nylon canopy. Fish Heid and CD are ahead, but now they turn back and are sprinting towards him, seeking shelter. They're giggling like a couple of kids. Jez wonders if their humour is more out of sheer relief that the service is over. Because that's how he feels. The three of them huddle together and quicken their step down the street. Jez raises his voice over the hammering raindrops, 'See that B&B over there… aye, where that parrot's sitting in the window. There's a guy staying there who works for the Met. Aye, he's a criminal profiler.'

'How do you know that, like?' asks CD.

'I met him on Saturday in the Cannon fish shop. Shared

a table with him. Got talking, y'know how it is. I had a copy of the *Advertiser* with me, so I showed him the headline about Kevin and we talked about it. Then I saw him again yesterday; he was walking the Walls. We ended up going for a pint in The Barrels.'

'What? Is he involved in the investigation?' asks Fish Heid.

'Nah. He's on holiday. Said he was here for some rest and recuperation.' Jez doesn't want to divulge too much about Elijah's reasons for getting out of London so leaves it at that.

'Well, I doubt our local cops would want an outsider digging about in their investigation, Jez, to be honest,' says Fish Heid.

'I think he feels the same, Heid. He seemed interested but, as he said, it wasn't on his manor. He's a cockney, by the way.'

'I wonder what those cops were saying to Colette, back there?' asks CD.

'Probably just offering their condolences, and that's fine. But if they say they're making progress, well, that's the pigs telling porkies,' responds Fish Heid.

To which Jez adds, 'Truth is, CD, I don't think they've got a fuckin' clue.'

'Bunch o' feckin' numbnuts,' concludes Fish Heid. Jez smiles at his friend's ongoing ability to be rude yet never swear. Glancing sideways he sees CD's smiling too and wonders if he's thinking the same. They're walking slightly hunched and peering out under the brolly as you do when you're caught in the pissing rain. And although they're talking, it's one of those odd conversations that on the surface sounds genuine and sincere, but actually their minds are elsewhere, preoccupied and numb from the service they've just attended. The town hall clock strikes noon. They pass the Cannon chip shop and Jez sneaks a glance in but doesn't see Josie. Fiona's there, behind the counter, talking on a mobile phone. He wonders if her son got out of police cells on Saturday. He's about to say that he's been on a date with a girl called Josie who works there but thinks better of it. Imagine if CD turned to him with one of his cocky little knowing smiles. Like he's been there. Jez would hate that so says nowt. Then Fish Heid shakes his muckle heid and says, 'I still can't believe he's deid. It's like a bad dream. Who would want to kill Kev? Like, what's it all aboot, eh?'

'God knows, Heid,' replies Jez. 'I feel so sorry for Colette and the bairns, like. They're just young kids, man. Too young to lose their dad.'

'It's no' just his death though, Jez,' says CD, 'it's the manner of his death. Some fucker was out to get him, like. Ah mean, this is Berwick, Northumberland, not fuckin' Brooklyn, New York, y'know? What the fuck's goin' on? Ah need a pint.'

They're quiet with their thoughts. The rain settles into a steady tempo and beats a heavy rhythm onto the brolly. They walk on, and Jez notices shoppers across the street, huddled together in twos and threes. They're looking over and talking in hushed tones. Obviously in reference to the procession of black-attired mourners and where they've just been. And why not? This town's been consumed with Kev's murder, so his funeral will have the gossipers going into overdrive.

Jez looks across the road and sees two old women sheltering in the entrance to Park's shoe shop and obviously having a good old chinwag. Recognition dawns. It's the two women he shared a table with on the train journey down here on Saturday. *Christ, was that only two days ago?!* He shakes his head in disbelief. And then he shivers and shakes his head again. He's thinking about the single black rose amongst the memorial flowers. And its meaning. And significance. *Who placed it there?* It could have been anyone. Friend, relative, disgruntled customer. He thinks of his friends, and goes through them in his mind, one by one: Bob, Cement Shoes, Bang Bang, Fifty Fifty, Fish Heid, The Hammer, Wacka, CD. But there's not a breath of suspicion on any of them.

'Christ, that rain's cracking out a great drum beat on your brolly, Jez,' says CD, smiling. 'Sounds like *"Dance with the Devil"*. You know, Cozy Powell.'

And maybe Fish Heid hears it too as he says, 'Aye, remember when we used to jump the train back from Edinburgh after the match? Honest, the noise of the train moving along the tracks was like the crowd chanting. Do you know what I mean? Like I could hear "*Hi-ber-nian, Hi-ber-nian, Hi-ber-nian*". Aye, going through places like Meadowbank, it was like the train was just swishing along, singing a song to the city.' CD and Jez both smile as they kind of know what he means. But behind Jez's smile he's thinking deeply.

'You okay, pal?' asks CD, as they near the entrance to The Brown Bear, its main door wedged open.

Jez responds, 'Aye. Just thinking, mate. Listen, can I ask you something?' They stop walking. 'That guy I mentioned, the profiler, staying up the road. Although he's on holiday here, I think he's intrigued with Kev's murder. He said that if he got a copy of the autopsy report then he'd have a look at it and give me his viewpoint. Obviously, Kev's family get a copy, and I'm wondering if you could work your charm, CD? I mean by speaking to Kev's mother.'

They smile, like lecherous old men. CD responds, 'I'll see what I can do, Jez. Aye, I'll speak to her, nae problem. Okay, Colette's put money behind the counter, remember. I need a piss, Jez, so do you want to go to the bar? Mine's a gin and tonic.'

'And mine's an Amstel, my friend,' adds Fish Heid as they reach the pub's entrance. Jez collapses the brolly and looks up. The sky's the colour of wet cement.

* * *

The Brown Bear public house is a local pub for local people. And it's always a busy boozer. Situated near the top of Hide Hill in the centre of town means it attracts a steady stream of customers day and night. There's no plastic plants, subtle lighting and smoked mirrors in this pub. The Devine family have hired it for the wake, although Jez doubts if they had to pay for it. And that's the thing about small towns: people pull together in a crisis. It's awkwardly quiet as he makes his way to the bar. Mourners are standing in small groups, gravitating towards the comfort of close friends. The hushed conversation seems at odds with the usual atmosphere in here. Jez sees the BUNDIG have taken up residence near the back, by the pool table which has been covered with a wooden board in preparation for the buffet.

'I'll have a Guinness, an Amstel and a gin and tonic, please,' he asks the barmaid, who plucks two pint glasses from the shelf behind. As she pours, he looks around and sees photographs of Kevin pinned and sellotaped to the wooden panelling along the back wall. He walks over and has a look. Images of Kevin with his family; with his young daughters. Him fly fishing under the Chain Bridge. There's a recent one of him sea fishing with Bob at Cocklawburn Beach. Jez returns to the bar as Fish Heid comes back from the toilet. He's obviously tried to dry his hair under the dryer, and it's gone all bouffant.

'There's no charge,' says the barmaid.

'Thanks,' he replies, setting the pints on the bar and waiting for them to settle.

But then Fish Heid raises his glass and says, 'To Kevin.'

'To Kevin,' Jez replies and takes a sip.

'Where's CD?' asks Fish Heid, and they both turn around and see him talking to Kevin's mum in an alcove next to the entrance, along with the girlfriends of Bang Bang and The Hammer.

'Ah, there he is with Naughty Norah,' Jez responds, a faint smile on his face.

'No' be the first time, Jez,' says Fish Heid. Then he nods his muckle heid towards the back of the pub. 'I see the boys have got themselves in a handy spot for the buffet. Shall we join them or do a bit of mingling here?'

'Let's join them first and see what the craic is, Heid. And I'm glad Bob's back there and oot the way cos he's got some fuckin' gob on him.'

The boys are sitting on stools and have pushed three small round tables together. And, as guys do, they all make a thing of moving out a bit and round a bit in order to create more space for them. They grab a couple of stools and shuffle into the company. Jez feels awkwardness as they all greet each other with solemn looks. He sits between Cement Shoes and Fifty and he likes that. They're less volatile, less edgy, always have been. Well, for the most part. He's expecting quiet, dignified small talk, as you would after such an emotional morning. But after about five minutes he senses the atmosphere's going to lift. And maybe they're all feeling a sense of relief as Bob shouts, 'Fuck's sake, Heid, what's happened to your hair?! You look like a cross between Fred West and Mungo Jerry!' They all look at Fish Heid then burst into stifled laughter, ducking their heads down to hide their laughing faces. Bob continues, 'Nice one, HEEEIIIDDD!'

Even Wacka, the notorious control freak, loses it but still manages a giggly, muffled, 'Shut the fuck up, Bob.'

Fish Heid looks serious and replies, 'Was that you wearing your tackety boots in the church, Bob? Some noise you made when you were walking in, like. Disrespectful, Bob, disrespectful. You're not down the flippin' coal mine now, y'know.'

Bob left Berwick in his twenties when he married a girl from Alnwick and moved down there, finding work as a coal miner nearby. His wife was a serial adulteress and it didn't last. CD once slagged him by saying that half the men in Alnwick had shagged her. To which he'd replied, 'Aye, but Alnwick's no' a big place.'

Fish Heid looks at Jez, shakes his empty glass, then gets up and makes his way to the bar. Jez looks down the pub and the place has filled up in the last ten minutes. He sees rough guys who look out of place in their suits, drinking in small groups. Then, through the crowd, Fergal "Fatlad" emerges and makes his way towards them. He greets them then grabs a stool from another table and there's a half-hearted attempt to make space for him. He sits down then pushes up the sleeve of his suit to check his watch and leaves it on show. It's a huge TAG Heuer.

Wacka leans forward and rests his meaty forearms on the table. 'Nice watch, Fergal.'

'Nice? It's better than nice, man, Wacka. It's fuckin' coostie! Look at it. Cost me nearly two grand, it did.'

'Oh, did it? Why?' responds Wacka, and he looks right through Fergal, whose smile freezes and he begins to redden with embarrassment.

'Well, it's a class watch, you know. It's... well, it's accurate to a hundredth of a second... water resistant down to 200 metres... and—'

'What does it do, like? Apart from tell the time,' asks Wacka, whose icy stare remains on the newcomer.

Then The Hammer leans over and grabs Fergal's wrist before pretending to have a good look at his watch. He shakes his head and says, 'Looks far too masculine on you, Fatlad. That's a man's watch. Pussies like you shouldn't be wearing watches like that. Fergal fuckin' Fatlad.' The Hammer still has Fatlad's wrist, and his other hand is wrapped round a pint tumbler. He suddenly laughs out loud then pushes Fergal away from him before sinking his drink in a oner. 'I'll stick to ma Casio Classic, if that's alright with you, like, Fatlad?'

The fat man's about to respond when Wacka leans over towards him and starts speaking, slowly and quietly. He's looking right at him. 'You know, Fatlad. Years ago, many years ago, I thought you were going to be part of this team. Like Kev was. But the fact is, you never got past being a hanger-on, a wannabe. And here we are, all these years later, and you've no' progressed from an arse-licking waste o' space.' He pauses, takes a long pull on his pint, then adds, 'Excuse me, but I only drink with friends.'

Perspiration beads on Fatlad's forehead. Shamed, belittled. And now shit-scared. He gets the message, rises and, without a word, makes his way back into the throng of mourners standing in the main bar. The Hammer shouts after him, 'Aye, get to fuck before you get poosled!'

They're all smiling, then Fifty Fifty laughs and says, 'I fuckin' loved that!' They all laugh and feel bonded within the comfort of the familiar.

Cement Shoes turns to Jez and says, 'Did you see the ring Fatlad was wearing?' Jez shakes his head. 'It was a Freemason's ring. You know, with the square and compass emblem. I bet he's used that a few times to keep him oot the nick.'

'I don't trust secret societies, Shoes. Never have. Can't be bothered with them. Open to corruption,' responds Jez. And Cement Shoes slowly nods his head with an expression of agreement and understanding.

He says, 'I was once approached to join them. But, and I think Groucho Marx said it first, I'd never join a club that would want me as a member.' They both smile and sip their pints.

'Anyway, pal,' says Jez, crossing his arms and changing the subject, 'with your degree in Theology and interest in religion, what's your view on funerals and the afterlife? I mean, what do you believe?'

'I believe that Jesus died for someone's sins.' Then he looks right at Jez and says, 'But not mine.' Jez is caught off balance with his comment so just slowly nods and looks serious. Cement Shoes was a real handful in the past and he dished out some terrible beatings to people. He always wore brogues back then as he reckoned you got a better kick out of them. But that was then. Like most of the guys who were wild in their youth, Shoes is a quiet man now.

Bang Bang's now sitting on the other side of Shoes and says 'Amen, brother,' before necking the remains of his pint and bringing the glass down heavy on the table. Jez thinks, *Aye, that's the difference between you two. Someone like Bang Bang, well, you can't categorise him as good or bad. He's violent cos that's all he's got left. I wonder what a shrink would make of him. I wonder if he's got his knife on him today. Probably, aye. Even today.*

CD appears with another gin and tonic and pints for Jez and Fish Heid. He takes the stool vacated by Fergal. Jez is expecting the conversation to centre around Kevin – his life, his death, the investigation – but it's as if they're all talked out on these themes. Time passes, drinks are drunk and the conversation becomes disjointed with guys trooping back and forth to the bar. Jez now has The Hammer sitting next to him and asks, 'What were you saying to the cops outside the church, before?'

'Me and Wacka were just asking them aboot how the investigation was going. Seems it's no' goin' well at all. They've interviewed the family, including Kev's cousins, and all his business associates, and come up with nowt. So they'll be contacting his friends soon to go in for a chat. Gettin' desperate now, if you ask me. Nae way was this just a random attack. You don't kill someone like that without a reason. So maybe he's fucked someone over and got taken out. That's why I thought they'd have caught him by now. Kev's crossed someone, like. I'm convinced of it. And anyway, the police have told Colette that they're sure Kev knew his killer. He's pissed someone off, that's for sure. Ah mean, aye, he still did a bit of drug dealing, like, but nothing serious. And nowt like the old days, y'know.'

Jez lets these words sink in, then adds, 'Fish Heid mentioned he was shagging his accountant. Maybe it's a crime of passion?'

'Aye, the minister never mentioned that, like,' The Hammer responds, 'and it's fairly common knowledge around town. I mean, his family haven't got a clue about that. Or the other women he was knocking off. I'm surprised he didn't have a condom on him when he was found. It was Savage who told me about the accountant. He used to drop Kev off at her flat in Ravensdowne.'

Just then Suzie appears, The Hammer's long-term girlfriend. Jez gets up and kisses her, then they try and work out when they last saw each other. It was at least a year ago. She looks over at her partner and says, 'How long you gonna be, Mr Steelhammer?'

'Ten minutes, hen,' he replies; 'just talking football with Jez. Gonna go to a Hibs game with him soon. Maybe spend a night in The Burgh.'

She smiles and replies, 'You think more of Hibernian Football Club than you do of me, Tony. Okay, I'll see you at the door in ten. See you, Jez,' who raises his hand in reply.

As she leaves, The Hammer turns to him and says, 'I think more of Heart of Midlothian Football Club than I think of her.' But they both know that's not true. He loves her; she loves him. And she's kind of tamed him. Fuck knows how, but she has.

The day becomes evening, and everything becomes hazy as alcohol loosens tongues and liberates emotions. At some point Jez returns to the buffet for a second time, overfilling his plate. He's back sitting next to Fifty Fifty and offers him some food, but Fifty shakes his head. He's pissed now and talking to Bang

Bang and CD. Jez has lost the thread of the conversation so just looks at Fifty and pretends he's taking it in. And it's only now that he's focusing on him that he realises how thin he is. He looks at Fifty's face, side-on. His skin looks tight and shiny and tinged with yellow. No, it's more like gold. He's thinking of the word to describe it, but he's too pissed now. He goes through the alphabet but the word won't come out.

He nearly stumbles on his way outside for a cigarette and realises darkness has fallen. Norah Devine's there, drawing heavily on a cigarette then blowing the smoke straight upwards. He tries to sound sober and passes on his sympathies and she looks appreciative. Her smile's bright but false, like a mask. Father Time has been busy on her face. She goes back inside and he finishes his cigarette alone. And he thinks, *To hell, I've had enough.* Just inside the pub's entrance is an alcove and mourners have deposited coats and bags there. He finds the brolly and stumbles outside.

He walks slowly up the high street. It's quiet. He feels the change within a minute of leaving the busy pub. It starts to rain again, a steady light drizzle that deadens the atmosphere. He walks down steep-sided West Street with its cold, black cobbles. The town hall clock tolls nine times. At least he thinks it was nine. He lights another cigarette and silently exhales up towards the streetlight's sodium glare. A car comes slowly down the narrow street behind him, illuminating the wet cobbles like a field of diamonds. He steps into a shop doorway and watches it go past. Tyres on the cobbles sounding like they're punctured. From somewhere a dog barks out.

Near the bottom of West Street he stumbles on the cobbles and nearly goes down. Cursing quietly, he regains his balance.

From here he can see the inky, black river and is drawn towards it. Passing The Barrels, he gets a heavy whiff of yeast and he's glad no one's outside having a smoke cos he can't be bothered to speak to anyone. He's all talked out. He walks up onto the section of the Walls that overlooks the river and stands there under the meagre light of a Victorian-looking streetlamp. He looks at the dark flowing water and thinks about Kevin Devine. And what he must have gone through. And what it must be like to drown. To go under. And he says out loud, as you do when you're pissed and no one's around, 'Kevin's dead. Trapped then drowned. Like a wasp in a jam jar. With no escape. Someone knows who killed him. Whoever left the black rose knows.'

CHAPTER 14

THE MORNING AFTER

TUESDAY

Jez doesn't as much wake up, it's more like regaining consciousness. His tongue feels thick and coated with gunge. Even the comfort of the well-sprung mattress and soft cotton sheets can't gloss over the fact he feels like shit. The full-blown hangover headache isn't here yet, but it's in the post. He rolls onto his back, presses the heels of his hands into his temples and quietly says, 'Ahh, fuck.'

He slowly rolls out of bed and then just sits there, motionless. On the bedside table lies debris from the day and night before: loose change, crumpled notes, room keys, mobile phone. He leans on the washbasin and looks at himself in the mirror, inspecting his face like a doctor searching for symptoms. He looks into his eyes, as if he has a secret and only his reflection knows it.

He glugs down a tumbler of water, along with a couple of

ibuprofen, before climbing back into bed and lets the events of yesterday pass through his mind: funeral, burial, wake. It's blurry and fuzzy and his memory seems reluctant to revisit the previous day with any sense of order. By the sound of things outside, the patrons of Bridge Street are up and going about their daily business. Voices chattering, a shop's awning being extended, the shrill of a bicycle bell. The duvet is lying perfectly over him with just the right amount of weight, warmth and softness. He drifts off again, and his mind takes him back to a child visiting Mr Hattem, the cobbler, on Bridge Street. The entrance bell always gave a loud solitary ding, then, once inside the dimly-lit shop, you were hit with the smell of leather and warm polish.

The transition from memory to vivid hangover dream is stilted and blurred. He's standing at the counter waiting on Mr Hattem to emerge from behind a screen at the rear of the shop. On the counter is a cobbler's anvil along with an assortment of shoes and boots to be repaired. The back wall consists of pigeon-hole racking, each compartment housing a pair of shoes. But the cobbler's not Mr Hattem. No, it's Wacka. And he's gone all fat. A dirty, leather apron clings to his extended waist. Jez takes off his shoes and gives them to him. Wacka puts one on the anvil and starts the repair. Hammering the heel, he tells Jez that cobblers are the last craftsmen on this street. He's laughing now. Jez asks him who placed the black rose at Kevin's graveside. He shakes his head and asks if he's ill, and Jez says, 'Yes I am.' Wacka reaches under the counter and produces a hot-water bottle and asks Jez to sit down and hold it to his stomach.

Then he tells him to go behind the screen and, when he gets round, he's in the Cannon chip shop! Josie's there and so is Fiona. Josie gives him a plate of alphabet spaghetti on toast and says he should try and eat it. Then he walks back round the screen and Fish Heid walks into the shop. He picks up the hammer and feels its weight in his hand. Wacka turns to Jez and smiles, saying his shoes are as good as new. Fish Heid strikes Wacka full in the face with the hammer and Jez is amazed, as it fits perfectly into the orbit of Wacka's eye. Fish Heid strikes him again in the face and he goes down. Then again, as he lies there. Fish Heid giggles, then extends his arm and gives Jez a single, black rose.

'HI!' Jez shouts in a loud scream, which shatters the peaceful, morning ambience. He sits up and feels cold sweat on his back. 'Fuck. I hope no one heard that.' He makes his way to the shower and turns on the power full-blast. Ice-cold spray pulses down on him, like polar needles. It hurts but he feels much better now. He dresses quickly and heads downstairs. The breakfast room's empty and the debris around the mahogany table says he's probably last down. *Good. Nae small talk and shan patter to deal with. Cos ah need food. Mmph, mmph.* Sounding like Oliver Hardy. First stop is the sideboard along the back wall, full of cold starters. He gulps down a glass of fresh orange juice then refills his glass. As he tucks into a bowl of muesli, the kitchen door opens and Lesley enters. She's wearing a white T-shirt, tucked into the tight, black jeans she wore when he arrived on Saturday.

'Morning, Jez. What fettle today?' She's smiling at him, yet her body language shows she's concerned. Must be because of the funeral yesterday. And he appreciates that.

'Ah've felt better, Lesley, that's for sure. It was a long day yesterday, y'know.'

'I'm sure it was. I hope the service went as well as expected... I mean, in the circumstances, y'know.'

She's nodding as she's saying these words, and he feels soothed by this. 'All things considered, it went about as well as expected. There was a big turnout... so he got a good send off, you know.'

'It means he was liked and respected, Jez. And you can't ask for more than that.'

Jez thinks, *Liked? Aye. Respected? Well, no' so sure about that if you really knew him.* 'Aye, he was a character, Lesley, we can definitely say that. And the wake was... well, it started fairly quiet but soon livened up. There were photographs of Kev and his family on the walls of The Brown Bear, which was a nice touch, but sad too. Anyway, I ended up having far too much to drink. Can't remember what time I got in, but I don't think it was too late.'

'Not that late, Jez. About half nine. I was in the sitting room when you came in. You were muttering something then off you went upstairs. Now then, is it tea or coffee this morning?'

'Oh, a pot of tea would be lovely, thanks.' And it's only now that he realises she's not wearing an apron. 'Listen, is it too late for a cooked breakfast?'

'No, not at all. It's not ten o'clock yet. Nearly, but not,' she responds with a laughing smile on her face. 'So, you had the full English hangover breakfast on Sunday; do you want the full Scottish one today?'

'Oh, yes please. I'm visiting my mum later on this morning, so I probably need the sustenance.' She giggles and disappears into the kitchen. In a minute she's back with a pot of tea, a pitcher of milk and a rack of toast.

'Back in five,' she says, smiling. There's a hypnotic sway about her gait. Definitely more Saturday night than Tuesday morning. The hot tea and hangover anxiety cause him to feel sweaty across the forehead. It's worse as there's just the two of them so he decides to hurry through the rest of breakfast then make a quick exit. He fishes out his mobile phone and, when Lesley returns with his cooked breakfast, he pretends he's texting so they just exchange smiles as she lays it down in front of him. Two texts have arrived. One's from his mum, a reminder that he's visiting her this morning. The other one's from Wacka and he's probably sent it out to all the BUNDIG.

Cops just phoned. Bringin' me in for interview. 2day

Jez thinks back to the drunken conversation he had with The Hammer at yesterday's wake, when he told him the cops were going to start questioning his friends now. He looks at the message and thinks, *I wonder if they'll interview me? Ah mean, he's a friend but I've not been close to him for yonks. They'll have to chase me to Edinburgh if they wanna talk to me.* He lays down the phone and tucks into the huge plate of streaky bacon, link sausages and tattie scones. He eats quickly, quelling the hangover munch, and washes it down with more tea. Satisfied, he rises silently and leaves the breakfast room, darts upstairs to his room, grabs some money and makes his way back downstairs. As he approaches the front door the doorbell rings. He opens it cautiously and there's CD standing there!

'CD! How's it goin'? Are you… eh… I take it you're here for me?'

'Unfortunately, pal,' he replies quietly while looking past him down the corridor. Jez turns around and sees Lesley approaching.

'It's okay, Lesley, it's for me,' Jez says. Then adds, 'Lovely breakfast, thanks.'

'Oh… oh thanks, Jez,' she responds, giving CD the once-over then returning to the kitchen.

CD watches her then says, 'So, that's your landlady, eh. Aye, Fifty told me where you were staying, like. What goes on behind closed doors, Jez, eh. You'll no' get that in The Burgh.'

Jez laughs quietly and says, 'Aye, right. Now, what do you fuckin' want?'

'Eh? I do you a favour and what do I get? Dogs' abuse, eh?' responds CD. 'What time did you leave last night, anyway?'

'Oh, aboot nine, something like that. Ah'd had enough, man. Ah was full as an egg.'

'Nine o'clock, lightweight,' he replies, smiling now as he's got the upper hand. And he knows Lesley got a good look at him, which he's finding pleasing, the posing bastard. 'Well, as you requested, Jeremy, I spoke to Norah last night and asked about the autopsy report. And she was fine about it. She said if it would help catch Kevin's killer then I could come round to hers this morning and she'd print off a copy.' He hands Jez a sealed envelope. 'Aye, she was true to her word. Makes a change for Naughty Norah.'

Jez lowers his voice as a couple of pedestrians pass by. 'Thanks for this, pal. I'll get it to the guy I was talking about yesterday. Listen, are you coming in for a coffee?'

'Love to, Jez, but I need to nash, pal. Ah've got a rewiring job on up at Prior Park. Fish Heid's there now. We divn't all get six weeks' holidays every summer, y'know. How long you here for?'

'Till Saturday.'

'Okay, pal. Hope to see you before you go. Maybe Friday night?'

'Aye, I'll keep in touch. Thanks again for the favour, CD. Much appreciated. See you. Keep a'had, mate.'

'Deeks ya, gadge.' And he's away.

Jez returns to his room and picks up the profile he'd compiled on Kevin. He's gonna walk up to Elijah's B&B this morning and give him the report and his profile. Then he'll dodge down Crawford's Alley as it's a shortcut to his mum's. He sits on the bed and looks at the envelope. Morbid fascination gets the better of him and he opens it up. He's never read an autopsy report before; and while he's aware of most of the detail, it still makes for grim reading. There's an information portfolio on the bedside table containing B&B information, including an envelope for visitors to put in their review comments. He puts the report inside and seals it.

On the way out he checks the display cabinet at the bottom of the stairs for a tide timetable, but the only ones he can find are for Holy Island. He steps outside, thankful for another glorious sunny morning. Near the top of Hide Hill there's a huddle of elderly people sitting at small tables outside a coffee shop. *Maybe a coach trip from Kelso*. The smell of strong ground coffee permeates the street.

'JEZ!'

He jerks his head round. It's Elijah! He emerges from the coffee shop and walks over the street towards him, a newspaper tucked under his arm. They shake hands, like old friends. And even though Jez only met this guy on Saturday, like three days ago, he *feels* like an old friend. Maybe because of the subjects they've discussed, including that appalling murder he had to deal with in London. So they stand there on the pavement, chewing the fat like old mates.

'Elijah, how's it goin'? You look like you've been up and about early.'

'It's going well, mate. Yeah, I was up early, then walked round the Walls after breakfast and nothing was stirring. Just how I like it. And what about this weather, eh? Lovely.'

'Well, it hasn't taken you long to settle into the local scene, eh? Early morning walks, then coffee with the tourists,' replies Jez.

'You know, I couldn't understand a damned word they were saying! It's a bit like being abroad.' Elijah's laughing and shaking his head. He reminds Jez of Cement Shoes for some reason. A powerful mix of strength and gentleness.

'Well, believe it or not, I was just on my way up to your B&B now.' Jez produces the envelope from his pocket. 'Here, it's for you. A copy of the autopsy report and my profile on Kev that I promised you.' Elijah takes the envelope and looks at it, while each side of his mouth turns down, like a sad clown.

'How did it go yesterday?' he asks quietly.

'All in all, probably as good as could be expected. I saw you, by the way. Up on the Walls. Where we'd stood the day before.'

'Yeah,' he answers uncomfortably, and sweeps a finger along his brow as if he's been caught gate-crashing a party. 'Yeah, well, it's kinda linked to this, Jez,' he says, touching the envelope, before continuing: 'As I say, or maybe I haven't said, but if you want me to help then I need to get to know the victim. So, I thought I'd take a wander along. Bloody pissed down for a while, didn't it? Anyway, anything unusual for you yesterday? Like a surprise mourner, you know, like: "Why is he or she here?" Or strange behaviour from anyone?'

Jez purses his lips so Elijah knows something's coming. 'No one stood out, but there was something strange. Well, at the graveside, all the wreaths and laurels had been laid out, and amongst them was a single flower. A black rose. Do you know what that means?' Elijah shrugs his shoulders. 'Nah, me neither. I had to look it up. It represents death. And vengeance.'

Elijah looks at him in surprise. 'The inquiring mind of a teacher, eh, Jez. Did anyone else notice it, or did you mention it to anyone?' Jez shakes his head. 'Good,' he continues, 'let's keep that to ourselves, then.'

'Somebody hated my friend, Elijah, that's why he was murdered and that's why that rose was placed there. You said murderers were clever fuckers. Well, someone's trying to be a clever fucker here. By the way, I was told yesterday that Kevin was doin' a bit of shaggin' around. His accountant for one. I didn't know that when I put the profile together. Aye, it's common knowledge around town. Well, apart from his family.'

'It's usually the way, Jez. You're the last one to find out. Okay, I'll keep that in mind. As for the rose… mmm… interesting. Could be just innocent naivety on the person who laid it there. Or it could be a clue. Yes, clever that. Well, in my experience, clever fuckers tend to trip themselves up eventually, so that's not a bad thing. So, what are your plans for today, then?'

'Well, I'm just on my way to see my mum. Spend the day with her. She's been away on holiday. Again. Aye, she gets around, does my mother.'

'It's good she's still fit and active, Jez. Well then, thanks for this information. Okay, I'm gonna spend a little time on this then I'll tell you what I've come up with. And I mean a little time. I'm in holiday mode, remember? So it's a bit of light reading for me, that's all.' Jez nods in approval, then Elijah says, 'Do you fancy meeting up for a pint tomorrow sometime?'

'Erm… Thursday would be better for me. I'm planning on meeting that girl from the chip shop tomorrow night. And whenever I visit my mum I end up with a list of wee jobs to do so I'll keep tomorrow free for that.'

'Thursday's fine for me, Jez. Do you fancy The Barrels again?'

'Aye. What about four o'clock?'

'That'll do,' replies Elijah. 'I like a late afternoon relaxing pint or two when I'm on holiday. And I am on holiday.'

'Perfect, pal,' replies Jez. 'Listen, I better get going. See you Thursday.' They set off in different directions. Jez's thoughts turn to meeting his mum and he salivates at the prospect of the coffee and cakes she'll lay on. When she lived up the Greenses he'd stay the weekend and not feel hungry again till about Thursday. And of course she'll want to know all about the funeral. What was it like? How am I about it? Who was there?

He turns down West Street as the sun emerges over the rooftops. Long slits of sunlight reflect off the shopfront windows. He thinks about Elijah's comment regarding strange behaviour at the funeral. Fifty Fifty saw that rose, he's sure of it. And why was CD last to leave the graveside? And for that matter, why did Elijah show up on the Walls to watch the burial? He thinks, *That's strange behaviour, isn't it?*

Arriving at his mum's he searches down the call points until he reaches her name, then presses the buzzer. Waiting for her to come to the door, he thinks back to his sister. The last time he saw her was in the undertakers, the day before her funeral. She'd physically deteriorated. White fabric trimming lined the interior of the coffin like a hungry mouth with rosewood lips, about to swallow her. He's about to press the buzzer again when he sees his mum approaching through the door's glass panel. He rearranges his expression and forces a smile, like an actor's mask.

CHAPTER 15

ELIJAH'S PROFILE

TUESDAY

Elijah Bootle strolls up the street, pleased he's bumped into Jez and already looking forward to a pint or two of Orkney Dark Island in The Barrels on Thursday. There's a lightness in his step. Yesterday was the first day in a long time where he hadn't woken up scratchy eyed and restless. This morning was the same. He feels refreshed and unburdened. Yes, the slow moving pace of this quaint Borders town is just what he needs. And he's noticed something else too. Unlike London, where everyone walks about in an aggressive hurry, up here people seem to have time to stop and talk. With smiles on their faces! Then, bang on cue, he has to sidestep three old women who are standing there, helpless with laughter about something one of them has said. Other shoppers are smiling infectiously as they detour round them. And their laughing eyes don't change when they see a black man. This is a white, parochial town, yet the only time he felt uncomfortable was on arrival at his B&B when his landlady was a bit off with him. Not now, though. Mrs Barraclough clearly likes him; and although he's told her half a dozen times to call him Elijah, she still calls him Mr Bootle. Not out of reverence; he thinks she just likes the name! *You know what? I could live here!* This place reminds him of family seaside holiday towns he went to as a child.

Yes, there's an innocence about this small, backwater town, as if time has rewound to a more innocent, contented age. Except for a vicious murder which seems no nearer to being solved. And as he saunters up the street with the hot sun on his back, he contemplates Kevin Devine's brutal murder. And with Elijah's years of experience, he views this case as highly unusual. Clearly there was no attempt to conceal the body. But why? To satisfy the fantasy needs of the killer, or to send a message to the police? Or to the public, for that matter. The killer coveted suffering and humiliation for the victim. Normally, these types of murders throw up forensic clues, yet this killer seems to have been organised and careful.

He enters Tommy's shop and breathes in the smell of warm newspaper print. It takes him back to his youth when he delivered papers around the streets of south London. Newspapers are laid out on the counter and a stack of them are bundled up with string behind the entrance door. Elijah gets a whiff of another nostalgic smell but can't quite place it. He's already been in here earlier to buy his paper. In fact, he's developed a morning routine. After breakfast he walks round the Walls, then comes in here to buy a paper and reads it while enjoying a coffee in the Harlequin café. 'Hello *again*. What did you forget?' Tommy asks with a broad grin as he ushers a white poodle off the glass-top counter. 'Get down, Maggie!'

'Oh, erm… I seem to have run out of cigarette papers,' Elijah responds. 'Do you have any? Erm… preferably the long ones, please.' He runs a hand through his hair, pretending to pat it down. Tommy's reaching up to replace a large sweet jar on an upper shelf. 'Is that a jar of Kola Kubes you're putting away there?'

'It sure is. Wanna quarter?'

'A quarter of Kola Kubes?! Yeah, go on, then. I smelt them when I came in but thought it was scented candles.'

Tommy pours the sweets onto a set of scales. 'Okay, then. A quarter of Kola Kubes and there's your king-size papers.' Elijah hands over a fiver. Tommy's gives him his change, then looks down at the dog. 'No, they're not for you, Maggie. Okay, thanks. See you tomorrow.'

'Yes, I'll see you tomorrow,' Elijah responds. He steps outside, narrowing his eyes in the bright sunshine. The road's been relaid with gravel, and a band of tarmac follows the kerbside along the street, shining black in the sun. Elijah's wondering if the tarmac's hot enough to bubble, when he hears a loud knocking from across the street. Looking over, he sees Savage inside the Cannon chip shop, giving him the thumbs up, so he returns the gesture. On the opposite side of the counter is the girl who served him the other day, the one who liked Jez. Elijah waves at her and she responds with a quick wave and a lovely smile as she wraps up food at the counter. Further up the street he sees the police station, so crosses the road and stands looking at the appeal poster of Kevin Devine. He talks quietly to the photograph. 'What triggered your death, Kevin? What was your killer's stressor? Did he get a thrill at how he left you? Battered and broken. Left to drown. Someone was angry with you, my friend.'

The police station main door bangs open and a man emerges onto the street. He's shaking his head and looks in a foul mood. He looks neither one way nor the other but focuses straight ahead on a red Ford pick-up truck which is parked half on the kerb, half on the road. He isn't a tall guy, but he's built like an ox. And he walks like a fighter. As he opens the driver's door, he shoots a glance at Elijah. Their eyes meet and Elijah thinks, *Yeah, you look like a hard man. Bet you've got "the rage".* Because on the subject of physicality Elijah has two categories: those who have the rage, and those who don't. His view isn't shaped by science or study, more by his life experiences, growing up on a tough south London estate. He's clutching his paper bag full of sweets and fishes one out then pops it into his mouth. In the back of the pick-up a dog has stirred. A huge, thickset Rottweiler, now standing with its front paws on the side hoarding of the vehicle. Elijah makes a mental note of the vehicle's livery along the side of the pick-up:

W. Short. Scrap Car and Scrap Metal. 01289 30**.**

The vehicle revs violently before moving off down the street; the horn sounds as it passes the Cannon chip shop. *Must be a friend of Savage's*, thinks Elijah, as he saunters up to his B&B. The Kola Kube in his mouth implodes into a delicious chewy centre. Stopping in front of the B&B he has a bit of a face-off with the parrot, who stares impassively at him then winks, so Elijah winks back and lets himself in. As he passes the reception, he sees a carousel full of brochures. Amongst them is a seasonal tide timetable. He pockets it then makes his way up to his room.

It's been cleaned and a window is open onto the street. He retrieves the envelope from his pocket and plonks himself down in the soft, slouchy armchair by the window. Kicking off his shoes, he opens the envelope and the autopsy report slips out onto his lap. It's a four-page document. He retrieves the tide timetable and runs his finger down the dates until he reaches Friday, 27th June. He nods his head in confirmation. The tide was indeed coming in on the night the victim died. High tide was forecast at 10pm.

It's that time of the day when the sunlight begins to peep over the rooftops across the road, so he turns the armchair to face the street, places a small notebook on his lap and begins to read the report. And because it's not his case and he's firmly in "holiday" mode, he approaches the report in a detached, almost carefree way. That's why he brought the criminal profiling book with him. He thought that reading it while on holiday when he's more relaxed and content could throw up something that might assist with the London murder. Occasionally he scribbles in his notebook.

After half an hour his attention wanes and he stops reading, pops another Kola Kube into his mouth, settles back and checks out the street below. Reading this report gets him thinking about work. Not his main remit, dealing with the death and violation of human beings. No, he thinks about the minutiae of work and how far removed he now feels. No telephones ringing here, no meetings to attend, no emails pinging into his inbox. Elijah thinks about the people he works with: the backstabbers, gobshites and sycophants. The young, ambitious workaholics, the gossips and the moaning face fuckers always on a downer.

He gets up, stretches tall and yawns loudly, then makes a coffee. He places it on a small bureau in the corner, along with his notebook, autopsy report and Jez's profile on Kevin Devine. He retrieves his criminal profiling book from the bedside table. Last night he'd read a chapter on brain waves and damage to the paralimbic regions of the brain, like the amygdala and medial temporal lobe, and its links to psychopathy. But it was all 'shrink talk' to Elijah and he got bored with the scientific terminology. He skips back the pages until he finds a chapter headed 'Staging, Posing and Signature of Killers'. He opens out the book and lays it on the table.

There's some notepaper on the desk with 'Oakwood B&B' as a header, plus Mrs Barraclough's contact details. He stares at the notepaper then draws a large circle on the page. Inside the circle he writes Profiling Inputs then creates sub-headings: Crime Scene, Forensic Information, Photographs. He cross-references the autopsy report with these three areas which include body position, physical evidence, weapons, wounds and cause of death. Alongside he jots down comments in his notebook. He takes a slug of coffee then winces, realising that the Kola Kubes have caused havoc with the roof of his mouth. There's a taste of blood on his tongue. But he's happy as he sees his mind map taking shape on the page. Alongside the word Photographs he puts a question mark. Elijah knows that a Scenes of Crime Officer would have been at the on-scene examination to photograph the victim and surrounding area.

He draws another circle and entitles it Victimology. He scans Jez's written profile, and although it's scant it covers the victim's domestic setting, employment, reputation, criminal history, hobbies and social conduct. Further circles are drawn, smaller than the first one. Some are joined to the big circle with a pencil line, others are out on their own, like planets round the sun. He glances at his watch, which prompts him to check the Evidence Collected section of the report, and is surprised that no watch or mobile phone was found on the victim. He goes to the bathroom then quickly returns to his seat at the desk. He's in the zone and knows from experience that everything in his mind has to appear on the page, regardless of how trivial it may seem. Underneath a circle entitled Crime Awareness he adds Staging/Posing, Motivation and Control of Victim. He refers to his criminal profiling book and jots down comments in the notebook while caressing the roof of his mouth with his tongue.

After a few minutes he stops and looks at the pictogram alongside his notes. He has all the information in front of him. Now he puts the pieces together like a jigsaw, with straight-edged facts framing a jumble of misshapen hunches and suspicions. Then he writes the word Conclusions in his notebook.

Conclusions
Killer is male and acting alone. He's local with knowledge of both the location and the victim's movements. Timing, victim, location and weapons used were all chosen. An organised offender. Not an opportunist. Blue collar and probably skilled or semi-skilled.

This killer is someone close to the victim. Excessive force used so it's personal. Possibly an extreme one-off killing, with no repetition. He will have a violent history but not for murder.

He's clever; a body exposed to the elements and tidal water destroys forensic evidence. Shackled to a stake with a cable tie means intent was to deliberately drown him. The victim was meant to suffer. Why?

He planned ahead and brought his own tools. Blunt weapon (unknown), cable tie and wooden stake. What caused the injuries to victim's skull? Have the police held back this information? Same weapon used to break both legs and cause head injuries.

Motivation – may only be known and understood by the killer. Not financial gain. Personal, so revenge. Family honour? If random then a sociopath or primary psychopath.

Precipitating events – what was the killer's stressor? Was there prior trauma, either physical or psychological?

Items taken from victim – no watch or mobile phone. Strange. Need an answer.

Victim lifestyle risk – low, no known enemies. Drug convictions in his past. No drugs in his system. Criminal record is petty. No violent record.

Crime scene assessment – one scene for all. Victim and killer make contact, assault scene, death scene and body location scene all on beach.

Location risk to victim – high risk. By himself on a deserted beach. Evening time, so quiet.

Location risk to killer – high risk. Murder in a public

place. Could have been disturbed, e.g. other fishermen on beach, dog walkers. Public footpath at clifftop. Near to holiday camp (Have police questioned holidaymakers?).

MO – what did killer have to do to commit the crime? He had to control the victim. Used violence to subdue, then tied victim to stake. If random then this could be his fantasy. Is this his signature? If so, victim was posed in position. Or posed to send a message to police or public.

Elijah sits back, pats his brow with a handkerchief, then reads through his notes. He looks at the autopsy report. In the section entitled External Examination he recites a sentence out loud. 'A quantity of sand and pebbles was found in the victim's mouth.' He mutters, 'Mmm, now that's interesting. Why do that? The blows to the head would have knocked him unconscious so no need to gag him. An example of posing, perhaps?'

He'd really like to see those crime scene photographs. He'd like to talk to someone working on the case. Walking to the window he looks out over the street, then up towards the Parade and can see part of the grassy park. He thinks about the buildings round the park. The church, the barracks and the Freemasons' Hall. A wind has got up, and in the sky above the park he sees an orange and blue kite idly drifting on the high wind current. Elijah sees its crucifix frame then follows the tail down to the kite flyer, a young boy. The boy lets out some slack and it soars vertically into the sky.

He pockets his notebook, puts on his shoes and gets ready to leave. He checks he's got his wallet. Checks he's got his phone. Checks he's got his keys. Check, check, check. He leaves the room, locks the door then nearly rives it off its hinges checking that it's actually locked and secure. Then, as he heads downstairs, he convinces himself that he needs to check the door again so heads back up again, and there's more riving and pushing on the door until he's finally satisfied. Only now does he feel he can leave. On his way out, Mrs Barraclough emerges from a back room. 'Oh, hello, Mr Bootle, off out for another walk? It's a lovely day again, though a bit windy now.'

'Hi, Mrs Barraclough. Yes, it is. Just off down into town,' Elijah replies without stopping.

'Mr Bootle... can I have a moment, please?' Elijah pauses, then returns to the reception desk, conscious of his landlady's smiling yet uncomfortable expression.

'Yeah, of course. What is it?'

'Mr Bootle,' she responds, 'my son, Terry, he's thirty-six now and lives across the river.' Elijah looks at Mrs Barraclough. *Where the hell's this going?*

'Yes,' she continues, 'he's got MS, had it for years now. Anyway, he... err... well, he smokes that wacky baccy... to relieve the symptoms, you know? It's just that... when I cleaned your room this morning, there was a... well a... a smell that reminded me of the stuff Terry smokes.' Elijah feels a warm glow creeping up his face, but his landlady already has her hands up in a defensive gesture. 'All I want to say, Mr Bootle, is by all means partake in it, but could you leave a window open in the morning? Just the small one will do. And let's keep this quiet, Mr Bootle. I've got my licence to think about.'

'Listen, Mrs Barraclough... I'll stop...'

'No, absolutely not, Mr Bootle,' she interrupts him. 'Terry smoked it quite often when he lived here. I don't mind at all. In fact, can I tell you, I love the smell of it!' She laughs then looks at Elijah as if to say *"I'm giving you permission"*.

Elijah smiles back and says with sincerity, 'Well… thanks for that, Mrs Barraclough. Yes, I'll definitely open that small window each morning. In fact, I might keep it open all the time.'

'Just you treat it as your own, Mr Bootle, treat it as your own. Now, go on and enjoy your afternoon.'

'Are you sure… sure you don't mind? I mean I can…'

'Mr Bootle, it helped my Terry. If it's good enough for him, then I'm sure it's good enough for you. Now, I'm away to put out some washing, and on a day like this it'll be out and in again in a couple of hours. Bye, Mr Bootle.' And she bustles out the door.

'Bye, Mrs Barraclough, and thanks.' He's still smiling as he lets himself out and walks down towards the police station. In his pocket he runs a finger along the notebook's edge. Behind him, high up, the kite is twisting from side to side.

CHAPTER 16
THE EVIDENCE
TUESDAY

Detective Constable Gordon Mackay sits back, drains his coffee in one gulp and looks out the window. He's having a bad day. DCI Hazelwood's presentation to the Major Investigation Team earlier this morning on the Kevin Devine murder case didn't tell them anything they didn't already know. *And Bawheid knows it. It's been nearly a month since the murder and we're runnin' oot o' leads and suspects.* The custody sergeant walks into the office, drops some files into a cabinet then shouts over at him on his way out. 'Hi, Goagsie, a bit of advice.' Goagsie swivels his chair round to face him, hoping for a positive comment or some guidance from the experienced police officer. 'Don't look out the window in the morning.' A pause, then he giggles and says, 'It gives you nowt to do in the afternoon, man!'

'Ho fuckin' ho,' replies Goagsie, with all the humour of a goth with depression. He feels about as enthusiastic as the cartoon cop lying flat out on his chipped, manky mug. He puts two fingers down the collar of his shirt then pulls on it to give him some relief. In defiance of the custody sergeant he looks out the window again and his mind drifts back to when he joined the force nearly five years ago. After four years on the beat he requested a transfer into criminal investigation, desperate for some real action. And here he is, on his first case, and it's a high-publicity murder! And it's not going well. Weeks of chasing dead-end leads have caused the fledgling detective to sense the first pangs of panic.

A tall black man passes the window. Goagsie's seen him before but can't place where. A moment later the main entrance door opens and there he is, standing behind the glass panel at the counter. The young detective rises to his full height, goes to the panel and slides it open.

'Yes?' he asks, abruptly.

'Hi. Erm… my name's Elijah Bootle. I'm here on holiday and err… yes, I was just wondering… if I could talk to someone about the Kevin Devine investigation. You know, informally. Err… there's a poster outside.' He points towards the poster which he can see from the counter.

'You want to speak to someone about the Kevin Devine investigation, do you? Well, you can speak to me. I'm working on the case. I'll come around and let you in.' Elijah stands back and waits. He's slightly uncomfortable at the way this discussion might go. Not at the profile he's created, which is an educated attempt to identify the killer. No, it's because this is a rural town in a rural region and the last thing these cops would want is a "big shot from down south" trying to interfere like some smart-arse.

Goagsie opens the door and says, 'Okay, I'm Detective Constable Mackay. Follow me through here, Mr err…'

'It's Bootle. Elijah Bootle.'

'Okay, Mr Bootle. I'll see if there's an interview room available.' They stroll down the corridor. 'So, you're here on holiday, then, eh? Got good weather for it. You sound like a Londoner?'

'Yes, I am. And it's been glorious here since I arrived last Saturday. Yeah, lovely.'

The corridor is painted bright canary yellow, its warm colour adding to the stifling hot atmosphere. The two men walk into a vacant interview room. The young detective offers Elijah a seat on one side of a chipped Formica table then sits down opposite him. He pulls out a notebook, places it on the table and says, 'Okay, Mr Bootle. You've got some information on the Kevin Devine murder?'

'Well, look… I need to tell you something about… well, about me first. I mean… Oh, don't worry. It's all relevant, Mr Mackay. I'll… I'll be brief,' replies Elijah with an open-hand gesture, implying that he's not here to waste anyone's time.

The young detective flashes a smile at Elijah, opens his notebook, then writes the date and time at the top of a new page. Underneath, he writes Elijah Bootle. 'Okay, Mr Bootle. What is it you want to tell me?' He doesn't look up, but stares at the page with pen poised, ready to write. And he thinks, *You'd better not be here to waste my time, cos I've got better things to do than listen to a fuckin' holidaymaker trying to be important.*

Elijah exhales noisily through puffed-out cheeks, then says, 'Well… I need to tell you about my job. I'm a criminal profiler. Employed by the Met.' Goagsie looks at Elijah, raises his eyebrows in surprise, then writes Criminal Profiler next to his name. 'I've... err... got my ID card with me. I have it in my wallet,' continues Elijah.

Goagsie looks at the card, then at Elijah, then nods in confirmation and says, 'Okaaay,' dragging out the second syllable as if to say, *"Where's this going?"*

'Yeah, I'm here for a couple of weeks. Stayin' just up the road. Well, this murder seems to be the talk of the town. The taxi driver who picked me up from the station mentioned it, then I got talking to a guy in the chip shop next door who had a copy of the local paper, you know, the *Berwick Advertiser.* As you probably know, it was front page news in last week's edition. Anyway, he talked to me about it too.' The young detective maintains eye contact with Elijah and nods at appropriate moments. *You could do a job for us, Mr Bootle.* His heart quickens with renewed optimism.

Elijah senses that Goagsie seems impressed with his occupation as a criminal profiler. He shrugs off the discomfort he felt on entering the police station and eases back into the plastic chair, then continues. 'So then... err... the next day, I bumped into him walking round the Walls and we ended up chatting in a pub. I'd told him what my job was and, well... we talked some more about the case.' He pauses, then looks right at Goagsie and adds, 'My way of taking my mind off things, you know?' And in that moment the young detective sees an expression in the older man's eyes. Glints of light that radiate anger. Anger and something else.

'A profile? Now, that's interesting, Mr Bootle. What's this guy's name?'

'Ehh... well, it's Jez. I don't know his surname,' responds

Elijah. 'He was an old friend of the deceased who came down from Edinburgh for the funeral.' He waits as Goagsie writes down the word "Jez" then a question mark. Elijah's decided he's not going to tell the young detective that he's seen a copy of the autopsy report. That sounds "too interested". Elijah carries on talking. 'So, he told me a bit about the victim, and that, plus what I've read in the paper, was enough to... kind of... put together a profile. If you want it. I mean, you may have enough leads on the killer already, and if that's the case, that's fine by me, Mr Mackay. I *am* on holiday, you know. But if you think it might assist you?'

'You got it with you?' asks Goagsie.

'Yeah, I've got it here,' replies Elijah, leaning forward and retrieving his notebook from a back pocket.

Goagsie says, 'Well, yes... I'd like to see your profile. And you never know, you might uncover something. Do you want a tea or coffee?'

'Oh, I'd love that, officer! Coffee please. Milk, two sugars and... err... not in a polystyrene cup, if possible,' requests Elijah, smiling now. Goagsie leaves the interview room. Someone opens a door in the corridor and a cool breeze enters the room. Elijah quickly smells under both armpits, and is pleased that they haven't turned damp and sour smelling. He reads through his profile notes again. Outside in the corridor he can hear Goagsie talking to someone in passing, like they're walking in different directions and talking over their shoulders.

'Hi, Stevie. How did it go with Wacka Short?'

'How did it go? Ah had to tell him to take his dog back ootside, first. Ah mean, imagine interviewing Wacka Short with a muckle Rottweiler sitting at his feet, eh?'

'Was he friendly and helpful? Wacka, I mean, no' the joogle,' says Goagsie, laughing out loud now.

'Aye, considering. The joogle was aboot as pally as a Caribbean reef shark. Catch you later, Goagsie boy.' A door bangs shut and the cool breeze disappears. Elijah picks up Goagsie's pen and makes some notes. He has questions for the detective and doesn't want to leave the station without getting all the information out. Because this is the only time he's coming in here. He thinks, *This is too much like work, Elijah. What the hell are you doing in here, eh? After this you'll get some cakes from that bakers down on the corner. They look great in the window!*

En route to the kitchen Goagsie knocks on the door of the Personnel Office. He enters and speaks to a young woman typing furiously. 'Hi, Jackie, how's it goin'? Another scorcher today, eh? You'll need that fan on full blast.' It's the usual niceties before he asks a favour. And Jackie knows it.

'Hi, Gordon. Oh, you know. Hard at it as always,' she responds with a mock exhausted smile.

'Could you do me a favour, Jackie? I've got a guy in Interview Room 2; he's just walked in off the street. He's here on holiday. Could you do a security check on him? He's called Elijah Bootle.'

'Oh, what a lovely name!' responds the personnel officer as she jots it down.

'Aye… he works for the Met,' continues Goagsie. 'I've seen his ID card so, you know, he's on the level. I think. But… could you just check him out… to be on the safe side? Could you do it now, if possible? You see… I'm in with him now.'

'No problem, Gordon,' Jackie responds, with a smile that says *"I'll never get this bloody report finished"*.

'Aww… thanks, Jackie. You're a star.'

Goagsie goes into the kitchen, makes the coffee and returns to the interview room with two mugs; his with the cartoon cop and a standard white one for Elijah. They each make a play of sipping their coffees then placing them down on the table. 'Okay, Mr Bootle. What you got?'

'Right, Mr Mackay. Obviously, I've not been privy to anything you guys have discovered. Y'know, evidence, leads, suspects,' responds Elijah, opening his notebook and laying it down on the table. 'But I'll tell you what I've got.' He's about to start, then pauses as Goagsie faffs about with his pen nib. Elijah sips his bitter coffee, then he continues: 'Okay. I think the killer is male, I think he's local and he's acting alone. And I think he's likely to be blue collar, possibly skilled. And he probably has a violent history.' He looks up, but Goagsie's scribbling away, so carries on but slows his diction. 'This is not opportunist. It's planned. This guy is an organised offender; the crime was premeditated and carefully planned. And he's clever.' Goagsie holds up a hand to indicate he's writing quickly now. Then he looks up and nods once. Elijah continues, 'No need to write this bit down. I'll just tell you. He's clever, cos he picked a perfect location. A lot of evidence and clues will have been washed away with the tide. The best cops in the land couldn't have preserved that crime scene, Mr Mackay. It was impossible.'

'The crime scene *was* beneath the high tide mark, Mr Bootle, so yeah, a lot of evidence was washed away,' responds Goagsie without looking up. He's writing and nodding, like he's getting the words down in a hurry. He looks at his scribbled notes, then says, 'We do have the crime scene photos taken by the Scenes of Crime Officer. Err… they're quite graphic.'

'I'm sure they are, Detective,' Elijah replies, then thinks, *If you really want "graphic", son, come and work with me some time!* He continues with his profile. 'I think he knows the victim. Excessive force was used and it was close-up and personal. So, this could be a one-off murder with no repetition.' He sneaks a quick peek at his armpits.

'That's good news, Mr Bootle. Dinnae really want a serial killer on our hands, do we? Is he married?'

'Married or divorced, I'd say,' replies Elijah.

'Colour?' asks Goagsie, blushing slightly after asking the question.

'Oh, this is a white man, Mr Mackay. You're dealing with a clever, white, violent bastard.' Goagsie eyes him with a questioning look. Elijah leans forward and says quietly, 'True story.' He sits back and drains his mug, lifting the front legs of his chair off the ground, then places the mug down hard on the table. 'And he knows the victim. And hates him. And his mission was to drown the victim. Specifically, to drown. So that could be his signature, but not necessarily his MO.'

Goagsie scribbles away, pleased that Elijah's paused his narrative. He looks at what he's written then asks, 'Could drowning not be one of the killer's characteristics? You know, that's him leaving his personal mark. His psychological imprint? That would be his MO?'

'I'm not convinced that it is, Detective. I think Kevin Devine was drowned to serve the needs of the killer.' Goagsie looks questioningly at him. Elijah elaborates, 'The question I always ask myself in regard to MO is: what must the offender do in order to commit the crime? So, tying the victim to a stake and using a cable tie to restrain him, now that's an MO. But drowning him, no; I think that comes from within the psyche of the killer.'

Goagsie writes this down in scrambled form, hoping he can decipher it all later. He looks at it all then says, 'What's the age range?'

Elijah puffs out his cheeks. 'If it's a psychopath, then mid-thirties to late forties. He'll have been fantasising and building up to this all his life. If it's revenge, well... any age really, from mid-twenties up to fifties, if he was fit enough. So, yeah, that's feasible.'

'You say he's clever, Mr Bootle, but do you see any weaknesses in his approach, any chinks in the armour?'

'Well, he chose an open place to carry out the killing. That's a risk, as he could have been seen from the clifftop, or been disturbed by a member of the public, say, walking their dog. The report in the paper said it was quite near a holiday camp.'

'That's right, it was. And we've interviewed holidaymakers whose caravans are nearest to the clifftop path but come up with nowt. We had a publicity board next to the wee onsite supermarket asking for information, but again... zilch. And a week after the crime we had a police presence on the beach itself... Nothing came up.' Goagsie shakes his head, looks through his hurriedly scribbled notes then asks, 'Anything else you could tell us, then, Mr Bootle?'

Elijah shakes his head then says, 'Have you got it all down?'

Goagsie nods and says, 'I think so. Listen, thanks for this, and I mean it. And thanks for not getting too scientific with your profile.'

'Oh... you mean dressing it up with "expert" jargon. No chance. Actually, I'm already slightly uncomfortable, you know… I mean, it's not my case and not my region.' Then Elijah asks, 'What do you have on the victim? I'm talking lifestyle issues, here.'

Goagsie nods once, then says, 'Well, he's got previous, but it's petty, to be honest. Possession of drugs, affray, breach of the peace, that sort of thing, but, well, we're talking over twenty years ago, here. In terms of criminality he's kept his nose clean for a long time. We're reliably informed he's had a few affairs and we're following that lead. You start sleeping around with other guys' wives, Mr Bootle, and sooner or later you're going to get found out. Especially in a small town like this. But, apart from that, he seems a regular guy living a normal life. Listen, do you have any questions for me?'

'Yes. Do you have a suspect?' asks Elijah.

Goagsie shuffles his feet, looks at Elijah, then says, 'The truth is… we don't have a horse in the race. Not as yet. Plenty leads, you know, all the usual suspects like family and business associates. But, so far, we've got nowt.'

'There's a way to get to everyone, Mr Mackay, you just need to work out what it is. You mentioned before you had a police presence at the crime scene a week after the murder. What about the monthly anniversary?'

'We had it staked out day and night last Friday, which was a month since the murder. Cops dressed as dog walkers, couples, joggers… you name it, but no, nothing. In fact, the place was deserted. Wonder why, eh?' There's a soft knocking on the door. 'Excuse me, Mr Bootle,' says Goagsie, rising from his chair and going to the door. It's Jackie, so he steps outside into the corridor and pulls the door shut.

'Okay, I've done the search,' says Jackie in hushed tones,

'and he's the real deal, Gordon. Been a profiler for over twenty years and he's worked on some heavy cases. Aye, but he's currently on sick leave.'

Goagsie thinks, *Sick leave? I wonder what for? He looks okay. Strange.* Then he says, 'Okay, Jackie. Thanks for this. Good, good. Okay, I know where I'm going with this now. Thanks again.' Goagsie steps back inside the interview room, apologising to Elijah for the interruption. Then he glances at his watch and says, 'Listen, I really appreciate you coming in here, Mr Bootle, and providing us with this information. Look, I'm gonna have to cut this interview short; I've got an appointment in twenty minutes and need to get going.' Then he says, 'But I'd really like to talk to you again, if possible. There are a few more aspects of this case that I'd like to get your view on. I know you're on holiday… but… would you mind meeting up again… say, tomorrow afternoon, if you're not busy?'

Elijah pulls out his wallet, finds a business card and slides it over the table. 'No problem, Mr Mackay. Not at all. In fact, I've got a few more questions I'd like to ask you. But not here. I mean… as you said, I'm on holiday, you know.'

Goagsie pockets the card and says, 'Thanks, Mr Bootle. I'll phone you tomorrow morning for a time and place if that's okay.'

'No problem at all, Mr Mackay. Don't phone till late morning though as I go for a walk round the Walls every day after breakfast. And I don't take my phone with me. Prefer the peace and quiet.' They rise and Goagsie walks him back to the reception. Elijah steps out into the sunny street, breathes in the warm air and catches a whiff of freshly baked cakes. He follows the aroma down the street to Ford's Bakers, on the corner. He feels good, he's done something positive today. And that all helps his mental well-being.

In the interview room Goagsie stares at the notes he's scribbled down. Reading from the bottom he eventually reaches the top of the page where he wrote his first words. 'Elijah Bootle, Criminal Profiler.' Alongside he adds a question mark.

CHAPTER 17

AND LIFE GOES ON

TUESDAY

And life goes on. You have a funeral. Then a wake. Next morning you "come to" with a heavy hangover… and your thoughts. Hangover thoughts, when you feel empty and lonely inside. It's Tuesday, and the morning sun rose above the horizon hours ago. And, as every day for a thousand years or so, the bustling little market town of Berwick Upon Tweed stirs itself from slumber. It's now mid-morning and the locals are moving through the gears as the sun rises above.

Usually, there's a sense of closure after a funeral. The mood lifts, conversations lighten and we "move on", as if the experience has made us more aware of death but thankful that it wasn't our turn. Even the weather's trying to assist. The gentle breeze blowing in off the North Sea tries to push away the heavy atmosphere that's shrouded the town for weeks like an unwanted, lingering guest. But not this funeral. There's no purging of emotion. A son of the town is buried, but the tension remains. The killer's still out there. A killer with a new target in sight. A killer with a double-bladed craft knife. Ready to wreak havoc.

* * *

Wacka Short wakes with a shout, reaches over and grabs his mobile from the bedside table. 'Yes?' he barks into the phone. He sits up in bed with a serious look on his face. 'What? Today? What time, like?' He hangs up, then lies back and sends a text to the BUNDIG.

Cops just phoned. Bringin me in 2 interview me. 2day

He crawls out of bed, scratches his arse and heads for the bathroom and Nurofen. Looking at himself in the mirror he shakes his head in disgust, cups a hand to his mouth and smells his stale alcohol breath. It's not good. He needs coffee; and while the kettle's boiling, he goes to the window, opens it and breathes in the warm summer air. From this viewpoint he looks out over the docks to the north side of the river and the old walled town. His fiefdom. Twenty years ago, he ruled this town and people lived under his jackboot. Well, under his nine-inch Doc Martens. Friends, enemies and associates. But time is catching up with him and he no longer wields the same power and fear. He makes a coffee, scratches his third nipple, then punches Bob's number into his phone. Bob's been working for him at the scrapyard for a couple of years now and has work to do today. 'Aye, fuckin' scrapyard doesn't run itself, pal,' he says out loud to himself. He looks at his mobile, as if to summon a response, but there's no answer.

'Ah bet the bastard's still in his kip.' He rings his secretary, Barbara, who goes in two days a week to do the admin. 'Hiya, Babs, it's me. Is Bob in yet?'

'You mean Bob Noxious? No, ah've no' seen him, Wacka,' she replies. 'Shall I ring his mobile?'

'Nae need, doll. I've just tried. I said to him yesterday, at the wake, like, just to go in later on today. But, ah mean, what's the time now? Fuckin' half past ten, Babs. Eh, what's goin' on? I give him a job cos I feel sorry for him. And when I need him, where is he, eh? In his fuckin' scratcher.'

The conversation moves on to ledgers, accounts and signatures. Wacka's nodding his head, waiting for a pause in the monologue. '...Aye, well I'm stopping in tonight so I'll look at it then. Listen, Babs. I need to go oot in aboot half an hour. I'm being interviewed at the police station. Aye, the cops want to talk to me. Like I've got time for their shite. Look, I'll take the pick-up and go straight out to East Ord after that. I've got that Audi A3 to look at. The one that was torched. So I'll see you about three this afternoon?'

'I'll still be here, Wacka,' she responds in a warm, inviting way, as if she's smiling as she says the words. And she is.

'See you then, Barbara. Bye.' Wacka slouches to the window again and looks down into his backyard. He opens the window and shouts, 'Atlas!' The huge Rottweiler looks up, barks with enthusiasm and begins to circle the yard, like a fighter in the ring. Wacka shouts down again, 'Aye, I've got a little away day lined up for you, son.' And he looks down on his beloved dog and wishes Bob could be as obedient. *Aye, twenty years ago Bob would have been in work today, on the dot, wake or no wake yesterday. Not taking the piss.* But he's not really thinking about

Bob. He's thinking about Babs. Big, blonde, busty Babs. He drains his coffee and heads for the shower.

* * *

CD was up early, despite the number of gin and tonics he'd had the day before. First stop, Kev's mum's house. He declined the offer of a coffee and got a copy of the autopsy report in a sealed envelope. He wasn't aware the family could request a copy from the coroner. Then he met up with Jez at his B&B before driving over to Prior Park to finish the rewiring job. Not that he left the house looking like a "workie". CD couldn't do that. If he has appointments before work then he dresses appropriately and takes his work clothes in a holdall, then changes into them on site. So today, it's Italian shoes, slim-fit 501s and a fitted white shirt. He looks good. And he feels good, like he's done his good deed for the day, getting the autopsy report to Jez.

Fish Heid's already there, repairing some trunking in the front garden and generally tidying up. He's been CD's occasional "sparky's mate" since the fishing industry died about a decade ago. 'Get the coffee on, Heid, I need a pick-me-up, pal,' shouts CD as he shuts the car door and approaches.

Fish Heid looks up from his work and says, 'Now, that's a good idea. I've bought some cakes too. By the way, you look okay to me, Chris. What time did you leave last night?'

'Must have been the back of eleven. Ah stayed on the G and Ts like, so no' too bad this morning. What about you?'

'Left before nine, pal. It was looking like it could get messy, guys falling aboot drunk, spilling drink, greetin' on each other.

That's alcohol for you. I thought Wacka was gonna batter Fatlad early on as well. Two sugars?'

'Oh, make it two big boys, Heid. I might look good to you, but you want to see me from this side.' They both laugh out loud. 'I'll just go and get changed.' Just then his mobile rings. '...Hi, yes. Yes it's... it's Christian. How are you?' He smiles at Fish Heid, who shakes his muckle head and makes for the kitchen. CD takes the call then changes into his "workie" clothes. Five minutes later, Fish Heid returns with two coffees. CD picks up his mug and says, 'I've just noticed a text from Wacka. He's bein' interviewed today.'

'Aye, I got one too,' responds Fish Heid. 'Well, Hammer mentioned yesterday that they were going to start interviewing Kev's friends, so no real surprise. Wonder why they started with Wacka? We'll all be getting quizzed soon, I suppose. So, who was that on the phone, *Christian*?'

CD sips his coffee and nods in appreciation. 'She's from Fife. Comes doon here every year with her pal. Ahm seein' her tonight. Oh, she's a hottie, Heid. They stay at the Cross Keys Hotel. Posh manishees. Ah mean, for Fife, like.' He lowers his voice. 'Aye, Hammer's been with the other one. Actually, it's a funny story.' He pauses, and sees the Heid looking at him, waiting, as if in judgement, so he continues. 'Aye, we met them in the Hunting Lodge last year. Went back to their hotel.' He takes a bite of cake then licks cream off his fingers.

Fish Heid smiles and says, 'Go on, Christopher.'

'So, aye. Hammer was on the job, geein' it laldy, and she *twice* shouted out, 'Oh, yes, Christian!' Fish Heid laughs, then chokes and splutters coffee onto his overalls. 'Aye, he was fuckin' furious. And he was already pissed off having to call me

Christian all night. Anyway, he said nowt, but the girl told the one I was with the next day.'

Fish Heid's muckle face cracks into a huge smile and he shakes his head. 'Oh dear! Poor old Tony Steelhammer, eh? By the way, your nose. It's got icing on it.'

'Oh, Heid, ah've had worse things on ma nose,' responds CD, now rubbing his face. And they both laugh. That dirty, raucous laugh that men do. And even though Fish Heid doesn't swear, he does have a loud, filthy laugh.

* * *

Fifty Fifty gets into the back seat of Savage's taxi and greets the two occupants. Savage whacks it into first gear and sets off. He looks uncomfortable and says nothing.

Cement Shoes turns and says, 'Morning, Fifty. How are you?'

'Well, a'hm no' deid yet, son,' replies Fifty and stretches out across the back seat. His cancer's returned, and this time it's determined to snatch him away. He looks thin and weak. Only his wife, Cement Shoes and Savage know the truth. Savage knows because he's been taking him back and forward to the hospital. Cement Shoes knows because, well, because he's the sort of person you'd confide in. You know, when your blood starts mutating inside you.

Savage glances at Fifty through the rear-view mirror, then says, 'It's eleven o'clock your appointment, aye?' He knows this, it's just that he gets uncomfortable with the heavy silence. So he says things, random things, to keep the conversation going. He turns to Cement Shoes and says, 'Aye, a've no' been able to take a bath for a week, Shoes.'

'Oh. Why like?' replies Cement Shoes.

'Because it's full o' fuckin' salmon, man! Aye, there's aboot four hundred pounds' worth of fish in ma bath. Aye, it's the en suite for me and the missus.'

'Nae wonder you're loaded, Sav,' replies Cement Shoes. Then he throws the driver a stern look and says, 'Don't they all belong to Berwick Salmon Fisheries Company, Mr Morrison?'

'Well, in all my years of poaching, I've never seen a salmon with that marked on it. They belong to God,' replies Savage.

A quiet pause, then from the back seat Fifty says, 'Fuck God.' And he sits back and looks at the back of their heads. He notices that Savage has his meter turned off. At the lights, Savage leans over, grabs a CD from the glove compartment and puts it on. He starts singing along to the catchy ska rhythm.

"An earthquake is erupting. But not in Orange Street.

A ghost-dance is preparing. You got to help us with your feet."

Fifty joins in. He's smiling now. The atmosphere lifts. Cement Shoes shoots little glances at the invalid through the rear-view mirror. The taxi pulls into the hospital car park. Cement Shoes gets out and stretches. Fifty leans forward and says, 'Listen, Sav, you might as well go. I don't know how long this is going to take and, well, they might admit me today.'

Savage turns and replies, 'Okay, Fifty.' They shake hands and Fifty starts to get out as Cement Shoes comes round and opens his door for him. Savage says, 'If you're admitted I'll come and visit, pal.' Then he adds, 'And I'll no' greet, honest.'

'Divn't fuckin' bother comin', then,' responds Fifty and shuts the door. Cement Shoes bursts out laughing. He likes that sort of humour. Bleak.

* * *

The Hammer's lying on Bang Bang's settee in his wee flat down Palace Green. After the wake they went back there and horsed four grams of speed up their noses, bought from Fatlad at the wake, who's obviously still doing a bit of this and a bit of that. And they talked and laughed and interrupted and shouted over each other all night. Every subject received deep analysis: Kev's murder and possible suspects; the afterlife; outer space; and music of the seventies, like punk, new wave and two-tone. Then they reminisced about the house music scene in Edinburgh during the nineties. Underground clubs like Taste and Joy where they got out their nuts on ecstasy. And how GHB and date-rape drugs ruined the whole scene. Then football, but relegated Hibs was too depressing, so they moved onto conspiracy theories. Basically talked shite all night. It's 9am. They've just shared a huge, conical joint the size of a small parsnip, and sleep is in the post. Bang Bang's in his bed, getting some shut-eye before his shift at Aldi's this afternoon. That's if he goes. The Hammer has the day off from his scaffolding job. He gets off the settee, finds Bang Bang's weed box, raids his stash and rolls another joint. Just for himself. Because you can do that, among friends. And the BUNDIG have been friends for years.

* * *

And the sun shines down onto the steep-sided roofs of the old town. Roofs packed so tightly together, from a distance they look like a group of hooded old men, deep in discussion. In the churchyard of the Trinity Church the tombstones stand to attention, waiting… for another burial.

And the killer waits. And life goes on.

CHAPTER 18

AN EARTHQUAKE IS ERUPTING...

TUESDAY

Fergal "Fatlad" Owens stirs from his drunken slumber. Without raising his thick head from the pillow, he fumbles about for his watch on the bedside table. Loose change spills onto the carpet. Through matted eyes he sees 11:38 on his TAG Heuer Carrera, precise to a gnat's baw hair of a second. He rolls out of bed, shuffles over to a full-length mirror and looks at himself. His huge belly hangs down, like he's swallowed a size five football. It looks bigger when he's naked. Bigger and uglier.

'Aye, fuckin' Fatlad, awright,' he says out loud to himself. He's been called it all his life. Well, since he arrived in Berwick as a child from Coleraine in Northern Ireland. Not that he was fat back then. In fact, he was a skinny little runt. But some smart-arse worked out that a mnemonic of the six counties – Fermanagh, Antrim, Tyrone, Londonderry, Armagh and Down – made a great nickname. Plus, he liked the use of

Londonderry as opposed to Derry, as it sat comfortably with his neo-Protestant beliefs and Masonic family history.

He moves close up to the scruffy, fingerprinted mirror and inspects his pockmarked face. His breath stinks of stale whisky. Fatlad likes whisky. He could drink it through a shitty cloot. He looks at his blood-red eyes, then suddenly jolts as a memory from yesterday explodes in his mind like a penny squib. Wacka Short's verbal annihilation of him at the wake makes him feel sick. In front of the BUNDIG too. He'd been totally humiliated and spent the rest of the night as far away from them as possible, slugging back pints of Guinness with whisky chasers. Later on, The Hammer and Bang Bang approached him and he feels again the panic and cold sweat on his back. But all they wanted was some speed, and of course he was the man to have a supply. And he gave them a good deal. Hopefully some brownie points had been earned.

He puts on a dressing gown and saunters into his kitchen, still rubbing sleep from his keekers. He needs a coffee to bring him round. He's on back shift at the abattoir, two to ten, which is good because it quietens down after five o'clock, when the bosses go home. So, he's got time to get his act together, have a shower, some food and then go to work. As the kettle boils he thinks about the funeral. About Kev Devine and how he was murdered. And who killed him? He thinks about the faces in the congregation and outside at the burial. He stares at the kettle, like he's in a trance. His mind freezes as a thought slithers into his brain like a cold worm.

He opens a window, breathing in lungfuls of air which immediately start to refresh him. The jet-black Jaguar sits on his drive, looking sleek and lithe, like a panther. Fatlad likes to express himself in what he owns. Flash cars, expensive watches and chunky Masonic rings. You know the type. But he needs the exercise so he's gonna shower, dress, walk to McDonald's on Park Road, then it's a wee hike to the abattoir on the industrial estate. He's already salivating at the thought of a Big Mac; he's got the hangover munchies. He gulps down his coffee, grabs a towel and heads for the shower, checking his watch on the way. 'Ah, loads of fuckin' time,' he says out loud to himself as he pulls the cubicle door closed and turns on the shower. But time is running out for Fatlad Owens. This is the last shower he'll ever have.

* * *

Elijah Bootle sits at the writing desk in his room, munching on a chocolate glazed doughnut he bought at the bakery after meeting with the detective. It soothes the roof of his mouth which still feels rough and delicate after his "Kola Kube fest" earlier on. Smiling broadly, he recalls the conversation with Mrs Barraclough, when she acknowledged his use of cannabis then gave him permission to smoke in his room. In fact, there's much to make Elijah smile since he arrived here a few days ago. A beautiful town, with lovely walks, and he's made a friend or two, like Jez, and Tommy down at the newsagents. And this local murder has given him an interest. It's keeping him occupied, like a hobby or a project. He feels more like an amateur sleuth than a criminal profiler. *Or a forensic detective,* he grandly thinks.

On the desk is the autopsy report and the mind map circles and notes he made earlier that morning. Wiping chocolate off his face he opens his notebook and turns to the page where he wrote his conclusions. He begins to work through his notes again, this time cross-referencing each comment with his mind map circles.

He looks at the circle entitled Victimology. Retrieving Jez's profile on the victim he places it alongside his mind map. Then he mutters, 'This man was not victim prone. We've either got a dangerous stranger, or this is a revenge killing.' He nods in confirmation then goes to the bathroom; the effects of several cups of coffee are playing havoc with his bladder. Returning to the desk he lays his big hands on the back of the chair and says, 'And if it's revenge, then what was the precipitating event? What stressed the killer?' He opens the autopsy report and looks for the section marked External Examination. He remembers that something had bothered him when he was compiling his profile. Furrowing his brow in thought he stands at the window overlooking the street. The small casement window above the main one is open, his side of the agreement with Mrs Barraclough. Looking out, he sees red-skinned holidaymakers idly looking in shop windows and sauntering up the street. Elijah thinks about the view from his office window in London, with its busy traffic, congested pavements and choking diesel fumes. And all its low life, nutters and psychopaths. But, as he grimly contends, evil seeds can be sown anywhere. Even in this picturesque holiday town.

He settles down again. And he suddenly remembers. He picks up the autopsy report and scans the narrative again, then says out loud, 'It's not a pebble beach. The sand and stones in the victim's mouth weren't to gag him, they were placed there deliberately.' His mind goes back to Saturday night when he got a taxi to Murphy's Beach and surveyed the scene. It looked like a sandy beach, right down to the seaweed-scattered shoreline. The killer must have hunted around for a couple of stones to shove into the victim's mouth. Or brought them with him. Why? He goes to his wallet, pulls out Savage's card and taps in a number. He gets a response immediately. 'Hello, Savage, it's Elijah, your old friend from London here. Are you free?'

A minute later he hangs up then makes his way downstairs and out onto the street. As he waits for Savage, he thinks about his arrival here, three days ago. A child had run down the street. She'd been dressed in similar clothes to Hayley, the young girl murdered in London. The case that broke him. He shakes his head to repel the thought as a taxi lurches up the street. He hails it, London style. The taxi draws up, the passenger's window winds down and Savage shouts through it, 'Nae need to stick your arm oot for me, gadge. You're no' exactly inconspicuous.' He gets in and Savage says to him, 'How's it goin', ma haga?'

Elijah hasn't a clue what he's saying but guesses it's some kind of local greeting so responds, 'I'm very well, thanks, Savage. Yes, I'm *very* well. Erm, to Murphy's Beach, please.'

'What, again? Fair enough, pal. Ah divn't ask questions, me. Ah just drive. Are you keeping oot the Burglar's Arms?'

'No need to visit that boozer, Savage. I'm a Barrels man.'

'Oh, good choice of peever, Elijah. Some lovely real ales, if that's your thing.'

On the way to the beach their conversation moves from pubs to alcohol, to legalisation of cannabis, to football, and they're there. Elijah gets out and walks to the beachhead. For the second time he stares down at the murder scene. It's quiet and the ebb tide is receding back out to sea, its waves long and lazy. Below him he sees two men picking winkles out among the newly exposed rock pools. Faces down with their backs to the sky. He makes his way down the concrete steps to the sandy beach below. But his slow, ponderous gait belies what's going on in his mind. He's buzzing like a fridge.

* * *

Fatlad Owens walks out of McDonald's and sets off through the Five Arches to the industrial estate. He feels full and satisfied as a Big Mac and Coke sloshes around in his belly. He enters the abattoir, clocks in, then goes to the changing room. He removes his watch and Masonic ring, puts them in his locker, then gets into his work clothes: overalls, plastic apron, a nylon hairnet and rubber boots. He walks out a side door into an enclosed yard and gets his phone out. As he waits for the connection he looks into the pen where a group of cattle has a date with death. They're huddled together in one corner, as if in fear. Fatlad isn't a fan of slaughtering cattle. Not that he feels for these beasts. He feels for nothing and no one, except himself. No, it's just they're so fucking boring. *No' like the sheep,* he smiles to himself. Fatlad loves sheep. Well, he loves kicking them full in the face. He loves spinning them round by the legs then hurling them against the back wall of the pen. He smirks as he remembers cutting a sheep's throat then watching it bleed to death with spectacles drawn round its eyes in yellow paint.

'Hiya,' he says into the phone, while looking at the ground. 'Aye, it's fuckin' me. Have you got? Ah need thirty grams of speed and ten grams of Charlie.... Aye, I'll chop it with the speed. Ma customers won't know the difference. And some grass, but

I'll see what you've got when I get there.' He listens then shouts out, 'AH NEED IT BEFORE FUCKIN' FRIDAY. Aye. Right, see ya, gadge.' He walks back into the main building and enters the processing zone, also known as the "kill floor". Because this is where animals come to die. His shift is getting its handover. Some of them are wearing chainmail gloves and are sharpening huge knives. There's a metallic smell of blood, mixed with the odour of disinfectant.

The two o'clock buzzer sounds and he walks to his station. He's slitting throats first. A few minutes later, the killing begins. In single file the cattle are forced down a corridor where a man waits for them on an overhead catwalk. He's holding a pneumatic "stunner" that looks like a nail gun. The fatted-up animals look like they're about to burst, and they walk with that slow lumbering movement shared by cattle and fat people. As they pass under the catwalk the man reaches down and shoots them between the eyes with a metal bolt, rendering them unconscious. Then they're shackled by a hind leg, hoisted above the ground and passed along to Fatlad. He slits the throat then stands back as the twitching animal's beating heart pumps out blood into a trough below.

As the shift continues the cattle look less like animals and more like what you'd see in a butcher's shop window. At four o'clock the shift has a meal break. He guzzles down mugs of tea while playing gin rummy in the rest room, then nips outside for a smoke. He walks over to the corner of the yard, idly peering into a skip half full of animal waste. Maggots squirm about on the ground. The slaughtermen call them "disco rice".

Fatlad has wangled half an hour's overtime each night to gather up the waste product from the day and take it out to the skip in a big green wheelie bin. Ten o'clock and everyone goes home, except Fatlad who begins the clear-up. He fills the bin with bits of membrane and strips of flesh and fat. The smell of blood hangs in the warm, muggy air. He wheels the bin outside and tips the foul-smelling contents into the skip, like feeding a hungry mouth. It's dark now and under a moonlit sky he lights up a cigarette and stares into the base of the blood-stained skip. He's reminded of the funeral, when he stared into the open grave of Kevin Devine. His stare becomes a trance as he thinks again about the congregation and the faces amongst the mourners.

Unseen and unnoticed, the rest room door opens and a figure emerges into the yard. Wearing overalls, hairnet, disposable dust mask and surgical gloves, the man walks silently towards the skip a dozen metres away. Fatlad's back is towards him. He's still staring into the skip, engrossed in his own dark thoughts. Suddenly his sixth sense kicks in, like he's being stared at. Fear jumps in his throat as he turns around. The person is right behind him. Fatlad, more confused than scared, shouts, 'Fuck's sake, man! Who the fuck are you?' The man smiles behind the mask then raises his arm and smashes down a ball-pein hammer full force onto Fatlad's skull. He crumples like a concertina into a sitting position, his back against the skip. Blood seeps out from his hairline. He looks up at the man with wide, fear-filled eyes. The man lowers the mask to reveal his face. And now Fatlad knows. He knows who murdered Kevin Devine. And why. He squeals in terror, like a tortured sheep. The killer is over him now, raining blows down onto his skull with sickening accuracy. The arc of the hammer showers crimson blood into the air. And again he strikes. And again. And now it's Fatlad's turn to look less like an animal. The killer stops; he's breathing heavily now. He reaches into his pocket and takes out his customised Stanley knife. Pushing forward the slide to reveal the double blades, he gets down low and looks closely at his victim's pockmarked face. Moonlight glints on the tool. The killer quietly asks, 'Where's your happy, smiley face, Fatlad? Lost it, have you? Here, I'll give you one.'

He sinks the blades into Fatlad's cheek before slitting the skin wide open, right down to the side of his mouth. Then he does the other cheek. Blood flows out fast; like an open sewer into a filthy river, it gushes out of his face. The two cuts make Fatlad look like he's smiling. Lower teeth show where the skin has folded away. Blood and brain matter pool around him on the ground. Maggots begin gyrating towards him. The killer stands back and admires his work. He could shout out loud with sheer joy. Justice has been done. Murdering Kevin Devine was a job half done. *Mission complete,* he thinks.

He lies the wheelie bin on its side, then pushes Fatlad in head first, like discarded roadkill. With effort, he heaves the bin upright. Nearby, there's a length of hose attached to a tap. He rinses off his tools and disposable gloves, hosing the blood-stained water down a drain. He walks back inside the building and clocks out Fatlad's card then locks the front door of the premises and turns off the lights. He goes to the changing room and locks Fatlad's locker before returning to the yard. He wheels the bin over to the low perimeter fence, then heaves it up and over, nearly spilling its contents in the process. It's now eleven o'clock and the industrial estate is eerily quiet. But the killer still needs to be watchful, still needs to be careful. Unlike Kevin, where he was left in situ, this body needs to be disposed of.

The hammer, Stanley knife, hairnet and mask go into his overall pockets. The killer wheels the bin across the deserted Ord Road then into a public park. He slants forward, dragging his haul behind him. It's fifty metres across the park, then he stops and looks down. Before him is a cornfield and, beyond, the black water of the River Tweed. He sets off along the perimeter of the field, where the soil has been worn down to make a rough path. It's slightly downhill to the river, which makes his job easier. A breeze runs through the corn like a moving snake.

He reaches the mudflats called Yarrow Slake. Coarse grass has colonised the mud, making it firm underfoot. The killer hauls the bin over the thick, dense grass. Over hundreds of years, creeks have formed that wind their way through the mudflats like black worms. The tide's rising and silty water fills these channels. He reaches a creek and stops, sweat running down his back. Relieved that his exertions are finally over, he tips the bin's bloody contents into the channel, then watches as Fatlad slowly sinks. Fatlad, with his appalling skull injuries and grotesque smiley face. He disappears beneath the dark water. The killer trundles the empty bin further out, to where the main river flows. He pushes it into the water and watches as the current takes it midstream, then it too sinks out of sight.

Hugging the contours of the river, the killer walks upstream. Soon he reaches the Union Bridge. Halfway over he removes the hammer from his overall pocket and hurls it into the fast-flowing water. He walks to the other side of the bridge, then scrambles down to the river's edge and begins walking back towards the old town. Among some scrubland up from the shore he digs a hole in the soft earth then removes his overalls and places them in it, along with the hairnet, gloves and mask, before setting the contents on fire. He fills in the hole and covers it with clumps of grass, then goes down to the shoreline. Taking out the Stanley knife he undoes the locking screw then throws the parts far out into the river. A startled duck cries out in the darkness then skims to the opposite shore.

And as the lights of Berwick draw closer, the killer thinks about violence. He thinks about retribution. And murder is the ultimate retribution. Not that he's a murderer. No. He's the executioner. The killer feels a quiet sense of power. It could be days or weeks before Fatlad's body is found, somewhere downstream. He'll be bloated and ugly, like a skinned cow. And by then it will be void of evidence. Just like Kevin Devine. The killer smiles again, in grim acknowledgement of his actions. But not as broad as the hideous smile he left on Fatlad Owen's pockmarked face.

CHAPTER 19

WORKPLACE WOES

WEDNESDAY

Fifty Fifty's pottering about in his wife's shop. She's out doing a few deliveries. The phone rings so he goes behind the counter to answer it.

'Angie's Flower Box… Yes… yes we do… yes of course. Gimme a minute and I'll write it doon.' He jams the phone behind his ear and scribbles down the order. 'So, that's a bouquet of carnations and, yes, we have those colours. We can deliver tomorrow, Thursday… Yes… Okay, bye.' He hangs up then stands there motionless, looking at the phone. He goes into one of those stares that becomes a trance and your mind goes elsewhere. Cancer does that. It invades your thoughts like it invades your body. Cancer. It exists to live off, then kill off, its host. And in killing the host, it kills itself. The ultimate parasite. In his mind he's back twenty-four hours and in the consultant's room. He hears again the gently spoken words:

'I have to tell you, Mr McDonald, that the diagnosis is serious. You have a very aggressive cancer of the pancreas.' He carried on talking about the prognosis and survival rates but Fifty wasn't within a mile of his own mind. He was scared. He remembers the consultant settling sad eyes on him and saying, quite deliberately, 'Is there anything else you want to know, Mr McDonald?' Fifty shook his head. He could have asked him, of course. But he didn't. Cement Shoes, who'd gone in with him, had sat motionless, totally focused on the consultant. At one point Fifty had to leave the room for a blood test and on his return he could hear them both talking quietly, almost a whisper. He could have put his ear to the door, but he didn't. Because he didn't want to know.

It was different when he was nineteen and diagnosed with testicular cancer. He was bolder back then, and stronger. Although he'd been scared at times he'd actually enjoyed the fight and had treated the illness like a game. A game of baseball, and God had pitched him a ball called cancer. And that young man had taken it on and batted it right out the fuckin' stadium. But that was thirty years ago and that fearless fighter is long gone.

He's told Angie. She's in denial, like she's living in hope, talking about treatments and weight-gain supplements. But Fifty knows his wife. He sees her desperation. And her fear. Cement Shoes sounded stoical afterwards, talking about his needing to be resilient and getting ready to do battle. And his last words on the phone last night were, 'Don't renounce this world, Fifty.'

He stands and looks around his wife's wee shop. Angie's had it for about twenty years now. When she started, it was to give her an interest more than anything else. Back then, Fifty and Cement Shoes were steel erecting all over Europe and the Middle East. Long contracts, hard work, big wages. But it's been nearly a year since he "walked out on the steel". The earthy smell of damp soil complements the sweet aromas of flowers sitting in buckets on the floor. Bouquets and wreaths sit on shelving around the wall. Bouquets for the new born; wreaths for the dead.

He grabs a brush and is sweeping soil off the floor when a familiar face passes the window. 'Hi, Johnny Boy,!' he shouts through the entrance door, which is wedged open on this warm summer morning. A moment later Johnny Bang Bang saunters in with his hands in his pockets. 'How's it goin', son?' asks Fifty.

'No' bad, considering, pal. Where's Angie?' replies Bang Bang, who starts mooching about.

'She's oot delivering. So I'm just holding the fort. I saw you looking at those sunflowers in the window. I did all that, Bang Bang. I *created* them.'

'You *created* them? You're a fuckin' steel erector, Fifty, no' a poxy flower arranger. Why don't you go and create me a cup of tea, eh?' replies Bang Bang. Fifty disappears into a cubbyhole at the back of the shop and puts the kettle on. He shouts through, 'What time did you finish up on Monday night? After the wake, I mean?'

'Oh, it was late, Fifty. Aboot eleven o'clock, I think. Me and The Hammer bought some speed off Fatlad then went back to mine. So I was fucked yesterday. Even missed ma shift at Aldi's, and that started at two in the afternoon! Aye, I felt like shit all day. But I'm glad it's over now. I mean Kev's funeral, you know.'

'Me too, son,' Fifty responds, coming back into the shop with two mugs of coffee. 'Not that there's any closure, really. There's still a nutcase oot there. Did you get a text from Wacka? He was getting interviewed yesterday.'

'Aye, I got it. They'll have us all in soon,' responds Bang Bang and takes a sip then pulls a face. 'I thought you were making tea?'

'Did I say tea? Sorry, pal. I've… eh… I've got a lot on my mind just now. Listen… me, Savage and Cement Shoes are away to Bamburgh later on this morning, if you fancy a trip down. You know, that holiday let we own. Aye, we're gonna lay a new carpet, then maybe go down to Craster for a bite to eat. Shoes phoned me last night and suggested it. Do you fancy?'

'Fifty, ah've already missed one shift this week, I cannae miss another one, pal. Thanks for asking though. Anyway, I thought it was just you and Cement Shoes who owned that holiday property?'

'It was,' replies Fifty, laughing, 'but Savage made that much lowie on the poaching a couple of years ago, he needed to launder it somewhere, so he bought into it.'

Bang Bang shakes his head and laughs out loud. Then he says, 'I remember going to Craster when I was a kid. It was a school trip, like. Aye, we went to that place where they smoke the herring to make Craster kippers. I was aboot ten years old. Do you know what happened?' Fifty shakes his head. 'At the back of the factory there's this gadgee stirring a muckle vat with a stick of some sort. I asked him what he was doing. Like you would. You know what he said to me? He said, "What does it fuckin' look like I'm doin'?" So I just stood there embarrassed, then he saw ma hands and said, "Now, you'd make a good fish filleter, eh?" Aye, the fucker thought it was funny. I hated him for that. Ah was just a kid, man. See if he came in here now, I'd fillet him. Probably never been oot o' Craster in his fuckin' puff. I was drivin' once and went past Craster, and I went to the factory to see if he was still there, but it had shut doon. I hope he fell in that vat o' fish shite he was swilling aboot, the fat fuck fanny.'

'Nice alliteration, Bang Bang,' says Cement Shoes, striding into the shop. 'How's it goin', boys?'

'No' bad, Shoes,' responds Bang Bang. 'Hi, you see those flower arrangements in the window. Fifty *created* them, y'know.'

'The act of creation is always an act of destruction,' responds Cement Shoes. 'No' ma words, actually. Pablo Picasso. Are you ready, Fifty? I've told Savage we'll pick him up at his hoose aboot elevenish.'

'Just waiting on Angie, son. She'll be back anytime now,' responds Fifty. And, on cue, his wife draws up outside. Bang Bang needs to get going so he says his goodbyes to Fifty and Cement Shoes, walks outside and talks to Angie for a minute, then heads off down the street.

She enters the shop and Cement Shoes goes to her and gives her a big hug. 'How are you?' he asks softly, with his head to one side.

'I've been better, Shoes,' she responds quietly. And her gentle, vulnerable smile fills the silence like a speech, each of them immersed in thoughts of Fifty's illness.

'What was Bang Bang saying ootside?' asks Fifty.

'Just talked about the funeral, really, darlin'. Then he said you looked like a stick insect and I need to get a pan of stovies down you. I take it you didn't tell him about... about... you?'

Fifty shakes his head. 'No sweetheart, only us three know. And Savage.'

There's another awkward silence so Cement Shoes moves towards the entrance door and says, 'Okay, Angie. We'll be back about seven, I think.'

'Thanks, Shoes,' she responds, 'and thanks for taking Fifty away for the day. Change of scenery will do him good.' Fifty just stands and smiles at his wife.

'Hi, Angie, this is no' a jolly, y'know,' replies Cement Shoes. 'He'll be on his hands and knees most of the day laying carpets.' He looks over to Fifty and says, 'I've got all the tools in the boot. Tape measures, a knee kicker and a couple of Stanley knives. Okay, let's get this show on the road. See you later, Angie.'

Cement Shoes walks out and he feels relieved. The damp smell of earth and plants had taken him back to Kev's burial, when he'd stood in the rain next to his graveside. He gets into his car. It's an old-style graphite grey Land Rover, powerful and understated. Like its owner.

Fifty kisses his wife then walks out and gets in the car. Angie stands there in the shop and waves as they pull away. Fifty looks as fragile as a spider's web. A tear glistens in her eye. Once out of sight her hand goes to her mouth and she stands there looking out the shop window, still as a tombstone. Her eyes move to the floral arrangements in the shop window; the tall, regal sunflowers and bouquets of roses in yellow, pink and black.

* * *

Wacka Short's scrapyard looks like something you'd see in a British gangland movie. A three-metre red-bricked wall encloses the site, with broken glass embedded in cement around the top. Above that, razor wire coils like a silver serpent. Just inside the entrance is a grey portacabin which serves as the office, kitchen and toilet. The site looks as friendly as a menacing mob.

It's mid-morning and Wacka's sitting at his desk, talking to a customer. He hangs up, cradles a huge mug of tea in his hands and wanders over to the open door. 'Bobby boy, tea's up!' he shouts. Bob's dismembering a Ford Escort using cutting equipment. He's still in the doghouse for not turning up for work yesterday. Wacka was furious with him this morning so he's working hard and looking as busy as the wasps buzzing around him. He takes off his goggles and walks towards the cabin along a muddy, potholed aisle. On each side of him, derelict vehicles are stacked three high. They look precarious, which adds to the general air of disregard for health and safety. Bob enters the portacabin and gets his tea. They sit apart from each other in grimy overalls, sipping noisily. Smells of oil and rubber waft into the room. Bob knows that Wacka's still pissed off with him. But Bob, being Bob, has a need to talk.

'Sooo… where did you pick that Audi up from yesterday?'

'East Ord,' snaps Wacka, 'not that it's any o' your fuckin' business.' Wacka glares at him in silence. Bob feels tension in the air. Wacka says, 'Aye, picked it up aboot two in the afternoon. You were still in your pit at that time, of course.' Bob feels nauseous as he thinks back to Monday night and Kev's wake. He'd got so pissed he'd started to weave when he went to the bar. He'd decided to walk up the high street and get a taxi home. On the way he'd met a woman who he used to casually sleep with on a Saturday night, but only when he was pissed. None of his mates knew. She was that ugly. Her two front teeth protruded so far over her bottom lip she was known as 'Bucky Beaver.' Aye, getting a blowjob was a scary experience. CD said she could eat a corn on the cob through a chain-link fence. Bob thinks, *Aww, imagine if CD found out I'd been there. Oh nooo!* Anyway, they'd shared a taxi back to her place and he'd spent the night with her. Didn't get out her flat until lunchtime yesterday and he was so fucked he just went home. Now he's shitting himself in case anyone saw them together on the high street. Wacka must have been reading his thoughts as he says, 'So, eh, what time did you get oot The Brown Bear after the wake, then? Someone saw you arguing with a lamppost on Hide Hill aboot midnight.'

'Oh, it was late, Wacka. Aye, I overdid it with the shorts, I think. Still, it was a good send-off. Loads of people there, eh?' He's trying to sound normal, but inside Bob's thinking, *Who saw me on Hide Hill? Was I with Bucky by then? Oh fuck, I hope no'.*

Wacka scratches his third nipple through his overalls, then says, 'Aye, well… when you were still in your pit, I was at the police station, helping those fuckers with their enquiries.'

'How long were you in there?' asks Bob.

'No' long, really. Asked what I was doing on the night Kev was murdered. To be honest, I haven't got an alibi. I stayed in that night, watched a bit of TV and went to bed early. So, I've no' really got an alibi. But you know what, Bob? I couldn't give a fuck. I didn't kill ma mate so if they want to waste their time investigating me, then bigger fools them, eh? Shows how desperate they're getting. I did speak to my ex aboot half nine, but apart from that, nowt.'

Bob quaffs down his tea, then replies, 'Fuck's sake, eh?

Weeks have gone by and they're still chasing shadows. Useless. Did they say why they asked you in?'

'Did they fuck. Desperation, I think.' Just then the phone rings and Wacka answers it. 'Short's Scrapyard. Yes. A *what*? Okay, where is it? Right, I'll send Bob up for it later on today. Okay.' He hangs up, then looks at Bob. 'That was the council. There's a Porsche needing picked up in Highfields.'

'A Porsche? In *Highfields*?' asks Bob in disbelief.

'Aye, it's been stolen, wrapped roond a lamppost, then torched,' responds Wacka, trying hard to hide a smile.

'That's more like it,' says Bob, relieved to see Wacka regaining his humour. Bob wipes a greasy forearm across his mouth then gets to his feet. 'Ah'll finish stripping doon the Escort, then I'll take the pick-up over.' He walks purposefully out of the portacabin, reinforcing the appearance of busyness. Atlas bounds along behind him, sensing a journey. Wacka walks to the open door of the portacabin, leans against the doorframe and watches Bob as he gets back to work. Although he's still pissed off with him for not turning up for work yesterday, deep down he's not bothered. Because yesterday he'd shut the site gates at about three o'clock, unplugged the phones, pulled down the portacabin blinds, then spent the rest of the afternoon with big, blonde, busty Babs…

* * *

Fish Heid pours himself a mug of tea. It's ten o'clock and he's on site in Prior Park. CD's still not showed up. He often had other jobs on the go or was away looking at other jobs. *Or he's still in bed at the Cross Keys Hotel with that slapper from Fife,* he contends. Not that he's bothered. He's got enough to be getting on with and it's good not having CD around saying "get this" and "get that" all the time. The perils of being a sparky's mate. A car pulls up and out jumps the man himself. He saunters in, still wearing last night's clobber, with that swagger that men have when they've been shaggin' all night.

'Sorry I'm late, Heid. Is that the kettle on? No, no, you're fine. I'll get ma'sel a cup. Were you here at eight o'clock?' asks CD, walking through to the kitchen.

'Eh… well, obviously, Christopher,' responds Fish Heid. 'That *is* my starting time. Aye, but the funny thing about being punctual is that no one's ever there to appreciate it.'

'Sorry, pal,' responds CD, slurping on a mug of tea as he walks back from the kitchen. 'I was… well… I didn't get oot the Cross Keys Hotel until about nine this morning.'

'Well, I didn't think you'd been in the hoose watchin' *Cash in the Attic*,' Fish Heid responds. 'So… how was your night, then?'

'Aaww, Heid, unbelievable,' CD responds, shaking his head slowly. He smiles then says, 'I ended up with both o' them!'

'Both of them?' replies Fish Heid, now smiling too. 'You're a dirty shagamuffin, aren't you?' There's a pause, then he says, 'Well, come on, then. Let's hear it.'

CD smiles at his mate. 'Well… for a start, I didn't know they swung both ways. Had no idea. So we got into the hotel room, got stripped off, then they said I had to watch them play.' Fish Heid shakes his muckle heid as if to say, *"You pervert"*. 'Aye, then I joined in. Oh, by the way, they were both wearing black body stockings.' The Heid's now nodding, a picture emerging in his mind. CD continues, 'Then, when I was with the blonde one, the other one filmed it on her mobile! By the way, that's a fuckin' turn-on, Heid. Close-ups and everything, man!'

'Jeezo,' responds Fish Heid, laughing, 'you're going to hell, Chris. Straight to hell. Are you sure you've got the energy to do a day's graft?' CD sits there laughing, thinking about the previous night's exploits. 'So they didn't enrol you in the Fife Flat Earth Society, then?' asks Fish Heid, who's got a view that only cave dwellers live north of the Forth.

'Naw, Heid. They're from St Andrews, man. Posh manishees, these. Hi, they knew Kev, you know. Aye, from years ago. They used to come here as kids with their parents and stay at the holiday camp. They knew The Hammer and Kev first. Aye, they said it was late seventies. One of them said the first time she met Kevin was in a booth in Boots on the high street. You remember those little booths where you could listen to music? Aye, she said she bought her first single there too. "Breakfast in America". Supertramp.'

'Good job she did, CD. It would have taken aboot a fubbin' year for that song to reach Fife.'

CD guzzles down his tea then says, 'Oh, by the way, I phoned The Hammer last night to see if he fancied a foursome. Suzie was oot so he could talk. Anyway, he wasn't interested but he told me the cops had contacted him and he's being interviewed today. This afternoon.'

Fish Heid nods his heid like the sage of wisdom. 'Obviously they're starting with the psychos then working doon. Wacka first, now it's Mr Steelhammer.'

'You're right, Heid. After all these years, those two are still fuckin' dangerous men. Did you see them with Fatlad at the wake? I thought either one of them was gonna batter him.'

'Me too,' responds Fish Heid. 'And last Friday night in The Brewers. When The Hammer was kicking chairs aboot and shouting, 'Up the BUNDIG.' He's still flippin' unpredictable, that knobstick.'

And they both sit there, deep in thought. CD says quietly, 'I wanna ask you a straight question, Heid. Just between me and you. Could someone like The Hammer have done it? Could he have murdered Kev? Ah mean, one of us?'

Fish Heid blows his cheeks out, then says, 'Oh, mate, that's a tough one. Funny you should ask about The Hammer. Alice and I were talking about this the other night. The night before the funeral.' He looks up at CD. 'Aye, married couples do a lot of that in bed. Talk.' He smiles, then continues, 'Ah don't just mean The Hammer. We went through all the names of The BUNDIG. Could The Hammer have done it? Aye, he could cross that line.'

'He'd cross a line in a colouring-in book, that fucker,' responds CD. 'Anyway, I've been thinking aboot Jez.'

'Jez?' asks Fish Heid. 'Jez is no' a killer, CD. Jez is soft, man. He's spent too much time aroond leftie liberal teachers up in Edinburgh. He's a pussy, man. Well, he is now. Ah mean, back in the day he was a complete radge.'

'Aaww listen. Ah didn't mean *that*,' responds CD, 'ah meant what he told us after the funeral, walking down to the wake. Do you no' remember? When we were under his big jessie brolly. He'd met some dude who worked for the Met. A criminal profiler gadgie.'

'Christ, you're right, CD. I'd forgotten about that. I was so messed up with the funeral that my mind was all over the place. But I remember it now you say. Aye, he met him in the Cannon chippie, didn't he?'

'That's right,' responds CD. 'Listen, ah've got something to tell you. Keep it to yourself, but Jez told me that if this guy got a copy of the autopsy report he'd have a look at it and put together some kind of profile. Well… I got a copy from Norah Devine and gave it to him at his digs yesterday morning. I had no idea the family could request a copy, did you? I'd find it hard to read if it was one of my own.'

'Hardly light reading, is it?' says Fish Heid. 'Well, I'm not up on criminal profiling, CD, but how would knowing how Kev died and his injuries tell him about, say, motive?'

'Aah now, motive. That's the tricky question. Why would someone want to kill Kev?' responds CD. And both men look at each other, as if searching for the answer in the other man's face.

CHAPTER 20

GOAGSIE MEETS ELIJAH

WEDNESDAY

Detective Constable "Goagsie" Mackay stifles a yawn and looks around at his colleagues. More to gauge how bored they look than anything else. He's in the Conference Room and DCI Hazelwood's giving his weekly briefing to the Major Investigation Team. It seems to Goagsie that Bawheid's merely regurgitating what he said yesterday at his update presentation. He sits back and looks at the cartoon cop on his mug. *Aye, that cop's got more chance of cracking this case than we have. Christ's sake, how much longer is Bawheid gonna slaver on for?*

He sneaks a peek at his watch. This morning he'd phoned Mr Bootle who suggested meeting for lunch in the Cannon chip shop. He'd like to see the crime scene photographs, which meant a bit of a run around for the young detective. During the phone call Mr Bootle had asked not to draw attention to anything on the photographs, but to make comments on the back of them. That way he wouldn't be influenced by someone else's observations. As requested, Goagsie added comments where appropriate. Then he'd reread his notes from their meeting yesterday and scribbled down further points he'd like to raise with him over lunch.

Bawheid's still droning on. His rural Durham accent jags the ears. As dull as a wet weekend in Seaham. Goagsie's mind wanders off. He thinks about the crime scene photographs, the appalling injuries and sheer graphic horror of the murder. Bawheid calls a five-minute comfort break. Around him people stand and stretch while others turn to colleagues and the busy hum of small talk begins. But almost immediately the chatter dies down to a whisper as all heads turn towards Chief Superintendent Jack "Bomber" Mills standing in the doorway. All six foot four of him. Bawheid blushes and looks flustered – the way sycophantic middle managers do when in the presence of a senior officer. And Jack Mills is certainly that. He's the force's Northern Area Commander. But he's still a cop, unchanged by success and promotion. A policeman's police officer. He makes his way to the front of the room, acknowledging staff he knows on the way.

He stops at Goagsie and points a finger right at him. 'Aye, Detective Constable Mackay. I dunno what you're looking so chuffed about, after that performance against Cumbria last month, eh? How many tries did they score? Was it six? Eh? You'll need to do better than that, young man.' Goagsie's flustered that The Boss, as Jack Mills is known, should even be talking to a rookie detective. He flushes bright red and says:

'We'll stuff them in the return leg, Boss.' Jack Mills smiles, then carries on walking to the front where Bawheid's waiting with a pathetic smile on his face, pretending he's pleased to see the senior officer. Pleasantries over, they begin to talk. Jack Mills is half sitting on a desk with his arms folded while Bawheid's almost standing to attention in front of him. The harsh fluorescent lighting picks out beads of sweat on his baldy wee heid. It's clear to Goagsie that Bawheid's doing all the talking. He's babbling like a child. Then The Boss starts talking quietly to Bawheid, whose expression changes with each turn of their discussion.

A couple of minutes later The Boss rises and turns to the now silent audience. A sense of respect hangs in the air. 'Well, guys,' he says, in a south Northumbrian accent, 'I'm up here on another matter but… well… it's not often I get to speak to a murder investigation team. I spend too much time behind a bloody desk these days. I'm not going to ask you how it's going because I know you've not made much headway.' Bawheid squirms behind him and Goagsie feels his discomfort.

'Now, two things. First, the media. It's important, guys, that any of you coming into contact with the media need to remember what we can and can't make public. So I've asked DCI Hazelwood to get an aide-memoire put together for everyone working on this case. So you're all singing from the same hymn sheet. Okay?' It wasn't a question. 'Secondly, the DCI's going to be on the news tomorrow night. The public wants to know what's going on and we're going to tell them. Or at least he is.' He points his thumb behind him. 'And he's going to announce a new lead. We don't have one but that's what we're going to say. That'll pacify the public, but more importantly it might draw the killer out. He might get scared, he might get careless, then we get our break. It's called the "ass pucker" factor. Once the information's out there then *you* all need to be out there, with your noses to the ground. Use your judgement, guys. This case will be solved using good old-fashioned detective work.'

He pauses and hauls a hanky out of his pocket. 'Bloody hay fever. What a summer it's been.' Then he looks at them all and says, 'Because the last thing I want is another murder on my patch.' He turns to Bawheid, thanks him for the time, then walks straight out of the room without another word.

Bawheid raises his voice and says, 'Okay, you heard the Area Commander. Let's get out there and find this killer.'

* * *

Elijah Bootle saunters down Church Street; there's a warm smell of frying fish in the air. Mrs Barraclough told him at breakfast that Wednesdays and Saturdays are market days in Berwick so the town will be busier than usual. And there does seem to be a few more people about but it's hardly Piccadilly Circus. His plan is to meet up with the detective, then wander up the high street and browse among the stalls. He fancies a book; he's got his reading head on which is always a sign that he's content.

He pushes open the Cannon chippie door and it's loud with busy chatter. The waitresses are flying about with plates of food. Elijah hopes there's an empty booth for himself and Mr Mackay. As he passes the frying range he sees the woman who served him last Saturday. She's behind the counter frying chips, and the heat has blushed her cheeks. She looks up and says, 'Hiya,' in a bright, friendly way. Like he's a local. She'd waved to him yesterday as he walked past the shop so feels familiar enough to walk over to the counter.

'Hi there. Yes… err… I was in here last Saturday and had the best fish and chips in a long while.'

Josie smiles and says, 'Yeah, I remember you. You dined with the lovely Jez Guinness, didn't you?!'

'Yeah, that's right. I did. Nice guy. Is that his surname? Guinness. I didn't know that,' responds Elijah.

'And how was the service?' Josie asks, smiling broadly.

'Top class,' responds Elijah, with a grin and a thumbs-up.

Josie laughs like she really means it. 'There are a few empty booths at the back. I'll be down in a minute.' Elijah walks down the aisle, looking for a free booth. In the distance, the potato peeler clatters like a windmill. Eventually he finds an empty booth and sits facing the front of the shop so he'll see Mr Mackay when he comes in. He pushes the condiments out of the way then retrieves his notebook and mind maps and places them on the table. He's mindful that the detective doesn't know that he's seen a copy of the autopsy report, courtesy of Jez.

'Mr Bootle, how are you?' Elijah looks up and there's Goagsie approaching him with an arm outstretched. Elijah rises and shakes the young man's shovel-sized hand.

'I'm well, Mr Mackay, very well. Sit down, sit down. And just call me Elijah.'

'And I'm Gordon, although I get called Goagsie by everyone round here,' responds the detective as he fits his huge frame into the seat opposite. He places a black folder on the seat next to him. 'Listen, thanks for meeting up with me again. I know you're on holiday, so this is appreciated.'

Elijah replies, 'Only too happy to help.'

'Well, I don't know about you, Elijah, but I'm famished. Three Weetabix this morning and that's been my lot.'

Elijah smiles and says, 'A man your size needs more than that. I recommend the fish and chips.'

Josie walks down the aisle to their table, digging a notebook out of her apron pocket. 'Now then, gents,' she says, looking at Elijah, 'fish and chips for you, I suppose?'

'They're the best in town. And a mug of tea, please.'

'Make that two,' says Goagsie, looking at her admiringly.

'We don't do mugs of tea, but you can have a large pot of tea between you?' says Josie.

'That's fine,' both men say in unison, then smile at each other. Josie walks off and both men sit there, looking around. There's a sudden burst of loud laughter from a booth down the front, like a monkey's treetop scream. They both laugh quietly. Then Elijah asks,

'Well, how's it goin' over the road?'

Goagsie blows out his cheeks, then says, 'We had our weekly briefing this morning and the Area Commander showed up. Said he was here on other business, but I'm no' so sure. Anyway, the cop leading the investigation – he's a DCI – he's giving a television interview tomorrow night on the local news.' Goagsie leans closer and Elijah reciprocates. In a low whisper, Goagsie says, 'He's gonna say that we've got a new lead, which we're following up. Truth is we've got sweet fuck all, but it might cause the killer to get anxious and drop the ball.'

'I like it,' responds Elijah with a nod. 'Proactive police work often pays dividends.'

'Aye. We're also getting aide-memoires done so we know

what we can and can't say to the public and the media. Not that a foot soldier like me will be facing the cameras anytime soon. And that suits me fine.'

'How long have you been a detective, then?' asks Elijah.

'Six months, and this is my first murder case. Why? Does it show?' responds Goagsie, blushing slightly.

'No, no, not at all,' responds Elijah, raising a hand to emphasise his sincerity. 'Do you work with a partner?'

'Aye. He's a detective sergeant. Good guy. He's on leave this week. Aye, he's asked me to put all the information we've gathered into a report for him. Like a review of our work so far.'

'Now, I like that, Goagsie. All orderly like. Get the facts then get a vessel to put them in. Like groceries in a well-ordered cupboard. Because it's facts and attention to detail that will crack this case.'

'Funnily enough, that's what the Area Commander said. Well, he said it would be good old-fashioned detective work but it's the same thing. Christ, ahm gagging for a cup of tea,' says Goagsie, looking around him with a gloomy expression.

Elijah looks hard at the young detective and says, 'Don't beat yourselves up, mate. I said yesterday you're dealing with a clever man. A very clever killer. Someone who covers their tracks well. I mean, look at the crime scene. Most of the clues have been washed out to sea. So that's your first obstacle. There's bugger all evidence. No wonder you're struggling and… err… oh… here comes our meal.'

Both men sit back as Josie sets down a tray with cups, saucers and a teapot. She smiles and says, 'Enjoy, guys.' Behind her a younger girl has two plates of fish and chips. She places them down then follows Josie back up the shop.

The two men move their heads towards each other again and Goagsie says quietly, 'We're still questioning potential suspects but nothing's come up yet. We had a guy in yesterday. His name's Short. William "Wacka" Short. He's an old friend of the deceased.' He points at the retro ketchup holder. 'Pass me that tomato sauce thing, will you? Aye, we had him in yesterday. And he doesn't have an alibi.' Elijah pours out two cups of tea and looks at Goagsie as if to encourage him to continue. 'Yeah, he runs a scrapyard over on the south side of town. A dangerous man with a history of violence. Aye, back in the day he ran a mob of dodgy boys. The BUNDIG, they were called. Kevin Devine was a member. To be honest with you, all that gang are on our radar. We've exhausted all the obvious leads, y'know, family, business associates, affairs, that sort of thing.' He takes a slug of tea and nods in appreciation. 'Okay, I'm going to demolish this meal in aboot five minutes. Look at that fish, Elijah. Michel Roux would be proud of that, eh?'

After the meal is finished and the table cleared, both men sit with their tea and Elijah says, 'Right, let's see these crime scene photos, then.' Goagsie reaches into his folder and pulls out a sheaf of A4-size colour photographs. Elijah takes them while glancing around him, pleased that the booth provides privacy. He sets them down in front of him, like a grotesque pack of cards, then looks down at the first photograph. It's a full body shot from about ten metres' distance. He looks up at Goagsie and asks, 'Is this how he was found? I mean, did the first cop on scene touch the victim, alter his position, you know, looking for clues under the body? Stuff like that?'

'Nah,' responds Goagsie. 'He was obviously dead so he was left in situ until the Scenes of Crime Officers arrived. So that's how the killer left him.' Elijah looks again at the battered body in a sitting position with both hands behind him. The top of the stake tethering him is visible above the victim's head. Elijah flips the photo over to see if Goagsie had made any comments, but there's nothing.

He looks at the next photograph; it's a close-up headshot. Elijah winces then says, 'Jesus Christ, what happened to his eyes?'

'There are rats on that beach, mate. They ate out his eyes. In fact, all the trauma to his eyes, nose and ears were rats,' responds Goagsie. 'You'll see them better in the next photo.'

But Elijah isn't listening. Unwanted, distressing memories of a sightless dead child fill his mind in gruesome technicolour. Sweat oozes out of his fingertips. He pretends to scrutinise the photo but he's focusing on his breathing, and controls it down, all the time hoping Goagsie doesn't notice. The flashback fades and, after what seems an age, the trauma passes. He's glad he's seeing these photographs *after* he's eaten. Composed now he says, 'Those wounds to the side of the head, they look high impact. And a small surface area.' He looks up at Goagsie and asks, 'A hammer?' The detective smiles then nods as if to say, *'Turn it over.'* On the back is written: *Four-pound ball-pein hammer.*

Goagsie leans forward. 'You know the type. Engineers use them for fabrication work. Panel beaters knock out dents with them. They're used in scrapyards to recover spare parts. Wacka Short owns a scrapyard. By the way, this information's not been made public, okay?' Elijah nods and taps his nose then looks down at a close-up frontal view of the victim's face. He sees the small grey stones amongst the sand in the victim's partially open mouth. Elijah turns the photograph over and says, 'There's nothing written on the back.' He passes the photograph over then says, 'Look at it.' Goagsie takes the photo in both hands and studies it intently. Elijah says, 'Now, look again at the first one. This one, from a few metres away.' Goagsie places the two images next to each other. He's still looking at them when Elijah says, 'Show me any pebbles on the beach around the victim in the first photograph.' Goagsie looks hard, then says:

'There aren't any.' He then looks at the second photo then shakes his head, 'So… are you saying…?'

'I'm saying, Detective,' cuts in Elijah, 'there are no pebbles on that part of the beach. I think they were placed in his mouth. It's called posing, mate. The murderer's telling you something. They weren't put there to choke him. The killer wanted this man to drown. No mistake. That's his signature but what's the message? Work that out and you'll get close to your killer.' Elijah looks at the next photograph. It's taken from behind and shows the victim's hands cable-tied to a stake about a metre high. He turns over the photograph to see the words: *Plastic Casio watch missing*. Elijah nods and says, 'The watch is missing as it could have helped you with the time of death.' Goagsie writes a comment in his notebook then scans back a page and says:

'Yep. High tide was at 10pm that night so it would have told us when he started to go under.' The next photograph shows a close-up of the victim's hands, restrained with a cable tie. On the back is written: *Black, plastic, 30cm long. Hardware stores?* Goagsie continues, 'The cable tie and stake are in the evidence locker at the station. With the victim's clothes. His wife confirmed that he didn't have a mobile phone on him.

The stake, if you're wondering, was a piece of driftwood. The hammer was used to drive it into the sand.'

'Mmm…' responds Elijah, 'the killer must have been confident of finding a piece of wood that would serve his needs. Another example of local knowledge.' The remaining photos are various shots of Kevin Devine from different angles. One has his trousers rolled up to reveal the broken fibulas beneath his knees. He gathers up the photos then passes them to Goagsie who places them back in his folder. Elijah leans forward, intertwines his fingers and says, 'Tell me about this gang.'

'Oh, the BUNDIG. They've been around forever. About twenty-odd strong back in their heyday. Maybe about ten of them still kicking about. Be in their late forties now. BUNDIG stands for Berwick United, Never Defeated In Green. They're Hibs fans. You know, Hibernian, Edinburgh club. I'm a rugby man, myself.'

'I'm Crystal Palace,' replies Elijah, a broad smile on his face.

'Funnily enough,' resumes Goagsie, 'your profile fits most of them to a tee.' He glances down at his notes. 'Male, local, blue collar, manual worker, knows the victim. The guy you met in here the other day. Jez. You told me about him yesterday at the station. He was one but he's a teacher and lives in Edinburgh so doesn't really fit your profile. Yeah… I asked a couple of old beat cops this morning. His name's Jez Guinness. One of them was in the same year as him at school. Aye, he nearly got murdered himself, when he was in the navy. The cop remembers seeing him when he was home on sick leave, his head all bandaged up. Long time ago now. But yeah, the rest of them fit your profile.'

'Are any of them capable of murder?' asks Elijah, wiping his mouth with a tissue.

Goagsie looks at him. 'Yes. I'd say some of them are. Some of them have done time. Some for violence, others were in and out of the nick for petty stuff. Y'know, revolving door criminals. I'm talking years ago, like.' A beep prompts Goagsie to check his phone. 'Christ, is that the time? Listen, I've got a meeting back across at the station in ten minutes, so I'd better get going. Is there anything else you'd like to ask me?'

Elijah leans forward and says, 'Just one question. How many flower shops are there in Berwick?'

Goagsie laughs then furrows his brow. 'There's two. One in West Street and one up Castlegate. Why?'

'I want to buy some flowers, Goagsie.'

The two men laugh, then rise and shake hands. Goagsie marches off, carrying his folder under his arm like a sergeant major's baton. Elijah walks up to the counter, pays for his meal and exchanges further pleasantries with Josie before exiting into the warm afternoon sunshine.

* * *

The market day stalls stretch out up the high street, bursting with the colours of fruit, veg and clothes. The conversation buzzes as buyers haggle with stallholders over quality and quantity. Customers dawdle under canvas awnings that dazzle white in the glaring sunshine. Elijah Bootle stands at a bookstall. He's got a Thomas Hardy novel under one arm. He picks up another book, its cover wrinkled like a dried apple. *Valley of the Dolls*; a cult classic set during the hedonistic sixties.

He idly turns it over to read the back page. *'Dolls: red or black; capsules or tablets…'* The narrative describes the lives of three struggling actresses in sex-fuelled, drug-addled New York. He looks again at the front cover. A woman's pink-glossed lips are parted to show a capsule held between her teeth. The town hall clock strikes twice. He looks up at it. He stares at it. And as the minute hand slowly moves, a thought takes shape in his mind. Did the pebbles in Kevin Devine's mouth signify capsules or pills? Still looking up, he mutters out loud, 'This is drug-related, my man. That's the killer's message. He was murdered because of drugs.' He remembers Goagsie telling him that Kevin Devine had a conviction for drug possession.

He puts the novel back, pays for the Hardy book and wanders off. He's going to pop into Tommy's for some lemon bon bons then it's an easy afternoon in his armchair by the window. But within his subconscious mind is the germ of a solution to the murder of Kevin Devine.

CHAPTER 21

MEMORIES OF ANOTHER DAY

WEDNESDAY

Jez lowers the newspaper and lets it rustle onto the contours of his lap. The chair's leather upholstery feels like a breath of cold air on his back. He can hear Lesley clearing away the breakfast dishes. She's singing quietly to herself. The only other sound is the metronomic ticking of a grandfather clock in the corner of the sitting room. The door opens and Lesley's standing there with a jug of coffee. It looks dark and enticing. The heavy smell of roasted beans wafts into the room.

'Would you like a refill, Jez? It's still hot.'

'Oh, go on, then. Why not,' he replies, lifting up his cup as she approaches him. 'Thanks, Lesley. Err… that's fine, thanks.'

She stands back then walks to the window and says, 'So, what're your plans for today, then? The forecast says sunny but it's a little cloudy out there just now.'

He senses she wants to talk so he sips his coffee then says,

'Well, to be honest I was expecting a few odd jobs to come my way this week after being at my mum's yesterday, but there was nothing. Not even a lightbulb to change. I was there all afternoon then she cooked a meal and we watched some TV. So, today I'm going to walk over to Tweedmouth, maybe catch up with a few old friends.'

'Oh, it's good to keep in touch, Jez. I suppose you saw a few of your friends at… at the… funeral on Monday,' she stutters.

'Yeah, they were all there. Aye, not exactly ideal circumstances for a nostalgic chinwag though, Lesley, y'know.'

'Of course, of course.' A pause, then she asks, 'Was that one of your old friends who called here yesterday morning, then?' she says, with a smile so false her top gum looks like bubblegum has been squeezed around it. Like you used to do as a kid.

Jez nods and suppresses a smile before answering, 'Yeah, his name's Chris Driver; although if he met you, he'd be calling himself Christian Dangerfield. That's his nom de plume, by the way.' Lesley's eyes widen, as if being pulled up by her increasingly arched brows. 'Aye, he's from over the river. I met him at Sunday School so that's how long I've known him!' They both smile and Jez thinks, *Here we go, another one for the list of CD's conquests. Another notch on his headboard. Bastard! Still, he's ma mate so I'm gonna put a word in for him. Cos that's what mates do.* 'Aye, he's an electrician and a good one too. I'd recommend him, Lesley.'

'Oh well, if I ever need one I'll look him up. Do you want a biscuit to go with that? Or is it too early?'

'It's never too early for a biscuit, Lesley.' She smiles then disappears, and he hears her laughing quietly in the kitchen. Jez leans back and plans his agenda for the day. He has an urge to see his old house in Ladykirk Lane. Then it's on to the cemetery at Sunnyside to visit his sister's grave. He wonders how many people visit Mandy's grave these days; it was all so long ago.

Then tonight he's seeing Josie after she finishes work. They're going to the cinema, or "the flicks" as she calls it. Wednesday's Nostalgia Night, and they're showing the 1971 classic *Get Carter* with Michael Caine. He saw the film advertised outside the Playhouse yesterday and decided to take her there. She loved the idea and he's looking forward to a second date. He sees her now in her tight jeans and high heels she wore on Sunday night, and that familiar sensation of excitement surges up from his stomach. He knows where he'd like to end the night. In her cosy little flat overlooking the Walls. In her warm bed. But that's the difference between men and women. Men never know how the night's gonna end. It's the woman who decides. Well, as long as it's a decent man. His thoughts are interrupted as Lesley returns with a plate of biscuits. 'There you go, Jez. Custard Creams. Top dunkers, those,' she says, pointing at them for added emphasis. She lays the plate on the arm of his chair. 'Well, enjoy your day. I'm away shopping.'

'See you later, Lesley,' he replies. She shuts the door and it's all quiet again in the sitting room. Cool and tranquil. He settles back, feeling a mid-morning nap is in the post. He drifts off thinking that you can have old friends and you can have new friends, but you can't have old, new friends. Because new friends have no shared history or past. He stretches out his legs and drifts off into a deep, dreamless sleep. The newspaper slides off his lap.

* * *

A couple of hours later he's standing on the cinder path between his old house and the one next door. White vertical blinds adorn the windows and the outside woodwork is eggshell blue and white. But it's still his old house, his home, and you only ever have one home. The lavender hedge is still there, after all these years, framing the edge of the garden. He brushes his hand along its spires of purple flowers, then breathes in its sharp smell. As refreshing as a sea breeze. And it's funny, cos every time he smells lavender he thinks of this hedge. He snaps off a sprig and sticks it in his back pocket. The garden looks neat and ordered, with its mowed lawns, bordered by red and yellow rose bushes. But in his mind's eye he sees the garden as his dad had it, forty odd years ago. There were rows of geraniums and chrysanthemums, bursting with colours, stretching right down to the back wall. Next to them were lines of top-heavy Brussels sprout plants. Jez hated sprouts; and if they had them for Sunday dinner, Dad used to make him sit at the table until he ate them. His memory's floating about now. He thinks about the day Dad left them. He'd felt scared, as a child does when they see a strong man broken down with emotion. He'd asked him to look after Mandy, and Jez had promised he would, although at the time he was more concerned about who was going to look after the leek bed.

Standing there today, only the lavender hedge and an apple tree remain from his childhood days. Mandy planted the tree. She must have been about five at the time. Jez remembers laughing at her and those few pips in her outstretched hands. *They won't grow into a tree,* he'd told her. Dad had dug down into the soil and she'd placed them in there. Jez sees the scene in his mind's eye and can smell the freshly dug soil. The three of them, standing there. Mandy had looked excited. Happy. Alive. And just like childhood haunts you like the memory of some former happiness, that memory becomes a permanent refuge. Jez stands there, clinging to the vision of that excited, happy, "bursting with life" little girl. His face begins to crumple with emotion, but he holds it together. His mind moves to Mum's wee flat and the photograph of Mandy when she's about sixteen, standing next to the tree with a tiny apple in her palm. He looks at the tree now, growing strong and bearing fruit as it lives out its long, peaceful life.

He takes in the garden and house one last time in a panoramic sweep. It becomes blurred as tears gather in his eyes. He wipes them away with his sleeve then locks the image in his mind, like an old photograph. He walks back along Ladykirk Lane, thinking about childhood games played out on this street when they were kids. The boys played football games like "tackly-shooty in" and "penalty prize". Mandy and her wee mates would play hopscotch, drawing numbers with white chalk onto the grey paving slabs. Or they would twirl a long skipping rope and one by one the rest of them would jump in, singing a rhyme or something. Innocent kids in innocent times.

* * *

A knee-high wall surrounds the cemetery, mounted by thin, spiky railings. They look newly painted in black gloss. Inside this enclosure are rows and rows of headstones. Jez walks through the entrance gates and views the sombre scene. He's the only living being amongst hundreds. Around him, sparrows dart from tree to tree. He's heading for the far corner of the cemetery. First on a black tarmac avenue, then it's a cracked, worn path. Some of the graves look neglected and overgrown. Crumbled headstones commemorating forgotten people. Eventually, like a pilgrim returning to a sacred place, he sees Mandy's headstone. As he gets closer he sees the grave is well tended and fresh flowers have been laid. Pink and blue forget-me-nots. He thinks, *Who put those flowers there? Mum's been on holiday so it couldn't be her.* Maybe it was one of his aunties or a friend of Mandy. There's a white note with biro writing but it's blurred with rainwater and unreadable.

He stands at the grave and reads the inscription. It's black marble with gold writing.

In Loving Memory
Mandy Guinness
5th February 1968 – 8th January 1986
Aged 17 years old
Precious daughter to Kathy and sister to Jeremy
"Deep in our hearts your memory is kept. To love and to cherish and never forget."

Emotional pain rises up in a wave and catches in his throat like a big lump. He looks around the deserted graveyard, then down at the ground where his sister lies. And he begins to talk to her, quietly. 'Hi, Mandy, it's me. Been a while since I was last here, I know. I've come to talk to you, sweetheart. Like brother to sister. Ah mean, I talk to you all the time.

In the bath. In the car. In my dreams. Aye, I've just been to the house in Ladykirk. Just looking. Aye, you're tree's doin' well, darlin'. I remember the day you planted it. Like it was yesterday. Me, you and Dad. And I was at Mum's yesterday. She's doin' fine, she's good.'

He gets down close and lays his hand on the headstone. 'Mandy, listen. It took a long time, darlin', but I found out in the end. Nearly thirty years it took me. How you died. And who did it. I know they put drugs in your drink. I know they abused you like a piece of meat. Mandy, listen. I've killed them. Both of them. I've fuckin' done them in, sis. You wanna play big boys' games you play by big boys' rules. And don't you worry about me. I'm in the clear. I won't be caught so you sleep on now and don't worry about me. And I love you, okay. And I always will.'

His voice starts to quiver and then it comes. Tears form in his eyes and his whole body seems to shudder and shake. His crying becomes a wail of grief as a sea of tears burst out of him. Slowly, he recovers, shoulders still heaving with emotion.

Eventually he stands up straight. He looks down at his sister's last resting place and says to her, 'You know, I still find it hard standing over your grave. I want to talk to you about mortgages, marriages and kids, but… but I can't.' Warm tears run down his face again. 'But I want you to rest easy now, okay? Cos justice has been done.' He lays the sprig of delicate lavender against the headstone and catches its freshness again. He turns away and heads back down the uneven flagstones, past unkempt and unloved plots, thinking that he's forty-eight and she'll always be seventeen, a child. And despite the warm sun radiating heat on this green and grey setting, the smells are of damp earth and wet grass. The tranquillity is broken by a heavy lorry chugging up Sunnyside Hill in a low gear, spewing out filthy blue and black smoke.

As he walks through the cemetery gates an ambulance screams past with blue lights flashing, heading south in a deafening hurry. He thinks about Fatlad Owens. The noise of the hammer splintering his skull excites his memory and sends a warm surge up from his belly. It's like panic, fear and pleasure combined. The more he struck him the harder he hit him. Like the power didn't fade. It intensified. That look on his face. He didn't ask why. He didn't plead for mercy. Because he knew. His skull looked like mush with bits of white bone poking out and brain matter running down his fat face. Fuckin' terrified, he was. His cheeks had sliced open so easily with the craft knife. *Aye, he's always got a smile on his face, has Fatlad. Well, he fuckin' has now.* He hopes the rats get to him, like they did Kev. He hopes they bite out *his* eyes. Will an ambulance respond like that when they find him? He wonders where he'll be found. Out on the stinking mudflats? Or washed up downstream? Or maybe never. The river gets turbulent as it meets the sea. Swirling currents and fast-flowing tides mean that the Tweed doesn't always give up its dead.

A thought comes to him. *Should've punctured his lungs with a shank. Don't want that fucker coming to the surface anytime soon.* He closes his eyes again; the physical exertion of last night has left him exhausted. Then he whispers, 'Aye, you didn't see that one coming, Fatlad, did you? No one did. Not even my new friend, Elijah, the washed-up criminal profiler, who I'm keeping close to my chest, as any double killer would. Maybe no' a serial killer, but there's time yet.'

Beep beep, goes his mobile. He digs it out of his pocket. It's from Josie.

Hi Jez. Really looking forward 2 seeing u 2nite! busy here today. Your friend from London's here. with a cop! C u at 7. Xxxx

He freezes. He reads it again. *With a cop. With a fuckin' cop.* Panic bristles across his forehead. *Elijah's talking to a fuckin' cop. Is he onto something? Is he onto me? Keep a cool heid. You're fine. You're in the clear.*

He walks on with a slow, methodical pace and goes over the conversations he's had with Elijah since he met him last Saturday. When he told him he was a criminal profiler. When he became wary of him. Very wary. He was confident that the local "boys in blue" wouldn't have a scooby regarding Kevin's killer. And he was right. But a specialist from the Met, a criminal profiler, now that's a different kettle of fish. Even if he is on holiday. And burnt out. He'd shown Elijah the story in the newspaper and he hadn't seemed interested. But then he'd met him on the Walls last Sunday and told him he'd visited the crime scene after seeing an appeal poster in the police station window. Then Jez knew he'd have to keep him close to him – in order to divert and distract. And he'd tried to dissuade him, pointing out to him his mental health problems which brought him here in the first place.

Elijah had said the method of killing was to deliberately drown. That was the killer's signature. Correct, Mr Criminal Profiler. But nothing Jez said could have linked Kev's murder to him. And by getting him the autopsy report and profile on Kev he would push his enquiring mind and suspicions far away from him. There was nothing in the autopsy for Jez to worry about. And he'd left a couple of clues. He thinks, *Wanna play games with me, Sherlock fuckin' Holmes? I've been playing games with you since I met you. Shame really, cos I like you. And that black rose at the funeral pushed me even further away. What a diversion. Because I don't know who the fuck placed it there. But someone knows. I'm meeting Elijah tomorrow afternoon in The Barrels so let's find out what he knows. And thinks.*

He decides to walk back over the Old Bridge to his digs, have a sleep then get ready to meet Josie tonight. And like a farmer who ploughs all day and longs for sunset and rest, once the thought of sleep is in his head, he wants his bed. He wants to feel fresh and energised when he meets Josie tonight. A ravishing distraction from his preoccupation with murder and revenge.

* * *

An hour later he's on the Old Bridge, looking out towards the river's estuary and the sea beyond. To his left, small fishing boats bob about in the harbour. To his right is Tweedmouth, with its ugly docks and crane gibbets. Berwick's bastard child. And this bridge joins them like a stone-built umbilical cord. Below him the tide's on the turn and the river's running fast and violent. He looks down into the swirling waters but there's no sign of a lifeless, mangled body. *Aye,* he thinks, *a good job well done.*

He thinks about Fatlad Owen's lifeless body sinking from view under the black river water last night. He thinks about looking at his slashed "smiley" face for the last time as it slowly disappeared. He shuts his eyes. A wave of intense pleasure washes over him, a pleasure so wonderful it feels physical. The feeling fades then returns again, before fading once more – as if he can only tolerate the intense joy in short bursts.

CHAPTER 22

DATE NIGHT

WEDNESDAY

Jez lies in bed with a headache like his skull's being sawn open with a blunt hacksaw. Sharp pain sweeps over him in waves. He feels sweaty and clammy. Walking back from the cemetery, dark clouds were rolling in from the sea and the atmosphere became dark and heavy. *It's close,* Mum would say. Behind the closed curtains he sees a flashing bright light, then thunder cracks across the sky.

Then it comes. Jagged lights form a prism in front of his eyes then start to turn in on themselves, like a kaleidoscope. It's a full-on fuck-off migraine. Shit. He crawls out of bed, staggers to the bathroom and swallows two Sumatran with a glass of water, then falls back into bed. There's no escape from the blinding pain, but a couple of these heavy duty bad boys usually do the trick, if he catches it early enough. He pulls the duvet over his head for complete darkness then thinks about that scumbag with the dimple pint mug, all those years ago. He grinds his teeth, fuckin' raging at the memory of it. Funnily enough, the man died three years later, just a week after he got out of prison. Well, Jez thought it was funny. He laughed out loud when he heard. Epileptic fit in his sleep. Aye, God's like that. He fuckin' hates scumbags who hurt the innocent. He's still disappointed that the boy died peacefully. Shame he wasn't thrown off the Tamar Bridge. *Anyway, thirty years on and thanks for the migraines, you fucker, but I'm still here. No one misses you. No one. Not even God. And God doesn't hate me, because my crimes are justified. So me and the Big Man are brand new! I'm going to heaven.*

He sticks an arm out from under the duvet and gets his phone. In the darkness he powers it up and checks his calendar. He's got his annual check-up with Mr Yogi, the neuro consultant at the Western General, a week on Wednesday, where focus on his "post offence behaviour" is required. He needs to sleep now so thinks nice thoughts to prompt drowsiness: Josie's slinky walk; her high heels and skinny jeans; Fatlad's fat face, all sliced up; Kev's broken legs. Windswept sprays of rain rattle against the window. He gets cosied up under the duvet and lets his mind get inside the noise. It becomes soothing and lulls him off to sleep. The sound of a hairdryer has the same effect.

He wakes about five o'clock and feels washed out and groggy. And that's understandable. Not just the after-effects of the migraine. He beat a man to death last night, then dragged him down to the river, for fuck's sake! He throws open the curtains and peers out onto the street. It's still pouring down and sheets of rain are being pushed around the pavement by a violent wind. He showers and feels better for it, singing to himself as he shaves. There's still a whiff of lavender on his hands. He looks close up and says to his reflection, 'I killed another man last night. Yeah, struck him down with a hammer. He killed my sister, you see. Spiked her drink. Him and his mate. Then they stripped her, aye, to cool her down. Yeah, sure. Then they touched her, you know. Touched her all over. They thought it was funny.' His nose touches the cold mirror. 'But I didn't think it was fuckin' funny. And what goes around, comes around. That's what I always say, Jez.' He sprays aftershave on his face and in his hair. He smells nice. CD nice. His mobile beeps on the bedside table.

This homework is killing me! Cant do anymore. Save me…xxx

He smiles and responds: I'll save u josie!! Xxx

It's a deal!! Lookin forward 2 it!

This is good. All of it. Not just seeing Josie again. No, after you kill someone you need to try and act normally. As if nothing happened. Normal service must resume.

It's quiet on the ground floor and he wanders over to the back window for a weather check. It's where he stood on Sunday when Lesley was sunbathing in the garden. The jam jar's still on the outside windowsill, and a pile of dead, bloated wasps now reaches the waterline. On top of the dead is a mass of black and yellow crawling animals. He bends down and looks closely at the scene. This is their hell on earth. No escape and certain death. He wonders how bloated Fatlad will be now, under the river for nearly a day. Squinting up he sees the storm's passed. The migraine's lifting too but food is needed to kick it into touch.

He lets himself out onto the street and starts salivating

at the spicy aromas seeping out of the Indian restaurant next door. A café stop is required for a sandwich and coffee. The sun's stretching long shadows across the pavements. Rainwater gurgles out the drainpipes and drips off the shop awnings. He checks the date on his watch. It's the 23rd. *Aye, in three days' time I'll be back in The Burgh. Back in Leith. Back home.* The new school term is just round the corner. So is the other Jez Guinness; the quiet, respected schoolteacher. The guy next door. The killer's back in his cage.

He's just finished eating when his mobile beeps.

Runnin wee bit late. Just come 2 flat. Hair 2 do! Xxx

Ok. Will do that xxx

He saunters up the street towards her flat, as casual as a double murderer could be. As he looks in a shop window, a car passes, beeps its horn then pulls over. It's Savage and he's lowering the driver's window. Before Jez can greet him, he says:

'Have you heard?' He looks straight at Jez, all serious. Shock surges through him like a blast of electricity.

'Heard what?' he responds, struggling to keep fear out of his voice. He prays he's not gonna tell him that a body's been found up the river. *Don't say that, Savage. Don't fuckin' say that to me.*

'Have you heard aboot Fifty?'

'Fifty... no. No, what... what's happened, Savage?' And now it's relief he feels.

'Get in,' responds Savage. Jez goes around the front of the car, gets in and looks at him.

'What's wrong, pal?' he asks, now fully back in control.

'Fifty's in hospital, Jez. Me, him and Cement Shoes went down to Bamburgh this morning. Just to fit a carpet at a holiday home we've got. He collapsed in the bathroom. We called an ambulance. He's in Berwick Infirmary now, like.' Jez is about to speak, then Savage says, 'Listen. This isn't public knowledge but… his cancer's back. It's in his pancreas this time.'

'Jesus Christ, Savage. I didn't know that. Oh, for fuck's sake. Who knows about it?'

'Until today, just me, Cement Shoes and Angie, but now he's in hospital it's no' gonna be a secret for long,' he replies.

'How long's he had it?' asks Jez.

'Aww, it's a few months now, like. We thought he was going to get over it. Like the last time, but…' he trails off, shrugs then slowly shakes his head.

'I thought he looked shabby at the funeral,' replies Jez. Then he asks the big question. 'Is it terminal, Sav?'

'Well, he doesn't know. That's cos he doesn't want to know. I think Shoes knows, but he's as deep as the fuckin' ocean so… but it's aggressive. The doc told him that, like.'

'Is he allowed any visitors?'

'No' sure, Jez. It's all happened so quick today. I'm going to ring Shoes later on. He's close with Angie so he'll know.'

'Okay, pal. Listen, here's my number. Could you ring me tomorrow? I'd like to visit him before I go back up to Edinburgh.'

'When you back up there, like?'

'Saturday, Sav.'

'Okay pal, I'll keep in touch.' And then Savage looks at him, as if for the first time, and says, 'Anyway, where you off to now, then? Eh? You're looking good, kid, smelling lovely, like a poofy wee rent boy.' He pats Jez's face, who knocks his arm away.

'I'm off on a date; and to answer your next question, never fuckin' mind who. Anyway, talking of smells, what's that smell in here, Savage? Have you got weed in this licensed taxi?'

Savage giggles like a wee boy. 'Hee hee, just picked up a stash of tidy Lemon Haze, ma man. Proper stinky stuff, this. Aye, that's why my taxi light's off, I'm no' for hire. Want some?' He peels back a photograph of his wife and kids on the dashboard to reveal a small compartment. He pulls out a bag of weed then digs into it with his muckle sausage fingers, pulls out a clump then puts it in an empty cigarette packet. 'There you go. Enough for a couple of joints. Now, take my advice as a top shagger, Jeremy. One joint before sex, one after. Okay?'

'Top fuckin' shagger, my arse.' Jez laughs and gets out, gives him the thumbs-up and mouths, *'Ring me tomorrow,'* then stands motionless and watches as he takes off through the Scotsgate. He thinks about Fifty. He did look ill at the funeral. Sallow! That's the word he was thinking of when they were all pissed at the wake. He looked *sallow*. Jez is shocked and worried about him. Fifty's one of his oldest friends. He wonders how Angie's taking it.

Jez walks up to the street then up the steps and onto the Walls. His mind moves on to what Elijah told him last Sunday when they walked along here. How Savage had taken him to Murphy's Beach. Aye, he'd talked a fair bit about crime scenes and modus operandi. Oh, and the Covenanters tying people to stakes and drowning them. And that's where Jez got the idea from. He'd learned it in a history lesson when he was about fourteen. Inspirational, it was! He repeats something Elijah said that morning: 'The killer certainly wanted your man to die by drowning.' *Well, you're right there, Mr Criminal Profiler. I certainly wanted Kev to drown. But you don't know why.*

He's meeting Elijah tomorrow afternoon in The Barrels so he'll leave a few red herrings for him to chase. Which is the main reason he befriended the man. It was a three-step process: gain his friendship, secure his confidence, then distract and divert him onto the wrong path and in the wrong direction.

And another thing. Josie saw him with a cop in the chippie today. So he's still sleuthing about. He told Jez in The Barrels that the killer lives locally and is probably blue collar. *Really? Well, do me a favour, Elijah, tell that to the cops. That case in London really messed with your head, didn't it? No wonder you were sent on gardening leave. Still, I can't help feeling sorry for you regarding that child killing. What a heinous crime, eh? Pure fuckin' evil. Killing the innocent should be punishable by death. It's justifiable.*

* * *

Jez's preoccupation with murder now has a rival. Fifty's illness is weighing heavy on him as he approaches Josie's front door. Then he sees her behind the glass panel so knocks quietly as he doesn't want to frighten her, but she still jumps with a start. She opens the door then points to an imaginary watch on her wrist and says, 'You're late, Mr Guinness!'

'I didn't want you to rush your hair, Josie. It's lovely to see you.' She pushes her face up to him and he kisses her lightly on the lips, careful not to smudge her lipstick. Then he stands back and takes in her long auburn hair, beautiful heart-shaped face and full lips. 'I think you look gorgeous, Josie.' She smiles then gives him a 'Mmmm' back, and pouts her lips in a Frankie Howerd way as if to say *"Oh, do you, now!"* Then she gives him an exaggerated once-over and he laughs out loud. It's a great ice-breaker.

'And it's lovely to see you too. I was just looking for a brolly behind the door. Do you think the rain's off for the night?' She peers past him at the sky, wiggling her dark eyebrows. It's blue skinny jeans this time, and a white floaty blouse. *Definitely a boho chick. And she likes a smoke. She told me last Sunday during our meal. Recreational of course.*

'Yeah, if that's the forecast you'd better bring one,' he replies. She disappears again then reappears with a small, collapsible brolly and pops it into her handbag. They link arms and set off.

'So, did you get your homework finished?' he asks.

'Nearly, nearly,' she replies breathily. 'It's the last year of the course so assignments are coming at me thick and fast now.'

'So, you're working in a chippie and studying for a diploma in nutrition.' And she gives a kind of "mmm" sound and they both smile. 'Well, forget nutrition tonight, Josie, cos in about an hour's time we'll be in the flicks, knocking back pick 'n' mix and Haagen Dazs ice cream. And definitely no broccoli.' She laughs then replies:

'Did you say Haagen Dazs? That beats a bunch of flowers any day! Oh, you know how to treat a woman, Jez! Now, this film. You said Michael Caine's in it.'

'Aye, and it's set on Tyneside so you'll recognise some of the places. It's a black and white cult classic. Probably one of my favourite films.'

'What? Michael Caine plays a Geordie?' she asks, furrowing her brow.

'Well, he is, but then he moved to London and became a villain. It starts with him taking a train back to the north-east to look for a murderer. Someone had killed his brother. And that's all I can tell you.' And he thinks, *Yeah, just like me. I took a train from Edinburgh down here to kill a guy who murdered my sister. And I had a funeral to attend.* Josie's mention of the word "flowers" takes him to another question in his mind. *That black rose at the funeral. Who put it there? Did it mean anything? Someone just might like black roses.* 'Anyway,' he continues, 'it must be hard, working a full-time job and doing all this studying.'

'It's just a case of managing my time. Truth is, I don't get out that much so it's okay. And I love my job. Fiona's a great boss and I'm meeting people all day. I love it,' she responds enthusiastically. 'I served your friend today. The black guy you were sitting with last Saturday. He was with a cop. Goagsie Mackay, he's often in the shop, that bugger. Looks too young to be a police officer, if you ask me. Aye, he's a rugby player, big guy. You probably won't know him, but he's local.'

'No, I don't, but I don't know many people here anymore. I joined the navy when I was eighteen and haven't lived here since.'

'Yeah, you were telling me about the navy last Sunday. Oh, I loved that meal, by the way,' she replies. 'Anyway, the… err… the funeral went okay on Monday, then?'

'Aye, it did, Josie. As well as could be expected, I suppose. There was a huge turnout. And the wake went well at The Brown Bear.'

'Yeah, there've been a few folk in the shop yesterday and today that were there. There's still no real closure though, is there? Not till they catch his killer. The police need to get their bloody fingers out! Like Goagsie today, eh? Maybe spend a bit more time solving this murder instead of sitting in the Cannon chippie with a holidaymaker, scoffing fish and chips, eh?'

Jez says, 'Aye, there were a couple of police officers at the funeral. Wacka Short and The Hammer were talking to them afterwards, but they seem clueless. Aye, they've even started interviewing his friends now. Wacka was in yesterday.'

'Was he? I saw him in his pick-up yesterday. Aye, with a muckle dog in the back. So you visited your mum yesterday, then?'

'Aye, I went to see the old boot yesterday,' he says, smiling. 'I had an easy day after the funeral on Monday, you know. So aye, we blethered and drank coffee all afternoon. Just catching up, really. Then she did a lovely meal and we watched TV last night. And blethered some more. It was late when I got back to the B&B. All very quiet.'

'Very quiet, Jez! Hi, welcome to my world!'

They arrive at the cinema. He buys some refreshments then they take their seats as the adverts start. He settles back. Josie takes some pick 'n' mix from the bag on his lap, then rests her hand on his thigh. He blushes in the dark, feeling awkward with her familiarity, like she's taking the lead. *You need to do something here, Jez.* He kisses her softly on the cheek. She turns and plants one square on his lips, and she's smiling when she's doing it. It's innocent, but a line's been crossed. His stomach somersaults with anticipation. And, in the circumstances, this is a perfect date. He's had a migraine and he butchered a man in a slaughterhouse last night, so he's happy to sit in the silent darkness.

* * *

It's after ten when they get out and it's warm and muggy, which suits Jez fine as a brolly can become a lethal weapon in a woman's hands. Well, maybe no' lethal. Stanley knives and hammers are lethal, in the wrong hands. They link arms and she leans on him as they walk slowly back to her place.

'Coming in for a coffee?' she asks, pushing the door open like she's *telling* him to come in for a coffee.

'Love to,' he replies.

She leads him along the corridor, then disappears into the kitchen. 'Just go straight through. I'll be back in five.' Jez walks into a large, wooden-floored sitting room. Prints adorn the wall and a Chinese cluster lantern provides warm, subtle lighting. It's cosy and relaxing. He turns on his mobile for any missed calls. There's a text.

Jez, got yor number from Sav. He told u about me. In hospital now. Tests tomoro. Come c me Friday. Fifty.

He reads it again. *Fifty wants to see me? Okay. It's time I saw him.*

Ok pal. hope tests go well. c u friday. Jez

Josie shouts through, 'Check out that box on the coffee table! It looks like a big book!' He opens it to reveal joint-making gear: weed, grinder, lighter and cigarette papers – and a large conical joint. She comes through with two coffees on a tray. 'Yes, that's one I made earlier,' she says with a smile. 'You said on Sunday you liked a smoke.'

'I did, and what a lovely surprise,' he replies, taking the coffee. 'Lovely place, Josie. Love that Chinese lantern over there.'

'I got that in Amsterdam a couple of years ago. You said you've been there loads, aye?' Jez nods and smiles. 'Aye, a wee shop on the Singel, by the flower market. Spark up, then, I'll put some music on.' He does, and it's strong gear and feels harsh on his throat before giving way to a soft mellowness which begins to spread slowly through him. 'Donna Summer or Grace Jones?' she asks.

'Oh, Grace Jones,' replies Jez and they both smile. Music on low, she joins him on the settee, takes the joint then eases back. A few tokes then she passes it over. They talk about the film, then it's music and past gigs. They were both at the same Sensational Alex Harvey Band gig at the Odeon in Edinburgh back in the seventies.

'Lovely weed, eh? Very relaxing,' she says.

'And that's what I like about weed, Josie. It enhances all pleasures.' He looks at her and says, 'You know, I've been wondering all week what it's like to kiss you properly.'

'Have you, now?' she responds, stubbing out the joint. He pulls her to him and she places her hand on his cheek. They kiss and it's slow, soft, almost tentative. It feels endless. They break off and look at each other; her eyes are bright and eager. He finds her mouth again, her open mouth. Their hands roam over one another, touching, teasing, caressing. The pace quickens; it becomes frantic as he undoes her blouse. A button pings onto the floor. Quickly now, they reveal themselves, lost in the sheer thrill of it all. It becomes urgent; their kisses hard and wild, her lips feel electric on his throat. He undoes her bra then runs his fingers up her back, then down and over her breasts. He teases her with his tongue and she quivers, eager to start. She drags him off the settee, undoes his belt then pulls down his jeans. He raises himself up as she tugs at his pants.

Jez pushes her onto a soft, woollen rug and slowly lowers himself onto her. Their eyes meet and she's done waiting. Her hands are on his chest and her feet round his legs; now they're up in the small of his back. He rolls her over so she's straddling him, and she's giggling in a gloriously dirty way. He massages her firm buttocks as she bites his neck and ear. She raises up slightly, then positions him, like a blade about to be sent to its scabbard. Jez thinks, *Stoned sex, man. It's so fuckin' good. Oh yes, oh yes, oh YES!*

Suddenly he thinks, *Oh fuck, no! Oh no, no. Not yet, not now!* Anxious sweat breaks out across his forehead. He immediately takes his brain elsewhere to repel the orgasm, to drive it back. Somewhere depressingly bad. Somewhere where he feels like total shit. And that's the only good thing to come out of the 2012 Scottish Cup Final, when Hibs were thrashed by Hearts. It works every time, but you have to hang a balance or you can go right off the boil. And that's not a good situation! Back in control he loses himself in the wonderful, rhythmic beauty of it all. He thinks, *What a night! What a week.*

CHAPTER 23

POLICE, PARROTS AND HOT GOSSIP

THURSDAY

Detective Chief Inspector Alan "Bawheid" Hazelwood breezes in to Northumbria Police HQ at around 10am on Thursday morning. It's been an hour's drive down from Berwick to Wallsend in North Tyneside. He's carrying a black briefcase containing file notes on the Kevin Devine murder.

The receptionist looks up. 'Hi, Alan. Long time no see. How's it goin' up there in the wilds of woolly?' There's no formality. DCIs are two a penny round here.

'No' bad, Joyce. No' bad. Aye, it's nice to be back in civilisation. Listen, I'm being interviewed by *North East News* at eleven o'clock. It's going out tonight and—'

'Aye, they phoned here earlier, Alan. They're gonna do it outside, they said. In front of the main doors. Ooh, how smart do you look, eh?' She gives him the once-over and thinks, *Aye, you're still a jumped-up little prick—*

'Aye… thanks,' responds Bawheid. 'Thought I'd make an effort. It's bloomin' warm in this uniform though.' He sticks a finger down his starched shirt collar and tugs it away from his neck. 'Listen, the Area Commander phoned me this morning before I left Berwick. Wants a word with me before the interview. Is it alright to go up to his office?'

'Hang on a minute, I'll check his diary.' She opens up a screen on her computer. 'Aye, he's in and got no appointments. Just go up.'

'Thanks, Joyce,' he responds, then sets off up the stairs. Following the Area Commander's surprise visit at the weekly briefing yesterday, the team put together a "media aide-memoire" regarding what information can be released to the press. Bawheid's got a laminated copy in his jacket pocket. And even though the investigation isn't making much progress, he's quietly pleased with his own management of the case. And the exposure gained from TV interviews is great for his promotion aspirations. He smiles the sickly smile of a toady sycophant. The sign on the door says: Chief Superintendent J. Mills. And beneath it, in upper case: NORTHERN AREA COMMANDER. Bawheid tugs at his collar again then digs out a hanky and dabs sweat off his brow. Then he knocks.

'Come in,' says a thundering voice from within.

Bawheid squirms with nervousness. He peeps his baldy wee heid around the door. 'Morning, Boss. You wanted to see me?'

Bomber Mills is at his desk, typing furiously at a keyboard. He looks up. 'Ahh ha, Mr Hazelwood. Come in, come in. Take a seat. I'll just finish this.' He points to a coffee table in the corner, with easy chairs around it. Bawheid sits down, opens his briefcase, removes the folder and places it on the table. He looks around his boss's spacious office and allows himself a pleasurable thought. *This could be my office one day. Aye, and I'd get rid of that shite straightaway,* looking at an aerial photograph of St James's Park football ground under floodlights. The phone on Bomber's desk rings and he pounces on it. 'Jack Mills,' he barks. A pause then, 'Phone me back in half an hour.' He slams the phone down then looks straight at Bawheid, who now senses a heavy atmosphere in the room. Bomber says quietly, 'That was your Crime Scene Manager.' He glares at Bawheid, whose stomach lurches with fear and panic. *What's the Crime Scene Manager doing talking to the Chief Super?* Bomber Mills rises from his desk and joins Bawheid at the small coffee table. Their close proximity unnerves the young DCI. 'What's that?' says Bomber, pointing to the folder on the table.

'It's my case file, Boss. Like a working copy, you know. Just so I can keep ahead of—'

'Your case file? Give me it here,' cuts in Bomber, with a beckoning hand signal. Bawheid passes the folder and watches as his boss begins to scan through it. He's glad he tidied it up yesterday afternoon; it's bang up to date and separated into relevant sections. The Boss is a stickler for order so he'll be impressed with the folder's arrangement. 'Okay, Alan, let's look at the crime scene information.'

'It's the third section in, Boss,' Bawheid replies, pleased at his instant response. Bomber opens the folder out and starts reading. Occasionally he checks back a page or two then carries on.

'So… in the evidence locker we've got the deceased's clothes, car keys, the stake and the cable tie?' asks Bomber.

'Yes, Boss. It's all there and—'

'How did you dry the wet clothes?' cuts in Bomber.

'Well… err… they… well, they were dried out in the morgue. Laid out on paper.'

Bomber nods once, without taking his eyes off Bawheid. Then he says, 'Good, good. And then who packaged them? I ask, because I looked at the evidence yesterday when I was up there, and the seals on some of those packages haven't been dated or initialled. And why were the deceased's underpants and socks placed in the same package? Was it your intention to cross-transfer the evidence?'

'I… I… didn't know that,' stammers Bawheid, wiping sweat off his hands onto his trousers, reluctant to meet Bomber's glare.

'You didn't know that? You're in charge of this damned investigation and you didn't know that?' replies Bomber, a blue vein visibly throbbing across his temple. 'A defence lawyer'll have a field day with this, eh? Ah mean, any DNA evidence, like blood, hair, whatever, is gonna be halfway across the fuckin' North Sea by now. So these items are all we've got. And it's a balls-up, Detective Chief Inspector.' Fear courses through Bawheid's nerves, like the chill of an icy wind. He begins to speak but all he does is blow out softly and shake his sweaty, baldy heid.

'Sir… I… I thought…'

'Let's move on,' responds Bomber, who hates being called sir. 'The stake that was recovered. It would still have moisture in it. Correct?'

'Yes, sir,' replies Bawheid quietly, whose confidence has vanished like snow in the sun.

'Then why wasn't it dried out first, then placed into a paper evidence bag, Alan? As you did with the victim's clothes. It looks like it was placed straight into a plastic container at the scene. Ah mean, any moisture trapped inside that plastic box will produce organisms that contaminate evidence. So, you tell me, why wasn't it dried out first?' says Bomber in a slow, clinical voice. Bawheid looks at his superior officer. The silence is heavy. Bomber continues, in a softer voice this time. 'Alan, we only get one shot at a crime scene. We don't get a rehearsal. One shot.' He lifts a finger to emphasise his point. Just then a tannoy message booms out: 'Could DCI Hazelwood report to the main reception. DCI Hazelwood.' The two men look at each other. Sweat glistens on Bawheid's forehead.

'That'll be for your television interview,' says Bomber. 'Don't mess *this* up.' He rises and returns to his desk. In silence Bawheid places his folder back in the briefcase, gets up and leaves. He was going to tell his boss about the new lead he's announcing. He was going to show him his aide-memoire. He walks along the corridor feeling sick and crushed. His starched, white shirt sticks to his back with cold sweat.

Bomber Mills dials a number. It's answered immediately. 'Detective Superintendent Johnson,' says the voice at the other end.

'Hi, Callum, it's Bomber here.'

'Morning, Boss. How can I help you?' replies the Detective Superintendent, sounding bright and breezy.

'I'm putting you on standby, pal,' responds Bomber.

'Standby, Boss?'

'Aye. The Kevin Devine investigation, up in Berwick. It's not going well. They've made bugger all progress and I've found out there're contamination issues with the evidence.

Last thing we needed. So… I'm thinking about replacing Alan Hazelwood as the Senior Investigating Officer. I thought he was ready for a case like this, now I'm no' so sure. And I'm looking at you, Callum. But if you replace him, pal, I'm telling you up front it's a dog's dinner of an investigation right now.'

'I'm fine with that, Boss. The further up the ladder you go in this job, the bigger the problems get,' responds Callum. 'I know the local press are having a field day with the lack of progress.'

'Listen, Callum. Keep all this under your hat for now. But I'll be looking to appoint you early next week. What you doing on Monday morning?'

'I'm on duty and at work here,' responds Callum.

'Oh, that's good, pal. Come up to my office first thing for a coffee and a blether. I'll brief you fully then. Is there anything you need to know now?'

'Erm… will Alan still be involved in the case?' asks Callum.

'Probably not. If I have my way, he'll be back on the beat somewhere down Mackem land, because he's ballsed up this investigation big time. And because of that, we may never get to the bottom of this case. So, be prepared for that. Which means we've still got a killer running loose in Berwick. Aye, before you say it, you're getting a right pig in a poke here. Will you take the job?'

'I'll take the job, Boss.'

'Okay, Callum. Have a good weekend and I'll see you Monday morning.' Bomber Mills hangs up the phone and walks to the window which overlooks the car park at the front of headquarters. He dabs his forehead with a hanky then violently sneezes into it. The TV company is setting up for the interview. Then he sees Bawheid heading towards them. He's walking unsteadily, like a blind man feeling his way.

* * *

Elijah Bootle concentrates hard on his leaving routine. Taps off, windows closed except the top one, and his room door's locked before going downstairs. Or is it? He goes back up and checks, then back down the stairs again.

'Mr Bootle! Mr Bootle!' Elijah stops at the front door. 'Mr Bootle!'

'Yes, Mrs Barraclough?' he responds, hesitantly. He's sure he just saw his landlady up on the first floor with a pile of laundry in her arms. He walks back in and pushes open the door to the front room from where he heard his name called. The big African Grey parrot sits there, motionless. As the penny drops, Elijah bursts out laughing and says, 'Hello! What's your name, then?'

The parrot replies, 'Mr Bootle!' in a loud, perfect imitation of Mrs Barraclough. Then it turns his back on him and looks out the window. Elijah chuckles to himself, then makes his way to the front door again. 'Don't forget your keys!' Elijah's still smiling as he lets himself out onto the street. He eyes up the parrot through the window. An upstairs window opens and Mrs Barraclough leans out.

'Mr Bootle!' she shouts down, and they both burst out laughing. 'I heard all that upstairs,' she continues. 'By the way, he's called Mr Whippy.'

'Mr Whippy,' replies Elijah. 'What a brilliant name.' Mrs

Barraclough is still looking down, hoping that Mr Whippy will talk to his new friend. But he's done with talking for now. Elijah looks up again and says, 'I'm just off up the high street for a walk.'

'Lovely day for it, Mr Bootle. All that rain yesterday is just what we needed. Freshens the place up a bit. See you later.' Elijah waves up to Mrs Barraclough then sets off down the street. And although he's just ambling along, he feels energised today. And happy. Five days in this lovely little town and the stress and fatigue he's felt for months is waning now – like an onion peeling off its skins, a layer at a time.

It's half-day closing on a Thursday and some of the shops are shut already. Elijah's disappointed. He preferred yesterday's market day bustle and bartering. He ambles down West Street to the flower shop that Goagsie mentioned to him in the chippy yesterday, only to find that it's closed too. He carries on down the narrow cobbled street towards the river and from here the water looks a brackish, brown colour. It's flowing fast too. 'All that rain yesterday must be washing a load of shit downriver, I suppose,' he muses out loud. He pushes his way up Bank Hill, then onto Castlegate, where Goagsie told him there's another flower shop. Approaching a young mother pushing a pram, he asks, 'Excuse me, can you tell me where the flower shop is on this street?'

'Oh, you mean Angie's. Aye, it's straight up there on this side,' she responds, pointing vaguely up the street. Five minutes later he pushes open the door to Angie's Flower Box, which prompts a bell to ding loudly. Elijah breathes in, savouring the earthy smell of damp soil and cut flowers.

Angie enters from the back of the shop and asks, 'Can I help you?'

'Hi there. Yeah, I'd like to buy a bouquet of flowers please. I heard this was the best flower shop in town,' replies Elijah, smiling.

'Thanks,' replies Angie and returns the smile, but it's laboured. She looks exhausted. Then she asks, 'How much would you like to spend?'

'Oh, about twenty pounds, I think. I'm on holiday and they're for my landlady at the B&B I'm staying at. Do you have bunches of flowers with a summer theme?'

Angie points behind him. 'Well, what about that rose and sunflower bouquet there, on the shelf?' responds Angie. 'It's called Sunset Bloom.'

He turns to see a bouquet of flowers in yellow, pink and coral. 'They're perfect! She'll love them. Yes, I'll have them,' he says with a flourish in his voice. As Angie wraps up the flowers, Elijah idly gazes around the shop. Then he spots something and says, 'You don't see many roses that colour, do you?' pointing to a bunch of black and red roses in the window. 'I mean the black ones in that bouquet there. I didn't know you could get black roses. I've not seen them before.'

Angie follows his gaze then nods in acknowledgement. 'Aah, you mean the Gothic bouquet. Yes, they go well with the red ones. Good contrast. A bit like your socks,' responds Angie, with a trace of a smile. Elijah looks down and he's got one blue sock on and one green one.

He looks up at Angie, laughs out loud, then replies, 'Hey, I'm in holiday mode.' A pause, then he asks, 'What do they symbolise? The black ones, I mean.'

'Death… and farewell,' responds Angie, her voice faltering. 'Or so they say. Usually for something like a gothic bride's bouquet. So, no... we don't sell too many.' The phone suddenly rings loudly. Angie's onto it in a second. 'Angie's Flower Box... Oh, Shoes, hiya. Yes... yes. Well, visiting times are two till eight so I'm shutting soon and going in. What time are you visiting?' A pause then she says, 'Oh, that's good, Shoes. Cos I don't want him left on his own for too long. You know Fifty, he likes a bit of company. And he's told me that Jez is going in tomorrow afternoon, then I'll visit him after work, so that's good. Okay, thanks, Shoes. Bye.' While this conversation is going on, Elijah takes a quick peep at the order book, which is open on the counter next to the till. The page goes back nearly a month and there's no sign of any Gothic bouquet sales. He pays for the flowers, wishes Angie a good day and leaves. He was going to tell her that he knew Jez and was meeting him later on for a drink but the telephone conversation seemed fraught and heavy, so he didn't mention it.

He heads back down Castlegate and into the old town. He smiles at the coincidence of the flower shop owner mentioning Jez's name. *Everyone seems to know everyone round here. Why would anyone be called "Shoes"? Yeah, Savage was right. Everyone in this town has a nickname.*

* * *

Elijah nearly trips over the white poodle as he enters Tommy's newsagents, which smells of warm ink.

'Maggie!' shouts Tommy, looking angrily at the wee dog. 'Get through the back now. Go on,' he says, pointing a thumb behind him. Maggie looks up at her human as if to say, *"Whae's he?"*

Tommy shakes his head, exasperated. 'You'd think it was

her shop, not mine. Now, how can I help you today? Lovely flowers, by the way.'

'For my landlady, actually. Mrs Barraclough. She owns the Oakwood B&B up the street. Could I have a quarter of lemon bon bons, please?'

'Oh, yes, Lily Barraclough. Lovely lady. And she knows everything about everyone in this town, I can tell you! Now then, bon bons, you say.' He climbs a stool and gets down a huge sweetie jar. Elijah's looking at the huge bundle of papers tied with string on the counter. 'Aye, they've just come in,' continues Tommy; 'it's the local weekly paper, the *Berwick Advertiser.* Want a copy to read with your sweets?'

'Okay,' replies Elijah, smiling at the thought of sitting in his comfy armchair by the window in his digs, bon bons on his lap and the nostalgic smell of newspaper ink on his fingers. He pays for his goods, steps out into the warm sunshine and walks back up to the B&B. Mr Whippy's on his usual perch and stares at him through the window. He lets himself in and walks along the corridor to the reception. Mrs Barraclough's sitting there, writing something down. She looks up, removes a pair of spectacles and says:

'Well, hello, Mr Bootle. How was your walk up the high street…? Oh, what beautiful flowers you've got there.'

'The high street was quiet today so I walked up to the flower shop in Castlegate. Here, they're for you, Mrs Barraclough.' He hands them over to her.

'They're for me? Oh, you shouldn't have, Mr Bootle. Oh, they're gorgeous. What lovely bright colours. I'll put them in a vase straight away. They'll look lovely here in the reception. Oh, thank you, Mr Bootle, you're so kind.'

'Oh, not at all. Not at all. I'm glad you like them. Well, I'm just popping in for a minute then I'm off down The Barrels to meet someone I've met here. His name's Jez Guinness, a local guy, although he lives up in Edinburgh now. He was down for the funeral of that man who was murdered recently. Yeah, I met him in the Cannon chip shop last Saturday and we got on well.'

'You said Guinness. Guinness? Now, let me think. Oh now, yes. Was his mother a teacher? She lives down West Street. Yes, I know her vaguely.'

'I can't remember if he mentioned that,' responds Elijah, furrowing his brow.

'Yes, she had two kids, if I remember correctly. A boy and a girl. Jeremy and… oh yes, I remember now, Mr Bootle.' She raises a hand to her cheek. 'Oh, it was a terrible tragedy. His sister died young, when she was a teenager… Mandy! That's her name. Aye, it was in all the papers. From memory, she went to a party and took some pills that killed her. It was an accident.' Then she lowers her voice and says, 'Supposedly.'

'Oh, what an awful thing to happen,' replies Elijah, genuinely shocked. He's getting the feeling that Mrs Barraclough wants to talk. Or better still, gossip. He tentatively asks, 'Supposedly? Why do you say that? Was there some suspicion around her death?'

Lily gives a furtive look around her, then crosses her arms and leans forward on the counter. Her voice drops another octave. 'Well, not at the time, Mr Bootle. She was from a good family, you know. Her mother was a teacher at the high school. She'd never taken drugs before. I remember the papers saying that. Aye, she took some pills. Oh, what are they called again…?

Aye, *destiny*, that's it. She took some destiny tablets and died.'

'Don't you mean *ecstasy*, Mrs Barraclough?'

'Ecstasy! That's it. Ecstasy. Well,' she says, pursing her lips before continuing, 'I always thought there was something odd about her death, Mr Bootle. Then I heard,' she says, looking around again then leaning closer to Elijah, 'keep this to yourself, but *I heard* on the grapevine, oh, this was years later, that it might not have been an accident at all. Aye, there were some dodgy folk at that party, apparently. Druggie types, you know.' Mrs Barraclough's tongue feels looser talking to Elijah as he's just a tourist, a stranger to these parts and people. He's not told her he's a criminal profiler from the Met. She continues on: 'Aye, my son Terry told me. He's been smoking that cannabis stuff for donkey's years to help his MS. I told you about him. Well, a guy who used to sell it to him was at that party. Oh, this was well over thirty years ago now, Mr Bootle, you know.'

'Believe it or not, that man was murdered a few weeks ago. Terrible, terrible.' She stands up straight and straightens her pinny. 'And murders in Berwick aren't good for business, I can tell you that. Well, I hope you enjoy your afternoon out, then. I'll just go and put these beauties in some water. And thanks again.' She bustles off through a back door behind the reception. It's been a long time since anyone bought Lily Barraclough flowers.

Elijah slowly climbs the stairs, absorbing what his landlady's just told him. Nigh on thirty years ago, Kevin Devine was at a party where Jez's sister died. He's meeting him in a couple of hours. Two steps from the top he suddenly stops and stands there, motionless. His stare glazes over as he has an anchoring thought. The profiler's mind becomes still. Thoughts "zone in" and begin to join up and connect. The focus is intense. He grasps the bannister and steadies himself. A mind map is forming. *Mandy Guinness. Drugs. Kevin Devine. Murder.* He walks quickly to his room. In a drawer in the desk he pulls out Jez's profile on Kevin. He scans down and sees the words in Jez's handwriting: *Used to like a drug.* So, Jez knew about Kevin's drug-related past.

He stands motionless and looks out the window, across and up to the red roofs over the street. His eyes flit back and forth, as if looking for a door into a hidden room. He licks his dry lips. Then a thought comes to him. Straight at him, like a sniper's bullet. He cries out loud, 'Oh Christ, no! Don't tell me that. Don't tell me that!'

CHAPTER 24

THE WALLS AGAIN

THURSDAY

Elijah Bootle stands on the Walls above the Scotsgate, looking down on the town. It's like an arena and he's up in the stalls. There's no one around and he starts to talk quietly to himself. 'Well, here's a story for you, Elijah. Once upon a time an unassuming criminal profiler and a likeable maths teacher set off together on a journey of discovery. Along the way, the former begins to realise that the latter could well be a cold-blooded killer.' He shakes his head at the utter absurdity of it all.

His mind rewinds to last Sunday when they'd walked round the Walls together, when he'd told Jez he'd been to Murphy's Beach after seeing the appeal poster on the police station window. And how Jez had tried to put him off the scent, telling him he should focus on his own problems instead. And Jez knew about the Covenanters too, although he pretended to be vague about it. *But surely he wouldn't go to the lengths he did in getting me the autopsy report if he was the killer. Why try and help a criminal profiler when you're the murderer? Why – because he's a very clever bastard playing a very clever game. With me. You fucker. Like I need this.*

Fuck's sake. If that's the case then my profile is so wrong. Blue collar, manual worker, lives locally, my arse. Christ, has the London child murder affected my professional reasoning too?

There's something else nagging at his vulnerable mind. Something Goagsie said to him yesterday. He mentioned that Jez had received a serious head injury many years ago. It's well documented that brain damage can cause people to act like psychopaths – to act in defiance of the laws of society. And vengeance can be a form of justice to psychopaths, who play by these different rules to the rest of us. They take revenge because they feel the law will not do justice. They take revenge because it's personal. It's about getting even, whereas justice is about being fair.

Do I speak to Goagsie? What'll I say? I mean, at best it's only conjecture and speculation. There's nothing on Jez regarding Kevin Devine's death. Nothing. I might be making a complete fool of myself. And that'll do your self-esteem a pile of good. Not.

Hey, it's not on my manor. I couldn't care less. Why should I move this investigation forward? I've got enough on my plate as it is.

He looks up at the town hall clock and realises he's meeting Jez in twenty minutes. The atmosphere's going to be surreal. He feels two-faced, duplicitous. He sets off, thinking, *Why should we try and punish people under laws laid down by civilised society when some people choose to live in an uncivilised way? Why shouldn't we try and punish them in an uncivilised way? If some humans choose to live like sub-humans then let's treat them like that, like rabid animals. Rapists and child killers, for instance.*

His mind flashes back to Hayley. Abducted, raped, blinded, murdered. She was eight years old. These dark thoughts are like a ship's stern light – illuminating only his past. He knows now that the only way to cure him of his post-traumatic hell is to solve the London crime. He has to be the one.

CHAPTER 25

NEMESIS APPROACHING

THURSDAY

'Do I look like a murderer?' Jez moves closer to the mirror and stares into his cold blue eyes. 'Is this the face of a man who's battered two men to death? Eh? Caved their skulls in with a hammer? Eh?' He smiles and watches wrinkles form around his eyes. 'Fuckin' no way. Look at you, man. You're Jez Guinness. A maths teacher. Dutiful son. Wouldn't hurt a fly, you, would you, now?' The smile fades out, replaced by a serious expression, as if he'd been asked the question by a detective. 'No, Officer. Of course not. Sorry, but I'm not your man.' He gets ready, and he's putting on his shoes when his mobile beeps. It's Josie.

Loved last nite. Movie, food, you! Xxxxx

He punches in a response. Loved it 2! Will ring u later. Meet for coffee tomoro? Xxxxx

Love 2! Speak later xxxx

He'd left her in bed this morning. And he'd walked back down through the town wearing a contented smile. The B&B was still serving breakfast when he got in so he'd scoffed down a "full English" and blethered to Lesley about the film he'd been to see last night, with 'a friend'. The conversation had moved onto favourite films. When he'd told her his was *Sexy Beast* her cheeks had coloured slightly, then she'd nodded and said, 'Sounds interesting. I must see it.' Hers was *Silence of the Lambs.* Masks, eh? We all wear them. Lesley's is a mask of respectability. Jez wears the mask of a law-abiding citizen. Hannibal Lecter's was a prison guard's face.

The *Berwick Advertiser* had dropped through the door as he'd left the breakfast room so he'd claimed it, poured himself another coffee and spent the rest of the morning in the sitting room.

He steps out onto Bridge Street as seagulls scream about overhead, diving like meteors onto a ripped-open bin bag. A couple of waiters from the restaurant next door run out onto the street and chase them, but the huge, ugly birds just seem to hang in the air above. Seagull shit splatters the pavement, so he crosses over and makes his way along to The Barrels on the corner. He thinks about last night at Josie's and a smile broadens across his face. 'Hey, this is "post offence behaviour", Elijah.' His mobile rings and CD's name pops up.

'Hi, Chris. How's it hangin'?'

'Ahm hangin' well, as always, pal. Actually, ahm groggy as fuck. Had some munchy gear last night. Anyway, how's you? Shagging that landlady yet?'

'Oh, she's oot ma league, CD. She had a good look at you the other morning. I think she's single, if you fancy it. I gave that report to the guy I was tellin' you aboot. The criminal profiler.'

'Well, why don't you give her ma number, then. I'll work ma charms on her. Anyway, I'm sitting here with Fish Heid and we couldn't remember when you're back up the road.'

'Saturday, CD. Train home on Saturday. Why? Are you oot on Friday night, like?'

'As always, Jez, as always. We'll be in The Brewers so see you there, pal. Oh, by the way, remember that Fatlad Owens? He was at the funeral. Remember, Wacka was going to batter him at the wake. Well, he went to work on Tuesday and he's no' been seen since. Fish Heid heard this morning when he was gettin' some supplies on the trading estate.' Jez thinks, *Okay, we're at Step 1 – he's officially missing. Good that it's taken two days before anyone's noticed. Very good.*

He mentally steadies himself, then replies, 'Wacka does put the fear of death into people, CD. He's probably done a runner somewhere. Anyway, see you Friday night, pal.'

'See you there.'

CD's news about Fatlad's disappearance kicks him up a gear. Not scared. Let's face it, this was inevitable. More like nervous excitement as this'll start the police investigation. They'll be asking questions. Where was he last seen? Who was the last person to see him alive? Phone records, that sort of thing. Nervous energy fizzes down to his fingertips. He checks his watch and walks into The Barrels. The dark, quiet atmosphere feels calming, in contrast to the bustling brightness outside.

'Jez!' He looks around and there's Elijah, at the bar. 'Amstel?'

'Cheers, Elijah.' He takes a seat in the snug where they sat last Sunday. Elijah approaches from the bar with two pints in his huge hands.

'Are you just in?' asks Jez.

'Yeah, first pint, mate.' Elijah settles down opposite him.

Jez raises his glass and says, 'Cheers. Well, I'm looking forward to this.'

'Cheers,' responds Elijah.

They clink glasses and, as Jez takes a sip, he checks him out. *What does he know? Is* he *wearing a mask?* He says, 'So… how's the holiday going?'

'Oh, it's goin' great. I *love* this little town. Lovely place, full of friendly people. Great walks. History. What more could you want? Oh, and lovely beer.' Elijah takes a pull on his Orkney Dark Island. 'And… yeah, it's done a lot for my state of mind. I told you why I had to get the hell out of London. Well, I'm in a better place now.'

Jez nods and answers, 'Good. I'm pleased to hear that, Elijah. Cos you looked troubled talking about that murder in London, pal. So… you're here for a fortnight, aren't you? Well, I hope there's enough to keep you occupied.'

'Oh, I think so, Jez. I'm certainly in no hurry to go back. Anyway, I feel I'm just getting to know the place. And I'm getting to know the people too. I mean, here I am, having a pint with you and I've only known you five minutes.' He laughs then takes another swallow. 'Yeah, you've become a friend although I only met you a few days ago. Shame that what got us together was the murder of your friend.' As he looks at Jez there's a mild intensity in his stare, eyes looking right at him. Then he says, 'So… what *you* been up to? Since the funeral, I mean.'

Jez nods, then replies, 'Yeah, the funeral went well, I suppose. In the circumstances, you know. I was dreading it in a way cos Kev's killer's still out there. So it's hard to move on, you know. But all in all, a decent send-off and the church was packed out. So, what have I done since then? Tuesday I was at my mum's and, oh, I was out with that girl from the chip shop last night. Took her to the pictures. She calls it the flicks.'

Elijah smiles and runs a hand through his hair. 'Very good. Very good. And how's your mum doing?'

'Oh, she's fine. Just back off her holidays. Thought I'd have a list of jobs to do but no, nothing.'

'Oh well, there's a result, mate. Maybe someone else has done them. Do you have any brothers or sisters?'

'No.' Again Jez senses him looking right at him. 'No, I don't.' There's a momentary silence. It feels awkward. Does he know about Mandy? 'Anyway,' Jez continues, 'was the report any help to you?'

'Yeah. Pretty helpful, yes. It gave me a starting point. And your profile. So I spent a bit of time yesterday going through it all. Lovely day yesterday, eh? Anyway, I made some notes.' He leans back and digs out his notebook. 'Bloody pockets are so tight, I must be piling the weight on! But who the fuck cares?! I'm on holiday.' He lays the notebook on the table then takes another drink. Jez does too; his mouth's dry. He looks at the notebook, then at Elijah.

'So…' says Jez, smiling, 'what's your take on it, then? From a police perspective.'

'Well,' Elijah responds, 'I'm a criminal profiler, not a detective, although I've enjoyed this stab at amateur sleuthing regarding your friend's murder, Jez.' When he says the word 'Jez' he looks right at him again. There's a charge in the air.

'What attracted you to becoming a criminal profiler, anyway? I've not asked you that.'

Elijah puffs out his cheeks. 'I've always been interested in the subject of crime. And we have to have a bit of crime, you know. It means we live in a free society where people make decisions of their own free will, even unlawful ones. Show me a society without crime and I'll show you a sick society. North Korea, for instance. As for the crime of murder, well, I've always been fascinated by people like us, me and you, and people who kill.'

Jez responds, 'Men are violent, Elijah. I watched *Mutiny on the Bounty* a while back, you know, with Mel Gibson. I mean, they were living in paradise, for fuck's sake, yet still ended up killing each other! What's that about, eh?'

Elijah smiles then takes another pull on his pint and sets it down. 'Oh, that's a lovely ale. Anyway,' he says, opening up his notebook, 'this is my take on it. You have to remember what a criminal profile is, Jez. It's not an exact science. More like an educated attempt at identifying a type of person that commits a type of crime. Murder, in this case. It's like a biography of personality and behavioural characteristics.'

'Aye, but what sort of process do you use? Like, where do you start?' asks Jez, shaking his head, as if it's all beyond him.

'I use mind maps first, just to get it roughed out in my head. It's rarely 100% correct so there'll be the odd error in here,' he responds, tapping a finger on his notes. 'But,' he continues, 'as the years go by my knowledge and experience grows, so there shouldn't be many. Sooo… Oh, and by the way, after I finished it on… What day was it now? Tuesday. Yes, Tuesday. I went down the police station and spoke to a young detective there. He's working on the case. It's his first murder. I met him again yesterday and he showed me the crime scene photos.'

'Yeah, Josie, that girl from the chippie, she said she'd seen you and a cop in there yesterday. So, you've seen the crime scene photos? What were they like?' He thinks, *My God. You've seen my handiwork. This is close to home.* His feet start to sweat. He needs to hold this together. Paranoia hovers over him.

'Oh, they were brutal to see. Grim viewing. The violence was... well, it was extreme, man. It was vicious. Whoever murdered this man really hated him. I'm glad I'd eaten *before* looking at them.' Their eyes meet momentarily, then Jez says:

'So... did they help you?' He's looking right at him, trying to sound as normal and casual as possible. He wants to hear his views. He wants to see that profile. He wants to see Elijah's mistakes and focus on them in order to divert and distract him and the police, although there's nothing to link him to Kev. Or Fatlad.

'Yeah, they were very helpful, although keep all this to yourself. Cos I work for the Met, I'm not sure if a rookie detective showing them to me would go down well with the senior investigating officer.' He lays his forearms on the table and looks down. 'Anyway, this is what I've got. Our killer is male and he's acting alone. He's a local guy with a sound knowledge of the area around the murder scene.'

'Well,' Jez cuts in, 'there're a few housing estates at that end of town near the beach: Highfields and Newfields, so—'

'By local,' interrupts Elijah, 'I mean he's a Berwick man. A townie. The victim knew his killer and don't be surprised if *you* know him too.' He fixes Jez with a look. 'And the killer knew his victim went sea fishing there on a Friday evening.' Jez focuses on looking relaxed, looking normal. But he can hear his pumping, thumping heart. Elijah looks at his notes, then up at Jez again. 'So, as I said in here last Sunday, my guess is it's a friend or family member. Or work-related. And I think he's blue collar as he seems comfortable working with his hands. Electrician, joiner, engineer, that sort of job. He'll be late thirties, early forties. And he's white.' He takes another sip of beer then scans down his notes and says, 'Our killer's a clever bastard, Jez. Oh, he's clever. Forensic evidence is destroyed when a body's left in water, especially tidal water. And he came well prepared. This was a premeditated and carefully planned murder. So, he's an organised killer.' His glance lingers a split second too long. Jez's heart rate's flying now and he concentrates on breathing it down.

'There's often three separate scenes to a murder. First scene,' says Elijah, raising a finger in the air, 'the killer approaches the victim; second scene,' another finger, like he's telling Jez to fuck off, 'the murder itself; and the third scene is where the body is disposed. In this case those three scenes merge together. Like a one-stop murder shop. So the killer spent next to no time with his victim. He approaches him, kills him and leaves him in about, what? Five minutes, maybe less. Yeah, I'm impressed, mate. Very impressed.' Elijah drains his pint in one then sits back in his chair looking right at the killer.

Jez puts a hand up and says, 'You said a profile features behaviour characteristics? What about previous behaviour. I mean, this man doesn't just wake up one morning and decide to kill someone. Wouldn't he have a violent past?'

'Almost definitely. Unless it's a crime of passion. You know, a one-off killing with no repetition. And you know something, it could be that. A husband being cheated on, a family member being abused, something like that. And if it was, then this profile could be worthless. Cos even the most mild-mannered of men can kill. Believe me, I've seen it. Revenge can do that to a man. Or a woman.' Jez thinks about that last comment. *Do you know? Do you fuckin' know? Are you playing a fuckin' game with me?* Then Elijah says, 'My view is he hasn't killed before and he won't kill again. A one-off. So it's for a reason. I'm talking revenge as a motive here.'

Jez looks down at the notebook then up at Elijah and asks, 'Is that why Kev was so badly injured? You know, revenge can make you mad with rage.'

'Can it?' Elijah glances up, then at his pint, like he doesn't want to look at him. The atmosphere's becoming taut, like a drawn bow. 'The injuries were all planned. Head wounds to knock his victim out. Legs smashed up to immobilise him. Makes it easier to drown a man with those injuries. Yeah, the killer treated his victim like a prop so he could send a message. What was the message? That's the big question. He's not mad with rage. He's just mad.' He takes another sip and their eyes meet over his glass. Then he smiles, but it's not genuine. Jez knows it's not.

Jez finishes his pint and wipes his mouth, then says to Elijah, 'So he lives locally, has a violent past, he knew Kev's movements and he's a manual worker. Late thirties. Is he married?'

'Married or divorced,' replies Elijah, then he sits forward so he's close to Jez. His clothes smell of warm wool and soap.

'Well,' Jez replies, 'your profile narrows down the field, but it still leaves a helluva lot of suspects.'

Elijah's still close and his brow furrows when he asks, in a slow deliberate way, 'Why was he drowned?' Jez looks hard at him. Emotions flash across his companion's face. Sometimes quizzical. Sometimes intense. Now it is something else.

Jez shifts in his seat then says, 'Well, I dunno. I'm a teacher, not a copper,' and he's pleased at the steadiness in his voice. Elijah sits back and gives himself a little smile, then says:

'That young detective I met. He mentioned a group of guys that the victim knew all his life. The BUNDIG. My profile fits most of them, he said.'

'Well,' Jez responds, 'I've known those boys most of my life. Yeah, there's some troublemakers among them but they're not killers. But hey, I've not been around them for twenty odd years so what would I know, eh?' He shakes his empty glass. 'Another pint?'

'Yeah, I'll have another.' Jez takes Elijah's glass and senses the rising tension between them. On the way to the bar he looks around at him but he's just sitting there, staring out onto the street. He orders the drinks and mops his brow with a beer towel off the counter.

The barman serves him then says, 'Aye, it's a hot one today. Err, that'll be six pound ninety, ma haga.'

As he pays for the pints he hears Elijah laughing quietly, like he's just got the punchline of a joke. He's shaking his head as Jez returns to the table and places the pints down. Elijah's smile feels false so Jez asks, 'What's so funny?' He's nervous now, his stomach's churning.

'Just having a good time, mate. That's all.' He sits down and Elijah's still looking at him with an odd smile on his face. Jez tries to look normal, but Elijah's eyes don't leave him. His smile slowly fades and they sit in silence and look at each other. There's a pain forming behind Jez's right eye. Bad sign. He thinks about that fucker who smashed a beer mug in his head. He changes the subject in his mind.

'So… you're a Palace fan, eh?'

'They're the pride of South London.' Elijah's expression doesn't change.

'I prefer Charlton Athletic, myself,' Jez responds. 'Charlton Covered Is Deadly. Well, that's what I heard. But you don't want to believe everything you hear, do you?'

Elijah leans forward on the table and quietly says, 'I'll tell you what I did hear. That *you had* a sister. She died young. At a party. Something to do with drugs, *I heard.* Kevin Devine was at that party. *So I heard.*'

'Is that what *you heard*?' Jez nods and holds his stare. An electric current jolts through his legs, right down to his feet.

Elijah's eyes don't leave him. He says, 'You asked me if the autopsy report helped me, yeah? Now I'm asking you if it helped you? I ask cos the envelope it was in had Apple House embossed on it. That's where you're staying, isn't it? You told me last Sunday when we walked the Walls. Why would you wanna read a fuckin' autopsy report?'

Jez sits motionless. You could cut the tension with a craft knife. Then he says, 'Morbid curiosity, mate. He was one of my oldest friends. I think anyone would be tempted to read it.'

But Elijah's past listening. He leans forward and lowers his voice. 'And I'm gonna tell you something else. Whoever left that black rose at the victim's grave knew who killed him. As a matter of interest, where were *you* on the night he was murdered?'

'At home,' replies Jez, shrugging his shoulders. He rubs his temple and takes a huge pull on his pint and thinks, *I'm fuckin' outta here in ten minutes.*

* * *

The town hall clock strikes midnight. Its chimes are muffled by fog winding its way up the river. In places the fog's thick, like a solid grey wall, elsewhere it's like vapour. Upstream, past the three bridges, the river curves elegantly to the south. On its northern shore two men appear. They're carrying a wee inflated rubber dinghy and talking in hushed tones.

'Right, Bang Bang. Once it's in the water, I'll get in it and grab the oars. You just hold the fuckin' thing steady, awright?'

'I know, I know. Fuck's sake. Calm doon, Savage. We're fine. Right, can you see the fishing shiel on the other side?' He points out, over the silent gliding water. 'See it? Good, that's where you're heading.'

Savage hisses a whispered response, 'Ah can hardly see a fuckin' thing in this mist, man.' They push the dinghy out until they're knee-high in water, then Savage gets in, careful to avoid the net which is lying folded along the stern of the dinghy. He grabs the oars then looks at Bang Bang. 'Aye, once again it's me doing all the fuckin' graft. Aye, you just stay here, Bang Bang, and look pretty.'

'Shut the fuck up and think aboot your bath full o' salmon in aboot two hours' time. And we've already got a buyer.' Bang Bang checks that the net is folded properly then takes hold of one end. 'Okay, Sav. Once the net's paid out, get back over here sharpish to help me draw it in.' He gives the dinghy a gently push.

'Ah know the drill, Bang Bang. Give me ten minutes. Count them on your fingers. Oh, maybe not, you'll be screwed after six.' Savage rows off across the river, muttering to himself.

In the distance a tug makes "oooo" sounds. It's eerie. Now enveloped in thick fog he carries on until the net fully pays out, its leaded bottom dragging it down before it's swept round in an arc by the current. Savage urgently rows back over, runs the dinghy onto the shore and rejoins Bang Bang, who is now pulling hard on the net and drawing it in. It feels heavy. They look at each other and start giggling like a couple of kids. Savage starts the *Jaws* theme tune. "Di di. Di di. Di di di di di di."

Bang Bang bursts into stifled laughter. 'Fuck's sake, Savage. You're gonna need a bigger bath.'

Savage whispers, 'I hope we've no' got a seal in here.'

'Where there's salmon, there's seals, my friend,' responds Bang Bang, the sage of wisdom.

Soon they see fish thrashing about in the bosom of the net, showering them with muddy river water. And then they see it. A huge, grey seal, all tangled up.

'Fuck's sake, I hope it's no' taken a bite oot any of the salmon,' says Savage, sounding alarmed. They haul the remaining net onto the silty shore then approach cautiously with felling sticks.

'WHAT THE FUCK'S THAT?!' shouts Savage. Bang Bang lets out a primeval wail then both men turn, grab the dinghy and flee from the scene.

It's not a grey seal. No. It's the grotesquely bloated body of a man. A cadaver clothed in grey overalls and an apron. And he's smiling.

CHAPTER 26

A TOWN IN TURMOIL

FRIDAY

Berwick Upon Tweed is a town in turmoil. It's boiling like a pot of lentils. Another man has been found savagely murdered, washed up in a tangle of fishing net on the river's shore. Found by a dog walker about seven o'clock this morning, the body's still there. Scene of Crime Officers are on site now, searching for clues, taking photographs and collecting samples. Initial examination of the body suggests the victim was battered to death with a hammer. His face has been mutilated. Two murders in a month. Hectic shit.

* * *

The custody sergeant leaps out of his seat at the front desk and rushes to open the double doors. He looks anxious as he greets the visitor.

'Morning, sir.' He doesn't prefix his salutation with "good" because there's nothing good about this morning. In fact, everything's bad. Very bad.

'Morning, Sergeant. Where's DCI Hazelwood?' scowls Chief Superintendent Jack "Bomber" Mills, with barely a glance at the officer. He doesn't stop to talk; there's no good-natured chatter like two days ago when he visited the station.

'He's in the conference room, sir, giving an emergency briefing—'

'Thank you, Sergeant,' interrupts the Chief Super; and without breaking stride, he marches down the corridor. A thick blue vein pulses on his forehead. He's mad as hell.

The custody sergeant calls after him. 'Sir, err… we've got a couple of reporters in the yard and—'

'Tell them to wait,' growls Bomber without turning. He silently opens the door to the conference room, steps inside and stands there. The Major Investigation Team are having an emergency briefing. DCI Hazelwood's giving a presentation on an overhead projector. He's got his back to the audience and talks to the screen, so doesn't see his senior officer. The fluorescent striplight above him casts a bright white circle on his shiny wee heid.

Ah cannae hear a word he's saying, thinks Detective Goagsie Mackay and, like most of his colleagues near the back of the room, he's sitting forward, straining to hear Bawheid's dull Durham voice. *He's fuckin' useless,* thinks Goagsie and slouches back in his seat, arms folded. Bawheid turns to the audience and says, 'Okay, let's recap, shall we? One measure we could… err…' He sees Bomber at the back and falls silent. A moment passes. He looks at his boss like a condemned calf in a pen.

'Carry on, Mr Hazelwood,' orders Bomber, scarcely controlling the anger in his voice. Bawheid stands there, still as a statue. The atmosphere becomes heavy. Sweat glistens on his forehead.

'Err, well,' continues Bawheid, now stuttering, 'err… one… one m-m-measure, guys, to err… to increase visible policing would be to p-put livery on our unmarked CID vehicles. The public would… err… well, they'd see these vehicles and feel safer and… err, yes… yes, sir?' He dabs at his head with a hanky.

Bomber's arm is still raised as he asks his question. 'But if you emblazon our unmarked CID cars with the word "POLICE" in big, bloody letters, how can they be used for undercover tasks?' Without waiting for an answer, he strides down the central aisle to the front. Each row of cops looks up at him as he makes his way past. His heavy footsteps ring around the silent room. He gets up close to Bawheid and says quietly, like giving an order, 'There're a couple of reporters outside. Go and *deal* with them.'

'What'll I say, sir?' asks Bawheid in a pathetic voice.

'You're a Detective Chief Inspector, get out there and do your job,' hisses Bomber. And as Bawheid walks out he shouts after him, 'And I need to see you in your office in fifteen minutes.' He waits until Bawheid's steps have receded along the corridor. Then he looks out and over everyone. 'By the way, guys, if you ever need to speak to the media following a murder, remember the three Ps. Pity for the victim; praise for the emergency services; promise to resolve the case.' The keener guys, including Goagsie, are scribbling his advice down on notepads.

Bomber continues: 'Okay. You all know the situation. We have another murder. Another local man. Another death in water. I don't believe they're unconnected. I believe we have a double killer on our hands. As a result, I'm increasing your resources and I'm raising the investigation's profile by appointing Detective Superintendent Callum Johnson to take over the investigation. You all know him, and he's starting here next Tuesday morning, with DCI Hazelwood as his deputy. That's his official start date but expect to see him here later on today and over the weekend to start to get a handle on things. Okay?' He scans the room before continuing. 'On Tuesday all leave is cancelled. We'll meet here at ten o'clock sharp. You might see your duties changing. You might be working with new staff drafted in. At this point that's all I want to say. Does anyone have any questions?' Silence. 'Okay. I'm going up to DCI Hazelwood's office now to start the ball rolling.' And he marches out without a further word. He had the Chief Constable phoning him at home this morning in a rage, asking what the fuck was going on up in Berwick. And, as Northern Area Commander, Bomber Mills needs answers fast.

* * *

Jez found out this morning. Over coffee in the breakfast room at Lesley's. He was talking to the Dutch couple about barge holidays when the news broke on Borders FM at ten o'clock. Funnily enough the song on before the news was 'Beautiful Girl' by INXS and he'd been thinking about Mandy. A shock wave shot through him when he heard the words. He nearly gasped but forced it back down his throat. He wasn't expecting

Fatlad to be found for at least a few more days. The report stated that a body had been found this morning, washed up on the riverbank. The police were on site but saying nothing more than it's a middle-aged man and this is a murder investigation. The newsreader went on to say that this is the second killing in the small seaside town in a few weeks. A wave of cold fear ran over his scalp.

Lesley was clearing dishes from the table and she stood there shaking her head with a hand over her mouth, then said, 'I can't believe it. This just doesn't happen in Berwick. I *honestly* can't believe it. Not here.' The conversation moved from barge holidays in the Netherlands to battered bodies in Berwick. The Dutch couple didn't know about the first murder and looked genuinely shocked. The consensus around the table was that it was probably the work of one man and surely the police will have enough evidence to catch him now. And when the old Dutchman wondered out loud what the motive could be, Jez listened with fascination as they discussed the case. He wanted to know what three members of the public thought about his work.

He knows that Elijah visited the police station on Tuesday then met a young cop in the chippie on Wednesday. He's hoping his profile on Kevin's murder has worked its way into the police investigation. You know, a blue collar, manually skilled local man who works with his hands and has a violent history – so far removed from a maths teacher living quietly in Edinburgh. He felt safe. He expected to be back up in Edinburgh when Fatlad was found. Never mind, nowt's been spoiled and, in a way, he's enjoying being here as the news breaks – just to see and feel the reaction.

* * *

He's about to leave for the hospital when his mobile rings. All morning he's been dreading a call from Elijah to tell him he's worked out that he's Kev's killer and he's gonna turn him in. But Jez knows he doesn't have enough on him. And Elijah knows he doesn't have enough on Jez. Then he sees it's CD and relaxes a bit.

'Hello, pal. How's it goin?' he tentatively inquires.

'Jez, it's CD. Have you heard?' He sounds breathless.

'Aye, I have. It was on the radio this morning.'

'Jez. Listen, keep this to yourself, right. It was Savage and Bang Bang.'

'What?! They killed the guy?' Jez asks, wondering what the fuck he's talking about.

'No, man! They were oot poaching last night and he was in their net. The body was in their fuckin' net! Cos they were poaching they didn't call the police. They just bolted and left it there. Aye, it was found by a dog walker this morning.'

'Aye, the report said that,' Jez answers. 'How did you find out?'

'Bang Bang phoned me before. He's shitting hisel'. Listen, this isn't official but the word on the street is it's Fatlad Owens. He was at the funeral. Aye, the cops are at the slaughterhouse now where he worked. They've got the yard cordoned off. Fish Heid saw them there aboot an hour ago.'

'Fuck's sake, CD. What the fuck's goin' on, eh? This is mental.' He deliberately sounds confused and angry.

CD says, 'Listen pal, I've gotta go. I need to finish this rewire job today. Are you still oot tonight?'

'Aye, pal. See you in The Brewers.'

'See you then,' responds CD, and they hang up. Jez didn't tell him he was off to see Fifty in hospital as he didn't know who knew about his cancer. He leaves the sanctuary of his B&B and steps out onto the street. And although the sky is clear and blue, and the air warm and soft, he senses a heavy atmosphere. People are talking. Whispering. Speculating. Looking scared. Heads are shaking. As if a tidal wave of fear has swamped the town's inhabitants. But it doesn't need to be like this! If only they knew that the killer in their midst was only interested in those who killed his sister. And his work's nearly done. He walks up Castlegate towards the Infirmary, avoiding eye contact. Fifty wants to see him. And he wants to see Fifty.

* * *

The receptionist points him in the direction of the oncology department. Fifty's in a private room on the first floor, just past Ward 5. Jez takes the stairs and walks along a creamy corridor that reeks of medication. Fluorescent light bounces off the squeaky, tiled floor. The ward doors are open and, as he passes, he gets a glimpse of the life and death dramas being played out between patients and staff.

He enters Fifty's room and closes the door gently behind him. He's propped up on pillows with a drip from his arm to a machine on wheels. The yellow pallor in his face has deepened. Jez smiles at his friend and he smiles back and points to a chair.

'How you doin', son?' Fifty asks, in a paternal way, like he's more interested in Jez than his own welfare. Jez should be comfortable now. He's looked forward to this for months. But now his mind's turned to mince. Fifty's gaunt, feeble condition has shocked him. His eyes have sunk back into their sockets and look small and far away. He's got *Columbo* on the overhead TV and mutes the sound. Around the room are vases of bright flowers.

Jez breathes in noisily, then says, 'Christ, it smells like an oilseed rape field in here! Is Angie running doon the profits or what? How is Angie? Ah mean, about your illness?'

Fifty shrugs and smiles. 'She's looking at it as a diagnosis. Not an illness.' They look intently at each other in silence.

Then Jez whispers, 'Odd word to use for a beautiful plant, eh? Rape. It's Latin for turnip, you know. *Rapum*.'

'Only a teacher would know that shit.' Fifty laughs nervously and shakes his head.

'Listen, pal. Savage told me about your... diagnosis. He said it was aggressive. So, how *are* you doin? I mean, *really* doin?'

'Well, it's pancreatic cancer we're talking aboot here, pal. Hard to detect. No' like the first time, when ma bollock was the size of a fuckin' tennis ball. It's spread, like... I know that much cos it showed up on the tests yesterday. Is it curable? Ask me after ma chemo course.' He's talking like he's come to terms with it. Jez slowly nods as he digests this information. Another silence. He's ready now.

'You texted me, Fifty. You wanted to see me. What about, pal?' Fifty looks at him and Jez sees something in the man's face. Fear? Sadness? Maybe both. Jez reaches out and takes hold of his bony, yellow hand and looks right at him. Then he says, 'Fatlad Owen's deid.' He grips Fifty's hand hard.

'EH?! FATLAD OWENS'S DEID?!' Fifty shouts out like it's a question. 'Fuck's sake. When?'

'Tuesday night,' Jez replies.

'Tuesday night?! How did he die?'

Jez looks into Fifty's sunken black eyes and holds the stare. 'He died screaming.' Silence. Jez repeats, 'He died screaming, Fifty. Unlike ma sister, who was unconscious when she died. But you know all about that, don't you? Because you were there the night ma sister died, weren't you? All those years ago. And that's what you want to talk to me about... isn't it?' He pats his arm gently.

'Jez... listen... I didn't, I... *honestly*... I... didn't know... what happened that night. I'd left by... by then.' The words come out like a clumsy dancer, one step at a time. His sweaty hand tightens hard around Jez's.

Jez pats his arm reassuringly, then whispers, 'I know, pal, I know. Do you wanna know how I know? Well, I'm going to tell you.'

* * *

'At the back end of last year ma mam visited an old friend in hospital. This hospital, actually, Fifty,' he says, pointing a thumb behind him. 'Aye, she was on her deathbed so both of them kinda knew this was the last time. Must be fuckin' hard that, eh? Seeing someone for the last time. Like you're *never* gonna see that person again. *Ever*. I struggle with infinity, Fifty, so... err... WHAT YOU FUCKIN' DOIN?!' Fifty's trying to pull his hand away from him, looking as scared as a sinner on Judgement Day. Jez grips his cold skinny arm, then whispers, 'It's okay, pal. I *know* the truth. That's why you're no' on ma radar, okay? Okay?' He's that close to Fifty's jaundiced face he can smell him. It's pungent, like sour milk. It's the smell of death.

'So… this woman. She's got a secret, Fifty. Big secret. A secret she's kept for… oh… nigh on thirty years now. Cos it's been that long since Mandy died. At that party, back in 1986. Long time to be fuckin' deid, eh?' He's back on track and it feels cathartic. 'Aye, she'd grown up with my mum and didn't want to die with this secret, you see. So, she told Mum the truth. Like, one mother to another, y'know the score. She told her that Mandy was *never* a druggie, like the gossips in this town wanted to believe. You see, her daughter was at that party, Fifty, so she knew the truth, and a few weeks after Mandy died she blurted it oot to her mam. Her daughter couldn't live with the lie, y'see. DIVN'T FUCKIN' LOOK AT ME LIKE YOU KNOW WHAT THAT'S LIKE, FIFTY! Cos you *have* lived with it. Awright?' His finger's an inch from Fifty's nose. The rage is rising. 'I COULD FUCKIN' PUNCH YOU RIGHT NOW!' Fifty cowers back into the pillow looking like a frightened child. Jez lowers his voice again.

'I say party, but it was just six teenage lassies there. You know the sort of thing – cheap drink, music, dancin' among themselves. The girl told her mam that they'd all tried ecstasy before. Except for Mandy, like. She was an innocent when it came to drugs. True story. Anyway, one of them knew Kev was dealing pills so she phoned him and he turned up with Fatlad. And by the time they got there the girls were all pissed and partying hard, so they decided to hang aboot. Probably thought they were gonna get a shag. Pair of fuckin' chancers. Oh… and she said there was another boy with them, but he'd had cancer and was still on medication and he left early. He wasn't involved, she said.' He pats Fifty's arm.

'Anyway, some of the girls wanted Mandy to try it. Just once, like. But she wasn't into drugs, Fifty. No' her scene. So Kev and Fatlad thought they'd play the wide boys, eh? Trying to be a couple of clever cunts, eh? So they dropped an ecstasy tab into a drink and gave it to her. They thought it was funny. Like, they were smirking. They did that to ma sister. *Ma* sister. You'd gone by then so stop looking' like you're gonna shite yourself, like ahm gonna fuckin' throttle you, *awright*?' Jez jabs a finger into Fifty's chest and says, '*My* sister. *My* sister. They did that to Jez Guinness's sister.'

He gets up and pours a glass of Lucozade from the bedside table and downs it in a oner. His mouth's as dry as dust. Then he looks at his helpless friend and shakes his head like he's *so* disappointed in him. He lays his hands on the foot of the bed and shouts, 'YOU SHOULD'VE TOLD ME, FIFTY!' He wipes the back of his hand across his mouth then sits down again. 'Anyway, Mandy overheated, drank a load of water then collapsed. Kev and Fatlad took her through to a back bedroom and stripped her off, supposedly to cool her doon. The girls were that pissed by then they didn't know what the fuck was going on.' Jez breathes in noisily, letting his nostrils flare. He could kill someone right now, just thinking about it. The rage is rising.

'Then they interfered with her, Fifty. They touched her. They touched her up, when she was lying there comatose. Violated her. Did things. *My* sister. The girls knew that cos one of them went through to see her and saw them with their hands all over her. Then when they came back through to the party they were laughing about it. They threatened to kill anyone who grassed them up. Fatlad had a knife at them. Ah mean, those wee lassies were fuckin' petrified. Nice company you were keeping that night, Fifty. Eh? Threatening teenage girls. Pair o' fuckin' wankers, if you ask me. Anyway, after they left, the girls ran through to the bedroom and Mandy was unconscious so they called an ambulance. When the paramedics got to her they thought… well, you know, just another fuckin' druggie on a bad trip. Like it was an accident. Aye, Fifty, this girl told her mum everything, pal. Her mum thought it best to keep it to herself. You know, let sleeping dogs lie and all that shite. Until she met my mum, that is. In here, all those years later. And she told my mum. And my mum told me. About six months ago.'

There's a buzzing noise from the drip machine and they both look at it, like it's a distraction. Fifty whispers, 'I… Jez… I didn't know that. About touching her. I knew they'd given her drugs but I—'

'When did you find out?' Jez cuts in, repositioning himself as his backside's sore from the plastic chair.

'Kev phoned me. He didn't tell anyone else. None of the BUNDIG know. It was… it was the day after your sister's funeral.'

'SHE'S CALLED MANDY!' Jez shouts. 'MANDY!' Fifty visibly shakes with fear. Sweat glistens on his yellow forehead like beads of gold.

'It was the day after Mandy's funeral, Jez. He told me it was an accident, y'know. Meant to be just a… bit of fun. It was… I don't know if you know this but… it was Fatlad who mixed the drink.'

Jez nods slowly. 'Kev supplied and Fatlad plied. Two cheeks o' the same arse, if you ask me. Go on.'

'Well… well… I—'

'Well, why didn't you tell me?'

'WHAT WOULD YOU HAVE DONE, JEZ?!' He hisses at him in anger now. 'You would have fuckin' killed them on the spot. Wouldn't you? Because the rage would've taken over. And you'd have been caught. And you would have been put inside for life.' Tears begin to well up in his eyes. His cold, clammy hand seizes Jez's arm. 'Your mum lost one child. I didn't want her to lose another. I wanted to tell you, Jez, but it... like... telling you would have destroyed *your* life too. It... it was too much. It was too much. IT WAS FUCKIN' MASSIVE, MAN!' He's shouting and tears suddenly burst out of him and run down his face. And Jez sees, etched in his features, the burden of carrying this terrible secret.

Without thinking, he leans forward and takes Fifty in his arms. He holds him close and feels his warm tears on his face. Then Jez gets that big, old lump in his throat and now he's crying too. Two grown men: one filled with sadness and rage, the other filled with sadness and cancer. They hold each other tight and greet like two wee boys. And you know, Jez hasn't cried openly like that for years. And when they're all cried out they just hold on to each other and let the silence heal them.

Above, on the overhead TV, it looks like Columbo's got his man. Jez smiles at his friend, nods at the screen and whispers, 'I'm glad he doesn't work for Berwick CID.'

Fifty smiles back, wipes tears from his face, then says, 'And the longer time went by it... it just seemed like, not the right thing to tell you. You'd become a teacher, you were doing well and... I just didn't... I couldn't tell you. I wanted to protect you from the truth. But I *fuckin'* hated them, Jez.'

Their eyes meet and in that stare Jez sees it all. There's no anger now. Just a sense of love and brotherhood for his dying friend. He says, 'Is that why you sent the black rose? I saw you looking at it. At the funeral.'

He purses his lips, then nods once.

'Is that why you leave flowers at Mandy's grave?' He nods again, looking right at him. 'Mandy drowned, Fifty. That's how she died. The condition's called "dilutional hyponatremia". The ecstasy affected her kidneys, so all the water she drank was retained in her system. Eventually the pressure shuts down functions like breathing and heartbeat. It's like drowning. Horrible way to die. Ma mum had to identify her, y'know. Think aboot that, Fifty. I know I have. Anyway, Mandy drowns so Kev Devine drowns.'

Fifty, calm now, slowly shakes his head as he absorbs what Jez is telling him. Then he says, 'When I heard about Kev's murder, I thought of you straight away. Cos I knew if you ever found out, you'd do them in. I just knew. Because I've known you all ma fuckin' life, mate. I remember… I remember being at matches when it was all gonna kick off. You were always on the frontline. Always steamin' in. You were a nutter, mate. So I knew the rage was there. So… it's no surprise for me. Obviously, I didn't know aboot Fatlad's death until you just told me there and—'

'And he squealed like the proverbial stuck pig when I got to him three nights ago,' Jez interrupts. 'Dirty little fuckin' pervert, that he is. Was. I cut a big smiley face in his fat chops. He likes E that much he can turn up in hell with it. By the way, ah've covered ma tracks well. Very well. So don't you worry aboot me doin' time for this, pal. It's no' gonna happen.'

Fifty smiles at him, then takes his hand again and says, 'I hope you're right, son. Because you were chasing something far worse than the cops are.'

Jez looks at him, digesting what he said, then says, 'I like that, Fifty. I like that. They took an innocent kid's life. I didn't.' He senses it's time to leave. It feels right. 'I'm gonna go now, pal. Okay?' They say their goodbyes. And when their eyes meet it's like Fifty's looking at him for the first time. Or the last.

Jez lets himself out and a warm draught blasts along the corridor. Sunlight hammers on the windows. Sweat runs down his back. He thinks about Fifty. It's like he's fatalistic. He couldn't care less about the future. Like an autumn leaf, he's turning yellow and preparing to die. Cos he knows. He steals a look into a ward on his way out. There's a crazy old woman with wild hair in a hospital smock singing tunelessly. Maybe it's better being insane. Then you don't know you're dying.

CHAPTER 27

PLAYING AGAINST THE WIND

FRIDAY

Jez necked a couple of painkillers when he got in from the hospital, then pulled the duvet over him and slept soundly. Now he feels good cos he's showered and smells clean and fresh. He lathers up his face for a shave then stops and looks at himself in the mirror. 'Well, here we are again. Anything you want to talk about? No, not really, I'm just practising my post-offence behaviour, that's all. I'm gonna ask Josie if she fancies coming up to Edinburgh next weekend. If that's alright with you? Good.'

He finishes his shave then sits on the edge of the bed with a towel around him, clutching the remote control. *Look North*, the BBC's regional news programme covering the north east and Cumbria, is about to start and it's bound to feature Fatlad's murder. He feels scary excited. His left foot's twitching nervously with a spasm. The opening credits roll and show north-east landmarks like the Tyne Bridge, Durham Cathedral and Roker Lighthouse. The confident-looking presenter smiles at him, then says:

'Welcome to Friday's *Look North*. In tonight's headlines. A murder victim is *washed up* on the River Tweed in Berwick. It's the *second* murder to hit the holiday town in a month. North-east public sector workers have voted for further strikes in a dispute over pay and conditions. And two Sunderland men are home after being held in a Damascus prison for three months.' She turns to another camera and looks straight at him again. 'Hello. A *second* man has been found murdered in Berwick Upon Tweed. His body was discovered this morning, on the river's northern shore. He's been named as Fergal Owens, a slaughterman from the Tweedmouth area of the town. Chris Paterson is there and reports from the scene.' She turns to a screen and asks the reporter, 'Chris, what can you tell us about this discovery?'

'Yes, Carol. Police were called to the scene at about seven o'clock this morning by a dog walker who'd discovered the body of a man tangled up in fishing tackle on the shore, just behind me here.' The camera pans to the right and shows an area of riverbank. Jez thinks, *Christ, the current's taken him right across the river.* The reporter continues: 'He's been identified as Fergal Owens, a forty-eight-year-old local man. An initial police examination here this morning confirmed that he had been murdered, although no further information was given regarding how and when Mr Owens lost his life.'

'And when was he last seen alive?' asks Carol.

'He was last seen at his workplace on an industrial estate in the Tweedmouth area of Berwick on Tuesday night. Police have that whole site cordoned off while staff are being questioned and forensic teams look for clues. Although, at this stage, we don't know if the victim was killed there, or elsewhere, then dumped in the river.'

'And is it too early to say if this killing and the murder in the town a month ago are linked?' pushes the anchorwoman.

'Well, a senior detective I spoke to here, an hour or so ago, said it was highly likely that these two killings *are* connected.' Just then the fluffy looking sound mike appears in the bottom-right corner of the screen. Jez shakes his head. 'Fuckin' amateurs, eh? It's like *Creature Comforts*, this.'

'And how is the investigation progressing regarding the *first* murder a month ago?' asks Carol, keen to gather as much information as possible for the viewers.

'Well, the investigation into the murder of Kevin Devine a month ago is still ongoing, Carol. He was found on a beach in the town. He'd been viciously attacked around the head and body, then tethered to a wooden stake and left to drown. The police have yet to make a breakthrough on that case. But now that there's been *a second murder*, hopefully the investigation will get the break it needs. But tonight, it seems, there's a double killer at large on the streets of Berwick.'

'How dramatic are you, Chris, you fuckin' slaver?' Jez hisses at the screen.

Carol turns back to face him and says, 'Chris Paterson there, reporting on a second murder in Berwick.' There's a pause as she composes herself, then says, 'North-east public sector workers have voted…'

He mutes the volume, looks at himself in the wardrobe mirror and says, 'I'm the double killer. Me. Jez Guinness.' He has an urge to go and pull up the sash window, put his head outside and shout, '*It was me!*' He drops the sweaty remote on the bed and gets dressed.

* * *

Jez pulls the heavy front door shut with a quiet "snick" as the Yale engages. Josie rang last night to say she'd been asked to work a late shift today so he's going to pop into the chippie and have a coffee with her. Then it's up to The Brewers Arms. A couple of waiters from the Indian restaurant are blethering on the pavement as he passes. He wonders what's Indian for "There's been another murder!" He wishes he was a fly on the wall at Berwick Police Station. Two murders and a bat in hell's chance of solving either. No evidence, no DNA, no witnesses, no fuck all. And this time tomorrow he'll be back in The Burgh.

He's got time to kill so heads down Dewar's Lane to the harbour. The dingy, cobbled lane is narrow and the walls are so high they almost meet overhead. The rat-infested granaries on both sides are long gone, but it still stinks of yeast and damp corn. Emerging onto the harbour he enjoys the warmth from an orange sun in the west. He passes through Shoregate and up Hide Hill. It's still and quiet as he focuses on the pavement and pushes up the street's steep incline. He turns up Church Street and begins to salivate as the smell of frying oil and fish batter drifts down the street and towards him. Outside the chippie he pauses and looks up the street to Elijah's B&B. There's been no contact since they met in The Barrels yesterday. He's tempted to walk up to the police station to see if they've got a poster up appealing for information on Fatlad's murder but decides against it.

* * *

The Cannon chippie is, as always, a bustling, noisy hive of activity. There's a herd of teenagers mucking about at the counter, and above their noise the manageress shouts, 'ARE YOU ALL FOR TAKEAWAYS?!' Then she sees Jez and shouts over the top of them, 'AND WHAT DO YOU WANT, MR GUINNESS?!' She's laughing now.

'Err… haggis and chips, please, Fiona. And a coffee. And err… is Josie in? She said she'd be on a break about now.'

Fiona smiles and points towards the rear of the shop. 'Last booth on the left, Jez.' He gives her the thumbs-up and walks down the aisle. Josie sees him approaching and smiles, but she looks flustered. A young guy in the booth across is looking over at her and talking in a raised voice. He can hear it from here.

'… Aye, nae fuckin' wonder it's taking ages to get served. Lazy staff like her sat on her fat arse!' He turns to his pluky faced mate and laughs. Pure rage rises up in Jez's throat. He could split the kid's face open. He stops dead and stands there, staring right at him. Their laughter fades.

Jez walks up to their table and bends down, so he's close to them. He quietly asks, 'Awright, lads, how's it goin'? Awright?' Louder this time. 'Who were you talking about just now?' Jez looks right at him. 'Divn't look at your mate for help, son. There's nothing he can do. *Nothing!*' He stares at the other one. 'Is there?' He puts his arms around both their shoulders and says, ever so quietly, 'Speak to her like that again and I'll kick your fuckin' teeth out, you pair of scrotes. Think ahm joking? Try it now, then. Go on. Fuckin' *now*!' He stands up straight and glares at them both. Other customers are peering out from their booths. A pain throbs behind his eye. He could smash the fuckin' table in two.

'It was… just a joke, mister. We… don't want any trouble,' says Pluky Face, hands up defensively.

Jez returns the gesture, widens his eyes and says, 'Hey, kids, neither do I.' From across the aisle he hears Josie calling his name. He goes to her and kisses her lightly on the mouth, then takes a seat opposite and says, 'I didn't like the way they were talking to you, that's all.'

She takes his hands in hers and says in a whisper, 'That's all?! Christ, Jez, I thought you were gonna, you know, attack them or something. Are you… okay? You nearly… lost it there.' She smiles uncomfortably, as if to say, *'Do I know you? Are you the guy I was with two nights ago?'*

'Even softie teachers can get annoyed, Josie. But I'm fine, I'm fine, I'm brand new,' he responds, keen to play it down now as he's unsettled her. 'Aye, Fiona said you were down here. I'm having haggis and… err… chips.' His voice tails off as he watches the two boys leave their booth and head for the exit.

'Talk of the devil,' responds Josie, smiling now. Jez swivels round just as Fiona arrives at the table with his meal.

'Here you are, Jez. And you need fattened up, son. What do you think, Josie?'

Josie gives him an exaggerated once-over, then replies, 'He looks good to me. Very good,' blushing as she says it.

'How's your son, Fiona?' Jez asks. 'I was here last Saturday when the police came in and told you they'd arrested him. Oh, and he wanted a fish supper.' He's laughing now.

'Aye, well that punch-up ootside the pub's got him a day in court next month. That'll teach him. And fancy asking the copper to get him a fish supper, eh? What a nerve that laddie's got.'

Jez shakes his head, then says to them both, 'Well, the police have more important things on their minds just now. I just watched the news about that guy, Fergal Owens.'

They respond in unison, 'Aww, it's *unbelievable* what's happened.' They're both shaking their heads, then Fiona adds, '*One* murder in this town's been bad enough. But *two*?! It's actually hard to take in. We've been talking about it all day, haven't we?' She's looking at Josie, who replies:

'The *whole* town will be talking about this. Aye, it was on the radio this morning. Christ, this is Berwick, you know. A quiet Borders toon!' She shakes her auburn hair, which takes Jez back to Wednesday night in her flat after the cinema. On the soft, woollen rug.

'Aye, well, the cops need to get a bloody grip of themselves cos there's a nutter out there,' replies Fiona, straightening her apron. 'Anyway, enjoy your meal, pal. When you back up the road?'

'Tomorrow, Fiona,' replies Jez, digging a fork into his haggis. 'The new term starts in a couple of weeks and I've still got a pile of marking to do.' Someone shouts her name and she hurries off to the front of the shop. He eats his meal with Josie and they talk murders, motives and suspects. And it's funny cos he feels completely relaxed – as if the switchboard in his mind is wired up to detach himself from these crimes. The killer's someone else. The conversation moves on to food then education, then their date night at the cinema. She's pinching chips from his plate and looks happy and relaxed now. Over a second coffee he invites her up to Edinburgh the following weekend and she accepts.

Break over, she puts on her hairnet and they get up together. A stray wisp of hair hangs down her cheek and he takes his time to gently tuck it in. Then he takes her face in his hands and kisses her softly on the lips. They step out of the booth and walk down to the front of the shop. As he pays for his meal an espresso machine hisses at him, as if it knows the truth. Jez couldn't care less. Justice has been done. But that's his secret.

* * *

He walks up Castlegate as the sun's evening rays turn the buildings amber. Pausing in a hairdresser's window he scans his features. *Do I look normal? Yes. Do I look like a double killer who's got every cop in a fifty mile radius looking for him? No.* He convinces himself with a nervous smile and runs a hand through his hair. A group of young men are standing smoking outside The Brewers Arms. They look intimidating with their aggressive postures as he pushes through the grey haze of Lambert & Butler and enters the pub. Boom boom music blares over the buzz of pub chat. Adrenaline surges through his system as he approaches the bar. Focusing on post-offence behaviour, he whispers to himself, 'I'm Jez Guinness, a maths teacher from Edinburgh. An innocent man.' But his heart's pounding like a drum.

A barman with old-school tattoos serves him, and the glass

feels cold and heavy in his hand. Now accustomed to the dim light he peers through the crowd and checks out the alcove where the BUNDIG gather. Wacka's there, with The Hammer, Bob, CD, Fish Heid and Cement Shoes. The talk will be about Fatlad and he needs to be composed. He breathes out noisily, trying to exhale the anxiety out of his system. This is his last night in Berwick. *Just act normal, have a couple of pints and get out of here.* And tomorrow he'll be outta this town on a train home. As he walks over to them he's jostled and bumped by happy, boisterous drunks. Cold beer spills onto his fingers. He fuckin' hates that, like he wants to wash his hands *immediately*. CD sees him approaching and pulls out a stool.

He glances over them all and they look serious, and why not? 'Alright, lads,' he says, placing his pint on a beermat that CD's put in front of him. He looks at them all, and they're all looking at him. *What do they know?*

'Have you heard?' inquires Wacka, ignoring his greeting.

'Course I've heard, it's all over the news, man,' replies Jez, trying to sound as normal as possible.

'Not that fucker!' barks Wacka, eyes glowing like blue coals. 'Ah don't give a flying fuck about that wee fat prick. Ah mean Fifty. Have you heard?' Jez contains his relief and loves the fact that Wacka's priority is Fifty's illness, not the murder of a low-life scumbag. Loves it. He's on Jez's side but doesn't know it.

'Aye, stop jumping the fuckin' gun, Jez!' shouts Bob, laughing. 'That's item number three on Wacka's agenda. Divn't fuck up his agenda, for fuck's sake. There'll be hell on!' Wacka's eyes don't leave Jez, like he didn't hear the piss-take.

'Aye, I've heard,' he responds. 'Savage told me. I saw

him in his taxi a couple of nights ago. He was just back from Bamburgh, so he put me straight about Fifty's cancer. Actually, I was up the hospital this afternoon seeing him.' His mouth's dry. He sips his pint and licks froth off his lip. Anxiety shrouds him like a black overcoat. He wants to divert attention away from him so he turns to Cement Shoes. 'You know him better than any of us, Shoes. What do you think?'

The big man looks at his pint with intent, as if the answer's in there but he's struggling to see it. Seconds pass. Then he says, 'This is pancreatic cancer, guys. This is major league, you know. No' like testicular. He's got a *massive* fight on his hands.'

'He'll be fuckin' fine, man,' responds The Hammer, glugging down his pint then belching out loud. 'You're a doom merchant, Shoes. He'll be fine. Now, whose having what? Ma roond.' He takes the order and heads off, barging a couple of revellers out the way. We talk about Fifty and how he fought off testicular cancer all those years ago. And his "never say die" attitude. He'd called it his "baby" due to the chemo giving him morning sickness.

'Aye, and just like having a bairn I bet he was chuffed to get it oot of him,' says Fish Heid, nodding his muckle heid.

'Who named him Fifty Fifty anyway?' asks Bob. 'I think it was you, CD?'

CD replies, 'Not guilty, Bobby Knobrot. I wanted to call him One Nut.' They smile at his cruel humour. 'Anyway,' he continues, 'why you called Bob? Cos you're a baldy old bastard?' They all laugh, then Fish Heid adds:

'It can't be that, CD. He was a *young* baldy.'

'Divn't *you* talk aboot hair, Fish Heid!' shouts Bob. 'What was yours like at the wake, eh? I thought you'd plugged yourself into the national grid. Aye, what did I say? Cross between Fred West and Mungo Jerry.'

Fish Heid responds, 'Bob, you had a combover at twenty-two, man! Mind, you used to put lacquer on it and it stuck up in the air when it was windy. Looked like a piece-box lid. Cross between Bobby Charlton and Ralph Coates.'

But Bob's shouting over the top of him. 'BOYS, DO YOU KNOW HEID'S FAVOURITE BAND?! EH?! FRED WESTLIFE! AYE, GO ON, HEEEEIIDDDD!'

Wacka raises a hand and shouts, 'BOYS, BOYS!' The laughter slowly dies away. Wacka leans forward and they follow suit. Close up to him Jez can see tension in his face. Quietly he says, 'Item number 2.' He looks at them all before continuing. 'We all know about Bang Bang and Savage. Yes? Yes?' They're serious now and nod like diligent schoolkids. Wacka's holding court, like he's been doing for over thirty years as the "de facto" leader of the BUNDIG. He rests his "Popeye"-size forearms on the table then beckons them closer to him. 'They found a body but didn't report it cos they were fuckin' poaching at the time. Now, I dunno if it's breaking the law not to report it but they're lying low and we need to keep schtum. Okay?' They nod in unison. 'So, no getting pissed and mouthing off, okay? Nae pillow talk with the missus. Nowt. Right?' He takes a quick sip then says, 'By the way, Bang Bang's finished with the poaching.' He pauses and a smile appears on his face. 'I think he was spooked! Anyway, he's bought a kebab van. Gonna call it SOS Kebabs.'

'SOS?' asks Bob.

'Aye. Straight Outta Spittal,' replies Wacka, smiling.

'More like shit on a stick,' answers Bob, with a face like

he'd just stepped in some. Behind them a group of young men have gathered; they're shouting, laughing and jostling each other. The BUNDIG Boys move closer in, straining to hear over the noise and commotion.

'Item number 3,' continues Wacka, quietly. 'Okay. Fatlad's been murdered. Personally, I couldn't give a fuck. Not one fuck. And can someone tell me how a poxy slaughterman can own a flat, a Jag and a TAG Heuer watch, eh? Cos he was a fuckin' drug-dealing scumbag. And now I'm beginning to think that Kev and Fatlad's murders are to do with drugs. Maybe they ripped off some fuckin' radge and this is their comeback. It's the only thing I can think of, boys.' He sits back, scratches his third nipple and looks at them all. Jez thinks, *He's right. It is drug-related. But not in the way he thinks it is.*

'Aye,' responds Bob, 'put like that, it would be a motive, like.'

'I could believe that of Fatlad. Never liked the man,' adds Cement Shoes. 'But not Kev. Surely not. But aye, maybe the cops need to cast their net further out. Like outside this town.'

'The cops haven't got a fuckin' scooby,' replies Wacka. 'You'll never guess what they've done.' He shakes his head in disgust. 'Item number 4. I was in the cop shop for an interview on Tuesday. You talk aboot stabbing aboot in the dark. Honest, they're fuckin' clueless. Anyway, I got a call yesterday at the scrapyard. They're eliminating me from their inquiries. Oh, there's a fuckin' relief, I said to him. You know what he said? He cautioned me. For carrying an insecure load in the back of ma pick-up.' Bob's giggling away, obviously in the know.

'What load were you carrying, like?' asks Fish Heid.

'MA DOG!' shouts out Wacka. 'Ma fuckin' dog, Atlas. He

was in the back of the pick-up when I went to the cop shop. *He's* the insecure load. Can you believe that, eh? *I'm fuckin' ragin'!* Aye, apparently it's against the law cos he might move around and I'd get distracted. Ah should have him in a cage in the back. Ma dog in a cage?! Ah mean, there's a sick fucker on the loose oot there killing folk and *he* needs to be put in a cage, but the cops seem more interested in putting ma dog in one. Can you believe that, eh?' He looks at them all then quaffs his pint and slams the empty glass down hard.

The Hammer returns with a tray of drinks, shouting to the group of boys behind them to make way. When he gets settled Jez asks, 'How did your interview go, Hammer?'

'Sweet as, Jez. Sweet as, ma man,' he replies. He's grinding his teeth and his pupils are like black saucers. The conversation returns to the theme of death and murder. Jez listens and doesn't get sucked into the vortex of speculation, debate and deliberation. Druggie theories sprout like magic mushrooms and he's liking what he hears and focuses on acting normal. Whatever that is. He wipes sweaty hands on his jeans.

CD turns to him and says, 'So that guy got the autopsy report okay?'

'Aye,' Jez responds. 'I saw him later on that morning, so aye, he's got it. Whether it'll help him, I've no idea. Ahm no' sure how interested he really is, CD, to be honest with you. By the way, how long you been wearing *them*?' he asks, pointing at his bold designer glasses.

CD moves closer and whispers, 'No' long. They've got clear lenses. Goes with the gear.' Jez glances at his clothes and he's looking immaculate. A good-looking, well-dressed man. He looks Jez up and down then shakes his head.

'What you saying like, you cheeky fucker?' replies Jez. 'I mean… am I no' smart enough to sit next to you?'

CD sips his G&T in contemplation, adjusts the angular frames then says, 'Ah wouldn't go oot for the coal dressed like that, Jeremy. And those black skinny jeans. How retro are they, eh? Do they no' make your balls sweat?'

'No they don't,' Jez replies, all serious, like an affronted wee laddie.

Wacka needs a piss and heads off with eyes blazing, still mad as fuck about his dog. As Jez is talking to CD there's a commotion behind them. 'EXCUSE ME! WHO YOU PUSHING, OLD MAN?!' shouts a smart twenty-something boy with a southern drawl and a puppy fat face. Wacka's standing there, head cocked to one side. He gets close to the boy and quietly says:

'You wanna have a go with me? Do you? Really?' The boy sizes up Wacka and realises he's way out his depth with this man. There's a menacing, hard-as-fuck look about him. Always has been. Smart Boy's mates are looking cocky until they see the BUNDIG in the alcove who are now on their feet, staring them out, waiting for it to kick off. They may be twenty years older, but they still look like hard dangerous men, used to mass brawls in public places. The tense silence is broken by The Hammer. 'Go on, Wacka son. Batter the slack-jawed southern fucker!' he says, sounding like an excited psychopath.

Wacka turns and says quietly, 'Hammer, cool it.' A pause, then he says to the boy, 'Well, what's it gonna be, son?' Smart Boy shakes his head, his double chin wobbling like a set jelly. Humiliated now, he and his friends back off and disappear.

'AYE GET ON THE SMACK, YOU FAT FUCK!' roars

The Hammer, giggling at his own joke. Bob joins Wacka and they both head off to the toilet. It's so busy that the staff are unaware of the commotion.

The BUNDIG settle back down and CD turns to Jez. 'Twenty odd years ago that boy's face would be looking like a margherita pizza by now. And you see what Wacka did there? That was more stylish than dragging the fucker down by the hair and kneeing him in the coupon. All getting older, I suppose. And there's nowt wrong with ageing, Jez, as long as you do it with style.'

'What, like you and your dodgy designer glasses, you mean?' asks Jez.

'Keep your jealous comments to yourself, Jeremy. Look at you. Fuckin' Man at Sue Ryder.'

Jez smiles and pretends he's listening, but he's having a flashback. He's back at the slaughterhouse last Tuesday night, watching Fatlad's blood and brains spill onto the concrete ground and the maggots closing in. Then his own blood loss at the hands of that cowardly thug, all those years ago. He runs a finger down the scar, from the top of his head down past his ear. He once thought of digging him up and pushing his bones through his mother's letterbox.

Suddenly he gets an urge to leave. He knew it was coming. Pounding heart, dry mouth, sweaty hands. And a desire to be alone. He needs peace and quiet, not noise and aggro. He turns to CD and says, 'Ahm just nashing oot for a smoke, pal.' He jostles his way through the mass of people and finally makes it to the pub door.

'Jez! Hang on.' He turns around and it's Cement Shoes. Fear surges through him like an electric shock, right down to his sweaty fingertips. He knows that Fifty's close to Cement Shoes. Has he said anything about Mandy's death? Shoes follows him out onto the street, digging out his mobile phone. Then he says, 'You visited Fifty today. How do you think he looked?'

'Oh, no' good, Shoes. No' good, mate.' Jez pulls out a packet of cigarettes. 'Ah mean, he sounds resilient and all that but physically he's… he's no' looking good, I thought.' He lights up, watching him over his cupped hands. *What does he fuckin' know?*

Cement Shoes breathes in deeply, then says, 'I've spoken to the doctor. Truth is he's no' got long, mate. Two months, ten weeks max. I'm telling you cos I know you're back up the road tomorrow. Keep this to yourself, Jez.' He nods his head back into the pub and says, 'I'll tell the boys when the time's right.' Jez looks up at him and shakes his head in disbelief. Inside, his emotions chop and change direction like a bat in silent woods. Pain and deep sadness at Fifty's prognosis mixed with sheer relief that he's said nothing. And with his death his secret stays safe. He smokes the cigarette and they talk about Fifty. And his wife, Angie, and how she's gonna cope. The sort of heavy conversation two people have when a lifelong friend's heading towards the exit door.

Jez throws the cigarette end into a bucket of sand and says, 'Listen, pal. This has been some week. Kev's funeral, another murder, and now this aboot Fifty. Ahm no' really in the mood for a night's drinking. So, I'm gonna head off, Shoes.' The Big Man understands and says he'll tell the rest of them that something's come up. They embrace and he promises to keep in touch about Fifty.

Jez walks off down Castlegate under a dark, crimson sky, wondering what it's like to know you're gonna die. For Fifty Fifty, death will be a gradual affair as he wastes away to nothing over several weeks. But he'll have the comfort of love from his family and friends. Kev Devine knew. He died alone and waited for death on the incoming tide. Fatlad Owens knew too, as his skull was being splintered and his face sliced open and his life flowed away like a red river. But like a dream in the night, that's behind Jez now.

Except for that person who's settled on his mind like a shadow. A nameless person who can't speak. He sits on a swing in his brain, at the edge of his vision. Sometimes their strides match as they walk together. They look up now as the town hall clock strikes nine and the stars wink down on them.

CHAPTER 28

DEPARTURE

SATURDAY

The tannoy booms out an announcement: 'The train now arriving at platform two is the eleven fifty-eight for Edinburgh, due to arrive in Edinburgh Waverley at twelve forty-one.' The tracks tingle as the train pulls in. And Jez tingles as he shoulders his holdall and boards. Tingles with excitement, satisfaction and fear. Fear because he's sure Elijah knows. And Jez doesn't know what he's gonna do. He feels nervous, scared cos this is out of his control.

He's booked a rear-facing seat and gets settled in. Then, as he idly looks out at the station platform, he sees Elijah! Running down the stairs two at a time with his holdall. Fear explodes inside Jez. *Jesus Christ! This is it. He's coming for me. Jesus.* Doom and dread cling to him like a wet coat. Then at the bottom of the stairs Elijah veers left, runs across to the other platform and jumps on the London train that's about to pull out. And as he turns to pull the door closed behind him, he looks up and their eyes meet. There's no acknowledgement from Elijah, no gesture of friendship, no hand wave. Then slowly, a hint of a smile. Jez stares back, like he's transfixed. *I thought he was here for another week. What's he playing at? What the fuck's going on? Has he turned me in, and this is him disappearing back down south?* Seconds pass then the London train jolts and glides off and Elijah smiles at him until he's out of sight.

There's a sick feeling in Jez's gut and his breathing's quick and shallow. Elijah's words about Mandy yesterday ring in his head like a tolling bell. A whistle blasts then the Edinburgh train eases out of the station, heading north and picking up speed. Jez watches the old town receding away from him, past the grey housing estates, then the industrial units, until the lighthouse at the end of the pier disappears from view.

The train hugs the coastline as it hurtles northwards. A faint, nervous smile plays on his lips. He can see it in his reflection as he looks out at the vast sea. He's front-page news in the Newcastle *Journal* and he starts reading the report with an off-centre gaze, like he's detached from the story. It's the usual who, what, when, where report. There's a quote from Detective Superintendent Callum Johnson, who's leading the case. *'We believe Mr. Owens was murdered elsewhere then dumped in the river between midnight and three o'clock this morning. At this stage we are working on possible motives and believe this killing and the murder of Kevin Devine in the town a month ago are linked.'* He then urges any member of the public who can assist with information to come forward. And he appeals to anyone who may have owned the fishing net to contact the police urgently.

Jez looks up and out the window as the train passes Burnmouth. His mind drifts back to the night he murdered Kevin Devine.

* * *

He knew Kev fished at Murphy's Beach every Friday night cos he'd posted something on social media a couple of months previously. The tricky bit was getting there unseen. So, on the afternoon of Friday, 27th June, he drove out of Edinburgh and onto the quiet country lanes of East Lothian. Not a camera in sight! Over the Lammermuir Hills then onto Burnmouth where he parked up unnoticed in a wee side street. He knew a quiet path down to the shore cos they used to pick winkles there as kids. It took a couple of hours to walk along the deserted shoreline to Murphy's Beach on the outskirts of Berwick. He passed the time thinking about the conversation he'd had with his mum a few months earlier. When he learnt the truth about Mandy's death. The rage was under control. He had a job to do.

He'd seen Kev from about fifty metres away, sitting on a blue tackle box. His fishing rod was next to him on a tripod pointing out to sea. Kev saw him approaching, then did a kind of double-take when he realised who it was. He'd looked uncomfortable, like the way he got to his feet and greeted him. Tried to sound normal, but he looked wary, like he could hardly look Jez in the eye. Jez played it pure calm though. Elijah would have been proud of his "pre-offence" behaviour. Told Kev he was down seeing his mum and fancied a wee hike up the coast. So, they stood there for a minute or two, chewing the fat like old friends do. He asked Jez what was in his poofy wee rucksack and Jez said sarnies and juice from his mum. Kev glanced at him and asked how she was. Jez focused on a gliding gull and said she was good and his mum and him were closer than ever. Another look up at the clifftop and no sign of anyone. It was just Jez, his sister's killer and a few crab corpses. He was looking out to sea when he asked Kev how his daughters were. He started talking and Jez stepped behind him, pulled out the hammer from his rucksack and smashed it full force across his head. Kev staggered sideways then dropped to his knees, then down onto all fours.

He was still conscious, which is how Jez wanted it. He wanted him to know. Kev was still on all fours, like he was gonna be sick. He could see his tongue; it had yellow sludge on it. Jez crouched down and whispered in his ear, 'Mum's still grieving over Mandy, Kev. So am I. You remember ma sister, don't you?' Kev made this funny wailing noise, like crying and screaming at the same time. It was pathetic. 'You gave her something once, Kev. Remember?' He shook his head and bright blood fell onto the yellow sand. 'You gave her ecstasy tabs, Kev. Can you no' mind? Anyway, this is from Mandy.' Jez got to his feet and Kev turned to look up at him. He cried like a wee terrified laddie. Jez struck him hard in the eye. The hammer head fitted perfectly and liquid ran out of his eye socket, then he dropped face down in the sand. Jez bent over him and said, 'You wanna violate *my* sister, then I'm gonna fuckin' violate *you*.'

He brought the hammer down hard on Kev's heid, making a loud crunching noise. 'That's from Mandy. And this.' And he struck him again. Then again. Then once more. Kev lay there, looking limp and lifeless. Now Jez couldn't muck about, basking in revenge. It was in, do the job, then out. He hammered the stake into the sand then turned Kev over, smashed up his legs then cable-tied his hands and got him tethered up. Then he shoved the two stones in his mouth, with a handful of sand. He was an inch from Kev's mangled, bloody face and said, 'They're from Mandy too. Goodbye, Kev. I need to go. Tide's coming in.'

There was blood on his hands and it had sprayed onto his face, so he went down to the incoming waves and washed it all off. Cleaned the hammer too, then set off back along the shoreline. He was about a hundred metres away when he got behind some rocks and pulled out a pair of binoculars from his rucksack. He scanned the clifftop path and saw no one there. Then he focused on Kev. Already the waves were lapping round his legs. Black, mottled froth licked at his waist like a cautious dog. And then he moved! He was conscious! Tried to struggle, but it was no good. Tried to shout, but the muffled screams didn't carry. The water rose and the terror on his face was a joy to see. Soon it was up to his neck and he was straining to stay above the water. Through the binoculars he could see the whites of his eyes. The terror of knowing you're going under. Like a condemned Covenanter. Then Kev jerked his head behind him. Jez panned right and saw what he saw. Huge, dirty rats. About six of them. They looked like miniature hyenas. One was bigger than the rest. Jez watched him doggy paddle out and grab the protruding stake. The others got bold and followed. They were clinging to the stake and nipping at Kev's scalp and ears. He shook his head violently to try to get them off. Then he saw Mighty Rat get onto Kev's head and start chewing his cheek. Another one was hanging off his lip. Then he went under. Cool to see.

He'd walked back to Burnmouth, all the time keeping out of sight. It was dark now and no one was about. He drove home under the starry face of a pure black sky. He felt bulletproof. Truth is, he thinks the minute Kev saw him on the beach he knew he was going to die.

* * *

Jez folds the paper then sits looking out the window. The train thunders on up the east coast. He looks at his watch. He'll ring Mum when he gets home. Tell her he got home safe. Suddenly his mobile beeps. It's a text from Elijah! A wave of pure dread runs through him then up over his scalp like icy water. He opens the message.

Hols over. Called back 2 london. Another child murder. Unfinished business. I'll see you around. Elijah

Jez responds with trembling hands as cold and clammy as death.

Sorry 2 hear that Elijah. Good luck. Wot u think of latest murder in Berwick? Do u think they'll get the guy?

He stares at the phone with a wooden face. Nausea rises up from his gut as the minutes crawl by like months.

Then another text from Elijah. Just three words.

Will remain unsolved.

Jez stares out the window and smiles at his reflection. It smiles back; but it's not hanging right, like it's at the wrong angle. The smile's distorted. Twisted.